Praise for *The Protégé*

"When it comes to high-finance intrigue, this series continues to look good on the bottom line."
—*Booklist*

"Fast-paced and full of plenty of twists and turns . . . If you are looking for a book with plenty of thrills, action and suspense, this is the one for you."
—*Mysteries Galore*

Praise for *The Chairman*

"A gripping story."
—*Wisconsin State Journal*

"Distinguished by colorful, well-drawn characters and an arresting, labyrinthine plot, this tenth novel by Frey . . . illuminates the machinations of big business and high finance."
—*Publishers Weekly*

Praise for Stephen Frey and his other novels

"He does for the trading floors what John Grisham has done for the bench."
—*Forbes*

"Danger and deception dominate."
—New York *Daily News*

"Action-packed . . . bookkeeping chicanery, insider trading and other big-business conspiracies abound."
—*The Wall Street Journal*

The
Protégé

A Novel

STEPHEN
FREY

BALLANTINE BOOKS • NEW YORK

2006 Fawcett Books Mass Market Edition

Published in the United States by Fawcett Books, an imprint of The Random House Publishing Group, a division of Random House, Inc., New York.

FAWCETT is a registered trademark and the Fawcett colophon is a trademark of Random House, Inc.

Originally published in hardcover in the United States by Ballantine Books, an imprint of The Random House Publishing Group, a division of Random House, Inc.

ISBN 0-345-48059-7

Cover design: Carl D. Galian
Cover photographs: woman © Luckypix; buildings © Alamy

This book contains an excerpt from the hardcover edition of *The Power Broker* by Stephen Frey. This excerpt has been set for this edition only and may not reflect the final content of the hardcover edition.

Printed in the United States of America

www.ballantinebooks.com

OPM 9 8 7 6 5 4 3 2 1

For Diana . . . I love you so much.

ACKNOWLEDGMENTS

A special thank you to Dr. Teo Forcht Dagi, a very busy man who was always available to talk and to offer tremendous help with technical guidance; Mark Tavani, my editor, for his tireless efforts; Cynthia Manson, my agent, for her tireless efforts; and Matt Malone, my great friend, for his suggestions on this book.

Thank you also to my daughters Ashley and Christina, whom I love very much, and to those who have always been there to answer questions and give encouragement: Stephen Watson, Kevin "Big Sky" Erdman, Gina Centrello, Jack Wallace, Bob Wieczorek, Scott Andrews, John Piazza, Kristin Malone, Gordon Eadon, Chris Andrews, Andy Brusman, Jeff Faville, Marvin Bush, Jim and Anmarie Galowski, Courtney, Walter Frey, Tony Brazely, John Grigg, Bart Begley, Barbara Fertig, Pat and Terry Lynch, Chris Tesoriero, Baron Stewart, Gerry Barton, and Mike Pocalyko.

And to Diana. I love you, sweetheart. You're my angel.

PROLOGUE

David Wright's eyes narrowed as he watched the woman struggle. She was standing on her tiptoes, hands high above her head, wrists chained to iron rings bolted into the ceiling. Her long dark hair cascaded past her naked shoulders as she held her head back, straining against the chains, trying to ease the pain.

Wright picked up the whip. Attached to its smooth wooden handle were ten narrow leather strands, each twelve inches long, each knotted at the tip. His breath turned quick and his heart raced as he drew the strands through his fingers, then passed them over her smooth skin. She moaned and shook her head when she felt the leather, trying to pull away, so afraid of what was coming. But her wrists were as high above her head as she could reach—she was almost hanging—so she could barely move. She was completely in his control.

Wright had first come to the sex store in the West Village several months ago, interested in toys to share with his wife, Peggy. After several visits, he'd gotten to know the owner, a slight, chain-smoking man with a thin mustache who'd casually asked from behind the counter one day if Wright would be interested in something "live." After a few moments, Wright had nodded and the man had led him through a hidden door in the back—into a bondage chamber.

Wright had watched the first session, then quickly decided to participate. Now he did it one-on-one, spending an hour alone with a woman he chose from a folder of photographs. The fee for the hour was five thousand dollars, but money like that was no object for him. This was his fourth session in the last six weeks. He took a gulp of water—it was hot in the room—as he gazed at the woman's slim arms and legs. He could see her muscles beginning to cramp, and he liked it.

He made the first lash hard, even though he'd been told to start slow. Not for her sake, but to excite him more. The owner had told Wright that if he took his time in the beginning, the thrill would build more consistently and thus be more intense when he began to deliver real pain. But he didn't care. He did what he wanted when he wanted.

The second lash was as hard as he could make it. She screamed into one arm, and a tremor shook her entire body. But there was no need to worry about anyone outside hearing her screams—the room was soundproof.

Wright took a deep breath. He'd used this woman the last three times. He liked her delicate features, her beautiful body, the way her skin rose quickly with the lashes. And he had no misgivings about the pain. She earned half the five grand—a lot of money for an hour's work, especially for a woman who by day was an administrative assistant at a law firm. She knew what she was getting into, she knew what he was going to do to her. There was no reason for remorse.

With the crack of the third lash, her head snapped back and she screamed at the top of her lungs, begging for mercy—which only made him want to hurt her more. He delivered the fourth, fifth, sixth, and seventh lashes in rapid succession, causing her skin to swell in long, narrow lines. After the seventh lash he rested, breathing hard, sweating profusely. He wiped the back of his hand across his forehead and took several more gulps of water, enjoying her sobs and moans.

When he was finished drinking, he put down the whip and forced the woman roughly up onto a block of wood, reaching for a noose hanging from a ceiling beam. Forcing it over her head and around her neck as she tried to keep it away by ducking. It was his first time doing this—the owner's suggestion. The owner had warned him to be very careful; things could easily go wrong. But he'd also told Wright what an incredible thrill it would be and how the woman had never had this done to her—so she'd be genuinely terrified.

Wright unhooked the woman's wrists from the iron rings, then brought her hands down behind her back and cuffed them. As he drew the noose firmly around her neck, she started to whimper. "Shut up!" he hissed, moving toward the wall where the other end of the rope was knotted to a cleat. He was going to tighten the rope, then pull the block of wood slowly out from under her and let her dangle for a few moments. Letting her think he was going to leave her there until she suffocated. Then push the block back beneath her feet when she started gasping hard. The owner was right: This was going to be incredible.

It was then that she panicked, struggling against the noose and screaming wildly.

He rushed toward her as she came perilously close to the edge of the wooden block, to steady her. But his foot slammed into the block as he reached for her, tripping him and knocking it from beneath her. He careened to the cement floor, then rolled quickly onto his back. Just in time to see her fall.

The drop was short, only eighteen inches. But it was enough.

Wright sprang up and rushed to the cleat on the wall, his fingers working madly to undo the knot. When he finally tore the loops free, he lowered her down, watching in horror as her limp body crumpled to the floor, the noose still draped around her broken neck. He knelt over her, staring into her empty eyes, his hands shaking horribly and blood pounding in his brain so hard that his vision blurred with each beat. "Christ," he whispered, sweat soaking his clothes. She wasn't breathing, and he couldn't find a pulse. He didn't know CPR, so he took her head in his hands and shook it gently. A pathetic attempt to revive her. But there was no response, not even a flicker of her eyelids. Just a dull mannequin gaze. "Shit!" he whined, panic seizing him for real now.

He crawled quickly to the door and cracked it, peering into the main part of the store. It was dark, as if the owner were gone. Which was strange. The other times, the guy had waited until Wright was finished—three in the morning a week ago. It was only a few minutes before midnight now.

He opened the door wider, allowing light from the chamber to illuminate the store. Still no sign of the owner. So strange, but he didn't have time to think on it now. He needed to take advantage of the opportunity.

He crawled back to where the woman lay, removed the noose from her neck, the cuffs from her wrists, then found a rag and wiped down everything in the room, erasing his fingerprints. Then he dressed the woman and carried her through the store, laying her down in front of the door before climbing three steps to the sidewalk, peering up and down the darkened West Village side street to make certain it was deserted. When he was satisfied all was clear, he hurried back to her body, scooped it up, and ran down the sidewalk as fast as he could, gasping with each stride.

When he'd gone fifty yards, he moved in between two parked cars and put her body down between them. He stepped back slowly, gazing down at her lifeless form, remorse overtaking him, hoping he'd wake up from this nightmare. A sudden sob racked his body, and he shook his head, then turned and raced back to the shop. It was about survival at this point. He had to stay focused on getting out of here.

Back inside the shop, Wright gathered up the noose, the cuffs, and the rag he'd used to wipe down the place, then bolted. He dropped everything in a trash can several blocks away and headed for Seventh Avenue to catch a taxi. But when he reached the brightly lit area, he realized he didn't want a driver identifying him later. So he half walked, half ran across Manhattan to Lexington Avenue and caught the subway, not looking anyone in the eye all the way home.

Wright finally got back to his apartment on the Upper East Side a little before two in the morning. He didn't want to wake up his wife, so he lay down on the couch and stared at the ceiling. Wondering when the police would come for him.

PART
ONE

CHAPTER 1

Christian Gillette strode purposefully down the long main corridor of Everest Capital, the Manhattan-based investment firm he ran.

"Christian."

Gillette ignored the voice calling him from behind.

"Christian!"

Louder this time, but Gillette still didn't stop. He glanced over at his assistant, Debbie, pen and pad in hand. She was struggling to keep up.

"*Mr. Chairman!*" Faraday huffed, finally catching up with Gillette, and grabbing him by the back of the arm. Faraday was second in command at Everest. A talented money raiser from Great Britain who had an Outlook full of high-level connections in the Wall Street world. His accent was heavy, though he'd been in the States for fifteen years. "Wait a minute."

"Morning, Nigel," Gillette said politely.

"A fucking magnificent pleasure to see you, too," Faraday muttered, breathing hard. He inhaled ice cream constantly—to fight stress, he claimed—but he'd been thirty pounds overweight since graduating from Eton. Long before he'd ever dealt with the pressures of a private equity investment firm. "I sent you three e-mails this morning," he grumbled. "You haven't replied to any of them."

"No time."

"One of them was *extremely* important."

"I'll get to it when I can."

Faraday scowled. "I'm the number two person here, Christian. I need access to you."

Gillette jabbed a thumb over his shoulder. "I've got three conference rooms waiting for me. A guy representing the Wallace Family in One, one of our accounting firms in Two, and—"

"The *Chicago* Wallaces?"

"Yeah."

"Jesus, they're worth like twenty double-large."

Following Gillette's lead, people at Everest sometimes referred to a million as "large" and a billion as "double-large."

"More than that."

"But they keep to themselves," Faraday continued. "They don't talk to other investors. I've been trying to get to them for years, to have them invest with us. But nothing, not even a return phone call. They're very secretive."

"I know."

Faraday hesitated, waiting for an explanation that didn't come. "Well, what do they want?"

"To hire you."

"Really?" Faraday leaned back, putting a chubby, pale hand on his chest.

"No, not really," Gillette answered, grinning.

Faraday sighed. "Well, what *do* they want?"

"I'll tell you this afternoon at three, when we're *sched-uled* to meet."

"But I have to talk to you *now*."

"All right," Gillette said, giving in. "Talk."

"Hey, it's fucking good news. I thought you'd want to hear right away."

Good news was always a welcome interruption. "What you got?"

"Two more commitments to the new fund," Faraday explained. "I got an e-mail late last night from the California Teachers Pension. They're in for six hundred large. And North America Guaranty agreed to invest one double-large five minutes ago." Faraday broke into a proud smile. "We're done, Christian. Everest Eight now has fifteen billion dollars of commitments. I'm happy to report to you that we've raised the largest private equity fund in history."

Incredible, Gillette thought. And fifteen billion of equity could be leveraged with at least sixty billion of debt from the banks and insurance companies that were constantly begging to partner with them. Which meant he had seventy-five billion dollars of fresh money to buy more companies with. To add to the thirty Everest already owned.

"What do you think?" Faraday asked. "Great, right?"

"It took a while."

Faraday's expression sagged. "It took ten months. That's pretty *fucking* good."

Eleven years Gillette had known Faraday, and he was still amazed at the Brit's language. He didn't care if the guy dropped the F-bomb when it was just the two of them, but there were others around now.

"The original target was a year," Faraday reminded Gillette. "We beat that by two months!"

Gillette spotted one of the receptionists coming up behind Faraday, a middle-aged woman who was waving, trying to get his attention. "Yes, Karen."

"Mr. Gillette, the commissioner of the National Football League is holding for you."

Gillette watched Faraday's face go pale. They'd been waiting a long time for this call. Two years of work lay in the balance. "Transfer Mr. Landry to my cell," he instructed calmly, pulling the tiny phone from his pocket.

"Right away," Karen called, hurrying off.

Gillette moved to where Faraday stood and shook his hand. "You did a great job on the fund, Nigel. You really did."

Faraday looked down, caught off guard by the compliment. "Thanks, that means a lot."

Gillette's cell phone rang, and Faraday glanced at it apprehensively. "God, I hope we get this."

Gillette pressed the "talk" button and put the phone to his ear, still staring at Faraday. "This is Christian Gillette."

"Christian, it's Kurt Landry."

"Hi, Kurt. What's up?"

"Well . . . Christian . . . the owners met last night." Landry hesitated. "And they voted to award the new Las Vegas expansion franchise to you, to Everest Capital. *You got it.*"

A thrill rushed through Gillette. They'd offered the NFL four hundred and fifty million dollars. A tremendous sum of money for a franchise with no history in a city that was nothing more than a dot in the desert. Lacking a large, permanent population that might justify such a stratospheric price elsewhere. But with the strategy he and his team had devised, Gillette was confident the franchise could be worth five times that in a few years. Maybe more. Maybe *much* more.

"Well?" Faraday whispered.

Gillette silently mouthed, *We got it.* "I have some ideas for the team's name, Kurt," he said, watching Faraday pump his fists, then raise both arms above his head and do an embarrassing dance in front of Debbie. Shaking his head and laughing at the Brit's exuberance. "How about the Craps?"

"Christian, I don't think that's—"

"Or the Twenty-ones," Gillette kept going, enjoying Landry's anxious response. "I can see the Super Bowl trailer now: The Twenty-ones and the Forty-niners for the world championship. Whose number is up?"

"Had that ready for me, right? In case I had good news."

"I *assumed* you had good news."

"Don't start designing logos yet," Landry advised, chuckling. "How about lunch on Monday? We'll talk details then."

Gillette already had a lunch Monday, but this was much more important. "Sure. I'll have Debbie call your EA to arrange it."

"Thanks."

Gillette slid the phone back in his pocket. "We're done, Nigel, it's ours."

Faraday was beaming. "Pretty good morning, huh?"

Gillette checked his watch: ten-thirty. Still plenty of time in the day for things to go wrong. "We'll see."

"Don't get so excited," Faraday said. "Wouldn't want you to have a heart attack here in front of everyone."

But Gillette was already striding down the corridor toward Conference Room One. "Cancel Monday's lunch," he said to Debbie as she trotted beside him, scribbling on her pad. "Then call Kurt Landry's executive assistant and—"

"I heard, Chris. I'll take care of everything."

Debbie was one of his best hiring decisions. She was always anticipating, always executing, and always pleasant—even when he wasn't. She was one of the few people he truly depended on. And one of the few people who called him Chris.

As Gillette reached the conference room door, his cell phone went off again. He pulled it out and checked the number: Harry Stein, CEO of Discount America, a fast-growing chain of megastores that had taken on Wal-Mart—and was winning. Everest Capital owned ninety percent of Discount America, and Gillette was chairman of the board.

As chairman of Everest, Gillette also chaired many of the companies Everest owned.

"Go in and see if they need anything," Gillette instructed, motioning toward the conference room. "Drinks, whatever. Tell them I'll be right in."

Debbie shook her head as his cell phone continued to buzz. "It's amazing."

"What?"

"How you handle so many things at once and keep everything straight."

He froze, unprepared for the praise.

"Okay, okay," she said, rolling her eyes, taking his reaction as impatience. "I'm going."

Gillette grimaced as she moved inside the conference room and closed the door. He'd always been terrible at accepting compliments. Just like his father. "What do you need, Harry?"

"Damn, Mr. Chairman, not even a 'good morning'?"

"*What do you need?*"

"How do you know I *need* anything?"

"You always do. What is it now?"

"It's what I told you about last week, but it's gotten worse. We're up to our eyeballs in alligators down in Maryland."

Stein constantly alluded to animals in conversation— which drove Gillette up a wall. "Remind me."

"We're trying to put up this great new store in a town called Chatham on the Eastern Shore. That's on the other side of the Chesapeake Bay from Bal—"

"I know where the Eastern Shore is."

"Right. Well, this'll be our first store in the region, and if we get in there, we'll give Wal-Mart fits. It'll really put us on the map."

"So, what's the problem?" Gillette asked.

"The mayor's rallying everybody against us."

"Why?"

"Chatham's this old fishing town from before the Revolutionary War that's built on some river called the Chester. Lots of boring history the locals want you to love, you know? Anyway, it's centrally located, very strategic. We'll draw from lots of other little towns. But this woman's all hot and bothered about us being the eight-hundred-pound gorilla. Got a bee in her bonnet because she thinks when the store goes up we'll run all her quaint little waterfront shops out of business and turn her Garden of Eden into strip mall heaven. Typical misguided small-town paranoia, but the woman's a damn pit bull. She's actually making progress, getting everybody stirred up, and—"

"That's normal, Harry, we've seen it before. Let it run its course," Gillette said gently.

"But she's calling mayors and town councils in other places we're trying to get into. She's already talked to people in New Jersey, Pennsylvania, Virginia, and North Carolina. Hell, she started some Web site, and she's spreading rumors on it about a class-action sex-bias suit she's going to hit us with. There's nothing to the suit, but that kind of crap can spin out of control."

"Why are you calling me?"

"You need to meet with her," Stein explained.

"Why me? *You're* the CEO."

"I did meet with her," Stein muttered. "I didn't do very well."

"Why would I do any better?"

"You're the ultimate decision maker, and she's a bottom-line nut. She was pissed off when I told her I had to go to you for permission to get some of the things she said might change her mind. She didn't have much use for me after that."

"What's she looking for?"

"For starters, she wants us to build her a new elementary school and a retirement home."

People always had their damn hands out looking for freebies. Sometimes the world seemed like one big scam-fest. "That's ridiculous," Gillette griped.

"But it's going to be an awesome store, Christian. A hundred thousand square feet of shelf-space heaven, our best location yet. A revolution in retailing. Everything a shopper could want under one roof in a region we've got to penetrate *right now*." Stein took a deep breath. "And we've got to stop this woman from talking to other towns. I need your help."

Gillette knew what "help" meant. It meant a day of palm pressing and ass kissing big-ego, small-town officials who'd try to pry everything they could out of him over a lunch of rubber chicken and some local high-carb dish that won last year's church bake-off. Nothing for the highlight reel and a black hole in terms of time, but Discount America was at a critical point. About to break out, about to make major noise in the retail industry. Which should enable Everest to take the chain public in the next twelve to eighteen months—or sell to Wal-Mart—at a *huge* profit.

"Call Debbie and set it up. Middle of next week some-time."

"Thanks, Mr. Chairman. You'll make the difference. You could charm a rattlesnake out of its fangs, and I—"

Gillette ended the call. He didn't have time for Stein's snow. The phone went off again as he was putting it back in his pocket. He cursed as he checked the display: Faith Cassidy. He was supposed to have called her earlier.

Faith was a pop star on a roll. Her first two albums had sold millions, and she was about to release her third. She was on the West Coast doing prerelease promotions. Her label was owned by an entertainment company controlled by Everest Capital and chaired by Gillette. She was also his girlfriend. Sort of.

"What's up?"

"Hi, Chris."

"Hi."

"God, you sound busy."

"Yeah. How's it going?"

"Great, it's going great. Thanks for calling the music execs out here. I'm getting the royal treatment."

"You should. You're hot."

"Well . . . I don't know about that," Faith said, being modest. "I miss you."

"Me too. When are you back?"

"I don't know yet. Depends on a couple of things. But I can't wait to see you."

"Yeah . . . it'll be nice."

"Just a bursting bud of romance this morning, aren't you?"

"Busy, baby. That's all."

She sighed. "I understand."

"Call me later, all right?"

"I love you, Chris."

He hesitated, waiting until a young associate heading up the hallway had passed by. "You too. See ya."

The man on the other side of the table stood up and held out his hand as Gillette walked into the conference room. "Gordon Meade, executive director of the Wallace Family office."

"Christian Gillette."

"It's a pleasure to meet you, Christian."

Meade looked to be in his late fifties, neatly groomed from his silver hair to his shiny shoes. For a man who managed over twenty billion, Meade had a relaxed air about him, and when he spoke he did so with a faint smile, as if he were recalling a secret about a Wallace Family member. Something that gave him job security, no matter what.

Families were always full of secrets, Gillette knew. Especially wealthy ones.

"The pleasure's mine," Gillette said, motioning for Meade to sit back down. "I know you don't talk to other firms very often, so I'm honored that you're here."

"Thank you." Meade gestured at the young woman sitting beside him. "Christian, this is Allison Wallace."

Allison was attractive, no two ways about it. Blond and slim, with pretty facial features: light blue eyes, a thin nose, full lips, and high cheekbones. Dressed conservatively in a dark blue skirt suit and a white blouse, top button buttoned. Late twenties, Gillette figured. "Hello."

She gave him a slight nod.

"Allison's on the board of the Wallace Family Trust," Meade explained. "Along with her uncle and her grandfather. The trust is the vehicle the Wallaces make most of their investments with. I report to Allison." His smile grew forced.

As if it were irritating to report to a woman half his age, Gillette thought. "Thank you both for coming. Like I said, I'm honored, but also curious," he admitted, sitting at the head of the table. "You weren't clear about what you wanted when you called, Gordon. Frankly, I don't usually take a meeting without a specific agenda. But this is the Wallace Family."

"Representing the Wallaces does have its advantages," Meade acknowledged. "How much do you know about the family?"

"I know they're hypersensitive about publicity. So hyper they don't even have a Web site. Most family offices do."

"I've tried to get them to set one up," Meade responded. "Better to control the flow of information than have people guess. But they won't do it. Are you at all familiar with the family history?" he asked.

"I know that Willard Wallace founded the Chicago and Western Railway back in the 1850s." Gillette loved railroads, so the Wallace Family history had piqued his interest when Debbie dropped the prep memo on his desk yesterday. "The family sold it to what's now the Burlington Northern in the early 1900s, but they kept a lot of the land Willard originally purchased for the railroad. They made a killing off it, too, selling it parcel by parcel for major bucks over the years. Then they struck gold again with the cell phone explosion." Gillette could tell that Meade was impressed.

"Nice job, Christian. That stuff isn't easy to find."

Everest Capital owned an investigation and personal protection firm—McGuire & Company—that could dig up almost anything on anybody. McGuire's CEO, Craig West, reported directly to Gillette. "I believe the family's worth over twenty billion."

"Can't comment on that," Meade said quickly, his expression turning serious.

"Which means I'm close." Gillette glanced at Allison. She still hadn't said a word—or taken her eyes off him.

"One thing you also figured out is the Wallace Family's political affiliation." Meade gestured at photos on the bookcases of Gillette shaking hands with both President Bushes, Rudy Giuliani, George Pataki, and several other Republican stars. "The Wallaces are big GOP supporters." Meade smiled. "Is there a conference room with pictures of you shaking Democratic hands as well?"

"Both Clintons, Kerry, Cuomo, and a few others," Gillette replied. "We have one for the independents, too." He checked his watch: five after eleven. He was supposed to have met with the accountants in Conference Room

Two at ten-thirty and the guy in Room Three five minutes ago. "So why did you want to get together?"

"You've become quite a story in the financial world," Meade began. "A hot commodity."

"We're a *team* around here, Gordon, no stars. My *team's* a hot commodity, not me."

"That's a nice piece of humble pie, Christian. Sincerely sliced, I'm sure. But you're the chairman of Everest Capital. You take hell for everyone's mistakes, so you get credit for their wins. That's the way it works." Meade eased back in his chair and crossed his legs at the knees. "How old are you?"

"Thirty-seven."

"So young." The older man sighed.

"I've done my time."

"Oh, I know. I saw that *People* magazine article a few weeks ago. The top fifty bachelors list issue. They called you one of the hardest-working men in America."

"I didn't speak to anyone at *People* about that list," Gillette said curtly. "They put it together on their own. They didn't even give me a courtesy call to tell me the article was coming out. I don't pay attention to that stuff, anyway."

Meade chuckled. "I guess it doesn't do much good to be one of the top fifty bachelors if you don't have time to do the things bachelors do."

"There's never enough time, Gordon."

Meade shook his head paternally. "I used to think that way, but I've learned to relax as my sun heads toward the horizon. Enjoy it while you can, Christian. Dust to dust, you know?"

"Uh-huh."

Meade flicked a piece of lint from his pants. "I want to ask you a few questions about Everest before I get into specifics of why Allison and I are here."

The people in the other conference rooms could wait. This man controlled twenty billion dollars, and Gillette smelled opportunity. "Go ahead."

"You took over as Everest's chairman, what? About a year ago?"

"Ten months."

"How long have you been here?"

"Eleven years." Gillette glanced over at Allison. She was still staring at him intently. "Before that I was with Goldman Sachs in their mergers and acquisitions department."

"Bill Donovan was chairman of Everest before you, right?"

"Yup. Bill founded Everest back in 1984 and was chairman until last November, when I took over. The first fund he raised was twenty-five million. We've raised seven more funds since then."

"*Seven more?*" Meade asked.

"Yes, eight in total since 1984."

"I thought Fund Seven was the last one you raised. That's what it says on your Web site."

"We just finished raising our eighth fund this morning. Literally right before I walked in here. The Web site should be updated by COB today."

"How big is this one?"

Out of the corner of his eye, Gillette noticed Allison lean forward slightly in her chair. "Fifteen billion."

Meade whistled. "Jesus, that's got to be the largest private equity fund ever raised."

"It is," Gillette agreed. "We're lucky."

"You aren't lucky," Allison spoke up, finally breaking her silence. "You're good. Investors don't care about luck, they care about performance, and your performance has been outstanding. Your funds have done at least forty percent a year. I hear the return for Everest Six was over *fifty* percent a year. In the past nine months, you've sold your grocery store chain and your waste management company to industry buyers and taken two other companies public. Your information management business in Los Angeles and that chip maker in La Jolla: All at very fat gains. The profit on those deals alone was over three billion."

"Closer to four," Gillette corrected. Maybe there was more to Allison Wallace than just a bloodline. "It's been a good run."

"It's been an *incredible* run, and you still haven't sold your grand slam, Laurel Energy. That should be a four-to-five-billion-dollar profit by itself."

Laurel Energy was a Canadian energy exploration and production company Everest had bought several years ago. Last fall, Laurel engineers had discovered a major oil and gas field on several option properties the company had acquired cheaply. Everest had put just three hundred million into Laurel, and Allison was right: According to the engineers, it was worth around five billion now. "How do you know about Laurel?" he asked.

"We have some oil and gas investments up there, too," she explained. "People can't keep their mouths shut. Everybody's always got to tell somebody their secret."

"Yeah, everybody wants to feel like they're in the know."

"Which you wouldn't understand, Christian," Meade observed, "because you're *always* in the know." His expression turned grave. "Let's talk about what happened here last November."

Gillette's gaze moved deliberately from Allison to Meade.

"About how you became chairman of Everest. About Miles Whitman."

Miles Whitman. Gillette hadn't heard that name in a long time.

A year ago, Whitman had been the chief investment officer and a board member of North America Guaranty—the country's largest insurance company and Everest's biggest investor. But Whitman had lost billions on some terrible investments he'd secretly made with NAG funds and was facing a long prison sentence if the internal accountants and the other board members figured out what he'd done. So he'd hatched a desperate plot to cover up his losses—which involved gaining control of Everest.

The plot hinged on Whitman having his own chairman of Everest, a puppet who'd do exactly what he was told. It had also hinged on getting Bill Donovan—*and then Gillette*—out of the way with help from the men who'd once run McGuire & Company—Tom and Vince McGuire. They'd gotten Donovan, but ultimately the plot had been uncovered and the conspirators had fled. The authorities had taken Vince in, but Whitman and Tom McGuire were still out there somewhere.

Donovan had been murdered on a remote area of his Connecticut estate. One hell of a way to get promoted, Gillette thought, shaking his head. "What happened last November was all over the news for weeks, Gordon," he said quietly.

"Yes, but—"

"You can read all about it on the Internet." Gillette could see that Meade wasn't happy.

"Any hangover from all that as far as North America Guaranty goes?" Meade asked. "Did they invest in the fund you just finished raising? In Everest Eight?"

"A billion dollars," Gillette replied. "We just got that commitment this morning."

"Good. It's important to have a relationship with the biggest pot of money around."

"Believe me," Gillette said firmly, "I understand."

"How much of Fund Seven is left?" Meade asked.

"Two billion."

"So you have seventeen billion of equity right now. Two billion from Seven and fifteen in the new fund."

"Seventeen. Right."

"How many companies do you own?"

"Thirty. We also own shares of other companies we've taken public but don't control anymore."

"What's that in total revenues for the control companies?"

"About seventy billion."

"How many of the thirty companies are you chairman of?"

Meade wasn't going to like this answer. "Eighteen."

"Holy crap!" the older man exclaimed. "Do you really have time to chair that many companies, chair Everest, *and* put seventeen billion dollars of new equity to work?"

"No," Gillette admitted. "We're going to hire at least two more managing partners in the next few weeks. We'll probably open a West Coast office before the end of the year, too, and staff that up fast with experienced people we pick off from other private equity firms. It'll cost more to do it that way, but it'll save time."

"L.A. or San Francisco?"

Gillette checked the clock on the wall. "Look, are you going to tell me why you're here?"

"We want to coinvest with you," Allison broke in before Meade could say anything.

Gillette considered her answer for a few moments. "What exactly does that mean?"

"We want you to call us when you're about to buy a company and give us the option to invest in the equity alongside you."

Gillette considered what she'd said for a moment. "What do I get for doing all the work? For finding the company and structuring the deal. For recruiting a management team to run the company after we take it over. What's in it for me?"

"More equity," Allison answered. "We'll commit five billion dollars to you so you'll have twenty-two billion instead of seventeen. You'll be able to buy more and bigger companies."

"It didn't sound like you were giving me a commitment a minute ago."

"Why not?"

"You used the word *option*. You said you wanted the *option* to invest with us."

"If we don't like the company you want to buy, we won't invest."

"That's not how it works at Everest. If you commit to us, you *have* to wire your share of the money when we call it to buy the company. If you don't, you forfeit what you've already invested. This is the big leagues. It doesn't work for me unless I know you're unconditionally committed. When I negotiate, I need to know I have firepower."

"What's the annual fee on Everest Eight?" Allison asked.

"One percent."

"*A hundred and fifty million a year?*"

"Most funds charge at least one and a *half* percent," Gillette pointed out. "As much as two, in some cases. You both know that. It's just that we're so big, we felt it was fairer to our investors to charge less."

"We'll pay a half a percent on our five billion," Allison offered.

"I don't cut special deals for anyone. I don't have to." Gillette looked at Meade, who was gazing down into his lap, then at Allison. She was staring straight back. So she was the decision maker after all. He hadn't been sure until just now.

"All right," Allison said deliberately. "We'll invest five

billion in Everest Capital Partners Eight under the same terms as everyone else."

"I'll have to go back to my investors," Gillette cautioned, "to the limited partners who've already committed to Eight. I have to make sure they're okay with the fund going from fifteen to twenty billion."

"At five billion, would we be your biggest investor?" Allison wanted to know.

"By far."

"Then I do want something."

Gillette figured this was coming. You didn't get five billion that easily. "What?"

"I want to be a managing partner here at Everest."

Including Faraday, four managing partners reported to Gillette. Beneath that were eight managing directors, then a number of vice presidents and associates reporting to the managing directors. One thing he hadn't anticipated from this meeting was adding anyone else to that pyramid.

"And I don't care about getting paid."

Ultimately, everybody wanted to get paid. Allison had some kind of angle here.

"I don't want a salary or a bonus," she continued. "I don't even want any of the ups."

Ups were pieces of profitable deals. When Everest made money—when it sold a portfolio company for more than it had paid—Gillette got to keep twenty percent of the gain. In the case of Laurel Energy, they'd paid $300 million. If they sold it for $5 billion, he'd keep twenty percent of the $4.7 billion gain—$940 million. As chairman, it was up to him to spread that around Everest as he saw fit. Under terms of the partnership's operating agreement, he could actually keep it all for himself if he chose to. He wouldn't, but he could.

"You want to see how we do it," Gillette said, thinking about Laurel. If the investment bankers could really get him five billion, it would be the best deal in Everest history. "You want to learn our secrets."

"Of course I do," Allison replied. "But in return you get five billion more of equity, fifty million more a year in fees, the ability to leverage that five billion with lots more debt, and a managing partner at no cost."

Gillette hesitated, going through the downside. As the biggest investor in the fund, Allison would assume she could barge into his office anytime. She'd probably feel she should have a bigger say than anyone else as far as strategy and investment decisions went, too. Still, as she'd pointed out, it was five billion in equity and fifty million a year in fees.

He took a deep breath. Major decisions all the time. "Done."

Moments later, Allison and Meade were gone and it was just Gillette and Debbie in the conference room.

"Well, that was interesting," Debbie said with a smug smile as they stood by the door.

"What was?"

"I've seen women try a lot of things to hook a man, but I've never seen one put up five billion dollars. That's a big piece of bait."

In the back of his mind he'd thought the same thing, but he didn't want to admit it to her. "It's not unusual for investors to want to have their people at a private equity firm when they make a huge commitment like that." Actually, it was, but she wouldn't know that. "And that's probably the biggest commitment any single investor ever made to a private equity firm."

Debbie groaned. "Give me a break. Did you see the way she was looking at you? She didn't take her eyes off you the whole time."

"Please."

"Come on, you two would make an incredible couple. Tall, dark, and handsome—slim and blond. Chairman of

Everest Capital—heiress to one of the greatest fortunes in this country. The dream couple, A-list for every party. That's what she was thinking, Chris. I could see it all over her face."

"You're just jealous."

Which they both knew wasn't true. Debbie was a lesbian. Gillette had been sure of that before he'd hired her—thanks to McGuire & Company. It was a perfect business relationship. No chance of her developing a silly crush on him, no chance of him getting any stupid ideas of his own.

"Do me a favor," he said. "Call Craig West over at McGuire and tell him to find out everything he can about Allison ASAP."

"Sure."

"And tell the guy in Three I'll be there in five minutes," he said over his shoulder as he moved toward the doorway. Then he stopped. "Oh."

Debbie looked up. "Yes?"

"What you said outside before we came in here."

She thought for a moment, trying to remember. "You mean about you being able to handle so much?"

Christian nodded. "Thanks," he said, his voice low. "That was nice."

"Christian!"

"Damn," Gillette muttered, almost running into David Wright as he turned to go.

Wright was an up-and-coming Everest managing director—thirty-one years old, tall and square-faced, with close-set eyes, short blond hair, and light skin. Aggressive to the point of arrogance, he was by far the most talented MD at the firm. And the only person at Everest who could give Gillette any competition at pool.

"I've got to talk to you, Christian. Now. *Right* now."

"What is it?" Gillette demanded. Seemed like everyone always needed to talk to him right away.

"We've got a chance to buy Hush-Hush Intimates," Wright explained. "You know, the Victoria's Secret competitor."

Gillette knew about Hush-Hush. The company was less than ten years old but had already racked up megasuccess by pushing the sex envelope even further than Victoria's Secret. Hush-Hush's catalog, published once a season, had become hotter than the *Sports Illustrated* swimsuit issue and the *Victoria's Secret* catalog combined.

"The company's privately held," Wright continued, "and the family just decided to sell."

"How do you know?"

"I just got off the phone with the guy who's head of corporate development there. His name's Frank Hobbs. We were pretty good friends in business school. He says he can get us the inside track to buy the company, but we've got to move fast."

"How big is it?" Gillette asked.

Wright shrugged. "I don't know. Who cares? It's growing like a tech firm, and we can get our hands on it."

Gillette eyed Wright carefully. They'd worked closely together for several years, and Wright had a haggard look about him Gillette had never seen. "You okay?"

Wright's gaze dropped to the floor. "Yeah, fine."

Gillette hesitated a beat, waiting for the younger man to look up. But he didn't. "Uh-huh, well, get more information on it," he instructed, brushing past.

"Hi, Marvin," Gillette said loudly, moving into Conference Room Two. Marvin Miller was a partner at White & Cross, a large public accounting firm.

"Hello, Christian," Miller said enthusiastically, rising from his seat and pumping Gillette's hand. "This is—"

Miller started to introduce a young associate who'd come with him, but Gillette waved it off. There wasn't time. "Relax," he said, recognizing Miller's anxiety. A lot of money was at stake here. "Sit down."

A nervous smile played across Miller's face. "Relax? Why would I need to do that?"

"You know why I wanted to see you."

"What do you mean?" Miller asked innocently as they both sat down.

"Come on, Marvin, you said there was a problem with the Laurel Energy financial statements. A problem that could get in the way of a sale. I'm about to get five billion for Laurel. Nothing's going to screw that up."

"I said it *might* get in the way."

"You guys have been doing Laurel's financial statements for the last three years. How could there *possibly* be a problem?"

"We depend on your management team to give us good numbers, Christian. One of my guys has a question about a couple of the admin figures we got last month. They don't seem right."

Gillette started to say something, then stopped. This was going to be a quick conversation, no screwing around. "How many of our companies do you audit, Marvin?"

"Um, nineteen."

"What do you make off us a year?"

"I . . . I . . . I don't know exactly, I'd have to—"

"Give me an estimate."

Miller swallowed hard before answering. "Around a hundred million, maybe more."

"A hundred million. That's a lot of fees, Marvin. A lot of fees to lose." Gillette watched Miller swallow even harder. "And we just finished raising another fund this morning. It's twenty billion, so we're going to be buying a lot more companies. Big companies with lots of accounting needs. You can have first crack at auditing those companies." He hesitated. "Or not."

"Christian, I—"

"Very soon I'm going to start the process to sell Laurel," Gillette cut in. "I'm going to retain Morgan Stanley, and the financials better be in perfect order," he warned, rising from his seat. "Got it?"

Miller nodded, resigned to doing whatever was necessary to stay in Gillette's good graces. "Yes, Christian, there won't be any problems," he said quietly. "Take this off your issue list."

"I will."

Gillette glanced at his watch as he headed toward Conference Room Three. It was eleven-thirty. He hoped the guy had waited.

He hadn't.

"Damn it!" As Gillette turned to go back to his office, Debbie was standing in front of him.

"You didn't miss Mr. Smith," Debbie explained. "He never showed."

"What?"

"Yeah, he called reception while you were in with the Wallace people. He's waiting for you in his hotel room at the Intercontinental." The Intercontinental Hotel was a couple of blocks from the Everest offices. "Room 1241." She smirked. "As if you're really going to drop everything and go running over there."

Gillette rolled his eyes. "Yeah, as if."

"Mr. Smith?" Gillette asked, moving through the hotel room doorway.

After Gillette had passed, the other man leaned into the hallway and glanced in both directions, then shut and locked the door. "Thank you for coming here, Mr. Gillette." The man moved into the suite and sat on a small sofa in front of a dark wood coffee table. He pointed at the matching sofa on the other side of the table. "I know you're busy, but it has to be this way."

Gillette sat down, not taking his eyes off the other man.

"By the way, my name isn't Smith, it's Ganze. Daniel Ganze."

"Okay."

"Would you like something to drink, Mr. Gillette? Coffee, Coke?"

"No."

Ganze was short, no more than five six, with closely cropped black hair that was thinning on top. He had dark, straight eyebrows and a small mouth with thin lips that barely moved when he spoke. His voice was low and precise, each syllable perfectly articulated. He didn't face you when he talked—his chin was pointed off at an angle, left or right. He didn't look you straight in the eye, either. Almost, but not quite.

"Why all the secrecy, Mr. Ganze?" It was the second time today Gillette had agreed to a meeting without a specific agenda, and it was killing him. "Senator Clark asked me to meet with you," he said when Ganze didn't answer right away. Michael Clark was the senior United States senator from California. Gillette had met Clark this past summer at a White House dinner, and they'd gotten together several times since to discuss ways in which Everest could do more business in California—and California could benefit. "I'm always happy to help the senator, but he didn't tell me what this was about. In fact, he didn't even tell me what you do, Mr. Ganze."

"I'm an attorney by training, but I don't practice anymore. Now I represent certain interests in Washington, D.C."

"Interests?"

"Yes, interests." Ganze leaned forward, over the table.

"I appreciate Senator Clark setting this meeting up, and I appreciate your time. I know how busy you are."

It was the second time Ganze had said that. "How exactly do you know how busy I am?"

"I just do." Ganze folded his hands tightly. "As I said before, I'm sorry for all the secrecy, but it has to be this way. That's all I can tell you about me and the interests I represent right now. If we proceed, you'll learn more."

Gillette was about to say something when Ganze spoke up again.

"Your father was a senator, Mr. Gillette."

Gillette's eyes raced to Ganze's, and his pulse exploded. He fought to contain himself, but it was impossible. "Yes, he was." He tried to say the words calmly, but he could tell Ganze had noticed the electric reaction and the rasp in his voice as his throat went dry. He hated being transparent, but he couldn't help it. This was his father.

"His name was Clayton Gillette," Ganze continued. "He founded and built a very successful Los Angeles–based investment bank, then sold it to one of the big Wall Street brokerage firms for a hundred million. Stayed on for a while after he sold out, then ran for Congress. One term there, then he won a Senate seat. He was killed in a private plane crash in the middle of that Senate term. The plane went down just after takeoff from Orange County Airport. It was a clear day. The official record says pilot error, but that explanation seems thin to me. To other people as well," Ganze added, his voice low.

Gillette had wondered about the crash for years but figured grief was making him paranoid. "What *other* people?"

"We have more information you'll want to hear," Ganze said, dodging Gillette's question.

"Like what?"

"Like the identity and location of a woman you've been trying to find for years."

Gillette froze, understanding immediately. His blood mother. "Ganze, I—"

"Mr. Gillette," Ganze cut in, "I know this is hard, but I can't tell you anything else at this time. I'm sorry. If you want to hear more, you'll have to come to Washington to meet with my superior and me. If that's agreeable, I'll be in touch." He hesitated, then motioned at the door. "Goodbye."

CHAPTER 2

Clayton was lighting his pipe when Christian got to the den—a hallowed room in the Bel Air mansion. He hesitated at the doorway, waiting for his father to see him.

"Come on in, Chris," Clayton called from behind the desk, clenching the pipe tightly between his teeth as he held a silver lighter over the bowl and sucked the flame down. "Close the door so we aren't interrupted, will you?"

"Yes, sir."

Christian loved this room. Dark wood paneling, big furniture, photographs of his father on hunting and fishing expeditions in exotic places with other famous people, dim lighting, the aroma of that pipe, a classic pool table off in one corner. A man's room. He sat in the leather chair in front of the desk.

Clayton tossed the lighter on the desk and took his first deep breath of the pungent smoke. The lighter landed beside the text of a speech he'd be making to the full Senate when they reconvened after the holidays. "Nice to get away from all the hubbub, huh?"

They'd just finished eating: thirty guests at the mansion for a formal Christmas Eve dinner. "Yeah," Christian agreed. Even nicer to spend time alone with his father. That rarely happened now that he was away on the East Coast at college.

"Your mother did a heck of a job with dinner. The food was great, wasn't it?"

Christian wanted to stop himself, but he couldn't. "My *step*mother, you mean." He'd had another run-in with Lana that afternoon, over something he couldn't even remember now, but it had burned out of control quickly. Like a small flame in a bone-dry forest, fanned by so much history.

Clayton looked up. "Chris, there's no reason—"

"And *you* did a heck of a job with dinner, Dad. *You* paid for the caterer. Lana didn't lift a finger." Christian watched for any signs of anger, but his father's handsome face stayed calm.

"Let's play some pool," Clayton suggested, nodding toward the table.

Christian had been hoping his father would say that. They had a long-running score he wanted to settle. "Sure."

As they got up, there was a knock on the door. "Yes?" Clayton called, clearly irritated at the interruption. "Come in."

The door burst open and Nikki rushed in. Nikki was Christian's younger half sister. She was a pretty brunette with a bubbly personality. They'd always been close.

She went to Clayton first and threw her arms around his neck. "Sorry to interrupt, Daddy," she said breathlessly, "but I wanted to say good-bye. I'm going to Kim's house, then a bunch of us are going out."

"*On Christmas Eve?*" Clayton asked, winking at Christian over her shoulder, feigning anger.

"Thanks for the bracelet, Daddy," she said, moving quickly to Christian and hugging him. "It's exactly what I wanted."

"There'll be more tomorrow."

"I can't wait to spend more time with you while you're home, Chris," she said, kissing his cheek.

Christian leaned back and smiled. "Ah, you'll be out with your friends all the time."

"No way." She shook her head hard, then headed for the door. "Bye, you two. Have fun."

When she was gone and the door was closed, they moved to the table.

"Eight ball?" Clayton suggested, putting his smoldering pipe in a large ashtray, then picking out his favorite cue stick from the wall rack. "Best of three, you break?"

"Okay, but I don't want any charity. You break."

Clayton nodded. "Fine, I'll take all the charity I can get," he said, leaning down and lining up the cue ball with the top of the triangle at the far end of the table. Then he hesitated, smiling serenely and straightening up. Looking at the ceiling as if he were deep in thought. "You've never taken a match from me, have you?"

They both knew Christian hadn't. *And* they both knew that such a victory was Christian's white whale. Reminding him of the streak was his father's way of playing with his mind, but he wasn't going to let himself be manipulated tonight. "This'll be interesting, Dad. I played a lot last semester."

"Is that all you guys at Princeton do?" Clayton wanted to know, breaking up the balls with a loud crack. "Play pool?"

"I'm keeping my grades up," Christian said quickly, sizing up the way the balls had come to rest. None in for his father on the break. A good way to start. "I'm fine."

Clayton chuckled. "I know you are. Four A's and a B plus in advanced calculus last semester. You're still on track to graduate with honors this May."

Christian had been about to take his first shot, but he stopped. "How do you know?" The semester had just ended last week. Final grades hadn't been released yet.

"I called my friend John Gray. He's one of the—"

"One of the assistant deans," Christian broke in, setting up for the shot again. "Yeah, I know." He made it easily. "Checking up, huh?"

"It's what I do, son. *Which reminds me.* While you're home I want you to have lunch with my friend Ted Stovall. He's a Stanford trustee. He'll be very helpful getting you into business school."

Stanford University had one of the nation's elite business schools. "I'll take care of that on my own, Dad," Christian said. "I appreciate it, but I don't need your help. Damn it!" He'd missed a shot he shouldn't have because he'd been distracted by the conversation.

"You mean you don't *want* my help," Clayton corrected, inhaling, then clenching the pipe between his teeth as he prepared to shoot. "Just have lunch with Ted," he pushed gently. "Okay?"

"Yes, sir."

"And when you graduate from Stanford, we're going to get you that job at Goldman Sachs. Mergers and acquisitions. That's the one you want, right?"

It was exactly the job Christian wanted after business school. The *only* job he wanted. "Yes, sir," he said, spying a large wooden box sitting on a table in front of the window. "Thanks." He knew this den like the back of his hand, and the box hadn't been there when he'd left for Princeton last September. "Is that a humidor?" he asked, pointing.

Clayton glanced in the direction Christian was pointing. "Yes."

"When did you start smoking cigars? I thought you hated them."

"I do. It's a gift from a friend in Cuba. I'm not supposed to keep those things, but, well, it was just so pretty."

Christian watched his father sink seven balls in a row, tapping the butt end of his cue on the floor faster and faster, harder and harder, until the eighth disappeared, too. "Damn," he muttered.

Clayton rose up as the black ball dropped and smiled from behind the pipe. "One down, one to go. This is going to be easy."

But Christian won the second game, and the third was hard fought. Finally, there were just three balls left on the tan felt—the cue, the eight, and a stripe—Clayton's. Christian smiled. His father was blocked. The striped ball lay directly on the opposite side of the eight from the cue, and his father couldn't use the eight in a combination.

Clayton grimaced. "Tough leave, huh? Nowhere for me to go."

Christian nodded, trying to mask the smile. His father had to do something, and the odds were good that once the cue ball came to rest, he'd have an easy next shot to win. The streak was almost over. He could feel it.

But Clayton did the impossible. He made the cue ball jump the eight and into the stripe, knocking the stripe cleanly into a far pocket. The cue ball caromed off two sides of the table and came to rest near the eight. Clayton dropped it into a side pocket easily for the win.

Christian just shook his head as Clayton replaced his cue stick in the rack on the wall and came around the table. He'd been so close.

"I know how you hate to lose," Clayton said, placing his hands on Christian's shoulders. "You're so much like me," he murmured, smiling. "So much."

"Christian."

Gillette heard the voice but didn't react. He was still far away, still in his father's study, wishing he could have an evening like that just once more. After pool, they'd talked until two in the morning. But there'd never be another evening like that. Six months later, Clayton was gone.

"Christian!"

Gillette finally looked up. Faraday was standing in his office doorway. "What is it, Nigel?"

"It's time for the meeting," Faraday replied, tapping his wristwatch. He cocked his head to one side. "You okay?"

"Let's go," Faraday snapped at the stragglers. "You're four minutes late."

The two managing directors hustled to their seats at the far end of the conference room table.

This was the Everest managers meeting: Gillette, four managing partners, eight managing directors, and Debbie; attendance required. The only exception—Gillette. If he needed to be elsewhere, Faraday was in charge.

Gillette ran the meeting from the head of the table, while the other managers sat down the sides in descending order of seniority. Debbie sat at the far end of the table, taking minutes. Donovan had never allowed anyone but the partners into this meeting, but Gillette had a different management style. He believed in open communication—most of the time, anyway.

"Everyone's here, Christian," Faraday reported. He sat immediately to Gillette's right.

Gillette had been reviewing a memo and glanced up into two rows of hungry eyes. They reminded him of a wolf pack. "A couple of updates," he began. "Nigel finished raising Everest Eight this morning. We now have fifteen billion dollars of signed commitments."

Everyone rapped the table with their knuckles—the customary show of approval. The news about Everest Eight had spread like wildfire this morning, so the announcement was just a formality.

"Nigel deserves more than that, people," Gillette urged as the sounds of congratulation faded. "I said *fifteen billion*."

The room broke into raucous applause and loud whistles. Gillette usually wanted controlled responses to everything at this meeting, even big news, but when he gave permission to celebrate, people responded. And this was tear-the-roof-off stuff.

Historically, Everest had achieved at least a three-to-one return, with the firm keeping twenty percent of the profits. So if the people around the table could turn fifteen billion into forty-five over the next few years, Gillette would have six billion—twenty percent of the thirty-billion-dollar profit—to spread around. It would be the biggest payout ever for a private equity firm. Some of the money would go to the Everest rank and file, but most of it would go to the people in this room.

Gillette nodded approvingly at their reactions, watching the hungry looks turn ravenous. He could see people calculating their potential share of the ups—as they should. Money was their driver, their reward for the intense stress and sacrifice—eighty to ninety hours a week away from family and friends. If they didn't get to enjoy the reward, they wouldn't last.

"That's better," Gillette said, motioning for quiet as he turned to Faraday, who was beaming. "Nigel, it's a tremendous achievement. The largest private equity fund ever raised. Thank you."

"Thank *you*, Mr. Chairman."

People began to clap and whistle again, but Gillette shut them down with a flash of his piercing gray eyes. "It gets better," he continued when the room was silent. "This morning, I met with representatives of the Wallace Family. They're out of Chicago, for any of you who *don't* know," he said, effectively telling anyone who didn't that they better research the Wallaces right after the meeting. "They're one of the wealthiest families in the country." He paused. "They've committed an additional five billion to Everest Eight, so it's now a *twenty*-billion-dollar fund."

There were gasps.

"And they've made their investment on the same terms and conditions as the other limited partners."

"They don't want *anything* special?" Maggie Carpenter asked warily. Maggie was one of the managing partners. Six months ago, Gillette had hired her away from Kohlberg Kravis & Roberts, another high-profile private equity firm in Manhattan. Thirty-five, Maggie was thin with dark red hair, a pale, freckled complexion, and stark facial features. Besides Gillette, she was usually the first one to ask tough questions in a meeting. "That's an awfully big commitment for them not to get some sizzle."

"They want one of their people on the ground here at Everest," Gillette replied, catching the uneasy looks appearing on the faces around the table. "Allison Wallace will join us as a managing partner. That's the only extra they want."

"The *only* extra?" asked Blair Johnson. Johnson was another of the four managing partners. He was African American and had grown up in an upper-middle-class Atlanta suburb. The son of a physician, he'd gone to the right schools: Harvard undergraduate and Columbia Business School. He'd been with Everest for seven years, and Gillette had promoted him to managing partner nine months ago. "That seems like a lot."

"Worried about the money?" Gillette asked.

Johnson cased the room quickly, making certain he wasn't the only one concerned about Allison Wallace. "Not the salary and bonus, really," he answered hesitantly. "After all, it's a twenty-billion-dollar fund. At one percent, we'll make two hundred million a year in fees alone."

"So it's the ups you're worried about."

"Yeah, the ups."

"Well, here's the deal, Blair," Gillette said sharply. "Allison doesn't want *any* money. No salary, no bonus, no ups.

All she wants is a front row seat at the game so she can see how her money's being used."

"What Allison Wallace wants," Tom O'Brien said in a professorial tone, "is to see how we do it." O'Brien was the fourth managing partner. He was forty-one but looked older. His hair was snow white, and he had a ruddy complexion. From Boston, he had a prickly New England accent. "She wants to go to school. She wants the keys to the castle."

"Of course she does," Gillette agreed. "But so what? Nigel and I planned on adding two more managing partners anyway. We'll need six of you to put twenty double-large to work in three years. At *least* six. This way we get one free, and we get an extra five billion to invest, plus the annual fee. It's like she's paying us fifty million a year to work here," he reasoned, liking the way it sounded. "It's a good deal, and it's not like she's going to be able to duplicate what we have when she goes back to her family office in Chicago." Gillette could see that people were apprehensive. "Another update," he said, switching subjects, not wanting to dwell on something that made people feel insecure. He'd made the decision about Allison Wallace, and it was final. "We got the Las Vegas NFL franchise."

"Hot damn!" yelled O'Brien, banging the table. He was a sports nut and had helped Gillette and Faraday during the bid process.

"Next week I'm meeting with Kurt Landry, the NFL commissioner, to work out a few things," Gillette continued, "but basically it's a done deal."

"And we're sure we've got the zoning to build the stadium?" Maggie wanted to know.

"Absolutely."

"Wait a minute," David Wright broke in. Typically, he was the only managing director that spoke without being asked a question by a managing partner first. "We're building the stadium?"

"I want to build it so we keep the extra revenue," Gillette explained. "Concessions, advertising rights, naming it. This way we have total control of everything."

"How much did we offer for the franchise?" Maggie asked. "I can't remember."

"Four hundred and fifty million."

"What's the strategy with this?" she continued. "I don't know much about sports teams, but four hundred fifty million seems like a lot, *and* you've got the cost of building the stadium. Which is what?"

"Three hundred million."

"So we're in for seven hundred and fifty million. Can we really get a decent return on that, Christian?"

Maggie was suspicious that this was just a "boys gone wild" investment, Gillette could tell. An excuse to jet to Las Vegas every few weeks and hang out with movie stars, corporate bigwigs, sports figures, politicians, and friends in a plush skybox. "The stadium will be finished in a year and a half, and it'll seat eighty thousand," Gillette answered, giving a quick overview of the numbers. "We'll charge an average of a hundred dollars a ticket. That's eight million dollars for each of the eight home games, sixty-four million a season. And that doesn't include a couple of preseason games we can probably get fifty bucks a ticket for. Plus, we get concessions, our share of the NFL TV contracts, and ad dollars. One of the big computer store chains already offered us ten million a year to put their name on the stadium. Nigel and Tom," he said, "figure we can generate at least three hundred million a year in revenues. Based on where other major league sports teams sell, that would make the franchise worth somewhere between two and three billion. That would be a hell of a return."

"But can you really fill up eighty thousand seats at a

hundred bucks a pop in that city?" Maggie pushed. "Vegas isn't that big, it's probably only got around a million permanent residents. I don't think eight percent of the population is going to a football game eight times a year for that kind of money."

"The population is closer to a million five," Gillette corrected, "but I hear what you're saying. Which is why we're already negotiating with a couple of the major airlines to add flights from Los Angeles to Vegas on game weekends. Remember, as crazy as it sounds, L.A. doesn't have a football team, and we've got assurances from the NFL that it won't get one in the next few years, until we're established. I think L.A. will adopt the Vegas franchise. It's a nothing flight for those people—you're up, you're down. We're also working with the casinos on promotions, and we're pretty far along with several of them. In fact—and what I'm about to tell you has to stay in this room," he said, giving everyone a warning glare. "We're looking at opening a casino ourselves. We've gotten to know the city officials very well over the last two years, and they've told us they can persuade the state gaming commission to give us a license."

"What about the Mafia?" Maggie asked bluntly.

Gillette had figured someone would ask about that. "We're checking, but I doubt the NFL would green-light the franchise if the Mafia was still a problem out there." He had better information than that but didn't want to alarm anyone. "I'll keep everyone up-to-date on what we find," he promised, looking around the room. It was time to end the cross-examination. Maggie was good, but she didn't get it this time. "This could turn out to be one of our best investments ever. Not Laurel Energy, but close."

People rapped on the table hard, nodding their approval, understanding that Gillette had ended the discussion on this topic.

"Another thing," he continued, holding up his hand for quiet. "I'm going to retain Morgan Stanley to sell Laurel Energy."

"Why Morgan Stanley?" Maggie asked.

"Why not?"

"I thought Goldman Sachs had the best mergers and acquisitions group for the energy industry."

"Morgan Stanley will do a great job for us," Gillette replied confidently.

"Is this payback?" Maggie looked over at Wright, then back at Gillette.

"For what?" Gillette demanded.

"You know what."

Gillette's eyes narrowed. "No." He stared at her for a few moments more, then resumed the meeting. "I want to get back to a point Blair made earlier. The fact that we'll be making two hundred million a year in fees on Everest Eight. I've decided to commit ten million of the first-year fee to St. Christopher's Hospital up on the West Side." He paused. "I want all of you to make personal contributions to your local charities, too. In your towns, your neighborhoods, whatever. That'll be something I'll talk about with each of you during your annual reviews in January. Frankly, the more you donate the better. All of us are lucky when it comes to money. I know everyone works hard and makes a lot of sacrifices, particularly those of you who have spouses and children. You don't see them much," he said, his voice dropping. "But it isn't like we dig ditches, either. While I'm chairman, this firm is going to be socially responsible, understood?"

His words were met with nods.

"Good." Gillette checked his agenda, scratching out the NFL, Laurel Energy, and charitable contribution items. The next topic was the L.A. office. "Just so everyone's clear, Nigel and I are looking into opening a Los Angeles office, but we haven't made any final decisions yet. I don't want rumors going around. When we do make a decision, we'll let everyone know right away." He grinned. "Anybody want to volunteer to go?"

Wright raised his hand immediately. "Can I get promoted to managing partner if I do?"

Gillette shot Faraday a quick look and shook his head, still grinning.

Faraday rolled his eyes.

"Always looking for a deal, aren't you, David." Gillette turned back to face Wright. "Stop by later and we'll talk about it. We can talk more about that other thing, too."

"Stop by later" meant they'd talk about it during a game of pool in the room adjoining Gillette's office.

"I'd rather talk about Hush-Hush *now*," Wright said, taking advantage of the fact that Gillette was speaking to him. "I don't want to wait. It's too hot."

To bring up a prospective investment in this meeting, a managing partner or managing director was supposed to run it by Faraday first, then send around a short memo on the company so the group had the basic facts—what the company did, how big it was, how profitable it was. Wright hadn't talked to Faraday or sent around a memo.

"Hush-Hush?" O'Brien piped up. "The intimate-apparel company?"

"Yeah, that's it," Wright said.

"What's the deal?"

"We've got the inside track to buy it. I have a friend in senior management who can help us ink it." Wright nodded at Gillette. "I spoke to Christian about it earlier. He likes it."

"*What I said was*, you should get more information," Gillette reminded the younger man, irritated that Wright had jumped the gun and was trying to make people in the room think he was already on board.

"I'll vote against that investment on principle alone,"

Maggie spoke up. "I don't care how great a deal it is. Their catalog is basically a porn magazine. It's insulting to women."

"If it's so insulting," Wright shot back, "there must be a lot of women who like being insulted. Hush-Hush is growing at over eighty percent a year, and—"

"I don't care how fast it's growing," Maggie interrupted. "It's not something we should get into."

"Hey, just because you don't care about looking sexy doesn't mean the rest of the female world doesn't—"

"*David.*" Gillette's sharp rebuke cut Wright off instantly.

Maggie glared at Wright for several moments, then turned to look at Gillette when Wright didn't look away. "Besides, it's the fashion business," she said, her voice cracking with anger. "There can be big revenue swings." She took a deep breath. "Christian, for Everest to make an investment, you and all four managing partners have to vote yes. I'm telling you right now, I'd vote no. So we can all save ourselves a lot of time by cutting off this discussion right now."

Gillette folded his arms over his chest. Maggie was right. Buying any fashion business was risky, especially one like Hush-Hush. But he didn't appreciate the way she'd tried to take control of the meeting. "Let me remind you," he said, "the chairman of this firm can overrule any single negative vote. Got that?"

She nodded quickly, understanding what he was saying— so much more than that he might overrule her if she chose to vote against the investment. "Yes."

Gillette looked back at Wright, irritated. "David, you know you're supposed to talk to Nigel before you bring up something like this."

"But I thought—"

"*David.*"

Wright's gaze fell to his lap. "Sorry."

* * *

"You give David Wright a lot of fucking rope," Faraday muttered as he sat down in front of Gillette's desk.

It was six-fifteen. The managers meeting had broken up ten minutes before, and Gillette was checking out a story on the Internet. He put his shoes up on the desk and locked his fingers behind his head. "David's a star, easily our top managing director. We both know that. He deserves some extra rope."

"Not as much as you give him."

"He's a thoroughbred."

"He's cocky as hell."

"He's young, he'll mellow with age. You and I can help him with that."

"Some of the other managing directors are grumbling."

"About what?" Gillette demanded, dropping his shoes to the floor. "Making a million dollars a year?"

"There's more to it than just the fucking money," Faraday retorted. "People around here are like puppies, okay? They don't like it when you pay a lot of attention to one person."

"Tell the whiners to find some investments for us," Gillette suggested. "Right now, David's the only managing director who does. We've already bought two companies he found, and now he's got us in the hunt for Hush-Hush. Which despite Maggie's objections might be a good deal. It's three hundred million in revenues, growing like mad, too. And I think you told me once you know people at some big apparel company in Paris. Your family is friends with the CEO's family, right?"

Faraday nodded, understanding immediately where Gillette was headed. "That's a good idea, I'll get in touch with him."

"He'd probably salivate at the chance to own Hush-

Hush," Gillette pointed out. "You know, increase his presence in the U.S. with a hot brand."

"Sure."

"It'll be an easy flip. We grab this thing quick, before other people find out it's on the block, then sell it in a few months for a couple-hundred-million-dollar gain. If it works, it'll be thanks to David."

"Yeah, but—"

"And remember, David's the one who got us in to see the California Teachers Pension," Gillette reminded Faraday. "The people who made that six-hundred-million-dollar commitment this morning. At one percent, that's six million a year of income for this firm. That ain't chump change."

"His fucking *father* got us in to see them."

Wright's father was a senior investment banker at Morgan Stanley. He'd introduced Faraday to the executives of the West Coast pension fund several months ago.

"But David made it happen. Now we have a great relationship with one of the biggest institutional investors in the country. Hell, they could have committed a couple of billion to us if they wanted. And they will next time around, to Everest Nine."

Faraday shook his head. "Christ, the ink isn't even dry on the Everest Eight subscription agreements and you're already thinking about Nine." He smoothed his tie. "Can I ask you something?"

Gillette heard an unusual tone in Faraday's voice. "What?"

"Was Maggie on point today?"

"About?"

"She didn't spin it out all the way, and frankly, I don't blame her. God, you looked like you were going to bite her head off when she started talking."

"You mean the Laurel Energy thing?" Gillette asked. "Giving the sell-side mandate to Morgan Stanley?"

"Yeah. Was that payback for David's father introducing us to the California Teachers Pension? Was she right?"

"Morgan Stanley will do a great job for us. I'm confident they'll get us five billion for Laurel." Gillette raised one eyebrow. "But if I can show appreciation for a favor at the same time and give them an incentive to do us more favors, well, that's just good business."

"Laurel Energy is so important to—"

"Enough." Gillette checked a stock price on his computer. "I'm thinking about promoting David to managing partner."

Faraday groaned. "But he's only thirty-one."

"He's on seven of our boards, five with me. I'm chairman of those companies, but he basically runs the quarterly meetings. He does a great job, too. Nobody on those boards seems to care that he's thirty-one."

Faraday exhaled heavily. "I guess it's better to promote from inside; at least you know what you're getting." He looked up. "But I don't think it would be a good idea to promote him, then send him to L.A. to open the office. We need to see how he does as a managing partner first."

"Agreed."

Faraday chuckled. "Can you imagine letting him go to L.A., what with all that beautiful, barely dressed tail running around, right after we promote him to managing partner? Jesus, we'd never be able to find him. Neither would his wife."

"I *said*, I agree."

"I just don't want you changing your mind over a game of pool with him. David can be very convincing."

"Won't happen." Gillette thought back to this morning when he was coming out of the conference room and he'd run into Wright. "Has David seemed a little off lately?"

"What do you mean?"

"Preoccupied. Subdued. Not himself."

Faraday hesitated, thinking. "No, I haven't noticed anything."

"I hope he's all right. I always worry that our top people are being wooed away."

Faraday's expression soured.

"What is it?" Gillette asked. He could tell that Faraday had started to say something but stopped.

"Nothing."

"Come on, Nigel."

Faraday fiddled with his tie for a moment, then dropped it on his shirt. "David Wright," he mumbled. "Are you grooming him to take over Everest when you leave?"

Gillette looked at Faraday hard for a few moments. "Every organization needs a succession plan."

"Why not me?" Faraday asked quietly. "You know I'm committed, and after all, I am second in command."

Gillette hesitated, thinking about whether or not to get into it. He needed Faraday to stay committed, and you had to be careful about how people would react if you were candid with them. Faraday might check out mentally if he thought he'd hit a ceiling. At the same time, you couldn't string someone along. Not someone as loyal as Nigel. Gillette took a deep breath. There were always so many major issues swirling around. So many split-second decisions he had to make.

"You're a hell of a money raiser, Nigel, and you've really come through for me over the last ten months as far as the admin side of the firm goes. But you don't have any deal experience," Gillette said gently. "You don't know how to find companies for us to buy, how to structure deals, or how to run the companies after we buy them."

"I can learn."

"That's a lot to learn."

"Listen, I'm—"

"Let's talk about Apex," Gillette interrupted.

Faraday hung his head, as though Apex were the last thing he wanted to talk about. "Not again."

"Yes," Gillette said strongly, "again."

"But we already have *twenty-two billion* to put to work now that you've got the Wallace Family in the corral. Do you really want more?"

"I always want more."

"And," Faraday kept going, "with Apex, we'd be inheriting more fucking problems. Why would you want to do that?"

Apex Capital was another large Manhattan-based private equity firm that owned twenty-two companies and had another five billion of dry powder—equity commitments from investors to buy more companies. Until last year, Apex had been run by a self-made moneyman named Paul Strazzi. But Strazzi had become the second casualty of Miles Whitman's war of desperation. Strazzi's fatal error: making a play for Everest, too.

Since Strazzi's murder, Apex had been run by a man named Russell Hughes, who couldn't fight his way out of a wet paper bag. Hughes looked the part—tall and dark, with sharp facial features, like Gillette—so he made a good first impression. But he couldn't make a decision to save his life. He put off everything, and the lack of leadership was severely affecting Apex. The firm had made only one investment under Hughes, and several of the portfolio companies had run into trouble over the last six months because he'd hesitated to replace incompetent executives. Apex was vulnerable, and Gillette knew it.

"We can pick Apex off cheap," Gillette said. "All we have to do is pay the general partners par, what they originally put in. Then we've got five billion more of dry powder and twenty-two more companies, several of which we could combine with our portfolio companies. By doing that, we'll pick up big savings axing back office jobs and getting more purchasing power with suppliers. I think I can clean up their dogs fast, too. I've looked at them, and I don't think they're beyond repair. If we fire a few of the execs and replace them with people we know, we can save them. But the most important thing is to get that five billion of unused equity. At that point, we'd have twenty-seven billion dollars of equity. Then we'll lever that twenty-seven with debt from the banks and insurance companies that are all over us to partner with them. I'd say we could get at least four times, wouldn't you?"

Faraday considered Gillette's guess. "That's probably right."

"Four times would be almost a hundred and ten billion dollars. Combined with the twenty-seven of equity, we'd control over a hundred and thirty-five billion of capital."

"How do you know we'd be able to get Apex so cheap?" Faraday asked.

"I spoke to Apex's controlling general partner. They hate Russell Hughes. They'd sell to us in a heartbeat if we offer par because they figure if he stays at the top, the family's money isn't going to be worth *anything*."

"Why don't they just replace Russell?"

"That would confirm to everyone in the financial world that Apex is in chaos. It would be impossible for them to raise any more funds, and who wants to be bought by a private equity firm in chaos?"

"I see what you're saying."

"So they're stuck with Russell," Gillette continued, "unless I show up. And I think I can get them to approve this thing fast."

"I bet you could," Faraday agreed. "How much would it cost?"

"A billion. It would have been a lot more a year ago, but Hughes has driven the thing into the ground."

"Would you collapse Apex into Everest after we bought it?"

"No. Not at first, anyway. I wouldn't give those people the opportunity to benefit from all the money you've raised. That wouldn't be fair."

"Good."

"Down the road, I might. Once you and I figure out who the keepers are over there."

"How are you going to do this? Who are you going to approach first?"

"Next week I'm meeting with Russell's largest limited partners, the institutional investors. I'm going to explain what I want, get their buy-in, and ask them to contact Russell and urge him not to fight us. Then I'm going back to the general partner, the Strazzi estate, to make a formal offer. After that I'll get a couple of the Apex managing partners in a room and make them an offer, too. Obviously Hughes won't want to sell his stake, but if I have everyone else in my corner, he won't have any choice."

"You've got it all figured out, don't you. Hughes is a dead man and he doesn't even know it."

"That's the way it has to be."

"You get what you fucking want, don't you, Christian."

"Usually. And one thing I want is for you to watch your mouth."

Faraday raised both eyebrows. "Huh?"

"You don't even know you're doing it, do you."

"Well, I . . ." Faraday's voice trailed off.

"Like I told you before, I don't care if 'fuck' is every other word when you and I are one-on-one like this, but I don't want you saying it in front of others in the office, especially the women."

"When did I—"

"This morning, okay?"

Faraday groaned. "Well, excuse me for getting excited."

"I don't care if you get excited. I don't even care if you do that silly dance you did in the hall this morning, which by the way has to be one of the most embarrassing things I've ever had the misfortune of witnessing. Just don't drop the F-bomb in public anymore."

"All right, all right." Faraday started to get up, then dropped his pudgy form back into the seat. "Is Allison Wallace qualified to be a managing partner at Everest Capital? Did you check her out?" he pushed. "I mean, it's great to add another five double-large to the new fund, but I don't want deadwood walking around here. Especially deadwood as pretty as her. She'll be a big distraction."

Gillette sighed. It seemed he was always pushing things uphill. "When did you see her?"

"When she was walking out this morning, after you met with her. How could I miss her? The whole office stopped to look."

"Give me a break."

"Legs up to her neck and a short little skirt to show them off," Faraday said smugly, holding one hand below his chin.

"Her skirt wasn't short. She was dressed very conservatively."

"Yeah, maybe you're right." Faraday chuckled. "But the important question is, does she have game or is she where she is just because of all the money? Even more important, are you letting her in here to get into her piggy bank or her panties?"

"Maybe both."

"At least you're honest."

"Oh, come on, Nigel. You know me better than that." Gillette's tone turned serious. "I'd never do something like that."

"I know."

"Hey, she's on the board of the family trust with her uncle and her grandfather. There's plenty of others in that generation of the Wallace Family they could have put on the board. She's qualified."

"Did you call Craig West?"

"As soon as Allison was out the door this morning," Gillette confirmed. "Craig called me back before we went into this afternoon's meeting. Allison went to Yale undergrad and Chicago's business school. You don't get much better than that."

"But what fucking university isn't going to accept her? Think about what she probably donates to those schools every year."

"She was top of her class both places."

"Really?" Faraday hesitated. "Did she go right to the family trust after business school?"

"No, Goldman Sachs after Chicago. Same department I was in before I came to Everest. There's still a couple of guys over there I know. They said she was good. Said she didn't try to shirk anything because of who she was."

Faraday held up his hands. "Okay, okay. You convinced me. But she will be a temptation."

"I'm still with Faith. You know that."

"Ah, yes, the lovely Miss Cassidy. Do I hear wedding bells?"

Gillette glanced out the window into the fading late afternoon light of midtown Manhattan.

Faraday let it ride for a few moments, then gave up, rising from his chair with a groan and heading toward the door. "I'm going downstairs to get some mint chocolate chip," he announced. "Nothing like a little instant fucking gratification."

"You better start watching your weight," Gillette called after him, grabbing his computer mouse.

"What are you, my father? First I have to watch my mouth, now I've got to watch my weight. *Oh, Jesus.*" Faraday snapped his fingers and turned around as he reached the door. "I meant to tell you, Christian."

Gillette was focused on the computer. "What?"

"I had the strangest experience this morning."

Gillette grinned. "Don't tell me, you actually ate something healthy for breakfast."

"I thought I saw Tom McGuire on Park Avenue."

The computer screen blurred. Tom McGuire. The former CEO of McGuire & Company who had teamed with Miles Whitman to kill Bill Donovan—and tried to kill Gillette. McGuire was still out there somewhere—filled with hatred of Gillette for uncovering the plot and costing him hundreds of millions in the process. "That's not funny, Nigel."

"I know it's not, but that's what I saw. At least I think I did. I was walking up Park Avenue from the subway, and I was almost to our building. I happened to look up, and he was coming the other way. I'm pretty sure it was McGuire, anyway. I mean, he'd put on some weight and his hair was longer, but I wouldn't forget that face. It was weird, too. I was going to start yelling for the cops, but when I turned around he was gone. It was like he'd evaporated into thin air." Faraday shrugged. "Hey, maybe I'm wrong, maybe it wasn't him."

Gillette glanced back at the screen. He had a bad feeling Faraday wasn't wrong.

CHAPTER 3

Norman Boyd studied Gillette's head shot. Black hair parted on the left side as he faced you, combed neatly back over the ears. Sharp facial features—a thin nose, strong jaw, prominent chin, defined cheekbones, and intense gray eyes that caught you right away, even from a photograph. It was the fourth time today Boyd had looked at Gillette's picture, trying to glean anything he could from the image. So much depended on his ability to manipulate this man. Based upon what he knew so far, that wasn't going to be easy. Not like many others he'd dealt with.

"How did it go?" Boyd asked, setting the photograph on the desk of the sparsely furnished office.

"Fine," Ganze answered. "He left Everest right away to come to my hotel room when he found out I hadn't shown up."

"He's interested."

"Very."

"You mentioned his father's plane crash, right?" Boyd asked.

"Yes. He wants to know more."

"Good."

"Much more," Ganze continued. "You should have seen his reaction when I mentioned Clayton. Gillette's thought about that crash every day for the last sixteen years. It's haunted him."

"*Haunted* him, Daniel?"

"A father's death haunts every son."

Boyd hesitated, thinking about his own father's death last year. Hadn't haunted him. "Tell me about Gillette."

Ganze reviewed his notes. "Went to Princeton under—"

"Yeah, yeah. Princeton undergrad, Stanford business school, Goldman Sachs M and A, then Everest. I read the short file. Tell me about the *man*."

"He's got a half brother and a half sister."

Boyd's eyebrows rose. *"Half?"*

"Thirty-eight years ago, Clayton Gillette had an affair with a nineteen-year-old Hollywood wannabe. The affair was short but important. That woman is Christian's blood mother."

"Does Gillette have a relationship with her?"

"He doesn't even know who she is." Ganze grimaced and shook his head. "It's got to be tough, you know?"

Boyd sneered. "It isn't *that* tough. Most of the planet would trade places with him in a heartbeat." Ganze came across as a cold fish when you first met him, Boyd knew, but beneath that plywood exterior was a compassionate heart. Which bothered Boyd. You couldn't be sentimental in this business. If Ganze wasn't such a tremendous sleuth, Boyd would never have kept him around all these years. "Does he know that Clayton's wife is his stepmother? Does he know he was born out of wedlock?"

"He found out when he was a teenager."

"I assume we know who Gillette's blood mother is."

"We do."

"Excellent."

"Christian's stepmother agreed to raise him," Ganze continued, "but she always hated him."

"What's her name?"

"Lana, after the actress. Lana's father was a Hollywood producer back in the fifties and sixties," Ganze explained.

"He had a couple of boys, too. Named them Wayne and Kirk."

"How do you know Lana hated Gillette?"

"She carved Christian out of the fortune as soon as Clayton was dead. The will, monthly allowance, credit cards, bank accounts. Everything. She didn't even send him cash to get home."

"Wow."

"Christian had just graduated from Princeton and was motorcycling back across the country to California. He'd stopped in a small town in western Pennsylvania to visit his grandfather. The second day he was there was the day of the crash. Lana called an hour after the plane went down to tell Christian he was cut off completely. The motorcycle was in the shop, and he had to sell it to the owner because he didn't have cash on him for the repairs. He had to ride freight trains back to the West Coast, had to take out big loans to pay for business school, had to get Goldman Sachs to advance him two months' salary so he could put down a security deposit on an apartment in a crappy section of Brooklyn. The irony is that he comes from a ton of money, but he's completely self-made. Everything he has he's earned himself."

"Tough?"

"As tungsten. And careful and calculating. But he's got a big heart."

Boyd scoffed. "Sure he does."

"No, no. I'm serious. He gives a lot to charity, personally and through the firm. He had Everest donate ten million dollars to a hospital in New York so it could build a new wing for kids with cancer."

"It's called publicity," Boyd observed. "You said he was calculating."

"People he's close to are very loyal to him," Ganze argued.

"He probably pays them a lot more than they could make anywhere else."

"Yeah, he does," Ganze agreed grudgingly.

Boyd bit his lower lip, thinking. "Lana Gillette sounds like a cold one. Do you think she was involved?"

Ganze's expression turned curious. "Involved, sir?"

"In Clayton's plane crash."

"Nothing I've turned up indicates that."

Music to Boyd's ears. "How did Lana and Clayton meet?"

"Lana's father sent her east for college, to the University of Virginia. Clayton was at UVA on a football scholarship. He was a star quarterback in high school, but his college career wasn't anything to write home about. He and Lana married a month after graduation and moved to Los Angeles, actually lived with her parents for a year. Clayton went to work for a local brokerage house that was owned by a friend of Lana's father. He got the hang of selling stocks and bonds fast and opened his own shop a few years later."

"Let me guess," Boyd spoke up. "He took all the guy's clients with him."

"Yup. He was smooth, could sell anything. That was his talent. After a few years, he got the firm into investment banking, too. Sold it for a hundred million dollars before he went into politics."

"So Lana's set financially."

"I haven't nailed that down yet," Ganze said after a few moments, "but I have to think so. She still lives in the same mansion in Bel Air."

"Does Gillette talk to Lana?"

"No."

Boyd hesitated. "Where is he politically?"

"Registered Republican, but he voted Democrat in the

last presidential election. He doesn't vote with his bank account anymore. It's so full at this point, it doesn't matter."

"How much money does he control?"

"They just closed a new fifteen-billion-dollar fund, and there's still money left over from the one before that. Plus Everest owns thirty companies. Some big-name ones." Ganze paused. "And get this. My information is that Christian's going to try to take over Apex Capital, too."

Boyd looked up. A potential pothole—and a big one. "That's interesting."

"You think it's a problem?"

"I don't know," Boyd replied calmly. "But we'll have to keep an eye on it. How about protection?"

"Protection, sir?"

"Bodyguards. Does Gillette use them?"

"All the time."

"Who does he use?"

"A firm called QS Security."

"Are they good?"

"Very. The firm's owned and run by a guy named Quentin Stiles, who's one of Gillette's inner circle. I've asked around, and he's as good as they get. Army Rangers and Secret Service before founding QS. But he's been out of commission for a while."

"Why?"

"He took a bullet to the chest last year. Finally about to get out of the hospital."

"Did he take the bullet for Gillette?"

Ganze nodded.

"Are there QS agents with Gillette all the time?" Boyd asked.

"Twenty-four/seven. Apparently, Christian and Stiles are worried about a guy named Tom McGuire."

Boyd's ears perked up. "Who's Tom McGuire?"

"The muscle for Miles Whitman when Whitman tried to

kill Christian last year. McGuire arranged the murder attempts." Ganze had researched everything he could find about Christian Gillette—as Boyd had instructed. "McGuire was never caught. Just like Miles Whitman wasn't."

Boyd snorted. *"Miles Whitman,"* he repeated, disgusted. "What an asshole. Is he still getting help from the inside?"

"Definitely."

"How much has he gotten so far?"

"About forty million dollars' worth."

"Jesus fucking Christ. Where is Whitman now, do you know?"

"Southern Europe, I think. I don't know exactly."

"What about Justice?" Boyd asked, still annoyed. "They must be pissed."

"It's definitely an embarrassment for them," Ganze agreed. "It's been ten months and they haven't been able to find either of those guys. The higher-ups are putting a lot of heat on people in the trenches, but it's not doing much good."

"Do you think they suspect that there's help from the inside?"

"My friend says they haven't asked yet. Too much pride."

Boyd chuckled. "Idiots." His smile faded. "Well, they'll get over their pride at some point." He thought for a moment. "Why are Gillette and Stiles so worried about this McGuire guy?"

"If the conspiracy had worked, McGuire and his brother, Vince, would have made hundreds of millions. But Gillette and Stiles figured out what was going on at the last minute and blew the thing wide open. Turned the feds onto McGuire. Like I said, McGuire was never caught, but he lost out on the money. And his brother," Ganze added.

"What happened?"

"Vince helped Tom arrange the murder attempts on Gillette, and the feds got him. He died in jail."

Boyd groaned. The last thing he needed was some psychopath out there stalking Gillette, hell-bent on revenge. "Should Gillette be worried about this guy?"

"I checked McGuire out," Ganze replied. "He's ex-FBI. A nasty son of a bitch."

"We need Gillette alive, Daniel."

"I understand, sir."

Boyd pointed at Ganze. "Monitor that situation *very* closely. We might have to move on it quickly."

"I will," Ganze promised.

Boyd glanced at Gillette's photograph once more. "When is our meeting with him?"

"Friday at eleven. I called him back this afternoon. He can do it then."

Boyd tapped the desk. "Unfortunately, something's come up since you spoke to him. I may have to go out of town on Friday. Would he come sooner?"

"He came right to the hotel."

"Mmm." Boyd took a long breath. "Think he'll cooperate with us?"

Ganze considered the question for a few moments. "You'll have to use what we've found, make him understand that we can tell him things he's been desperate to know for a long time. Then you might be able to bend him."

"But then we might have to tell him *how* we know all those things. He'll ask. He won't take us at our word. We might have to bring him inside."

Ganze shrugged. "Which is the bigger risk? Disclosing our secrets or detection from the outside?"

"Yes," Boyd said quietly. "That's the question, isn't it. Which is the bigger risk? But then, that's always the question for us."

* * *

Gillette drew the pool cue through the loop of his curled forefinger, aimed at a group of three tightly packed, brightly colored balls, and fired. With the crack of the cue, the seven, twelve, and fourteen split like a molecule, atoms racing and ricocheting in all directions. Then each ball slowed to a crawl and dropped neatly into different pockets. Running the table wasn't fun anymore, so he practiced trick shots now.

He straightened up slowly and checked his watch—almost eleven. The day had started eighteen hours ago, at five this morning. It had been a long one, but as Faraday had said in the corridor, overall pretty fucking good. The new fund was closed, with an extra five billion from the Wallace Family, and they'd gotten the Vegas NFL franchise.

There'd been some challenges, too—there always were. A product liability suit had been filed by an aggressive Detroit watchdog group against Everest's Ohio-based auto parts manufacturer, and the CEO of another portfolio company headquartered in Texas had resigned suddenly for personal reasons. Truth was, the guy was banging his executive assistant on his office desk and Gillette had given him no choice but to resign. However, the attorneys for the Ohio company—the best in the country for this type of litigation—had given him airtight guarantees that the suit had zero merit, and the Texas CEO could easily be replaced by several other high-level executives at the company whom Gillette had groomed personally in case there was ever a problem. Just as he did at all their portfolio companies.

Just as he ought to be doing at Everest, he thought ruefully, tapping the butt end of the cue stick on the floor. The conversation with Faraday this afternoon about succession had gotten him thinking. There needed to be a plan in place, especially if Tom McGuire was really lurking around out there. He owed his investors that.

Gillette snapped his fingers as he moved to rack the balls. "Damn it." He was supposed to have called Faith this evening, but it was too late now. She was at some award dinner until eleven o'clock West Coast time.

He took a deep breath and leaned against the table. He hated to admit it, but he missed Faith. She was wonderful—beautiful, sexy, caring, unpretentious despite her fame. But he didn't like missing someone, feeling so vulnerable. Didn't like caring about someone that much despite how good it made him feel inside. He'd adored—no, idolized—his father, and look where that had gotten him. Left him in an emotional abyss for years. All he could do for his father now was solve the mystery of his death. Which was why he planned to be available for Daniel Ganze whenever Ganze wanted. Ganze seemed to know something. That was enough.

Gillette glanced around the ornate billiard room, connected to his office by a short hallway. The hallway was the only access to the room, so he controlled who came and went. This was the one big perk he'd allowed himself after becoming chairman last year. He loved pool—he'd funded his trip back to the West Coast after Lana had cut him off by beating small-town patsies for fifty bucks a game. And he found there were times during stressful days that a couple of quick games against David Wright were therapeutic.

Gillette shook his head and smiled. He never had beaten his father in pool. Which he was glad about now. It seemed right.

His cell phone rang. Probably Wright, he figured. The young MD had promised to stop by and shoot a few games. During the match, Gillette was going to tell him he wouldn't be going to Los Angeles to open the office, but that he'd be promoted to managing partner. However,

Wright had already left when Gillette buzzed a few hours ago, which was strange. Wright rarely missed a chance at face time.

"Hello."

"Christian?"

"Yes."

"It's Allison Wallace."

"Oh, hi. Where are you?" he asked.

"Still in New York. I'm staying at the Parker Meridien."

"I thought you and Gordon were flying back to Chicago this afternoon."

"Gordon did," she answered, "but I decided to stay the weekend to see some friends."

"How did you get this number?" Gillette asked. He hadn't given her the number, and Debbie would never give it out without permission.

"I'm Allison Wallace," she answered.

Not smugly, he noticed, just matter-of-factly. He could tell by her tone she wasn't going to say anything more about it, either. The same way he wouldn't. "Look, I—"

"Let's have lunch Monday," she suggested.

"Can't."

"Why not?"

"I'm having lunch with the commissioner of the NFL. We got the new Las Vegas franchise today, and he wants to go over a few things."

"Fantastic," she said breathlessly. "That's really exciting. You better make that investment with Everest Eight, the fund I'm going to be in."

Gillette hesitated. He was planning to make the franchise purchase out of Seven, then issue Everest-guaranteed bonds to finance stadium construction. There wouldn't be any need to use Eight for this deal. "I'm not sure how we're going to fund it yet. We still have two billion left in Seven."

"Well, I think—"

"How about breakfast?" he interrupted. He could hear her tone flexing, and he didn't want to get into it now. He could understand why she'd want the NFL opportunity for the fund she was investing in—there was so much upside—but he had to be fair to all his investors. The best way to do that was to invest sequentially—use all of Seven, then go to Eight. Of course, he didn't know Allison well, and she might turn out to be emotional. She might pull the Wallace Family investment if she thought he was jerking her around so soon after committing five billion.

He took a deep breath. Conflict, always conflict in this world.

"I have a breakfast," Allison answered. "How about dinner? I could stay another night."

Gillette couldn't remember if he already had a dinner scheduled, but if he did and he couldn't remember, then it couldn't be important. "Okay."

"Great," she said, her voice turning pleasant again. "Come get me around seven at the Parker."

As he slid the phone back in his pocket, there was a knock on the hallway door. "Yes?"

"Open up!"

Gillette's gaze snapped toward the door. He knew that voice: Quentin Stiles. He hurried over and yanked on the knob. Suddenly, Stiles was standing before him.

Quentin Stiles was African American: handsome, light skinned, six four, and normally a rock-hard 240 pounds. He was from Harlem, a self-made man who'd never been to college but now owned a fast-growing security firm with fifty agents.

Gillette embraced him immediately, unable to remember the last time he'd been so glad to see someone.

"Hey," Stiles said, stepping back. "What are you doing?"

"I'm . . . I'm welcoming you back."

"Don't get so emotional."

"I just . . . well, I just—"

Stiles broke into a loud, good-natured laugh and wrapped his arms around Gillette. "Hey, brother, I'm just playing. It's good to be back."

"You look great," Gillette said. "A lot better than you did in the hospital bed the last time I visited."

"I don't look great," Stiles answered irritably, "I look terrible. I'm down thirty pounds from my normal weight. I probably can't even bench-press three hundred at this point. Christ, none of my clothes fit. Look at me," he said, holding out his arms. The black blazer hung loosely from his frame.

"We'll fatten you up fast." Gillette moved toward two comfortable chairs in front of a plasma television screen hanging from the wall. "Sit down," he said, pointing at one of the chairs as he sat in the other, "and tell me what the hell you're doing out of the hospital. Saturday, the nurses told me it was going to be at least another two weeks before you'd be released." He watched Stiles wince as he lowered himself slowly into the chair.

"If I'd stayed in the hospital another two weeks, I'd have gone crazy," he answered. "Hell, if I'd stayed there another *ten minutes,* I'd have gone crazy. The mattress was like cement, the nurses were even harder, I hate the way hospitals smell, and the food was awful. Let me tell you something, what I need is a big fat juicy steak. How about Monday lunch?"

"I can't, I—" Gillette interrupted himself. Lunch with the commissioner was at noon and would go no later than one-thirty. Landry's executive assistant had told Debbie that he had to catch a four o'clock flight to the West Coast and couldn't stay longer than that. "Can we do it later on? Say, one forty-five? Can you hold out till then?"

"Sure."

"How'd you know I was here?" Gillette asked, relaxing.

"I called the main number about an hour ago and Faraday picked up. He said you were going to be here for a while. He let me know where to find you," Stiles explained, looking around. "Hey, this is quite a place."

Gillette had built the pool room last spring—it had originally been O'Brien's office, but Gillette had kicked him out to get the space. Stiles had already been in the hospital several months at that point and hadn't seen it. "Thanks."

"You lost a match in here yet?" Stiles asked.

"Of course not."

"Well, what you need," Stiles declared, starting to get up, "is a good old-fashioned ass whipping on your home court."

Gillette reached over and caught Stiles, forcing him gently back into the chair. "Not now."

"Why not?"

"We need to talk."

Stiles cocked his head to the side, recognizing Gillette's serious tone. "What is it?"

"Last week I told you about a meeting I was going to have this morning with a man from Washington, remember?"

"Yeah."

During hospital visits with Stiles, Gillette had kept him up to speed with everything at Everest. Since last fall, Stiles had become as much a partner as Faraday, not just the man in charge of Gillette's personal protection.

"So how'd it go?" Stiles asked.

"It was strange; he didn't really tell me anything. I don't know much more about him or the people he represents than I did before the meeting, but I'm still going to Washington next week to meet with them."

Stiles's face contorted into a curious expression. "Sounds like he's a waste of time. Why would you bother?"

"Senator Clark arranged the meeting. I trust his judgment." Gillette hesitated. "More important, the guy I met with this morning mentioned my father's plane crash."

Gillette had told Stiles about Clayton's plane crash many times. How Gillette had been cut off from the family money immediately afterward, how he'd been born out of wedlock, and how he desperately wanted answers to so many questions surrounding all of that. "Now I get it."

"The guy also said he didn't buy the official explanation for the crash," Gillette continued. "Said pilot error seemed 'thin' to him."

"Christian, be care—"

"To others as well."

"They want something," Stiles warned.

"Everyone always does."

"I guess that's true," Stiles agreed quietly, "at least in your world."

Gillette nodded, then closed his eyes and pushed the thoughts away. "So, how are you?" he asked. "Really, shouldn't you still be in the hospital?"

"No, I'm fine."

"Well, when can you go a hundred percent? The guys you've had with me have done a great job, but I want you back full time as soon as possible." Gillette tapped the arm of the chair. "And Nigel's really raised his game. Like I told you, I'm surprised how dedicated he's gotten. This time last year, he was in at nine and gone by six, the latest. Now he's in early and here most nights until ten. I depend on him." Gillette hesitated. "But Nigel isn't you. Like I said, I need you here full time as soon as possible—but I don't want you coming back too soon, either," he added quickly. "No relapses, or worse."

"I'm fine," Stiles replied firmly. "We'll need to keep your current security detail with you because I won't be back to full speed for a few months, but they'd have had to stick around anyway. You need three to four men around you constantly."

"Amen," Gillette agreed. He'd stared down the barrel of an assassin's gun last fall, and he didn't want to do it again. "Monday at lunch we'll talk about your role at Everest. Debbie can arrange temporary space for you. It won't be great, but we'll get you into a big office quick."

"Whoa, whoa," Stiles said, holding up both hands. "Not so fast, Christian. I've got QS Security to run."

"It's done fine the last ten months without you."

"*Without me?*"

"Yeah."

"Are you kidding? I've been running it from the hospital. I've still been hands-on."

"I didn't know that."

"We're almost ten million in revenues at this point."

The number caught Gillette's attention, and he started going through his options. But there was only one that made sense. "Okay, I'll buy it."

"*What?*"

"Yeah. I'll use McGuire and Company, the security company we already own. How much do you want?"

"Jesus, Christian, is this how you negotiate? I thought you were supposed to be a hard-assed motherfucker when it came to buying and selling."

"This is different."

"Why?"

"Don't worry about it."

Stiles shook his head, fighting back a grin. "I'm not ready to sell."

Gillette did a few quick calculations. At ten million in revenues, QS Security probably netted around half a million dollars. "Any debt on the business?" he asked.

"Three hundred grand."

"Okay, I'll give you five million for it."

"*Five million,*" Stiles repeated incredulously.

Gillette chuckled. "Now who's the bad negotiator?"

"I just didn't . . . well, I . . . I just thought—"

"Take it, Quentin," Gillette advised. "It's the best deal you're going to get, at least anytime soon. In the morning I'll call Craig West and tell him what we're doing, that we're buying you out. And I'm going to pay you a million a year here at Everest, plus bonus, plus ups."

"Christ. That's incredible, but why?" Stiles asked. "I don't know anything about finance."

"I trust you more than anyone else on the planet. From where I sit, that's worth every penny I just offered. Plus, you know a lot about running companies. You just grew one and sold it for five million dollars."

"What exactly will I do here?"

"For starters, you'll get me everything on the guy I met with this morning and the people he reports to. And you'll go with me to Washington next week."

"Why don't you have Craig West get the info and go with you?"

"Craig's a good man, but I don't trust him like I trust you. It's not the same. And something tells me I'm going to need to be *very* careful with these people." Gillette took a deep breath. "There's something else, Quentin."

"What?"

"Faraday thought he saw Tom McGuire on Park Avenue this morning."

Stiles's eyes shot to Gillette's. "You're kidding."

"Nope."

Stiles looked down and was silent for a moment. Finally he glanced up. "Chris, I don't think a million bucks is going to cut it."

David Wright rose up on one elbow and ran his fingers gently through his wife's hair as she slept on the bed beside him. A half hour ago, Peggy had wanted to make love, but it hadn't happened. He was too distracted, expecting detectives from the New York Police Department to pound on their apartment door at any moment. Salivating to arrest him for the murder of the woman at the sex shop.

A half hour ago he couldn't perform; now he couldn't sleep. He kept replaying that awful scene in the bondage chamber in his mind. His foot hitting the block of wood, the awful sound of her neck snapping like a brand-new Ticonderoga pencil between two thumbs. A quick crack, then her body going limp. God, if he could only have those few seconds back.

Wright groaned and reclined slowly on the mattress until his head settled onto the pillow, listening to Peggy's heavy breathing, staring at the ceiling through the gloom. She'd tried hard to arouse him, going down on him for a full five minutes—which she didn't really like to do—but nothing. He'd blamed it on work, on Gillette being a slave driver, and she'd bought it, at least for tonight. But she wouldn't buy it for long. Typically, he couldn't go a day without sex. Soon she'd figure out something else, something more important, was wrong. Maybe the cops would have already led him off in shackles by then.

He tried to take a deep breath but couldn't. It was as if he had something heavy constantly pressing on his chest now. "Shit!" he hissed, rolling away from Peggy and grabbing the sheet. When he'd run into Gillette in the hallway at Everest this morning and talked about Hush-Hush, it was as if the older man had seen right through him. As if he'd known something was wrong. Wright still had that question ringing in his ears: "You okay?" And that look in Gillette's eyes was etched into his memory: like a spinning drill bit coming at him, ready to splay him wide open for everyone to see.

It was the damnedest thing about Gillette. It was as if he

could tell exactly what you were thinking—or what you'd done. Probably one of the reasons he was chairman of Everest Capital at just thirty-seven. He was different. He had an edge others didn't. As if he were ten steps ahead of you all the time.

Well, Wright thought, forcing his eyes shut. He was going to get away for the weekend and take Monday off. He was going to avoid the apartment and Everest just in case the police decided to visit. What he'd do if he found out they'd come by either place looking for him, he wasn't sure. But there was one thing he knew: He wasn't going to jail. At least not for a few days.

Suddenly there was a furious banging, a loud fist slamming against a door over and over.

"Jesus Christ!" Wright shot up in bed.

"What's wrong?" Peggy was up instantly beside him, rubbing her eyes. "My God, what is it?"

As quickly as it had started, the banging subsided, and Wright realized that the knocking had been on the door across the hall. He swallowed hard and ran his hand over his forehead. He was sweating like a leaky faucet. "It's all right," he murmured.

"David, what's wrong?" Peggy asked fearfully, putting a hand on his shoulder.

"Nothing, baby, nothing," Wright assured her, lying back down and pulling her beside him. He wanted to tell her so badly, but he couldn't. He couldn't tell anyone. Which was the hardest part of it all.

CHAPTER 4

"So, you excited?"

Gillette watched Kurt Landry shove a cell phone–size forkful of sirloin steak into his mouth as they sat at a back table of Sparks Steak House in midtown Manhattan. Landry had starred as a defensive end for the New York Jets in the eighties, then caught on with the National Football League's front office after a couple of high-profile stints—a two-year deal as a booth analyst for NBC's primary Sunday game and some heavily marketed rental car commercials. So he was instantly recognizable to the public, a perfect spokesman. Once at the league office, he'd played his cards right by doing a lot of palm pressing and behind-the-scenes lobbying at off-season meetings, and he'd been elected commissioner two years ago in a close vote by the owners. He'd beaten out the senior partner of a prominent Wall Street law firm in the election, mostly because the bloc of owners backing Landry believed he'd act as their puppet—they didn't want someone who would think independently.

Craig West had done some checking for Gillette, and apparently Landry's backers had been right, he was doing exactly as they wanted. There were strings everywhere.

But Landry's backers weren't here today.

As he watched Landry gorge, Gillette noticed how many of the man's physical features seemed oversize: his head, his mouth, his ears, his hands. He barely fit in a chair made for a normal-size man.

"How tall are you?" Gillette asked, ignoring Landry's question.

"Six seven."

"How much do you weigh?"

Landry laughed, a baritone rumble. "Two fifty, but that's forty pounds under my playing weight. I'm damn proud of myself for taking off all that weight and *keeping* it off." He scooped up a greasy spoonful of home fries and downed them with one swallow. "Come on," he said, slapping Gillette on the back with a bear paw of a hand after putting down the spoon. "You excited?"

Gillette nodded. "Sure."

"Doesn't seem like it. Hey, you've got a lot of fun coming your way with this thing. I mean, what could possibly be better than owning an NFL team?"

"I don't like getting ahead of myself."

"What does that mean?" Landry asked, scooping creamed spinach onto his plate out of a serving bowl.

"I want this to be a good investment for my partners," Gillette answered. "Four hundred and fifty million is a ton to pay for something that's never generated a dime of income. When we've done well financially, when we've made a good return on our money, then I'll get excited."

"Money-schmoney," Landry said, smirking. "Think about all the perks, especially with a Vegas franchise."

"There's a downside to that city, too."

"Hey, you're the youngest owner in the NFL," Landry pointed out, paying no attention to Gillette's caution. "Everybody wants to see you again, too, especially after that article in *People*."

Gillette pushed his plate of half-eaten filet and steamed broccoli into the middle of the table so he could put his elbows down. "Look, I'm not the owner, Everest Capital is.

And I was never even interviewed for that article. *People* did that all on their own." He was starting to feel like sic-cing Stiles on the guy who wrote the thing.

"I wouldn't be complaining if I were you," Landry said, wiping his mouth with a white linen napkin. "What was the story line? 'Most eligible bachelors in the country'? Jesus, most guys would die for that kind of pub. I bet that article's opened some doors, especially to some very attractive women. You've got it going on, don't you, boy?"

"You know, I'm just not into personal publicity, Kurt."

A concerned look came over Landry's face. "But you're going to be chairman of the team, right? You're going to be making the major decisions, aren't you?"

"Yes."

Landry seemed relieved. "Uh-huh, well, I would have liked it if that article had been written about me." He waved at one of the waiters, indicating that he wanted more water. "So, tell me about Everest. The *Reader's Digest* version, please, I don't know much about the investment world."

Clearly, Landry hadn't been very involved in the selection process. If he had, he wouldn't have needed the Everest primer. His minions—or the owners' minions—must have done the heavy lifting as far as analyzing the different bids. "We're an investment firm," Gillette began. "We usually buy and manage companies that manufacture things or provide services. And they've usually been around for a while before we get involved, so this situation is different for us. Which is why we have to be extra careful here. Not that we aren't always careful, but we want to be extremely cautious in this situation. Anything goes wrong with this thing and my investors will be on my ass. That's why I don't want to get ahead of myself."

"Ah, don't worry about it. You're going to make a boat-load of money on this thing," Landry said confidently. "Besides, that article said you have the magic touch when it comes to investing."

"I do all right."

"There were lots of people trying to get this franchise."

"What won it for us?" Gillette asked directly. "Was it price alone, or were there other things?"

Landry put down his napkin and leaned back, folding his thick arms over his barrel chest. "I really can't comment on that, Christian. There were lots of criteria; obviously price was very important. But the owners don't want me to talk about what went on behind closed doors."

"Who were the other bidders?" Gillette asked, ignoring the soft warning.

"Mostly wealthy individuals."

"Who?"

Landry chuckled nervously.

Obviously, he wasn't used to this kind of cross-examination. In his position as commissioner, he probably didn't sit on the hot seat often. When there was a controversial issue, the owners probably handled it for him. They must have anticipated that today's lunch would be just a formality. They probably figured the winner would be so happy at getting the franchise that he wouldn't dig for information. But Gillette was always digging. Having information others didn't was a surefire way to make money. "It really would be helpful to know," he pushed. "I don't understand why it'd be a problem to tell me now that the selection process is over."

"All names I'm sure you'd recognize. I mean, there aren't that many individuals around who could afford an NFL team." Landry held up his hands. "But I, I really can't say any more. League policy." He grimaced.

Like all of a sudden the meeting wasn't going the way he thought it would; or like he wished it were one-thirty and he could leave, Gillette thought, interpreting Landry's grimace.

"Let's talk some more logistics," Landry suggested, picking at something between his teeth.

"Okay."

"Tell me about the stadium construction. What's the timing there?"

Another indication Landry hadn't been one of the decision makers. All that information had been spelled out in the final bid package Everest had submitted to the NFL two months ago. "The architectural plans for the stadium were in the bid package. We still need to choose a primary contractor, but that shouldn't take long. There are only three or four serious players for this job. Our advisers tell us that once we've chosen the contractor, the stadium can be finished in eighteen months."

Landry rested his chin in his palm, as though he were thinking hard. "So, then, the plan is for your team to start playing not next season, but the season after that. We'll have the expansion draft a few weeks after next year's Super Bowl. That'll give you time to see what veterans you've got before the college draft." Landry grinned. "Damn, I wish I were in your shoes." His grin grew even wider. "If I were you, I'd make sure I was there for cheerleader tryouts."

Gillette broke into a halfhearted laugh. Landry had no conception of what it meant to be in charge, no idea of the pressure involved. "I'll remember that, Kurt."

"Now you're getting into the spirit," Landry said enthusiastically. "The NFL is fun, a marketing machine, the biggest damn party in all sports, and now you're at the center of it." He pointed at Gillette. "You beat out some people who've been trying to get one of these teams for a long time. There's folks out there who are pissed off right now, but the NFL made the right choice. It always does."

Gillette picked up his fork and pushed the broccoli around his plate. "Why are they so pissed off?"

"Because they lost," Landry said, as if the answer were obvious.

"Well, they didn't bid enough, so they've only got themselves to blame, right?"

Landry shrugged. "Right . . . I guess."

Suddenly, Gillette wished he could have been a fly on the wall during the selection meetings. Wished he could get his hands on all the bid packages. Something didn't smell right. "There's one more thing I want to talk to you about today," he said, glancing at his watch: one twenty-three.

"What's that?"

"Organized crime."

Landry's body went stiff in the chair, water glass halfway between the tablecloth and his mouth. "Huh?"

"The Mafia."

"What about it?" Landry kept his voice low, his eyes flickering around.

"Do you have any information about how active they are in Las Vegas?"

"No. I mean, I don't, specifically, have any information."

"Does someone else at the NFL office have that?"

Landry hesitated. "What do you mean?"

"Well, you guys must have looked at that hard before you decided it was all right to have a franchise in Las Vegas."

"Of course we did," Landry agreed emphatically.

"And?"

Landry hesitated again. "And I'll talk to our people who are in charge of franchise development later this week, when I get back from my trip. But what the hell are you worried about? We've never had a problem with the Mafia."

"You've never been in Las Vegas."

"No, but we're in New York, Chicago, and Florida," Landry argued. "What do you think they'd do, try to make players fix games? We monitor that very carefully. We have a team of people who review every game tape with a microscope to make certain there wasn't anything shady going on. Experts who can spot quarterbacks just barely under- or overthrowing receivers, running backs going down without really being hit, linebackers missing easy tackles, placekickers going wide on purpose. I don't understand what you're worried about."

"It has nothing to do with the actual operation of the team," Gillette explained. "I'm more concerned about the casino and the Mafia trying to influence the regulators on license renewals and things like that. And what they might gouge me for during construction of the casino and the stadium because they control the unions. You know, slow-downs and sick-outs if I don't pay them."

"Oh."

"I've done some checking," Gillette continued, "and I think they're still active out there, maybe more so than people think. I'll have better information on that in the next day or two. I'm willing to share that with you as long as you share what you have with me." He looked at Landry intently.

"Of course, of course." Landry cleared his throat as he checked his watch. "Look, maybe the best thing is for you to back off on this casino idea for a while? Get the franchise established first, then we'll talk about the casino again in a few years."

Landry suddenly seemed nervous, pulling the napkin through his fingers, bouncing one knee.

"No way," Gillette said firmly. "The only reason we offered four hundred and fifty million for the franchise was so we could build the casino. Without that, the bid doesn't make sense." Not entirely true, but Landry didn't know that. "That was clearly stated in the bid package."

"Right, right, but things change. We all know that. Everything's always up for renegotiation, right?"

"Not this," Gillette answered coldly. Landry gazed back for a few seconds, then glanced away, unable to stare Gillette down. "I hope I'm making myself clear."

"Let me get back to you."

Gillette shook his head. "No, I need an ironclad yes right now, or I go to our friends in the press and let them know you've reneged. If I do, you won't get close to four hundred fifty million when you reoffer the franchise. People will smell a problem, especially when I tell them why we backed off."

Landry blinked. "No, no, don't do that."

"What's your answer, Kurt?" Gillette demanded, glad the Wall Street lawyer hadn't won the election for commissioner. "I need to know right now."

Landry took several gulps of water, then nodded. "Okay, okay, you got your casino."

Wright moved slowly through Saks Fifth Avenue's main entrance across from Rockefeller Center, then meandered through a maze of glass counters full of perfumes and body lotions. He gazed emptily at the perfectly made-up women behind the counters who were smiling back, ready to sell him something outrageously expensive.

He stopped and rubbed his face hard in the middle of an aisle, hoping he'd wake up in his bed beside his wife and realize that what had happened at the sex shop had all been just an awful nightmare. He took a deep breath and closed his eyes, praying, knowing he was being irrational—which he prided himself on never being—but unable to calm down. He was holding on to anything at this point, anything that might give him a shred of hope. But when he opened his eyes, he was still in Saks, still in trouble.

"You all right?" asked a pretty, dark-haired woman from behind one of the counters.

Wright glanced over at her. "Huh?" He'd been thinking

about how he hadn't seen or heard anything on TV or radio about a woman being found dead between two parked cars in the West Village. Which seemed strange. The story might not be enough for CNN, but it should have made the local news.

"You look like you're having a bad day," said the saleswoman. "Girl trouble?"

Wright gazed at her, the horrible image of the woman dropping from the block of wood still vivid in his mind.

"You know," the saleswoman continued, "you should give her something nice." She reached for a small bottle on a purple velvet cloth. "This is called Allure," she said. "It's one of our best sellers."

Wright moved to the counter slowly. "It would be for my wife," he murmured.

"Of course it would," the saleswoman said, brushing her fingers over Wright's left hand and his wedding band. "You two having a little tiff?"

"Well, we—"

"Hi, David."

Wright's gaze shot from the woman's fingers into the eyes of a man he'd never seen before. A stocky, swarthy man with dark hair and a crooked nose. "Who are you?"

The man snickered and looked at the saleswoman. "What a joker," he said in a thick New York accent, spreading his arms wide and smiling. "He always does this to me. Acts like he doesn't know me. It's his thing, ya know?"

The saleswoman shrugged.

The man patted Wright on the shoulder, then reached into his jacket, pulled out a photograph, and held it up so Wright could see.

As Wright focused on the photo, his heart rose in his throat and his upper lip curled. It was a picture of him whipping the woman as she hung from the iron rings.

"Follow me," he ordered, his tone gruff. He wheeled around and headed toward the elevators.

Wright followed him like a puppy after its mother, head down and in the same tracks, all the way to a waiting elevator. Moving into the car obediently when the man waved him in. As the doors closed, the man turned toward Wright, resting his finger on the "stop" button. Pushing it hard when the elevator had risen a few feet, halting it between the first and second floors.

"What's going on?" Wright asked. "Please," he begged, "tell me."

The man smiled, his demeanor becoming pleasant again. "Everything's going to be fine, David, as long as you cooperate."

"How did you get that?" Wright asked, gesturing at the photo the man was still holding.

"We were there, in a side room. We saw everything. We got pictures *and* a tape of the whole thing." The man shook his head. "Poor woman."

"It was an accident," Wright muttered.

"Of course it was," the man agreed, "but the cops might not think so when they see the tape up to the point you put the noose around her neck."

Wright started to say something, but the man held up a finger and cut him off.

"Don't worry, David, your secret's safe as long as you work with us. Right now, all the cops have on their hands is a missing persons case. We picked the woman up and put her in cold storage. We took care of the owner, too, so he couldn't point the cops at you." The man chuckled snidely. "I doubt anybody will miss him, though. Pretty much a scumbag."

Wright shut his eyes tightly. "I didn't kill her," he said, gritting his teeth. "It was an accident."

"Of course it was," the man said, pulling a pocketful of

pictures from his jacket and tossing them so they scattered on the floor of the elevator. "But try telling the cops that when they see these."

Wright dropped to his knees, scooping them up quickly. "This is crazy," he muttered over and over. "Crazy."

"And don't worry about the shop, we cleaned everything up." The man laughed harshly and pushed the elevator's "start" button. "The NYPD crime lab won't find nothing."

Wright picked up the last picture as the car jerked to a start. "What's going on?" he whispered, looking up at the man. "Please tell me."

The car came to a stop and the doors parted on the second floor. "We'll be in touch soon," the man said as he moved past several people waiting to get on. "By the way, David, my name's Paul. Remember that, because we're going to be talking a lot from now on."

Déjà vu, Gillette thought, watching Stiles hoist a juicy piece of steak to his mouth. Stiles was sitting in the same chair Landry had used and had ordered the same meal—he'd shown up ten minutes after Landry left and hadn't stopped eating or said a word since the food was served. "Taste good?" he asked, glad to see Stiles enjoying himself.

Stiles finished chewing and swallowed, then leaned back and patted his stomach gently. "I don't think I've ever tasted anything better in my life."

"I'm just glad you *have* your life," Gillette said quietly, leaning over and touching Stiles on the shoulder. "I was worried about you." Worried was an understatement. Stiles had gone critical several times during the week after he was shot. The hospital chaplain had read him the last rites twice. "It was my fault you got hit."

Stiles pointed at Gillette. "That's crap and you know it. I signed up to protect you, you paid me a lot of money to do it, and I took the money. I did it out of my own free will,

out of complete self-interest. It's my job, I'd do it again."
He paused. "For a guy who's big on personal accountability, I can't believe you said that."

Stiles was right. It was his job, it was what he was supposed to do, and he had taken money. But right now, that didn't seem to matter. "I still feel bad."

"Then pay me more money."

"Yeah, good one." Gillette looked around the restaurant, checking for his security detail—over by the bus stand. Since Whitman and McGuire had tried to kill him last fall, he checked every few minutes whenever he was in public. It had been ten months, but the most dangerous person involved in the Laurel Energy conspiracy—Tom McGuire—was still out there somewhere. And if Faraday was right, McGuire might be close. "You're my friend, Quentin, my good friend." Gillette took a measured breath. "I don't let many people in," he admitted, his voice going low. "I can't."

"I know."

"Some people think I'm lonely," Gillette murmured.

"I know," Stiles agreed. "They want the money and all the perks, but they don't know what you go through. The pressure of making so many important decisions all the time. It's got to be tough."

"It is sometimes." Stiles understood. One of the few people who did. Gillette had to at least appear to be immune to it, but there were moments when he felt the walls closing in around him, and it felt good to tell someone that.

"It could have been very different," Stiles pointed out. "The guy aimed at the first person he saw in that room. It could have been *you* in the hospital for the last ten months."

"Maybe." Gillette replayed the scene in his head. It had been the wildest few seconds he had ever experienced. "But the most important thing is, you're okay. Judging by the way you're inhaling that steak, anyway."

"It'll be a while until I'm a hundred percent, but meals like this will definitely speed up the recovery."

"Good. Well, since you're feeling better, let's talk business."

Stiles nodded. "Sure."

"First of all, I want to close our deal."

"Our deal?"

"Yeah, for your company."

Stiles's jaw dropped. "I didn't think you were serious."

"When have you ever known me to be anything but serious about Everest business?"

"Not often."

"Try never," Gillette said sharply. "Look, McGuire and Company will pay five million dollars for a hundred percent of QS. I spoke to Craig West this morning, and he's fine with it."

"If he wasn't, he'd be fired."

"It's not like that."

"Sure it is, Chris. Craig knows where his bread's buttered."

"Whatever," Gillette muttered. But Stiles was right. It hadn't even crossed his mind that West would object to the deal.

"You're doing me a favor," Stiles said. "A five-million-dollar favor, and I don't want you getting in trouble with your investors. People get pretty crazy when it comes to money."

"You're telling *me*?" Gillette chuckled. "Look, I'm about to make my investors five billion dollars on Laurel Energy."

Stiles caught his breath. "Five *billion*?"

"Yeah, so I don't think they'll give me too much trouble over five million. That's chicken scratch to them."

"Jesus."

"And five million's a fair price for QS, anyway. It's full, but fair, and Craig and I think it'll be a nice tuck-in to round out McGuire's service offerings. McGuire has a high-end protection division, but it caters mostly to business executives. You've got connections in the sports and entertainment industry Craig doesn't. After we close, I'll expect you to work with him on those relationships, make all the introductions."

"Of course."

"Good. See, everybody wins. McGuire and Company gets a new business line at a decent price, you get five million bucks, and I get all your time. Okay?"

Stiles made a face as though he were trying to work through a calculus problem. "Okay."

Gillette could see it was all just beginning to sink in. Stiles had grown up dirt poor in Harlem, and now he was about to make five million dollars. More money than he probably could have dreamed of as a kid. But Gillette didn't want there to be any appearance of impropriety, either. They'd have to go through all the normal due diligence. "As part of the deal, you'll sign a noncompete."

"A what?"

"A noncompetition agreement. It'll stipulate that you can't start, or work for, another personal security company for at least five years."

"Well, I—"

"And you'll sign all the normal reps and warranties as part of the purchase agreement."

"The normal *whats?*"

"Representations and warranties. Promises that you alone have the power to sell the company and that you've been a good corporate citizen while you owned it. Specifically, that you're the only owner of QS stock and, if you're not, that the others can't block you, that you've paid all your corporate and personal taxes, and that you don't have any lawsuits pending against you. Things like that. If it turns out some of those things aren't accurate, and I find out about it after we do the deal, you'll owe me my money back and then some."

"So, I'm gonna need a lawyer," Stiles said glumly.

"It's all standard stuff in the deal business."

"I don't know deals, I know personal security and investigations."

"You'll be fine."

"You wouldn't take advantage of me, Chris."

Gillette grinned. "Sure I would. It's what I do. That's why you're going to get a lawyer." He could see Stiles was struggling, unsure of himself in this situation but trying to maintain his signature cool. Stiles didn't want to insult the man who was going to make him rich, but he'd sacrificed and risked a great deal to get QS where it was now, and he wasn't going to throw caution out the window for anyone. "I'd never take advantage of you, Quentin," Gillette said seriously. "You'll get your five million, and you'll never have to pay me back anything. Unless you lie to me, and we both know you'd never do that."

"Of course not."

"I'll get the lawyers started on the documents. We should have everything finished up in thirty days, okay?"

Stiles nodded deliberately. "Thanks, Chris. This is all pretty amazing."

"Don't worry about it. You've worked hard, you deserve it. Most people fail where you've prospered." Gillette could see Stiles appreciated that someone else understood how much sacrifice it had taken to make QS successful. Just as he appreciated Stiles understanding how isolated he felt sometimes as chairman of Everest. It was one of the reasons they'd gotten so close. Each took the time to understand the other's situation.

Stiles cut another piece of steak and put it in his mouth. "How did your meeting with Landry go?"

"The guy tried to back me off on the casino."

"*What?*"

"Yeah. I had a feeling he'd try that," Gillette said, folding his napkin. "I figured the owners agreed to the casino initially to get the four hundred and fifty million, then thought they could jerk it away once they gave us the franchise. You know, they thought I'd be so happy to be an NFL owner, I'd do anything they wanted after the fact."

"What tipped you off that they'd try the bait and switch?"

"I figured they knew the Mafia was still active out there, and I know they don't want any chance that the same people who own one of their franchises would be tempted to get in bed with organized crime. That's one of the last things they want to see splashed across the front page of *The New York Times*."

"Why did you think they were on to the Mob in Vegas?" Stiles asked.

"*You* were. I figured if *you* knew, *they* must."

Stiles's expression sagged. "You think their people are better than mine?"

"That's a fucking joke. You figured it out in a few hours, so I figured they could do it in a few months." Gillette pulled out his Blackberry and scrolled through his e-mails. "You find out anything more about what's going on? Anything specific about what we're likely to run into?"

Stiles nodded and leaned forward in his chair, motioning for Gillette to do the same.

"What is it?" Gillette asked, putting his elbows on the table and looking around suspiciously.

"Hey, this is Sparks Steak House," Stiles said quietly.

"Yep. Best steak place in Manhattan. So what?"

"There's probably Mob guys in here right now," Stiles said, looking around.

"Oh, come on."

"Hey, don't you remember?"

"Remember what?"

"John Gotti shot Paul Castellano dead on the steps of this place one night as Castellano was coming in to eat dinner. Castellano was godfather of the Gambino family. Ultimately, Gotti became don of the Gambinos. He used to eat here, too. Before the feds finally took Gotti down and sent him away for life." Stiles glanced around at a few tables. "But, like we all know, you take one wiseguy down and a new one takes his place, so I figure the walls here have ears."

Gillette nodded. "Yeah, but any ears in this place probably belong to the feds. If any Mob guy talked business in this place, he'd probably be killed by his own family before the feds could get to him."

"But they can hear what we're talking about if they're around, and I figure you don't want that." Stiles glanced at one table in particular, four tough-looking guys dressed in silk suits.

Gillette followed Stiles's glance. "Okay," he said quietly, "what do you have?"

"There's three families active in Vegas right now," Stiles answered. "Branches of the Chicago Treviso and Barducci families are there, but they're small-time. Penny-ante stuff, mostly, like retail 'protection.' They target off-the-strip restaurants and shops owned by foreigners who can't go to the authorities for help because most of their workers are illegal aliens and they haven't paid FICA in years. Easy pickings for extortionists who kill somebody every once in a while just to make a statement, whether he pays his arm-twist money or not. They've been targeting mainly Asians, from what I'm hearing. So, of course, the Asian Mob sees an opportunity and they're moving in to 'protect' their people. Problem is, these guys are worse than the Italians. They charge more and kill for less." Stiles paused for a moment. "The family you need to watch out for in Vegas is the Carbone family. They're out of New York, and they've got all the local construction companies tied up, so you got to make certain everyone wants to work hard all the time. If you try to bring someone in from the outside who doesn't gouge you for the extra incentive, you find out your equipment breaks down real often. They're also close to the gaming commission and the other state regulators involved with the gambling industry, so you'll run into them whenever you need licenses and approvals. Don't believe the local city officials who tell you everything's clean. It isn't."

"It's all like you thought."

"Yeah, but now two other sources have confirmed it. People I trust."

"How did you find out this stuff, Quentin? Who did you talk to?"

Stiles shook his head. "Don't ask."

"Come on," Gillette pushed.

"Before I started QS, I wasn't just with the Army Rangers and the Secret Service. I worked in another area of the government, too. We had dealings with some of these people."

"What area was it?"

"I can't tell you."

"Quentin, I—"

"Don't push it, Chris. Really."

Gillette took a deep breath. "So, if I don't play ball with the Carbones, I'll have problems with the construction of both the stadium and the casino, and I might be denied the ability to operate the casino when it's ready to open."

"Exactly. But there are . . . *consulting* firms that can take care of all that for you." Stiles smirked. "If you get my drift. You pay them a flat fee for something called 'general business services,' and they make the payoffs for you. They skim a little off the top, but you don't get your hands dirty and they make sure you don't have any . . . *interruptions*."

"I bet it isn't just a little off the top, either."

"It's not as bad as you think. Over time, markets get efficient. This one's no different. There's enough of those firms now that the skim isn't outrageous."

"The problem is," Gillette explained, "I want to bring in a construction group from the outside. There aren't any based in Vegas that can handle both jobs at the same time and get them done as fast as I want."

"I think as long as you hire one of these consulting firms, it doesn't matter that much. Might be a little more expensive, but as long as the Carbones get their pound of flesh, they don't care if you use someone outside."

Gillette brightened. "Good, then talk to a few of them for me. Are they all out in Las Vegas?"

"The ones you want to deal with."

"I'm going out there soon. Do phone interviews with the best ones and narrow it down to two, then we'll meet with them while I'm in town."

"Got it."

Gillette took another drink of water. "Some of these other New York crime families are in the paper every week. Somebody's being arrested for something, but I've never heard much about the Carbones."

"They're run by a guy named Joseph Celino who hates publicity as much as you do."

"Get some more on them from your contacts, will you? As much as you can. Specifically on Celino."

"Sure, sure." Stiles pushed his plate away, a few bites of the steak uneaten. "Man," he said loudly, "that wouldn't have happened a year ago. Wasting food like that, I mean. Hell, I would have had seconds."

"Like you said, it'll take a while." Gillette slipped the Blackberry back into his pocket. "Listen, Friday morning you and I are going to Washington. Then, in the afternoon, we're going to the Eastern Shore of Maryland to meet with the mayor of a small town down there."

"You're really going to follow up with those people in D.C.?"

There was no choice. Gillette had a gut feeling that Daniel Ganze really did know something about his father, and he wasn't going to miss even the *slightest* opportunity to find out what had happened to that plane sixteen years ago. "I'm going to meet with them at least once more," he replied. "I don't think I've got anything to lose doing that. Just the time if it turns out to be a dead end."

"I hope it's just the time."

"What do you mean?"

"I think you need to be careful."

"Always, and I'll have you there."

"Why the meeting with the mayor?" Stiles asked.

Gillette liked the fact that Stiles recognized when he didn't want to talk about something. If only most people he knew understood him so well. "She's getting in the way of a store Discount America is trying to build in her town, stirring up the natives. She's calling people in other towns, too. We can't have that."

"You going to bring her up to New York for a big, all-expenses-paid weekend? Turn on the Gillette charm at some swanky dinner? Make her an offer she can't refuse?" Stiles smiled. "If I know you, you'll have her begging you to bring that store to her town by the time the weekend's over."

"I wish." It wasn't going to be that easy—not according to Harry Stein, anyway. "I've got to get going. I've got this ground-breaking ceremony for the new hospital wing we're building at St. Christopher's," he explained, standing. "Why don't you come with me? We can talk more about the QS deal on the way over. It would probably help for me to let you in on all the things to expect when you sell your business. There's more to it than you think."

"Sure, and thanks for lunch."

Gillette grinned as he pushed in his chair. "Lunch is on you, pal. You're about to bank five large. You can afford it."

Boyd looked up from his desk when he heard the rap on the door. "What is it, Daniel?"

"I did some checking on that Miles Whitman situation," Ganze replied, moving into the office. "Called over to Justice to see what was what."

Boyd put down the report he'd been working on. "And?"

"They're not as stupid as we thought."

"What do you mean?" Boyd asked.

"It's taken them some time, but they've started to figure out that Whitman must have had help hiding his forty million. It's hard to hide that big a money transfer these days with the way banks have to report transactions."

"That doesn't sound good."

"They've put out feelers to several different agencies, including the right one. It could take them a few days, maybe even a week, to run it high enough up the flagpole to get an answer, but they'll get a bite if they have information to trade. Then we're screwed."

"We need this."

"I know."

Boyd groaned and rubbed his eyes. "Okay, let's move."

Gillette stood behind a raised podium erected in a field beside St. Christopher's Memorial Hospital on the Upper West Side of Manhattan. It was a beautiful early fall afternoon, the sky a deep blue, the air crisp, the summer humidity gone. *Football weather,* Gillette thought as he looked out over the hundred invited guests. Several of the hospital executive officers and board members had already stepped to the microphone to thank him for his personal generosity, and it was his turn to say a few words, which included reminding everyone that it was Everest Capital making the ten-million-dollar donation, not him.

He said a few more things—he hoped the new wing could make a difference to more than a few people's lives, hoped the research lab, which the wing would include, could produce results, and assured the hospital executives that Everest Capital would continue to support them in the future with their new projects. Gillette was close to several of the hospital executives—people he'd dealt with for years—so he knew the money would be used for the right purposes and not be siphoned off into some leech's pocket. He was generous with money he controlled, but careful. Because he knew how easily money could fall into the wrong hands. It was like water, always following the path of least resistance.

As Gillette stepped down from the podium, one of the construction company's representatives moved forward with a gold shovel that Gillette would use for the ceremonial ground breaking, and handed it to him.

"Thanks," Gillette said.

The man smiled from beneath his yellow hard hat, not letting go of the shovel right away.

"What is it?" Gillette asked.

"We're looking forward to having you in Las Vegas, Mr. Gillette," the man said quietly. "For everybody's sake, go with the flow when you get there. Make things easy." His smile faded. "Or we can make them very hard."

CHAPTER 5

David Wright drew back the pool cue, hesitated for a moment as he aimed, then struck the white ball hard. A tiny puff of blue chalk flew in the air, and the white ball raced across the table and careered into the seven, sending it toward the far corner pocket. But it skidded against the rail just in front of the pocket and bounced left, then rolled back almost a foot. "Damn it!"

"Too hard," Gillette observed, checking out the table as the seven came to rest. The ten was all he had to drop—Wright still had five balls on the table. If he knocked the ten in just right, he could set himself up perfectly for the eight and the match would be over. Three games for him—none for Wright.

"*Way* too hard," Stiles agreed. He was leaning against the wall beside the mahogany cue stand, sipping the iced tea Debbie had brought him.

"I don't need any coaching from the cheap seats," Wright snapped.

Stiles laughed. "Just trying to help, my man. I want to see your boss go down as bad as you do. He tells me he's never been beaten on this table." He winked at Gillette when Wright wasn't looking. "I get tired of hearing how good he is."

"Yeah, well, I almost beat him a couple of times, so screw you."

Wright and Stiles had just met, but Wright didn't care about first impressions, Gillette knew. He cared about winning.

"Why don't *you* play him," Wright said, gesturing at Stiles.

"I will when he's done with you," Stiles answered. "Which looks like it'll be in about thirty seconds, thanks to that last sorry-ass shot of yours. I thought Chris told me you had game."

Wright glared at Stiles. "Hey, you can—"

"Enough," Gillette interrupted, hiding a grin. He dropped the ten and eight quickly, then straightened up. "Looks like Quentin was wrong," he said. "Only took fifteen seconds."

"Yeah, well."

"Rack 'em, David," Gillette ordered. He picked up a bottled water off the table in front of the cue stand and took several swallows. "You and Quentin are going to play first," he said, wiping his mouth with the back of his hand. "One game, then the winner gets me. We're going to settle who's best right now with a little tournament, but it's my table so I get a first-round bye."

"What's he doing here, anyway?" Wright grumbled, gathering the balls into the rack.

"Quentin's in charge of my personal security."

"I thought we had a company doing that."

"Right, QS. *Quentin Stiles*. He's the one who got shot in Mississippi last fall. He's the one who saved my life down there."

Wright stopped gathering the balls and looked over at Stiles. "Oh, Jesus, I'm sorry."

Gillette had introduced Stiles to Wright only by his first name.

"I didn't put two and two together," Wright continued. "God, you're a legend around here." He hesitated. "No offense."

Stiles pulled a stick from the cue stand. "None taken. I got skin like a rhino."

Gillette sat at the table as Stiles prepared to break. "McGuire and Company is going to buy QS, and Quentin's going to join us at Everest when the deal's done. Which should be in about thirty days. I'm going to propose that he become a special partner at that time. Not a full partner like Faraday and me, but he's going to have some of the same privileges."

Wright's eyebrows rose, but he said nothing.

"One thing I'm going to do right away is give Quentin a piece of the ups on Everest Eight. You okay with that, David?" Gillette assumed Wright wouldn't be okay with that. Ups allocated to anyone meant less for everyone else, but Gillette had asked because he wanted to see Wright's reaction. "Well?"

Wright was waiting for Stiles to break. Stiles gestured for Wright to answer first.

"It's up to you, Christian," Wright replied, his voice uncharacteristically subdued. "It's your firm. If you think it's the right thing, do it. We've been damn successful with you as chairman."

But Gillette could see Wright wasn't on board a hundred percent. Which was fine—he wanted Wright to think for himself. He didn't want his most valuable people doing what they thought he wanted them to do or saying what they thought he wanted them to say. "You sure you don't have any issues with that?"

Before Wright could say anything, Stiles drew back his stick and sent the cue ball flying toward the triangle of balls at the other end of the table. It exploded with a thunderous crack and four balls dropped—three solids, one stripe.

Gillette had assumed Stiles was good—Stiles had told him how he'd hustled older guys in Harlem pool halls as a teenager, and another QS agent had said he'd been whipped by Stiles when they were on an assignment in Dallas one time—but Gillette had never actually seen Stiles in action. "Pretty good, Quentin." You could tell by the way he broke that he knew what he was doing. His stroke seemed effortless, but the cue ball had rocketed to the other end of the table. And the result had been impressive—four balls off the break. A lot of that was because he was strong as hell, even in his weakened condition, but you still had to have the coordination to make it all come together.

"Pretty good?" Stiles ambled down one side of the table toward the spot where the cue ball had ended up. "You only wish you could break like that, Christian," he said, sizing up the way the balls lay, figuring out the best way to play things. "I'll take stripes," he announced.

"But you dropped three solids off the break," Wright pointed out.

"Yeah, but we've got to even this up somehow. If I took solids, it'd be over in two minutes, judging from what I've seen of your play." Stiles grinned. "No offense."

"None taken."

"That's the other reason I'm going to be around more," Stiles said, "to keep Chris humble when it comes to pool."

"We'll see," Gillette said.

"That would be nice," Wright mumbled.

"Chris."

The three men glanced toward the door at the sound of Debbie's voice.

"Yeah, Deb."

"Kurt Landry is on the phone. Says it'll only take a second."

"Okay. Transfer him in here."

"Right away."

When the cordless phone on the table in front of the cue stand rang, Gillette picked it up. "Hi, Kurt."

"Hello, Christian. Two quick things. First, thanks for lunch."

"Sure."

"Second, I want to let you know that I spoke to several of the owners about the casino issue, and they wanted me to assure you that you can move forward on that. Everything's fine there."

Gillette's mind raced back to the man who had handed him the shovel at the ground-breaking ceremony, wondering how that encounter fit into all of this. "Good."

"Other than that, welcome to the NFL. Don't hesitate to call me if you have any questions or issues."

"Thanks."

"What did he want?" Stiles asked as Gillette hung up.

Gillette shook his head, indicating they'd speak later about it. "So, David, no issues with Quentin joining the firm?" he asked again as Stiles bent to line up his next shot. He watched Wright struggle. It was obvious that the younger man still wanted to say something, but it was also clear he understood how close Gillette and Stiles were and didn't want Gillette to think hiring Stiles was bad.

"Well . . ." Wright paused. "What exactly are you going to do for us, Quentin?"

Gillette liked the way Wright was going directly at Stiles, shifting the conversation away from them, not using him as the intermediary. Efficiency was the key in business. And no matter what anyone else at Everest said about Wright, about his arrogance or his brash manner, he was direct as hell. People who were direct made progress, and progress—whether the results were good or bad—was the only way to get to the bottom line.

"I'm going to focus on disaster planning, risk mitigation, and recovery alternatives," Stiles answered. "I've had a lot of experience in those areas both in the private sector and when I was with the Secret Service and the Army Rangers.

I've found that most entities aren't really prepared for disasters, even big corporations. Whether the threat is terrorism, internal fraud, fire, bad weather, whatever. Most companies haven't focused on protecting the entire entity against a disaster. Whether that means the physical plant, computer networks, or employees, they just haven't done enough. In some cases, they haven't even analyzed what disasters they face." He gestured toward Gillette. "Chris wants me to do a full review of all the Everest portfolio companies to make sure your investments are protected as much as possible."

Wright's gaze flickered back and forth between Gillette and Stiles. "How much of the ups are you giving him, Christian?"

"One percent." Gillette saw Wright's relief immediately. With a twenty-billion-dollar fund, one percent could be a meaningful number, but it was probably well south of what Wright had feared. "I'm going to pay Quentin a million a year in salary, too. He'll stay in charge of my personal security as well as doing all the other things he just talked about. I think a million's fair."

"Of course, of course," Wright agreed.

"Any more questions?" Gillette asked.

Wright shook his head.

"Will you back me internally on this?"

"Absolutely," Wright said, "but I'm not sure that's very important. I mean, I'll be glad to say something positive about it at the managers meeting, if that's what you want me to do. But I don't know if that'll help much."

"I'm going to have the managing partners vote on it before then," Gillette said.

"You probably don't have to do that," Wright pointed out. "This is probably something you can do on your own, as chairman. I can take a look at the partnership documents if you want. To make sure."

"Thanks, but don't bother," Gillette said. "I'm going to be extra careful here. Since Quentin's a friend, I'll feel better if the partners vote, even if the documents say I can do it on my own."

"Okay, but then what do you want me to do? I can't vote, I'm just a managing director."

"Not anymore."

Wright's eyes shot to Gillette's. "Huh?"

"David, I've got good news and bad news. Here's the bad. Nigel and I have decided to open a Los Angeles office. I know how much you love L.A., but you won't be going." Gillette held up his hand when he saw that Wright was about to speak. "But here's the good: I've promoted you to managing partner. I need to talk to Nigel one more time about your compensation, but the promotion's done."

"Jesus," Wright whispered. "Thanks."

"You deserve it. And I will need your vote as far as Stiles goes."

"You got it."

"Of course," Gillette continued, "this means there won't be any more incidents like this morning."

"Incidents?" Wright asked hesitantly, swallowing hard.

"Not being able to reach you." Wright had finally called Gillette back as he and Stiles were headed to the hospital for the ceremony. "Debbie started calling you at nine this morning, but I didn't hear from you until three-fifteen. What the hell happened?"

"Sorry."

"Where were you?"

Wright looked down. "I was shopping for my wife. Our wedding anniversary is coming up."

Gillette looked over at Stiles, who had stopped playing. "That took all day?"

"I'm buying her a diamond ring, and I was designing it with the jeweler."

"You didn't have cell phone reception at the jewelry store? Where was this place, in a fallout shelter?"

"I kept getting calls. The guy got pissed and told me to turn it off." Wright looked up. "Sorry, it won't happen again." He took a deep breath. "Thanks again for making me a managing partner; it means a lot to me. A hell of a lot."

"You're the youngest managing partner in Everest Capital history," Gillette said, not completely satisfied with Wright's explanation. "Beat me by a year."

Wright gave Gillette a grateful nod for the comment. "Does this mean I can call you Chris from now on?"

"No. In fact, if you take more than thirty minutes to call me back again, you'll be calling me 'Mr. Gillette.' "

Wright rolled his eyes and motioned for Stiles to start playing again. "By the way, Christian, I meant to tell you, I was able to get a meeting with the Hush-Hush CEO. It's tomorrow morning. I know this is last minute, but can you come with me?"

"Sure." Faraday had already called his contact at the French clothing company. As Gillette had suspected, they'd been ecstatic about the possibility of picking up a hot U.S. women's clothing company. Gillette figured they could bang a big profit on a quick flip here, maybe three to four hundred million without a lot of work, so he wanted to make certain everything went right. "What time is the meeting?"

"Ten o'clock." Wright watched Stiles sink one striped ball after another. "It should go about two hours."

"Okay, then I want you to come with me to my Apex meeting. That's at one."

"Apex meeting?"

Until now, Gillette had discussed his plans to buy Apex only with Faraday. "Yes, I'm getting together with Russell Hughes tomorrow."

"He's the chairman, isn't he? Why are you meeting with him?"

"I'm gonna buy Apex."

Wright's mouth fell slowly open. *"Buy it?"*

"Yup."

"They aren't doing very well right now. In fact, from what I hear, they're doing awful."

"Which gives us an opportunity. Plus they've got five billion dollars of dry powder. And if we shoot some of the operating people at their dog investments and put our people in, I think we can turn those companies around fast. I've talked to the Strazzi Trust, the people who control Apex, and they're interested in my offer."

"Which is?" Wright asked.

"Par, what they have in it."

"How much is that in dollars?"

"A billion."

Wright chewed on the figure. "Doesn't seem too bad for twenty-two companies and five billion of equity commitments."

Gillette had known Wright would come around fast. The great thing about David was that it was what he really thought, too. He wasn't agreeing just to ingratiate. "The trust people are worried that if they keep Hughes as chairman much longer, their investment won't be worth anything. Par sounded good."

"Why don't they fire Hughes?"

"Faraday asked the same thing. If they do, their investors will pull out," Gillette answered, "and Apex would die on the vine. The good thing for us is that a lot of Apex's investors are our investors, too. I've spoken to a number of them, and they'd support an Everest takeover of Apex. They wouldn't pull out if we were in charge."

"You mean if *you* were in charge," Wright said.

"I don't have time," Gillette replied, "I have to focus on our new fund."

"You can't keep Hughes around."

"No," Gillette confirmed. "Not for the long term, anyway."

"You going to bring in someone from the outside?" Wright asked.

"I'm bringing you in," Gillette said, smiling. "This is going to be your first assignment as a managing partner. You're going to be the next chairman of Apex Capital."

"My God," Wright whispered.

"We'll need to talk at least five or six times a day, maybe more at the beginning," Gillette continued. "Which is why I can't have another episode like this morning."

"I told you, it'll never happen again."

"The other managing partners may have a problem with this." Gillette rose from his chair. Stiles was about to finish Wright off without even letting him take a shot. "They'll think they should have been tapped. Especially Maggie. But I—"

"Screw her," Wright retorted sharply. "She couldn't handle Apex. You know I'm better than her. Better than Blair and O'Brien, too. They couldn't handle this assignment, either. I doubt even Faraday could. But you know I can."

Gillette glanced over at Stiles. "I'm worried about his self-confidence, Quentin."

Stiles smirked as he dropped the eight ball, winning the game. "I know what you mean. He just got his ass kicked at pool."

"Big fucking deal," Wright snapped, his bravado back. "I'll alert the media, I'm sure it'll be front-page news."

"Come on, Quentin, rack 'em," Gillette ordered, ignoring Wright. "Let's go."

"You sure you want to do this?" Stiles asked. "Sure you

want to have your unbeaten streak on your home table go bye-bye?"

Gillette smiled, paying no attention to Stiles's attempt to get in his grill. "Just rack them," he repeated calmly, and turned back to Wright. "Where are the Hush-Hush offices?"

"In the garment district, down on Thirty-eighth Street near Penn Station."

"All right, we'll leave here at nine-thirty. You can brief me on the big issues on the way. After the meeting, we'll get a bite somewhere and talk about how we're going to handle the Russell Hughes meeting."

"Why even bother meeting with him?" Wright wanted to know. "Just go around him."

"First, the Strazzi Trust people asked me to meet with him. Like everyone else in the world, they hate confrontation, so they want me to let him know what's coming. As if he doesn't already," Gillette added. "Second, as poorly as he's run Apex, he knows more about it than anyone else simply because he's chairman. I want to get as much of a debrief out of him as we can before we lower the boom. He won't help much after that."

"Are you going to let him know he's gone tomorrow?"

"Haven't decided yet, but I will let him know that you're the new sheriff in town." Stiles had finished racking, and Gillette reached in his pocket for a quarter. "That's all, David, I—"

"There's one more thing I forgot to tell you, Christian," Wright spoke up, interrupting again. "I've got a line on another big investor, a Bermuda-based insurance company. I know you said Everest Eight was closed at the meeting, but these guys are looking to invest five hundred large. You should think about letting them in like we did with the Wallaces. They could probably do even more in Nine."

Gillette broke into a wide smile and moved to where

Wright stood. "This is why I promoted him, Quentin," he said, touching the younger man's shoulder. The same way his father had done when he'd done something well. A couple of light pats, then a squeeze. "He's the only person at this firm, besides Faraday and me, who's raised a dime for the new fund, and he's got us going in to see the Hush-Hush CEO tomorrow. Impressive, huh?"

Stiles grunted.

"What do you think about the Wallaces coming into the new fund?" Gillette asked Wright.

"The more the merrier," he answered immediately.

"I love it," Gillette said, beaming. "You worried about Allison Wallace being on the ground here at Everest?"

"Only if she starts to distract you."

"Excuse me?"

"I got a load of her the other day. She's pretty, and she's worth billions. You two would make a hell of a couple."

First Debbie, then Faraday, now Wright. This was getting old. "There's nothing to worry about," he assured Wright.

Wright shrugged. "Okay."

"Let's go," Stiles called impatiently. "I'm going to show you how to play pool, Chris."

Gillette picked up Wright's wallet off the table. Wright took it with him everywhere he went, even if he was just going to someone else's office at Everest. "You can go now."

Wright grabbed the wallet. "I want to stay. I want to see you—"

"Let him stay," Stiles said, laughing. "Every protégé needs to see his mentor go down once in a while."

Gillette smiled thinly. He knew what Stiles was trying to do, but it wasn't going to work. In fact, he was going to turn the tables on Stiles, take him where he didn't want to go. "Okay, David, you can stay. Tell you what, Quentin," he said, "let's make this interesting."

Stiles stopped chalking his cue. "What do you mean?"

Gillette grinned. Stiles knew exactly what he meant. "You're about to come into some money," he said. "Let's bet."

"How much?"

Gillette's grin widened. He had Stiles right where he wanted him. "How about a hundred grand?" A lot, but not too much.

Wright's eyes flashed to Stiles's.

"*A hundred grand?*" Stiles glanced at Wright, then back at Gillette.

Gillette shrugged apologetically. "Fine, fine. Let's make it two hundred."

Stiles swallowed hard. "I thought this was about pride."

"It was until you got cocky."

"Isn't pride more important than money?"

Gillette shook his head. "Pride's for pussies."

Wright laughed out loud, happy to see Stiles sweating.

Stiles leaned on the table with both hands and dropped his head. "Two hundred grand, huh?"

"Unless you want—"

"No, no. Two hundred's fine."

"Good." Gillette held up the quarter he'd pulled from his pocket. "Flip for the break?"

"Sure."

"I assume you want heads."

"Of course," Stiles confirmed. "Coins always come up heads more often than tails. That's a fact."

Gillette tossed the quarter in the air so it landed on the pool table. It bounced several times, then rolled to a stop.

Wright leaned over the table. "Tails," he announced.

Stiles glanced at the quarter and shrugged, as though he didn't really care. "Go ahead, Chris."

It was over quickly. As Stiles had done to Wright, Gillette didn't even give Stiles a chance to shoot once. He ran the table cleanly, dropping all seven solid balls, then the eight.

"Double or nothing?" Gillette asked as the eight fell into a side pocket, watching Stiles try to figure out how he'd let himself get taken for two hundred grand so easily.

"Nah."

Gillette placed his cue back in the wall rack and picked up his coat off the back of the chair. "I've got to get going, I'm taking Allison to dinner to talk about our new working relationship."

Wright whistled. "I hope Faith doesn't find out."

"Easy, David, that's how rumors get started." Gillette took a few steps toward the door, then stopped. "By the way, I want both you guys to come out on the boat this weekend. We'll board over on the West Side around noon, at the Forty-fourth Street pier. Plan to spend the night. Bring wives or sweethearts." He winked at them. "But not both. I'm inviting Nigel, too. We'll celebrate your promotion," he said, pointing at Wright.

"Thanks, Christian."

"Come on, Quentin," Gillette said, waving at Stiles. "Let's go." He followed Stiles out, then stopped at the door and leaned back in the room. "By the way, David. Call me Chris."

CHAPTER 6

"Where's Allison staying?" Stiles asked as they pushed through the crowded Park Avenue sidewalk toward a black limousine idling in front of the Everest Capital building.

"Parker Meridien," Gillette answered, checking for the two sedans—one in front and one in back of the limousine, his full security detail. They were there.

Gillette wasn't worried about Miles Whitman. He probably wasn't even in the country. He was probably in South America or Europe, living under an assumed name, living off the money he'd stolen from North America Guaranty as the feds were closing in on him last fall. He was probably much more interested in not going to prison than he was in revenge. When it really came down to it, most white-collars were.

But Tom McGuire was another story.

McGuire had spent years in the FBI as a field agent before founding McGuire & Company. Revenge drove him, he was tough as nails, and he had no fear of prison. The feds had been watching his house on Long Island and listening to his wife's and children's telephone calls for the last ten months, but he hadn't made contact—as far as they could tell. However, Gillette had no doubt that McGuire had been in touch with them somehow. He was clever enough to keep it concealed.

And McGuire had one more big motivator—his brother,

Vince. Vince had been co-CEO of McGuire & Company before the conspiracy, and he'd helped Tom with the assassination attempts. He'd been as deeply involved in the plot as Tom and Whitman. But Stiles's men had caught Vince and turned him over to the feds just as the whole conspiracy was collapsing last year, and Vince had been killed in a prison riot three months ago. Knifed in the back and left to bleed to death on a basketball court.

Gillette climbed into the limousine ahead of Stiles and eased onto the wide rear seat. "What did you think of David?" he asked as Stiles relaxed onto the bench seat along the driver's side.

"Cocky as hell." Stiles shrugged apologetically. "Hope you didn't think I was too tough on him."

"Tough? You were like a Boy Scout helping a little old lady across the street, for Christ's sake," Gillette grumbled. "You were a bigger prick to *me* with all that jawing before our game. Never seen that side before."

"I was just having fun. Besides, it didn't do me any good."

"No, it didn't."

"You know, it seemed like something was bothering Wright," Stiles observed.

"What do you mean?"

"He seemed *on edge*. Preoccupied."

"How could you tell? You've never met him."

"I've watched a lot of nervous people in my career," Stiles explained. "I'd never met most of them before, but I could still tell they were nervous. To me, Wright seemed like he was about to take a polygraph test."

Gillette gazed at Stiles for a few moments as the limousine pulled away from the curb, following the lead sedan. He was sorry to hear this, but he'd learned to trust Stiles's instincts.

"What did Kurt Landry want?" Stiles asked as they headed down Park Avenue.

Gillette had started making notes in a date book, jotting down names of people he needed to call tomorrow before the Hush-Hush meeting. "To tell me he'd spoken to the NFL owners and they were fine with the casino idea. Everything's a go there."

"Why didn't you want Wright to hear that?"

Gillette shrugged as he slipped the date book back in his pocket. "He's one of those guys who keeps asking questions until he gets answers."

"Like you," Stiles said.

That was what everyone always said. "Yeah. Thing is, he wasn't involved in the bid process, and I didn't want to have to go through it all again. How the casino works in with the franchise and all that. He would have tried to push me on that, especially after I told him he'd been promoted." Gillette hesitated. "Hey, do you remember the guy who handed me the shovel at the ceremony this afternoon?"

"Yeah. Why?"

"When he handed it to me, he said they were looking forward to seeing me in Las Vegas. He told me not to make any waves. He said it so no one else would hear, but he definitely said it."

Stiles had been reaching for a small refrigerator across from the bench seat but stopped. "Really?"

"Think he's with the Carbones?"

"Maybe."

"How the hell would they find out so fast?"

Stiles shrugged. "People talk. That's the biggest problem with them. If they'd just shut up, everything would be fine." He shook his head. "I'll talk to my guys. I'm sure they checked everybody for weapons before they let them anywhere near you, but I guess they should have done background checks, too."

"Don't give them a hard time about it," Gillette ordered. "You're the one who always tells me if somebody really wanted to take out the president, it wouldn't be that hard."

"Sure, but—"

"Your guys do a great job. I don't want you getting on their case for that. Nothing happened. Just run a check on the guy."

"Right."

The limousine turned onto Fifty-seventh Street and headed west. Traffic had been heavy on Park, but it cleared as they made the turn.

"So, you want me to actually sit at the table with you and Allison at dinner?"

"Yup."

Stiles grinned. "I'm like your chaperone."

"More like my alibi."

"I don't get it."

"Some people are under the impression that I'm going to be distracted by Allison Wallace. You heard David. They think she's going to try to make our relationship more than just a business partnership, *and* that I'm going to let it happen. It's ridiculous, I'm not going to let it happen, even if that's what she wants. Which I doubt she does. But I want you there so I have a witness that tonight was just business."

"Okay, son."

"I know it sounds silly, but I gotta do what I gotta do." They were almost to the Parker Meridien. Gillette reached into his suit jacket. "This is for you," he said, handing a coin to Stiles.

"What the . . . ?"

"It's the quarter I flipped before our pool game, you know, to see who went first. I had it specially made while you were in the hospital. Check it out."

Stiles turned on a reading light behind his shoulder and held up the coin, then flipped it. "Son of a bitch. Tails on both sides."

Gillette laughed. "You always call heads when you flip anyone for anything. I've seen you do it so many times. And you always say I'm predictable." He gestured at Stiles. "Keep the two hundred grand, of course. Boy, it was fun to see your face when I dropped the eight."

Wright tossed a ten-dollar bill onto the front seat of the cab, then hopped out and headed down the shadowy sidewalk toward the entrance of his apartment building.

"David."

"Jesus!" Wright's head snapped left, toward the voice, and he staggered back a few steps. Like a ghost, the man who'd shown up at Saks that morning appeared out of a darkened doorway. "What do you want, Paul?" Wright demanded angrily, trying to regain control.

"From now on, I want to know where Christian Gillette is at all times."

Suddenly Wright was exhausted. He just wanted to go to bed. "Why?" he asked, his voice hoarse.

The man pointed a thick finger at Wright, holding it inches from his face. "Listen to me good, pal. If you aren't helpful with this, the cops will get answers to all those questions they have. Missing persons questions right now, but they'll be murder questions real fast." He grabbed a crumpled piece of paper out of his coat pocket and put it in Wright's hand, then curled Wright's fingers around it. "That's my number. Don't lose it, don't be a stranger, and don't be stupid."

Wright watched Paul walk away until he faded into the darkness. This had been one of the best days of his life—and one of the worst.

* * *

Gillette spotted Allison Wallace the moment he walked into the Parker Meridien lobby. Stunning. It was the only word. She wore a low-cut black dress, high heels at the end of her long legs, and a diamond choker—night and day from the conservative Wall Street outfit she'd worn to Everest. Two well-tailored men were trying to talk to her, but she wasn't paying much attention, giving them disinterested nods at inappropriate times in the conversation.

"Hi," she called, waving to Gillette with her champagne glass when she saw him over the men's shoulders. Spilling a little on one as she sidled between them. "What's this?" she asked, pointing at the agents standing on either side of Gillette, hands clasped behind their backs.

"Security."

She raised one eyebrow. "I'm the one worth twenty-two billion, and I don't have security. What's your excuse?"

"I'm careful."

"Think it might be a little much?"

"Nope."

"Sure you aren't compensating for a lack of something somewhere else?"

Gillette attempted a coy smile, but it didn't work. "Quite sure. There've never been any complaints about that."

"What *have* there been complaints about?"

"You can probably guess."

"Your girlfriends probably bitch about never seeing you, Mr. Workaholic."

"Very good, Captain Obvious. You win a prize."

"Which is?"

"Dinner with me."

"Whoopee. So, who pays for your security?" she asked.

"You," Gillette answered, noticing that she'd slurred her words slightly. This wasn't the night's first glass of champagne. "Now that you're an Everest limited partner." He wondered if she'd been drinking because she was nervous about dinner, if this was how she handled being worth twenty-two billion, or if she was just having fun. "Let's go."

"You have my office ready yet?" Allison asked as they walked. "I'll be there bright and early next Monday morning."

"What's 'bright and early' for you?"

"Seven o'clock."

"Sure it is. See you at nine."

"I'll beat *you* in."

"Are you going to stay here at the Parker Meridien for a few weeks until you get your apartment?" Gillette asked.

"I've already got my apartment. I move in next week."

"Oh, where is it?"

"On Fifth, right off Central Park."

Gillette jerked back as though he'd been slapped in the forehead. "Hey, I live on Fifth off the park."

"I know. I'm in the same building as you, two floors up."

He took a deep breath. "Great."

"Same elevator and all." Allison laughed. "What a coincidence, huh?"

"Yeah," he muttered, "amazing."

"You didn't answer my question," Allison said. "Is my office ready? I really am going to be there first thing next Monday morning, maybe sooner. I might not go back to Chicago at all."

They moved through the hotel's main door.

"It's ready. And it's at the other end of the hallway from mine."

"We'll just see about that," she said, climbing into the limousine ahead of Gillette. At the sight of Stiles, she jumped. "Who's this?" she demanded as Gillette eased next to her on the backseat.

Stiles leaned forward to take her hand. "Quentin Stiles."

"What are you doing here?"

"Quentin's in charge of my security," Gillette explained as the chauffeur shut the door.

"Fantastic, but what's he doing here?"

"Having dinner with us."

"Oh no, he's not." She smiled at Stiles politely. "Don't take this wrong, Mr. Stiles. I'm sure you're a very nice and interesting man, but I didn't come out tonight to have dinner with you. I'm here to have dinner with Christian. I need to talk to him about a lot of things, some of which are very confidential."

"Anything you say to me you can—"

"Don't give me that, Christian." Allison looked back at Stiles. "Could you sit in the front?" she asked courteously, reaching up and turning on the stereo. "Driver," she called over the music, "please pull over."

Stiles looked at Gillette as the chauffeur steered the limo to the curb.

"Go on," Gillette said quietly. So the real cost of the Wallace five billion wasn't going to be monetary, it was going to be something else. Something that might end up being far more expensive—his time and attention. He thought about Debbie's take on the meeting with Allison and Gordon. Maybe she'd been right after all.

"Just so we're clear, these aren't my real boobs," Allison said when Stiles was in the front seat and they were back in traffic. She put down the champagne glass in a holder in the armrest, then cupped her hands beneath her breasts. "I had the surgery two years ago."

Gillette searched for anything to look at inside the limousine besides her breasts. "Uh, why are you telling me this?"

"I noticed you staring at them."

"I wasn't staring."

"All right, you *glanced* at them a few times. But you would have stared sooner or later."

"Yeah, well, there isn't much to that dress."

"I figure it's better to be direct, about everything," she continued. "Full disclosure, you know? I just want the same thing from you."

"Well, these *are* my breasts."

"Funny."

"Thanks." This Allison Wallace was a firecracker, much different from the one he'd met at the office. Despite all the warnings, including a faint alarm going off in the back of his own head, Gillette kind of liked it.

Allison picked up her champagne again and took a long swallow, then pushed the button that elevated the partition between the front and back. "I was so flat before I got the implants. You have no idea how much better I feel about myself now."

"You're very pretty, Allison, with or without them."

"Ooh, a charmer. I like that." She held up her glass to him. "So, where are we going for dinner?" she asked after taking another sip.

"I made a reservation at a new restaurant here in midtown called Chez Madam." Gillette noticed how familiar Allison was with what buttons to push in a limousine. Which only made sense. She'd been riding in them since she was a baby. She probably didn't even have a driver's license. "It's popular, you'll like it."

"It's too quiet," she said, pushing the button that lowered the partition. "I went there on Saturday and it was a raging bore. I had to eat everything with silverware, and the bloody background music almost put me to sleep. I want to have fun tonight, I want to go off the hook. I know exactly where we're going. Driver," she called, "we're going down to TriBeCa."

Stiles looked back from the front seat. "Christian?"

Gillette shrugged, conceding. "I need to know where we're going," he said to her, "so my guys can check it out."

"It's called the Grill. It's down on Hudson Street some-where, and it's casual. A lot more fun than Chez Madman, or whatever the heck that place is called. They do a great mahimahi, which is what *you'll* have, Christian. I know you like fish, and this thing is to die for. Franky's the head chef. He'll prepare it for you himself, as a favor to me." She ran her tongue around her lips, as if she were already sa-voring a bite of something. "I'm having their bacon cheese-burger, it's the best in the city." She raised the partition and Stiles disappeared again.

"You want a *cheeseburger*?" Gillette asked.

"Yeah. So?"

He smiled. "It's just surprising. You don't look like a woman who'd want a cheeseburger for dinner, much less know where the best one in the city is."

"I'm full of surprises."

"So I see. How exactly do you know where the best cheese-burger in New York is, anyway? You're from Chicago."

"When you're worth as much as I am, you're always in New York. Big as Chicago is, it isn't New York. By the way," she said, leaning down and pulling a champagne bottle from the refrigerator, "I've already had my people at the Grill for a half hour making sure everything's okay." She handed the bottle to Gillette. "Open that, please. Re-member, turn the bottle, not the cork."

"I know how to open a champagne—"

"Of course you do. Look," she said, her voice turning se-rious, "I was kidding back at the hotel. I understand why you need protection. After our meeting at Everest, I had one of my staff back in Chicago put together a full report on what happened to you last fall. The way I see it, the guy you still have to worry about is Tom McGuire. Whitman's just trying to stay ahead of the law. Besides, based on what I read, he doesn't have the know-how or the guts to come after you. But McGuire's different. He's experienced with this stuff, and he's vindictive."

The cork popped loudly as Gillette gave the bottle a third twist. "You've been busy," he said, trying not to show her how impressed he was. "How did you know what I'd want for dinner?"

"You're in great shape, that's obvious," she said, brazenly giving him the once-over. "Guys in great shape eat healthy. And I spoke to Debbie this morning."

"You what?"

"Hey, girls gotta stick together. You wouldn't understand. Truth is, if I really want to be up to speed all the time with what's going on at Everest Capital, it's probably more important for me to have a good relationship with Debbie than you. If there's one person who might actually know more about what's going on at the firm than you, it's her." The limousine pulled up in front of the restaurant. Allison slid across the seat to the door and opened it. "Come on," she said over her shoulder.

Gillette liked that she didn't wait for the driver to get the door. He followed as she climbed out, looking away as her short dress rode high on her thighs. As he stood up, she grabbed his arm and pulled him toward the restaurant.

Then the paparazzi descended. Suddenly photographers were rushing at them from all directions and cameras were flashing everywhere. Four QS agents raced to form a wall around Gillette and Allison, then quickly ushered them into the restaurant. But not before fifty pictures had been snapped. People in the restaurant stopped and gazed as the couple came through the door, straining to see what the commotion was about.

Allison was still hanging on Gillette's arm. "Everyone's looking," she whispered. "God, this is fun."

Gillette turned around toward Stiles, who was behind

them. "Go back out there and talk to one of those guys, will you? Find out how they knew we were coming."

"Right."

When Stiles was gone, the maître d' led them to a secluded table in a back corner of the place.

"You arrange this, too?" Gillette asked, sitting down.

"Of course." Allison looked up at the maître d' when she was seated. "We'll have a bottle of Veuve Clicquot," she ordered over the music.

The maître d' nodded and moved off.

"So, I'm obviously a little different than you thought," she said after they'd relaxed into their chairs. "Not that quiet thing you met at Everest."

"Well, I—"

"I do the prim and proper routine for Gordon. He goes back to my uncle and grandfather and reports on me all the time. He thinks I don't know that. Fortunately, I've got him snowed, and he tells them mostly good things. They'd probably have heart attacks if they knew the truth."

"Your uncle and grandfather aren't stupid, Allison. They know the truth. They've probably had you followed."

"No way. I'd know if they did."

"How?"

"I pay the maids and the chauffeurs at home to tell me everything."

So she wasn't beyond bribery. A rich girl who didn't hesitate to put out money when she wanted information. He'd have to be careful about that. Maybe even have to give Debbie a raise.

"And my grandfather and uncle *are* that stupid," she continued, "which is why they have Gordon. At least they've got enough brains to understand how stupid they are."

A waiter appeared quickly with the champagne. When it was poured and he was gone, Gillette raised his glass.

"Here's to our partnership. At the very least, it's going to be interesting."

She tapped her glass to his and took a long swallow. "What do you mean by 'interesting'? Fun, or a pain in the ass?"

"I guess we'll find out. But I can tell you one thing: I've never been used like this before."

"Don't give me that," she snapped. "You're getting five billion dollars."

"And you're getting the education of a lifetime."

"Pretty sure of yourself, aren't you? Starting to believe the press clippings."

"I never believe press clippings. That puts you right on the road to ruin. All I believe in is profits."

"Like I said before, you're on a roll right now. But the economy's been good the last few years. Things'll get rougher when the GDP boards the down elevator."

"We'll be fine."

Allison sighed. "Yeah, guys like you always are. You're Mr. Consistency, aren't you." She pointed at his glass.

He'd put the glass back on the table without drinking. "What do you mean?"

"You know exactly what I mean. You don't drink alcohol. I wanted to see if you'd at least put it to your lips to try to con me."

Gillette rubbed his chin for a second. He wondered if there was anything she didn't know about him. "You've done *a lot* of homework."

"I invested five billion dollars in your fund, Christian. Almost a quarter of my family's net worth." She leaned over the table, swirling the champagne around in her glass. "I love a great time, I love to go crazy every once in a while, but I'm also very careful when it comes to my family's money."

"You should be."

"I put my grandfather and uncle down, but they're watching this move carefully. Investing so much in Everest, I mean. They aren't a hundred percent convinced it's the right thing to do. I'm taking a big risk."

"Then why do it?"

"I want to leave *my* mark on my family," Allison explained, her expression hardening. "I want to take twenty-two billion and make it fifty, maybe even a hundred. I want to be the one they talk about at Christmas dinner a hundred years from now. The one that made us a true dynasty." She laughed. "I want them to raise their glasses to a big oil painting of me hanging on the wall over the table." She pointed at him. "And you're the one who's going to teach me how to do it."

Always let people talk, Gillette thought. They'll tell you so much if you just let them go.

"Of course," she continued, "I'll be wearing a dress like this in the painting, maybe even shorter. Not one of those long things. I'll probably get the painter to make my boobs look a little bigger than they really are, too. That way I'll drive the young boys crazy." She put her head back and laughed loudly at her own idea.

"I'm surprised you haven't had the painting done yet," Gillette said.

"That's a good point. I should."

He watched Allison pull out her Blackberry and send a message to herself. A reminder to have the portrait done. It took everything he had not to laugh himself. "Remind me how your family got so rich." He wanted to keep her talking, hoping he'd get a few tidbits Craig West hadn't dug up.

"You already know all that. You told Gordon."

"Come on," he pushed.

"The railroad, real estate, then my father's brother, the smart one, got us into the cell phone explosion. He's dead now, unfortunately. He wasn't a very nice man, but he was wicked smart. The only thing my generation's done is invest in the public markets. We did okay in the late nineties with the tech boom because we got a lot of opportunities to invest in IPOs, thanks to the relationships we had with the investment banks doing the offerings. But we stayed in too long. We were actually worth almost twenty-five billion at one point in 2000. Thanks to my cousin Ricky, we lost a lot of the paper gains we'd racked up when the bottom fell out of the NASDAQ."

"Ricky is one of your uncle's sons? The one that's on the family trust's board now?"

"Right."

"How many uncles do you have?"

"My father had three brothers. Uncle Tad's the one who got us into cell phones and died. Then there's the one that's on the board now, and there's another one who lives on a beach in Tahiti. Literally sleeps at night in a hammock that's tied up between two palm trees. He's useless."

"And your dad, where's he?"

"He runs a cattle ranch in Montana. It's what he always wanted to do. The ranch loses money every year, but the family trust makes it whole."

"Do you talk to him much?"

"No. We're different," Allison said, her tone softening. "And don't give me the speech about how I should talk to him all the time and count my lucky stars he's alive," she warned, her voice growing strong again. "I know about your father. I'm sorry about it, but my father and I can't make it work. We've tried and it just doesn't click."

Gillette stared back for a few moments, then cleared his throat. "How old is your cousin Ricky?"

"Thirty-one, a year older than me. My father's generation had eleven kids, but Ricky and I are the only ones really involved in the family business affairs. The rest of them are just leeches. Ricky was the golden child of my generation and on the board," she continued, "until he lost that three billion. Which is why I'm on the board now. My father and the brother that lives in Tahiti screamed bloody murder until my grandfather made the switch. Now that I'm on it, I want to show everyone what I can do. I want to make it big." She patted Gillette's arm as she stood up. "Which is where you come in."

"Where are you going?" he asked, standing with her.

"Ladies' room." She smiled at him. "I like your manners, standing up when a woman leaves the table. Somebody raised you right."

Yeah, he thought. My dad.

Gillette watched her walk through the restaurant, watched men's heads turn as though they were on swivels. She was attractive but moved as if she didn't know or care, paying no attention to the stares or the elbows being jabbed. Or maybe she paid no attention because she was so used to it. If the guys in this restaurant only knew what she was worth, they wouldn't just ogle, they'd stampede the table when she got back.

"Excuse me."

Gillette glanced to his right at the voice. A young woman was waving at him while one of the security agents kept her at bay.

"Will you sign my *People* magazine?" she called, waving it as the man stayed between her and Gillette. "Please."

Gillette nodded to the agent as Stiles sat in Allison's chair. "What did you find out?" he asked, taking a pen from the young woman. She already had the magazine opened to the article.

"Nice mug," he said, pointing at Gillette's picture on the page.

"They must have gotten it off the Internet. I didn't send them anything." He signed his name along the bottom of the page, then handed the pen and the magazine back to the woman. "There you go."

"Thank you so much."

"Sure."

"She must have thought you were the rock star they put on that list," Stiles said, nodding at the magazine. "She couldn't have thought it was you. You aren't that exciting."

Gillette grinned. "Ah, you're just jealous. So, did you find out anything?"

Stiles nodded. "Yeah, it took a few minutes and a hundred bucks, but the guys outside found out you two were coming here from Allison. One of them finally came clean."

"He said she called?" Gillette asked incredulously.

"He said the call was anonymous, but it came from the Parker Meridien, so it had to be her. Otherwise one of the operators would have had to be listening to her phone, and I doubt that happened."

"How did the guy know the call came from the Parker?"

"Caller ID."

Gillette spotted Allison coming back from the ladies' room. "Thanks."

Stiles saw her, too, and stood up. "Have fun."

"Did you miss me?" Allison asked as Gillette held out her chair.

"Sure." He noticed that she was sniffing as he sat back down. "You okay?"

"Huh?"

"You're sniffing. You okay?"

"Oh, I'm fine. It's allergies. Happens every fall."

Gillette watched her closely. Please, he thought, please tell me I didn't partner with a woman who has this problem. "Why did you call the paparazzi on us?"

She put a hand on her chest. "What?"

"Why'd you do it?"

"I didn't."

"Come on."

She squinted at him for a moment, then smiled and shrugged. "I thought it would be fun."

"And I thought you didn't want your family knowing you were such a party animal."

An irritated look came to her face. "First of all, they don't read the kind of rags those pictures will show up in. Second, even if they did find out about them, I'd say the photographers were following you because of that *People* article. I'd tell my grandfather I was appalled at the pictures and that I'd already told you to be more low-key."

"Why did you call them, Allison?"

"I told you," she said, sniffing again. "I thought it would be fun." She cased the restaurant, eyes darting from table to table. "How's that pop-star girlfriend of yours? Still peddling her CDs?"

So that was Allison's game. She wanted Faith to see pictures of them coming into the Grill, arm in arm. Deb was beginning to look awfully smart. "She's doing fine."

"Where is she tonight?"

"On the West Coast doing some publicity. She's back tomorrow."

"How often do you see her? Is it an every night thing when she's in town?"

"Are you asking me if it's serious?"

"I'm just asking," Allison replied, wiping her nose with her napkin. "I'm not trying to get personal."

"Well, you are."

Allison rolled her eyes. "*Puleeease.* Don't flatter yourself. I'm not asking because I want to move in on her. Gawd, it would be awful to date you. You love your work way too much. A woman would always run second to Everest. Honestly, I just want to make sure it *stays* that way. I want my five billion to be twenty or forty billion in a few years. And for that to happen, your pecker needs to stay right where it is. In your pants."

She seemed sincere, which was good news. "Everyone will be very relieved."

"Everyone?"

"A lot of people at Everest think you're after me, and, well . . ."

"Well *what*?"

"You know."

Allison ground her teeth together for a few moments. "I'll pretend I didn't hear that."

"Okay."

"What's going on with that new NFL franchise you won?" she asked.

"Going on?"

"Like I said on the phone the other night, I want Everest Eight to make that investment."

Gillette shook his head. "No, we'll do it out of Seven. It has to be that way. I've got to be fair to my investors. The ones in Seven were in first."

"So do it fifty-fifty. I want a chunk of that."

"I'll think about it."

"I mean it."

"I heard you."

Her cell phone rang, and she pulled it from her purse. "What?" she said loudly, putting her purse back on the table and pressing her hand to her ear. "*What?*" But the music was too loud and she still couldn't hear. She got up and trotted through the restaurant.

Gillette watched her until she'd moved into the restaurant foyer, then his eyes shifted to the purse she'd left on the table.

Tom McGuire sat in the Explorer, parked on a darkened side street a few blocks from the Grill. Since everything had blown up last fall, he'd taken on a new identity—which wasn't hard if you knew what you were doing. He had a New Jersey driver's license, a Social Security card, and a passport—all of which made clear that he was William Cooper. He wore his hair longer now, had grown a goatee, and had put on twenty-five pounds. Even his children hadn't recognized him at first at the park on Long Island where he'd surprised them last month—the first time he'd seen them and his wife in nine months. The feds had been watching them twenty-four/seven since last November, but he'd found out from friends inside the Bureau that the tail had been called off at the end of August—almost a month ago. The feds were still listening in on calls, but not following the family anymore. It had been wonderful to see the kids.

Nigel Faraday's double take on Park Avenue the other morning was still bothering him. A stupid mistake, he thought. He shouldn't have been anywhere near there at that time of day, but he was trying to assess, trying to nail down routines. There was no need to worry, he told himself. The fat Brit probably hadn't noticed him anyway.

He shut his eyes as he sat in the SUV, clenching the steering wheel until his knuckles turned white. He and his brother had been so close to hundreds of millions, but Gillette and Stiles had destroyed everything at the last second. Now his brother was dead, and he had the rest of his life to look forward to an assumed existence and sporadic, short visits with his family.

McGuire took a deep breath. He'd been waiting ten months for tonight, and it was all coming together perfectly.

"You ready to go?" Gillette asked, checking his watch. It was nine-thirty, and he wanted to get home so he could go through the Hush-Hush material Wright had given him to prepare for tomorrow morning. "I'll give you a lift back to the Parker."

Allison looked at him as if he were crazy. "Are you nuts? We're going out. We'll start at the China Club, then figure out our plan from there. I don't go home at nine-thirty when I'm in New York."

Gillette checked the front of the restaurant. Through the large windows facing Hudson Street, he thought he could see the paparazzi still waiting, which seemed strange. They'd gotten their pictures, but it looked as though they were still hanging around. He motioned to Stiles.

"What's the matter?" she asked, noticing his wave.

"Nothing."

Stiles leaned down when he reached the table. The music was louder than when they had come in. "What is it, Chris?"

"Are the photographers still out front?"

"Yeah."

"But why? They got their pictures. You think they're waiting for somebody else?"

"I doubt it. This isn't a big place with celebrities. Besides, it's almost ten o'clock."

"Doesn't make any sense."

Stiles shrugged. "Nothing makes sense with these clowns."

Gillette thought for a moment. "Find out if there's a back way out of this place. I don't want any more pictures," he said, gesturing subtly at Allison. "You know?"

Stiles nodded, understanding. "There has to be another exit. It's building code, I think. When I find out, I'll have the driver bring the limo around. I'll have him waiting for us so we'll be able to get right in."

"What if they follow the guy?"

"I don't think—"

"Let's get out there," Gillette suggested, "then call him."

"But—"

"Just do it."

Stiles nodded.

When he was gone, Allison leaned toward Gillette. "What was all that about?"

Gillette eyed her. She was still sniffing, still blaming it on allergies. "Business."

"Well, I'm your *business* partner, so talk to me."

"It wasn't that kind of business," Gillette answered, watching Stiles as he spoke to the maître d', who seemed willing to help, judging by the way he was pointing and nodding.

"Maybe not, but it brings up an important point."

"What's that?"

"As a managing partner, I need to know everything that's going on at Everest Capital."

"Then talk to Debbie. Sounds like you think she's going to be your best source of information."

"I'm being serious, *Christian.*"

"So am I."

"We need to meet every two days," she demanded, "just the two of us, to go over everything that's happening. We'll make those meetings on Mondays, Wednesdays, and Fridays, and we'll talk one day over the weekend. Of course, if something really important happens, you'll call me right away."

The cost of Wallace money was going to be even greater than he'd expected, he thought, rubbing his eyes. "We meet once a week as a group in the main conference room. The meeting usually lasts several hours. Believe me," he said, emphasizing the words, "after a few weeks, you'll know more than you want to know about Everest Capital."

She shook her head. "That's not good enough. Nowhere near good enough."

"It's good enough for everyone else."

"Everyone else hasn't invested five billion dollars. I told

you, I'm very careful with my family's money. And my family is watching this thing very closely."

"Which I understand," Gillette said calmly. "I hope you can understand that I'm busy. If I had to spend that much time talking to you, I wouldn't have enough time to run the firm."

"I want to help, too. The only way I can do that is if I know what's going on."

"You know how you could really help?"

"How?"

"Find me a deal. Find a good company for us to buy at a great price."

Allison finished the last sip of champagne in her glass and reached for the bottle in the ice bucket. But it was empty. "Let's get another bottle," she suggested.

"I told you, we're leaving."

"If you don't get another bottle, I won't tell you about the deal I've got working."

He studied her, trying to determine if there was any truth to what she'd said or if she'd tossed it out there just so he'd get another bottle. He couldn't tell; her face was impassive. "You play poker?" he asked.

She nodded. "Love to."

That figured. "Want to play sometime?"

"Absolutely. Are you in on a regular game?"

"I know a few guys who run a game every Monday night. I go once a month or so. It's a bunch of Wall Streeters. It's a serious game, so you need to know what you're doing."

"I'd love to take some money from the Hermès tie and suspender set. How about next Monday?"

"First, tell me about the deal you've got working." There probably wasn't anything to this, just smoke. After all, if the deal was so great, she'd do it using the Wallace Family Trust money so she could keep all the upside for herself.

She grinned. "I know what you're thinking. If the deal's so awesome, why share it with Everest? Well, I'm your partner, and when I partner with someone, whether it's business or personal, I commit. So, here it is. The company's name is Veramax. They're a—"

"A drug company based outside Chicago," Gillette interrupted. "Owned by a family named Mitchell." He'd been following the company for two years. "Very fast growing. They were going public last spring, but the family couldn't get the valuation they wanted because some of their new products were being held up by the FDA."

"Held up by a lot of red tape crap," Allison confirmed. "Some higher-up at the FDA doesn't like Jack Mitchell, Veramax's main shareholder. The company did over a billion dollars in revenue last year, but they could be doing three to four billion if they could just get these new products to the market. Some of them are incredible. They've got an Alzheimer's drug that's supposed to be fantastic."

"Why the bad blood between the Mitchells and the FDA?"

"I don't know exactly, but I think you could help."

"How?" he asked, becoming interested. This was another way you made money in the private equity world—bringing something to the table others couldn't.

"You and Michael Clark, the senator from California, are friends. You know him pretty well, actually."

"How do you know that?"

She groaned. "If I have to tell you how I know something every time we talk, we're never going to get anywhere, Mr. I Don't Even Have Time to Keep My Five-Billion-Dollar Partner Up to Speed."

"All right, all right," he said. "How does knowing Senator Clark help?"

"He's got pull with the FDA. One of the big guys over there is a golfing buddy of his from California."

"So, I broker a deal."

"Yes."

"What do I get in return?"

"Even if Clark can convince his buddy at the FDA to finish approving Veramax's products quickly, my understanding is that it'll still take six to nine months to get everything finished. The company has some big opportunities they need funding for, and the family wants to do some estate planning. They need money for all that, about a half a billion, and they need it *now*. You get to be that investor, then cash out in the IPO, which should be next fall if you can get the FDA in line. You'd probably make five to six times your money in the IPO. Your investors, me included, will like that."

"I won't pay a premium, especially if I'm the one who gets the FDA off their ass."

"I'm with you," Allison agreed.

"And I want control, I want at least fifty-one percent of the stock."

"I'll arrange a meeting with Jack Mitchell. Talk to him about that."

This actually sounded good, and Gillette was surprised. He hated surprises. "What's your in? Why will Mitchell listen to you?"

"First, I'm bringing you and your connection to Senator Clark. Second, our families have been friends for years. We've vacationed together on the Upper Peninsula of Michigan ever since I was a little girl."

"When can you arrange a—"

"Chris."

Gillette looked up at Stiles. "Yes."

"Got a back door through the kitchen. Let's go."

"Okay. Send your guys out to the front, like we're about to come out."

"I think we should keep at least two of them with us."

Gillette shook his head. "We'll only be out there for a few minutes, we'll be fine. I don't want any more pictures."

"Still, I—"

"No," Gillette said sharply, standing. "And make your guys think we really are coming out that way. They'll sell it better."

Allison grabbed her purse. "Hey."

"Come on," he said, holding his arm out for her, "I'm not leaving you."

"You scared me," she said, standing up unsteadily and slipping her arm into his. "I thought you'd forgotten those beautiful manners for a second."

"You sure you want to stick to that allergy story?" he asked as they followed Stiles through the restaurant.

"Why wouldn't I?" she asked, holding on to his arm tightly as they climbed a few steps to the kitchen level. "It's the truth."

"Maybe you're getting sick."

"I feel fine."

"Then maybe it's something you're putting up your nose in the bathroom."

"*What*? Listen, I—"

"Nose drops, I don't know."

"Christian, I'm not a—"

"Look," he cut in, "if you tell me it's allergies, it's allergies. I'm not accusing you of anything. I'm just telling you, no drugs at Everest. No marijuana, no cocaine, no nothing. Got it?"

"Of course. I've never done drugs in my life, and I never will. I love to party, but I don't do that."

"Just so we're clear."

"We're clear."

"Perfectly clear?"

"*Perfectly.*"

"Then get me an appointment with Jack Mitchell."

"Maybe I will," she said testily, "and maybe I won't."

"Make it soon," he said, ignoring her. "Work with Debbie."

"Yes, sir. Is there anything else I can do for you? Maybe shine your shoes in between my snorting sessions?"

"And before we meet with him, I want to know two things," he said, ignoring her. "First, what's the source of the bad blood between Mitchell and the FDA, and second, how you know about my connection to Senator Clark."

Three steps led down from the back of the kitchen to the alley, which was littered with paper and broken glass that sparkled in the dim light cast by a single bulb affixed to the brick wall beside the door.

"This doesn't look good," Allison muttered, peering both ways.

"Come on," Stiles called, pulling his cell phone from his pocket, "I don't want to be out here long. Hustle!"

Allison tapped Gillette on the shoulder as they walked quickly to keep up with Stiles. "Just so you know, I didn't call the paparazzi."

Gillette's eyes shot to hers. "What?"

"I didn't call them."

"But you told me you did."

"You actually thought I'd go to the trouble of putting together some big plan so your girlfriend would see us together in the newspapers? You think I'm at Everest to get a husband, but I'm not. I'm here to make money for my family. That's it."

Gillette looked ahead at Stiles, who was staring at his cell phone as he walked. "Quentin, what's up?"

"The reception sucks back here. I haven't been able to get the driver or my guys."

Gillette pulled out his phone as they rounded the corner of the building at the end of the alley. "I think I've got—" He almost ran into Stiles, who'd stopped short.

"Jesus," Allison whispered.

Gillette counted five of them, about twenty feet away. Shadowy figures on the sidewalk, standing side by side, their faces obscured. His eyes darted around, looking for help, but the street was deserted. No one here but the three of them and the figures ahead—moving slowly toward them now.

"Give me a number, Quentin," he urged, stepping ahead of Allison and next to Stiles. "For one of your guys."

"We aren't going to have time for that."

Gillette looked up from the phone. The men had stopped a few feet away. They were close enough now that he could make out their faces.

"What do you want?" Stiles asked calmly.

"Your money," demanded the one in the middle. "Everything you got."

"Look, we don't want any trouble."

"We don't want no trouble, either," said the one on the far left as the others chuckled, "we just want your money."

"We don't have anything," Gillette said defiantly.

"Of course not. I can tell that by those cheap-ass threads."

As the gang laughed again, Stiles went for his gun, a Glock .40 caliber pistol in the shoulder holster inside his jacket.

"Hold it!" warned the one in the middle, raising his right arm and pointing a revolver at Stiles. "I got you covered. I'll kill you, I swear."

Stiles froze, hand over his heart.

"Down," the man ordered.

Slowly, Stiles dropped his hand back to his side.

"All right, now—"

Gillette hurled his cell phone at the man in the middle, nailing him on the forehead, and rushed him as he brought both hands to his face. Gillette hunched down as he closed in, driving his shoulder into the man's gut, hurling him to the sidewalk. The man let out a loud groan as he hit the ground. As they rolled, Gillette heard the gun clatter away on the cement, and he heard Stiles yelling and Allison screaming.

Gillette was yanked up instantly. He swung blindly as he got his feet under him, clipping someone's chin, then he was tackled hard by a shoulder that felt like the front end of a Mack truck. For a moment, Gillette and his attacker were airborne, then they landed on the street in a heap, tumbling over and over. He felt hands close tightly around his throat, and he brought his arms up, breaking the hold, kneeing the guy in the stomach at the same time and tossing him away. He jumped to his feet and saw Stiles wrestling on the ground with two of the men.

"Stop it!" Allison screamed. She was clutching the gun the man had lost when Gillette tackled him. Aiming the barrel in different directions frantically—at the men attacking Stiles, at the guy on the ground beside Gillette, then at a man coming toward her. "Right now!"

The man coming at her froze a few feet away when he saw the gun.

Suddenly Gillette heard the sound of an engine roaring to life, then squealing tires.

"Christian!" Allison screamed. "Look out!"

He turned into a pair of high beams just as the man who had tackled him grabbed him around the legs, bringing him down again. He grabbed the guy by the hair and slammed his head into the pavement, then scrambled for the sidewalk as the SUV raced past, running over the man lying in the street. The man's body shook for several seconds, then went still.

The SUV screeched to a halt, and the driver's-side window began to come down. Then the driver punched the accelerator and the vehicle roared away.

"Hands behind your head!" someone yelled. "Now!"

Gillette glanced toward Stiles and saw two QS agents racing toward their boss, guns drawn. Then two sedans skidded around the corner—opposite the one the SUV was headed toward—headlights illuminating the scene brightly. The other two QS agents jumped from the sedans, guns drawn, too. It was over as quickly as it had begun.

Gillette bent over, hands on his knees as he sucked in air, watching the SUV's taillights disappear around the corner.

CHAPTER 7

CHAPTER

"I got five minutes," Gillette said to Stiles, checking his watch. "Then I have to go." He and Wright were leaving at nine-thirty to meet with the Hush-Hush CEO at the company's headquarters down in the garment district. "What did you find out?"

"Nice." Stiles pointed at the fresh scab on the left side of Gillette's head near his eye. "Not as bad as a bullet to the chest, but it'll do."

It had happened when the guy had tackled Gillette and they'd tumbled into the street.

"For a rich guy, you're pretty ballsy," Stiles continued. "Chucking your cell phone at somebody pointing a gun, then going after him like that? Most rich guys I know are pussies. Which only makes sense. Why fight your way out of something when you can buy your way out? I was impressed."

"Thanks."

"With your *guts*," Stiles said, grinning, "not your *smarts*. What in the hell were you thinking about, anyway? Two on five?"

"Those aren't bad odds when it's you and me. Besides, we had Allison. That tipped everything in our favor."

Stiles rolled his eyes.

"Look, it was my fault, Quentin. I told you not to have your men come with us. That was stupid. I had to do some-

137

thing. Figured all we had on our side was surprise. Besides," Gillette said with a chuckle, "the guy was aiming at *you*. Now, what did you find out?"

"Sure, sure. Those guys last night? Hired guns. According to my people inside the NYPD, they're part of a Brooklyn gang called the Fire. Pretty nasty crew. The Mob doesn't even screw with them. They admitted taking money to assault us."

"What does that mean? Were they supposed to kill us or just hurt us?"

"They weren't supposed to kill us," Stiles answered, "just beat the crap out of you and me, steal our wallets, and leave us there on the sidewalk. They were supposed to take Allison with them."

Now it made sense. "Must have been a kidnapping. Well, looks like you've got another client. She ought to pay well, too. Maybe a few hundred thousand bucks a year for everything."

"I don't think it was a kidnapping," Stiles said quietly.

"Why not?"

"The gang claimed they were supposed to drop Allison off a few blocks away, unhurt."

"What?"

"Weird, huh?"

"That doesn't make any sense. Who hired them?" Gillette asked.

"The gang never knew his name, they just took his money."

"Or your sources inside the NYPD aren't telling you the whole story," Gillette observed, flexing his right hand. His knuckles were killing him from hitting whoever's chin he'd nailed during the melee.

"No, my sources are good. The gang claimed it was an all-cash deal, everything up front. They said they'd never seen the guy before."

"Well, if it wasn't a kidnapping, there's a good chance Tom McGuire was behind it," Gillette said. "He could have tipped the paparazzi off, probably paid a Parker Meridien hotel operator to tell him where Allison was going. He would have finished us off while we were lying there on the street. Allison would have been the gang's witness that they didn't kill us, and he would have gotten her out of there so he wouldn't have had to kill her, too. He didn't care about getting her, and he wouldn't want the Wallaces on his ass."

"The gang described the guy, but it didn't sound like Tom McGuire."

"At this point, I doubt Tom McGuire looks like the Tom McGuire we knew."

"Probably not," Stiles admitted. "It's interesting," he said after a short pause. "I told you I was in a gang when I was a teenager."

"Yeah, up in Harlem. So?"

"We used to scam people by agreeing to roll a mark. Mostly guys who came to us pissed off because their girl was cheating on them, and they wanted us to beat the shit out of the other guy. We'd get the money up front, but we wouldn't actually do it. I mean, why go through the hassle? You've got the dude's cash, so what's he going to do if you don't beat the guy up? If he screws with one of your gang, he knows he's dead." Stiles paused. "But these guys from Brooklyn did it, and they're one of the toughest gangs in the city. Why would they follow through?"

"Any ideas?" Gillette asked.

"Probably supports your Tom McGuire theory."

"Why?"

"Whoever convinced them to come after us must have had something on them. You know, information he threatened them with so that if they didn't do it, they'd go to jail. That's the only way I can see it happening. McGuire might still have friends inside the FBI, people who might even be helping him stay hidden. Even with everything he did. He could have gotten information from them." Stiles hesitated. "Just a theory, but it's possible."

"Yeah," Gillette said quietly, a bad feeling snaking up his spine—as if he was being stalked. With each day that had passed without a murder attempt, he'd felt safer. Suddenly he didn't feel safe anymore, even with Stiles back. "Why would the gang have talked? Why wouldn't they just shut up and post bail?"

"Good question. Maybe they were so pissed off about losing one of their own. You know, the guy that died? They said the SUV that ran him over was driven by the guy who paid them."

"Stop worrying about it," Gillette said as they walked through the double glass doorway and into the Hush-Hush lobby. He'd caught Wright checking out the scab on the side of his face several times. "They want our money, they won't care about a scratch."

"What happened?" Wright asked, still staring.

"I got into it with a few idiots outside a restaurant last night." Stiles had been able to keep their names out of the newspapers. But he realized that Allison might blab about it later, so he couldn't make something up.

"What happened to your posse? The QS guys. Why weren't they around?"

They reached the receptionist desk, and Gillette motioned for Wright to speak to the young woman.

"Can I help you?" she asked, not bothering to look up from her computer. She was pretty, dressed to show it all off. Her silk top hung low over her breasts, revealing the top of a lacy dark purple bra.

"We're here to see Tony Maddox."

The young woman looked up at Wright, then Gillette,

seemingly impressed with anyone who was here to see the CEO. "Your names?" she asked, giving Gillette a friendly smile, her voice more respectful.

"I'm Christian Gillette, this is David Wright."

"Thank you, Mr. Gillette. Just a moment."

"Why weren't Stiles's guys around to protect you?" Wright asked again as the woman buzzed Maddox's assistant.

Gillette glanced around the lobby. The walls were covered with pictures of women in lingerie. "I got careless; it wasn't Quentin's fault."

"What happened?"

"I told you, I got into a fight."

"How's the other guy?"

"Dead."

Wright laughed loudly. "No, seriously."

"David, let's talk about the meeting," Gillette said. "Given that you were on your phone the whole way down here and we've only got about ten seconds."

"Hey, I'm trying to get us in to see these guys at that Bermuda insurance company. They've got a big operation up here in New York, and like I said, they can probably do half a billion. I figure you want me to run that down as fast as possible, Chris."

"Do you want me to lead this meeting?"

"No, I'll do it."

"Don't screw up," Gillette warned. "I think we'll be able to flip this company in a couple of months for two to three times our investment. Faraday and I have it all arranged."

"*What?*"

Gillette hadn't told Wright about Faraday's connection to the French apparel company. "We'll talk about it later," he said, spotting a young woman coming toward them. Probably Maddox's assistant. "Just make sure the meeting goes well. There'll be a big bonus in this for you if the deal works out."

"Hello, gentlemen." Like the receptionist, Maddox's assistant was pretty and well dressed. "Please come this way."

They followed her down a short hallway and into an impressive office, expansive and modern-looking.

"Hey, guys," Tony Maddox called in a friendly voice, standing up and dropping the headset he was wearing onto the desk. He was short, silver haired, deeply tanned, and dressed casually. "This is Frank Hobbs, my director of corporate development."

"I know Frank," Wright said, stepping in front of Gillette and shaking Maddox's hand, then Hobbs's. "Frank and I went to business school together. How are you, pal?"

"Good." Hobbs was tall, dark, and thin and wore plastic-rimmed glasses. Unlike Maddox, Hobbs was in a suit and tie.

"Thanks for giving me the heads-up on this, Frank."

"Sure."

"Guess it paid off to be in study group together first year, huh?"

Hobbs smiled and looked at the others. "Paid off for me," he said appreciatively. "David taught me how to value stocks. I don't know what I would have done without him."

Gillette winked at Hobbs. "Well, I hope you didn't take *everything* he said seriously. David tends to overpay. Which is why I'm here."

When the laughter had died down, Maddox stepped around Wright. "You must be Christian Gillette," he said, extending his hand.

"That's right," Gillette acknowledged, noticing Maddox's gold bracelet and pinkie ring as they shook hands. Also noticing his quick glance at the scab. But Maddox said nothing.

"I've read a lot about you lately."

"Yeah, thanks to that damn freedom of the press thing."
Maddox laughed heartily. "A real bitch, huh? Bitten me
in the ass a few times, too." He pointed at two comfortable-
looking couches in a corner of the office. "Let's sit down."

As they did, Maddox's assistant came back into the
room and poured coffee, then picked up a tray from a table
near the couches and served croissants.

As the young woman leaned over in front of Gillette, her
loose blouse hung low, exposing her breasts. He looked
away, over at Maddox, who was smiling back.

"This is a fun business, Christian," Maddox said. "If we
can find a price that works for both of us today, you're
going to have a great time."

"Tony, what's the ownership structure of Hush-Hush?"
Wright asked.

"I own ninety-five percent," Maddox answered, giving
Wright a cursory glance, then refocusing on Gillette. "My
brother owns the other five, but he hasn't been active in the
business for a few years and I control the board. I made the
decision to sell the company. He has to go along with whatever I say."

"Why sell now?" Wright wanted to know.

This time Maddox didn't even bother looking over at
Wright, just kept talking to Gillette. "I know I look a lot
younger, but I'm fifty-five. I'm getting tired. This thing has
been my baby for the last eight years, and I love it, but it's
worn me out. Plus, we're growing so damn fast at this point.
Faster than we were a few years ago. The problem is—and
I didn't realize this when I started the company—but the
faster you grow, the more money you gotta put *in* the business. I'm old, Christian, I want to be taking money *out*."

"Sure." Gillette could see that Wright was aggravated at
the lack of attention from Maddox. "Tony," he said, pointing at Wright, "I want you to know that if we do a deal,

David will be responsible for Hush-Hush. He'll be the chairman. He's just been promoted to managing partner. He's one of our top guns."

"Oh." Maddox turned slightly toward Wright and gave him a respectful nod. "I see."

"Could you give me a snapshot of the company's financials?" Wright asked.

"I'll handle that one, Tony," Hobbs spoke up. "This year we'll do around four hundred million in revenues and thirty in net income. That's up from two hundred twenty-five and ten last year."

"Sweet," Wright said, turning to Maddox. "So, what do you want for it?" he asked bluntly.

Maddox shoved his hands in his pockets and shrugged. "Jeez, I thought you'd make me an offer."

Before Wright could say anything, there was a knock on the door and Maddox's assistant stuck her head into the office. "Tony, we're ready."

"Okay." Maddox nodded. "Guys, I thought before we got into any hard-core negotiations, we'd have a little presentation. You should have a firsthand look at what we do. That okay with you, David?"

Gillette saw the gleam in Maddox's eyes and knew exactly what was coming.

"Yeah, sure."

Maddox waved at his assistant.

She pushed the door wide open, then stepped back to let a statuesque woman whisk into the room. The young brunette wore just a sheer white bra, a lacy white thong, and high heels. She walked seductively to where the men sat, hesitated in front of them for a few moments, hands on her hips, chest pushed out, then turned her back to them and stood still again for a few seconds in the same pose. As she walked out, another woman entered. A blonde this time, wearing a black teddy.

Gillette glanced over at Hobbs, who was looking down, then at Wright, whose chin was in his lap. Finally he looked at Maddox, who was grinning from ear to ear.

"You did an excellent job with the Hush-Hush meeting," Gillette said. He and Wright were headed into an elevator to go up to the Apex Capital offices for their meeting with Russell Hughes. "I liked the way you cut off the show after the third woman."

"I knew what Maddox was doing, obviously." Wright shook his head as the doors closed and the elevator began to rise. "But, Jesus, those women were incredible."

"That's the fashion business." Gillette had been worried that Wright would give away the farm, but he'd handled himself well. The way a protégé should. "Six hundred million's a fair price, especially since it's growing fast. I was proud of you for not offering too much."

Wright smiled. "Trust me, I thought about offering Maddox whatever he wanted when I saw that first woman."

Gillette laughed. "You should have seen your face. Your jaw was in your lap."

"You think he'll take six hundred?"

"I think he'll call his investment banker, who'll tell him it's worth more."

Wright nodded glumly. "Like they always do."

"But Tony's sharp," Gillette spoke up. "He'll understand that he might get more if he tried really hard. But it wouldn't be that much more, and it would take a while to get. I talked to him for a few seconds as we were leaving, and I made it clear that we could wrap things up quickly. I also told him I could get him into the White House for a personal visit with the president. He's a big Republican."

"How are you going to do that?"

"Senator Clark told me he'd help with that if we ever

needed it. Only a couple of times a year max, but this is one of those times we need him."

Wright whistled. "That would be incredible."

The elevator doors parted on the forty-ninth floor.

"Better not tell your wife about Hush-Hush," Gillette joked. "She'll never let you go to work."

"Yeah," Wright said distractedly.

Gillette's cell phone rang.

"I'll let Hughes know we're here," Wright volunteered, moving to the receptionist's desk.

"Thanks." Gillette pulled the phone from his pocket and glanced at the digits: It was the Everest main number. "Hello."

"Christian, it's Nigel. Hope I'm not interrupting."

"David and I are about to head into our Apex meeting with Russell Hughes."

"Then I'll keep it quick. How did the Hush-Hush thing go?"

"Very well. David did a good job."

"Next steps?" Faraday asked.

"We offered six hundred million. It's in the CEO's court to get back to us at this point."

"Odds?"

"Fifty-fifty."

"I'm looking forward to the day you don't say that. Look"—Faraday's voice dropped—"I just wanted to give you a heads-up. One of the receptionists brought a copy of the *Daily News* into the office this morning. There's a couple of pictures of you and Allison on the celebrity page. She's hanging all over you." He hesitated. "I wanted to get to you before Faith did."

Gillette felt his jaw tighten. That was going to be tough to explain. "Thanks."

"Christian," Wright called from the receptionist's desk, "Hughes is ready for us."

"Yeah, all right." Gillette gave Wright a quick wave. "Thanks for the call, Nigel."

"Sure."

Gillette ended the call but didn't put the phone back in his pocket right away. Instead, he gazed at it for a moment, considering whether or not to call Faith. The proactive approach was always better, but—

"Christian," Wright called again impatiently.

Gillette let out a quick breath and shoved the phone in his pocket. Never enough time. "Coming."

The three men sat at a round table in Hughes's office overlooking the East River from forty-nine stories up. Hughes sat with his legs crossed at the knees, arms folded tightly across his chest, chin touching his tie. Clearly, some of his investors had alerted him to what was coming. Probably told him to try to negotiate some kind of settlement, Gillette thought. Then ride off quietly into the sunset.

"Thanks for meeting with us today," Gillette began.

"I didn't want to," Hughes answered candidly, his voice shaking with emotion. "But the Strazzi estate people basically gave me no choice."

"They're getting impatient."

"*They're getting impatient,*" Hughes repeated, his voice rising, "because you're going out and stirring them up. I have a plan."

"The plan's not working."

"I need time."

"Russell, I've looked at your portfolio. You got some dogs, and that's because you've let management teams stay on that you should have fired a long time ago. We have top-notch people who can step in right away and make a difference."

"You've already had in-depth discussions with the Strazzi estate representatives," Hughes accused Gillette.

"I wouldn't call them 'in-depth.' "

"They want you to buy Apex. They want out."

"They actually said that to you?"

"They didn't have to, it was obvious." Hughes leaned forward and folded his hands on the table, head down. "Give me six months, Christian. If I haven't improved things after six months, then buy the firm. I won't put up a fight."

"There might not be anything to buy at that point."

"You'll be able to get it for almost nothing if the portfolio companies keep getting worse."

"I'm not a vulture," Gillette said. "I like buying things that have a pulse."

Hughes cleared his throat. "If you bought it, how would you run it? I mean, would you fold it into Everest?"

"Not right away. For at least the first year, I'd keep Apex independent. Like I said, I'd hire some of my own people and replace some of yours at the portfolio companies. But I wouldn't physically combine the offices or integrate the staffs of Apex and Everest."

"What about me?" Hughes asked, his voice hoarse.

"I haven't decided yet, but I know that whoever's running this for us will report to David." Gillette nodded at Wright, who up to this point had said nothing.

Hughes took a deep breath. "I know what I'm doing, David. People here respect me." He hesitated, then glanced at Wright. "I need this job."

"Christian."

Gillette looked up from the Veramax report he was reading. The company was doing very well. If he could get the FDA off their ass, the thing would go white hot. Allison was right. "Yes, Nigel."

"Sorry to bother you, but Faith is in the lobby."

"Thanks." Faith had called earlier and asked if she could

stop by. She'd just gotten in from the West Coast. "Tell her to come on back."

"Sure."

Gillette stood up and stretched. It was eight-thirty, and suddenly he realized he was hungry. He'd eaten nothing that day but a bowl of cereal for breakfast and a quick salad with Wright in between the Hush-Hush and Apex meetings. He came out from behind the desk and leaned against the front of it. When Faith called, she'd been short. He could tell by her tone something was wrong, and he was pretty sure he knew what.

The door opened and Faith Cassidy was standing in front of him. She was so vivacious, blond with large green eyes and a voluptuous figure. Not at all impressed with herself, either, even though she had every right to be since her first two albums had gone platinum. Normally, when she hadn't seen him for a while, she would have rushed right into his arms, but today she lingered by the door. Normally, her eyes sparkled when she looked at him, too, but today the fire was missing.

"What's wrong, sweetheart?" Gillette asked, moving toward her. He'd missed her. Hadn't realized until just now how much. Been too busy. "You okay?"

"I'm a little tired." Her voice was soft, subdued. "It was a long trip. You know the deal."

"You hungry?" he asked, stopping a few feet away. He wanted to give her a hug, but not if she didn't want to hug him. "Want to get something to eat?"

"I ate on the plane."

"Oh, okay." She never ate airline food. "So, the new album's doing well," Gillette said, keeping the conversation going. "I checked this afternoon with the label."

"Yeah, they're putting a ton of money into advertising on this album, even more than they did with the first two."

Faith smiled stiffly. "I'm sure you had a lot to do with that."

After taking over as chairman of Everest last fall, Gillette had personally stepped in to increase the advertising budget for her second album—which had paid off in a huge way, kick-starting sales so the album jumped to the number one spot in the country for three weeks. "Actually, no, I didn't," he admitted. "Your execs figured it out all on their own this time."

She leaned slightly to get a better look at the side of his head. "Jesus, Chris, what happened?"

Gillette gave Faith his warmest smile. "I turned down one of David Wright's deals, and he didn't like it." But she didn't smile back.

"Seriously."

Normally, she would have laughed. She knew Wright, and they joked about how aggressive he was all the time. "Stiles and I got into it with some idiots outside the place we went to dinner last night. It was stupid."

"You okay?"

"It's just a scratch."

They were silent for a few moments.

"Faith, I—"

There was a sharp knock, and Allison appeared in the doorway. "Christian, I—Oh, I'm sorry," she said, "I'll come—"

"Allison," Christian interrupted, "this is Faith Cassidy. Faith, meet Allison Wallace."

Faith and Allison forced uncomfortable smiles and shook hands.

"What do you want?" Gillette asked, sensing the tension that suddenly swirled through the room.

"I heard back from Jack Mitchell," Allison answered. "You and I are going to meet him in Pittsburgh tomorrow night for dinner. He's going to be there on business." She giggled. "I've known Jack for so long. He's my dad's age. He taught me how to swim the year I was five up in Michigan. It'll be fun. He's staying at the William Penn Hotel, so I told him we'd meet him there. They have a nice restaurant. I'll make a reservation and get us rooms."

"Thanks." Gillette glanced at Faith. She was clutching her hands tightly together, the way she always did right before going onstage at one of her concerts. "Let's talk in the morning," he suggested.

"Sure. Um, do you want the door closed?"

Gillette nodded.

"Nice to meet you," Allison called sweetly to Faith as she was leaving.

"You too," said Faith. When the door was closed, she ran a finger under her eyes. "You *work* with her?" she asked, her voice full of emotion.

"Faith, it's not—"

"Can you even begin to understand how hard it was for me when the two of you were splashed across the celebrity pages of the L.A. papers? She was all over you in those pictures."

"Allison's a new managing partner here at Everest," Gillette explained. "Her family committed five billion dollars to us. We had a business dinner so we could talk about her responsibilities, that was all. You know how the damn paparazzi are."

"It didn't look like she was dressed for business to me."

"Stiles was there. Ask him about it."

She shook her head and bit her lip. "Like he'd tell me the truth," she whispered.

"What?"

"Nothing."

"Look, it isn't—"

"I want to take a break, Christian," Faith said suddenly.

"Spend some time away from each other. Maybe then we'll figure out if we're really committed to each other."

"We just spent a week away from each other."

"And apparently you enjoyed yourself a lot."

"Faith, you can't be serious. I don't want that."

She moved to him and reached into her bag. Her lower eyelids were glistening. "Here," she said softly, handing him a photograph. "I found it in a knickknack shop on Ventura when I had an afternoon to myself. I thought of you."

"Faith, let's talk about—"

But she turned and left before he could finish. He stared at the empty doorway, trying to convince himself to go after her and work it out. But he couldn't. He'd never been able to run after anyone in his life.

He looked down at what she'd given him. It was a faded picture of his father as a newly inducted senator, standing next to President Reagan.

CHAPTER 8

"Change of plans," Gillette barked into the phone at Harry Stein, Discount America's CEO. "I need to meet with the mayor of that town in Maryland this afternoon, not Friday." He had to talk loudly to be heard over the whine of jet engines as he hurried up the stairs toward the larger of Everest's two planes. His directive was met with stony silence. "Did you hear me, Harry?"

"I heard you, Christian, but this is really short notice."

Gillette ducked down to enter the cabin, then eased into a wide black leather swivel chair near the front. Stiles followed him onto the plane and sat in the chair beside his. There were already three QS agents in the back of the plane, but two more appeared at the door. Stiles was taking no chances, and Gillette was glad. Especially after the other night.

"It has to be this way," Gillette said, nodding to the agents as they headed toward the others in the back. "My meeting in Washington got moved up, and I need to do both of these things on the same day. I don't have time to make two trips down there."

Daniel Ganze had called at seven this morning and told Gillette to come to Washington immediately. Norman Boyd, Ganze's boss, had to travel unexpectedly for a week out of the country and didn't want to wait to meet until he got back. Things were too urgent, Ganze claimed. So Gillette agreed to come, though he still had no idea what they wanted.

It irritated the hell out of him to be anybody's beck-and-call boy, but there was no choice. He had to know about his father, and he had to know *now*. For the first time since Lana had cut him out of the family so long ago, he was desperate. He sensed that Ganze was for real, and he'd been waiting a long time for a break like this.

"I doubt I'll reach this woman for a while," Stein complained. "Her day's probably jammed. After all, she is the mayor."

"What would the mayor of a town half the size of a New York City block possibly have to do on a Wednesday afternoon that could be so important she wouldn't juggle a few things around?"

"Beats me, but remember, she doesn't like us. She's not going to do us any favors."

"Make it happen, Harry."

"Okay, okay."

Gillette ended the call abruptly and answered one coming in from Wright's cell phone. "What's up, David?"

"I just talked to Tony Maddox at Hush-Hush. He says if we up the offer to six fifty, we got a deal. He wants a few reps and warranties that aren't standard, but I can talk him down off the ledge on those. What do you want me to do about the price tag?"

Gillette considered going back to Maddox at six twenty-five, then acknowledged that, in this case, giving in to his natural urge not to leave a penny on the table would be shortsighted. There was no reason to waste time and potentially lose the deal over twenty-five million bucks. Not when they could probably flip the thing for at least a billion by March. "Hit it," he instructed, "but tell Maddox we want a signed letter of intent by three this afternoon. I want him locked up by then, or we pass. Tell him that's the price of a quick negotiation, got it?"

"Yup."

"After you talk to him, call me back. I'll be on the plane phone for the next hour, then on my cell again once we land at Reagan, which oughta be around nine-thirty. I'm at a meeting in D.C. starting at ten. After that, I'm going to the Eastern Shore of Maryland to meet with the mayor of a town over there."

"Is that the Discount America thing?"

"Yeah."

"What's the name of the town?" Wright asked.

"Why?"

"Oh, I've got relatives on the Eastern Shore. Just wondering if I'd recognize the name."

"It's Chatham." Gillette paused. "Mean anything to you?"

"Nope."

"It's not very big."

"Not many of them are down there."

"What town do your relatives live in?" Gillette asked.

"You know," Wright said slowly, "I can never remember. That's why I asked. Thought it might ring a bell when you said it. You coming back to New York when you leave Maryland?"

"No, after Chatham I'm going to Pittsburgh. Allison's got me hooked up with a deal that sounds pretty good. We're meeting the owner for dinner."

"What kind of company is it?"

"I'll tell you about it tomorrow if it's good." No need to go into it now in case it turned out to be nothing. "I'll probably fly back to New York after dinner, but if it goes late, I'll stay over in Pittsburgh and come back in the morning. Did you get in touch with that Bermuda insurance company?"

"Yep," Wright confirmed, "and they want to meet next week, Tuesday or Wednesday. Can you do it?"

Gillette checked his schedule on the Blackberry. "Yeah, I should be okay."

"If the meeting goes well, they want to invest five hundred million in Everest Eight. I sent them the offering memorandum and all the subscription documents by messenger fifteen minutes ago."

"Did you tell them about the Wallace Family coming in for five double-large?"

"Yeah, that was big for them."

"I bet."

"What about Apex?" Wright asked. "Where do we stand with them?"

"I spoke to the Strazzi estate people late last night. We've got a deal if we pay par."

"How much is that again?"

"A billion."

"And?"

"I told them we were in." Technically, Gillette was supposed to have a vote of the managing partners to move forward on a deal, but he knew none of them would dare fight him on it with the sale of Laurel Energy looming. They wouldn't want to be on his bad side as he was divvying up nine hundred million dollars.

"How are you going to fund it?"

Gillette thought for a second. "Five hundred out of Seven and five hundred out of Eight." He was still going to do the entire Vegas NFL franchise out of Seven, no matter what Allison said, but maybe this would help. Apex could end up being a great deal, too. "That'll leave a little over a billion left in Seven in case we need dry powder for the existing portfolio companies in Seven. You know, for add-on acquisitions or rainy day stuff."

"So from now on, all new investments will come out of Eight?"

Another major decision made. "That's right."

"What about Russell Hughes?" Wright asked. "Want me to go over there today and fire his ass?"

Gillette chuckled. He loved Wright's toughness, the way he was so damn direct. So efficient. So fearless. His father had always told him he was the same way. "Nah, let's wait. We're going to meet with him again Friday to go over a few things."

"What time? I mean, I assume you want me to go."

"Eleven. You know, we should do this every day now that we're buying Apex and Hush-Hush," Gillette suggested.

"Okay. Should I call you?"

"No, I'll call you. It'll be between seven and eight. Have your cell on if you aren't in the office or at your apartment. If you haven't heard from me by eight, then call me."

"Right."

"And great job on Hush-Hush again, David. Really. This is going to be another big win for us."

"Thanks."

Gillette hung up and glanced at Stiles.

"Everything okay?" Stiles asked.

"Yeah, fine." He pulled out his date book and went through a long list of calls he wanted to make while they were in the air. Thinking about how Wright was so much better than any of the other managing partners. "By the way, I got the lawyers started on your deal last night. Like I said, we should be done in thirty days."

Stiles shook his head. "How do you keep it all straight, pal?"

Wright hung up with Maddox. The Hush-Hush CEO had just agreed to sign an exclusive letter of intent after getting the news that Everest would up its offer by fifty million. All Wright had to do now was draft the letter and fax it over. Everything was beautiful, he thought, gazing at the scrawled telephone number on the crumpled piece of paper the guy calling himself "Paul" had pressed into his hand before—everything except this.

Wright dialed the number slowly, hoping Paul wouldn't pick up.

"Yeah?" the voice said gruffly.

"It's David, David Wright. You—"

"Well, hello there, Davy," Paul interrupted, "good to hear from you. You're making the right decision. So, what you got for me today? What's your boss's itinerary?"

Wright swallowed hard, wishing to God he'd never gone to that shop in the West Village. Wishing he could have controlled his urges. How many times had his wife warned him?

Christ. Peggy. If she ever found out about any of this . . .

He pushed all that from his mind. "Gillette's going to be in Washington this morning," Wright said in a low voice.

Christian, too, for God's sake. The guy had been so good to him. Why had he risked it all?

"And?"

Wright said nothing.

"Davy?"

Wright thought about hanging up and never calling again. Then he thought about the dead girl dangling by her neck and the photos they had of it. He hadn't heard a whisper on the news about a woman being found dead in the Village, and the shop was closed—he'd gone down and checked after Paul had shown up outside the apartment. Obviously, as Paul claimed, they'd taken care of the mess.

Suddenly it was clear to him. He had to play ball, because in the end it had to be about self-preservation. It was the only way. He'd fought too hard to get where he was.

"*David.*"

"Gillette's landing at Reagan around nine-thirty for a meeting in D.C. that starts at ten. This afternoon he's going to a town on Maryland's Eastern Shore called Chatham. After that, it's out to Pittsburgh. He may or may not stay the night. Either way, it's back to New York. I think he's in the city all day tomorrow."

"What hotel in Pittsburgh is he staying at if he doesn't go back to New York tonight?"

"I don't know."

"Find out."

Wright hesitated. "All right."

"And find out what he's doing tomorrow, just in case. You hear me?"

"Yes."

"You say 'Yes, sir' to me, understand?"

Wright bit his tongue so hard that it almost bled. "Yes, sir."

Paul chuckled harshly. "Good boy, Davy, good boy. Talk to you later."

Wright hung up and put the cell phone back in his pocket slowly, wondering if Gillette would make it back to New York alive. Wondering what it meant for him if these people did anything to his boss.

The address Ganze had given Gillette on the phone was in Alexandria, Virginia, ten miles west of Washington. Not downtown, as Gillette had expected. And Ganze still hadn't given him the name of the company, consulting firm, or whatever it was he worked for or represented.

The place turned out to be nothing special. Just a plain suite on the fifth floor of a nondescript office building, a long walk down the corridor from the elevators. There was no receptionist, no logo, and no sign identifying what or who they were—just Ganze waiting outside the numbered door. Ganze wouldn't allow Stiles into Boyd's office for the meeting but did agree to let Stiles and another agent wait in the small reception area. There were three individual offices in the stark space, each sparsely furnished—Ganze had to lug a chair into Boyd's office from another one so they could all sit down.

"Why all the cloak-and-dagger crap?" Gillette asked as he sat, noticing that the blinds on the window behind Boyd's desk were down. "What is all this?"

"First, you need to sign something," Boyd announced, handing Gillette a single sheet of paper with a signature line at the bottom. Gillette's name was typed in bold capital letters beneath the line.

Gillette scanned the paper quickly, then handed it back to Boyd with a smile. It was a blind confidentiality agreement covering anything and everything discussed in the meeting—or at any time afterward with Boyd and Ganze. "No way I'm signing that." The penalty for violating the agreement was incarceration in a federal penitentiary for up to thirty years. "No way in hell."

"We have to know you'll keep your mouth shut," Boyd snapped. "You're going to be privy to top-secret information, information even the brass at the CIA and the FBI don't have."

"Let's assume for a moment I'd even consider signing something like that. Paragraph five says that the government has the right, in its sole discretion, to determine whether or not I've violated the agreement, and that I have no right to trial or due process." He shook his head. "You've *got* to be kidding me."

"That's the only way it works," Boyd said. "If you had the right to due process, you'd threaten to tell everybody what you knew in court, and we'd have to back down. It's for your protection, too."

"Bullshit."

"I know it seems a little over-the-top," Ganze spoke up gently, "but we've never had a problem. No one's ever gone to jail because they signed one of these."

"There's always a first time."

"Just consider it," Ganze urged.

"You've got my word," Gillette said, "and that's all you're going to get."

"That's not enough," Boyd growled.

"Too bad."

"Mr. Gillette," Ganze said, "I really think—"

"Well, this was a huge waste of time," Gillette interrupted, standing up.

"Sit down," Boyd ordered.

Gillette turned to go.

"Don't leave," Ganze pleaded.

Gillette turned back around.

"Do we have your word?" Ganze asked.

"I just told you that."

"Mr. Boyd needs to hear it once more," Ganze said, gesturing at his superior.

Gillette glanced at Boyd.

Boyd nodded.

"Okay, you've got my word."

"Prison isn't our only option," Boyd warned. "I assume you understand that."

"Come on, Norman," Ganze said. "We don't have to—"

"I understand that," Gillette said grimly, sitting down. They could always take that step whenever they wanted. But he wasn't going to give them the ability to unilaterally stick him in Leavenworth for the rest of his life. That would be worse than death.

Boyd made an irritated face and shook his head wearily.

As though he were dead tired of taking on so much responsibility, Gillette thought. At least they had that in common.

"Have you ever heard of DARPA?" Boyd asked.

Gillette thought for a second. "I'm not sure. What does it stand for?"

"Defense Advanced Research Projects Agency."

"Oh, sure." Gillette recognized the full name. "The guys who invented GPS and the Internet, right?"

"Yeah. It's basically the Defense Department's dream tank," Ganze explained. "They contract with chemists, engineers, biochemists, physicists, and other kinds of doctors from the best universities and companies in the country, then let them loose to develop next-generation weapons and systems for the armed forces. But, as you pointed out, Christian, lots of great things they've invented have ultimately gotten into the hands of the public, too. Things that have made everyday life more efficient, safer, and, in some cases, more fun. The computer mouse, the Hummer. A lot of people don't know that the government invents this stuff, then gives it away when it's declassified."

"Sells it, too," Gillette added. "A lot of people don't know that, either."

"What's wrong with the government getting a return on its money?" Boyd demanded. "Companies do."

Ganze rolled his eyes. "Norman, don't—"

"The government isn't in business to make a profit," Gillette shot back. "At least, it isn't supposed to be."

"Don't be naïve," Boyd warned.

"Believe me," Gillette said forcefully, "I'm not. Look, I wouldn't care if those government profits reduced taxes, but from what I hear there are bureaucrats walking around D.C. making a damn good living off selling what the government invents. I doubt that's what Washington and Jefferson had in mind."

"Washington and Jefferson didn't have to worry about profits," Boyd snapped, "they were already rich."

Gillette said nothing.

Boyd fumed for a second, then put his hands flat on the desk. "Let's not get off track here. I don't want to get into some damn philosophical discussion about what the government might or might not be in business to do. Let's talk about one thing we'd all agree the government is in business to do, and that's protect our country from its enemies." He held out his arms, palms up. "All right?"

Gillette nodded.

"Good." Boyd took a moment to gather his thoughts. "Like I said, DARPA's mission is to come up with next-generation defense technologies. Star Wars stuff. Body armor that can start healing wounds even before soldiers make it to a forward hospital; telepathic command systems for fighter pilots; research on hemispheric sleep that allows one side of the brain to function while the other rests, so a soldier can effectively fight twenty-four hours a day. Darkening glass that can save at least one of a pilot's eyes during a nuclear blast. Cutting-edge projects that might seem like science fiction today but could ultimately become reality."

"Are you guys DARPA?" Gillette asked.

"Not technically," Ganze answered, "but we work closely with them. We're called GARD, the Government Advanced Research Department. We're set up to take on projects that are too secret for DARPA to handle."

"Why can't DARPA handle projects that are so secret?"

"Like most agencies," Boyd spoke up again, "over time, DARPA's developed an infrastructure and, worse, a reputation. For excellence, I'll grant you, but in this business you want to run quiet like a nuclear sub. You don't want *any* reputation. Another reason they run into problems on the supersecret stuff is the temporary nature of the agency's employees. Like I told you, we pull experts out of the private sector, which the companies and universities aren't happy about, so we have to plug them back in at some point. But that revolving door facilitates information flow, if you get my drift."

"Sure."

"So we need an agency that can handle the very top-secret stuff when there's a problem."

"Like what?" Gillette asked.

"Spies, basically. On projects that involve national security. I mean, we don't care much if our enemies find out about little things DARPA invents before they're declassified." Boyd's expression turned grave. "But there are certain projects that have to stay hidden from everyone. From terrorists right on down to some of our own senators and congressmen," he said. "I don't like hiding important things from our own lawmakers, but some of them just can't keep secrets. Sad, but true."

"I can relate to that," Gillette muttered. "I assume you have that situation now," he said, anticipating where Boyd was headed. "A spy issue, I mean."

"Right. And this project involves one of the most incredible technologies I've ever seen. We've got to keep this thing protected."

Gillette was interested now. "What is it?"

Boyd stared at Gillette evenly for several moments before answering. "Nanotechnology."

Gillette nodded. He'd heard about nanotech.

"The ability to produce structures at the molecular level," Boyd continued. "I'm talking about being able to build self-assembling micromachines with a diameter eighty thousand times smaller than the diameter of a human hair."

Gillette had talked to several venture capitalists who'd set up pools of money to fund preliminary research on nanotech. "I know there's a lot of work going on in that space, but people I talk to say that stuff is way out in the future. At least thirty to forty years before anything meaningful is developed. They say it might not even be real at all, just hype so scientists and institutes can get research dollars and maintain lifestyles. And the guys I've talked to would know."

"Forget for a second *when* and think about *what*," Boyd suggested. "Think about what it could do for us, for our military and intelligence capabilities, specifically." His eyes were flashing. "We could develop supersoldiers. Using nano-tech machines, men could carry hundreds of pounds of the latest battlefield equipment but still run three times faster than the fastest men we have today. They'd be able to wear thick armor that could withstand almost anything while remaining agile. They'd be able to carry computers and heavy weapons that would make today's soldiers look like minutemen. They'd be almost invincible."

"How would nanotechnology help us develop super-soldiers?" Gillette asked.

"Scientists could develop exoskeletons, like intelligent armor that would fortify with artificial muscles what the body could do. They would synchronize with microsensors injected into the soldiers' bodies."

"But *how*?"

"The machines carry micro-microcomputers, nanocom-puters, that take their cues from what the brain wants to do. They transmit those cues from the soldier's body as signals to the exoskeleton. The exoskeleton amplifies the physical abilities of the soldier. It's much faster and tremendously more effective than any kind of physical training. It's superhero shit come to life, Christian." Boyd took a breath. "Then there's the whole repair side. Scalpels and stitches will seem like butcher tools after we perfect nano-tech. We'll be able to direct cells to discard the dead, then reform and renew. Fast. There'll be no such things as scars anymore, external or internal. More important, we'll be able to fight diseases at the molecular level. We'll send armies of nanoterminators into the body to kill cancer cells, AIDS cells, whatever." Boyd spread his arms wide. "Things we can't come close to doing now. The possibilities are endless."

Gillette's mind was humming. He was fascinated. "You mentioned intelligence, too. What's the application there?"

"We'll be able to inject undetectable nanochips into the bodies of our undercover agents. Like microcameras, they'll record everything. Audio and video, so that the information can be retrieved later. Nothing will be left to memory. No mistakes will be made." He held up his hand. "Better still, in situations where we can't penetrate, we can actually use the enemy to help us without them even knowing."

"How?"

"Say we want to listen in on the Russian embassy here in Washington. We can put a nanochip into the nose drops or cold medicine of a Russian secretary who's sick, or into the aspirin of the ambassador or one of his or her staff who suffers from migraines. The machine that the chip is attached to directs the chip to become lodged in a certain sector of the target's body—the eye, the ear—and suddenly we have a direct line into the embassy without the host or his associates ever knowing. No more digging tunnels beneath streets, no more clandestine missions trying to plant bugs that are detected within hours anyway and put people's lives at risk."

There were negative implications to all this, too. *How* negative was the question. "What do you want from me?" Gillette asked.

"Remember how you said that the people you talked to, those people who would know, told you that nanotechnology was decades off? That maybe it was just hype so researchers could maintain lifestyles by taking dollars from investors, including the government, who desperately want to see it happen?"

"I don't think I said all that," Gillette answered, "but I understand what you're saying."

"It isn't just hype, Christian. We're close." Boyd glanced over at Ganze. "*Very* close."

Gillette's eyes flickered between Boyd and Ganze. He wondered how many other secrets of this magnitude they kept. "How do *I* fit in?"

"I'm getting to that," Boyd answered. "So far, this project has been housed inside DARPA, not actually at DARPA's headquarters, which is over in Arlington and not far from here, but at a university in the Northeast. Unfortunately, as you guessed, we think we have a spy problem. One of the senior biochemists on the project has been contacted by someone with close ties to al-Qaeda. The top people on the project don't know it, but we watch them constantly. The biochemist and the terrorist link have met three times. We haven't been able to record their conversations yet, but we don't have the luxury of time or giving our guy the benefit of the doubt."

"What are you going to do?"

"That's where you come in, Christian. We need to strip the project out of DARPA and use a cutout."

Gillette was familiar with the term. At one of their dinners, Senator Clark had described how the government sometimes used private companies to hide, or as fronts for, clandestine operations involving the CIA, the DIA, the NSA, and other intelligence agencies. How back in the sixties the International Telephone and Telegraph Company had bugged foreign embassies for the United States government, mostly in South America, while installing telephone systems for profit. How cutouts had become even more prevalent today and how typically only a few of the top officers in the company knew what was really going on. How numerous Fortune 500 companies were involved in such projects.

"You want to use an Everest company?" Gillette asked, anticipating what they were looking for.

"That's right."

"Why don't you just take the guy who's been contacted by the terrorist link off the project? Or take out the terrorist link?"

Boyd shook his head. "That would alert al-Qaeda that we know what's going on. Then they might try to get to someone else, or panic and do something crazy. We think it's a better idea to quietly lift the vital components of the nanotech project out of DARPA and slip it into one of your companies. We've already identified it."

"Which one do you want to use?"

"Beezer Johnson. Your medical products company. Specifically the division that develops and manufactures pacemakers, heart valves, and other very specialized products. That division works well for us from a number of different perspectives. First, and most important, it's based in Minneapolis. One of the leaders of the nanotech project, one of the people we trust implicitly, is from Minneapolis and has very good connections at the university's medical school and at the Mayo Clinic down in Rochester. Both will be excellent resources as the team finishes this thing. We intend to remove her and two other members of her team from the group and relocate them into space at Beezer in Minneapolis. We'll add a few people she's selected from a couple of other universities and companies in the U.S. to replace the people who will remain where the project is based now."

"Where is that?"

"Doesn't matter."

"Won't the people who stay, including the person who's been contacted by the terrorist link, won't they be suspicious when those people don't show up one day?" Gillette asked.

"No," Boyd answered quickly. "There's going to be an accident, Christian, a plane crash. No one, including their families, will know that they are really alive and well until after the project is complete. When it's done, they'll be able to go home. Hopefully within six months."

"Do these people have families? Spouses and kids, I mean."

"They're all married, and they all have children," Ganze spoke up. "Unfortunately."

Gillette groaned. "Shouldn't you at least tell the spouses what's really going on?"

"I can't risk detection," Boyd snapped.

"What if one of the spouses is so upset they commit suicide?"

"We're going to monitor that carefully," Ganze said. "Hopefully we'll recognize the signs and be able to stop anything—"

"But ultimately I can't worry about it," Boyd interrupted, his voice rising. "My job is to protect the project and this country. I can't allow what we have to get into our enemies' hands. It has to be kept secret at all costs. If someone is so weak they have to kill themselves because of the loss of a loved one, well, that's not my problem. And I won't lose a minute of sleep over it. I'm trying to make the world better for millions here, not individuals." He stuck his chin out fiercely. "Will you cooperate with us?"

"I don't know."

"You better decide fast."

Gillette eased back into his chair. "What about *my* questions?"

Boyd pointed at Ganze. "Daniel."

Ganze took out a small notepad from his jacket pocket. "Here's what I can tell you right now."

Gillette looked up. He'd been staring down, considering everything he'd heard.

"Your blood mother still lives in Los Angeles. Her name's Marilyn McRae."

"How do you know?"

Ganze held up his hand. "Don't try to contact her yet. We need to talk to her again first. Give us twenty-four hours."

"Okay," Gillette agreed, his blood pressure ticking up with each passing moment. "What about my father?"

"What I've been able to find out, what my sources have uncovered, is that sixteen years ago your father may have stumbled onto a plot to assassinate the president. This is still sketchy, and I should know more in the next few days, but it appears that he uncovered a left-wing conspiracy to kill George Bush. Obviously, it didn't go anywhere, but your father was killed so he couldn't tell anyone."

The room blurred in front of Gillette. "What?" he whispered hoarsely.

"I know it sounds incredible, but we think that's what happened. Like I said, we should have more information in the next few days."

"So, you gonna help us?" Boyd growled.

Gillette looked across the desk.

"Well?" Boyd demanded.

Gillette glanced from Boyd to Ganze several times. He'd made a career out of taking risks. But never one like this.

The flight to the Eastern Shore would take no more than a few minutes. As the jet powered up and began accelerating down the runway, Gillette put his head back and tried to relax. But it was hard. So many things were running through his mind. Apparently, his father had been murdered after all. He'd felt that in his gut for so long, but now he was close to proving it. And he was finally going to meet his blood mother.

He desperately wished Faith would call him back. He couldn't tell her much about what had happened, but he wanted to share with her the part about meeting his real mother.

"What's wrong?"

Gillette swiveled toward Stiles. He stared at the other man for a few moments but said nothing.

"Come on, Chris," Stiles urged. "What happened in the meeting?"

Gillette ran both hands through his hair. "I made a deal."

"So? You make deals every day."

"Not like this." He looked out the window as the plane lifted off. It was a crystal clear day, and suddenly he had a beautiful view of Washington, D.C. "I agreed to let them use one of our companies in return for information that's only important to me." He thought about how he could justify the deal in the name of national security, but that wasn't why he'd done it. "That's a first for me, and it doesn't feel good. But I've *got* to know what happened to my dad," he said under his breath.

"Who are these guys?"

"Can't tell you."

"Why not?"

Stiles would never tell anyone anything Gillette didn't want him to, but it wasn't about that. Men like Boyd didn't make vague threats. If Boyd thought Stiles knew what he and Ganze were about, Stiles would be in danger. As long as Stiles really didn't know, he'd have a chance if things got sticky. "It's for your own good."

"Oh, come—"

"I'm not kidding."

"Did they tell you anything good?"

Gillette nodded. "Yeah. They know who my real mother is. At least they say they do," he muttered.

"When do you talk to her?"

"Tomorrow. They're going to give me her number then."

"What about your father's plane crash?" Stiles asked. "Anything about that?"

"They gave me a little information on that. They said they'd know more in the next few days."

"So they're for real?"

"I'll let you know after I talk to this woman they claim is my mother." Gillette exhaled heavily. "Quentin, I need you to do me a favor, and this has to stay very quiet."

"What?"

"I need you to check out Allison for me."

"I thought Craig West already did."

"You've got to check on something he didn't. If she's into drugs. Cocaine."

"What makes you think she might be?"

Gillette shrugged. He felt bad even bringing this up, but he had no choice. He had to protect the investors. "She was sniffing up a hurricane at dinner, especially after she came back from the restroom. She said it was allergies, but I'm not so sure."

Stiles grimaced. "You always think the worst," he said quietly.

"I have to."

"Sure," Stiles agreed, his voice intensifying, "I'll check it out. But why do you care so much? You've got her family's money. She gets caught with the white powder, you let her go, but you keep the money." He paused. "Is there something else going on here?"

Gillette knew what that meant. "No."

"Come on, Chris. Are you interested in her? You can tell me."

"It's not that, Quentin. I'm serious. What I'm thinking is, she's good. *Very* good. And she's connected as hell." Gillette paused. "She'd make a great permanent addition to Everest. Might even be capable of running the show at some point." He shook his head. "But not if she's into coke."

"*Running the show*? Where are *you* going?"

"Nowhere. Not anytime soon. At least, I hope I'm not. 'Course, as long as Tom McGuire's out there, you never know."

"I thought you were grooming David Wright. I thought he was your guy."

"Never hurts to have another option."

"Isn't it a little early to start thinking about Allison being the next chairman?" Stiles asked. "Jesus, you just met her."

"I trust my gut. You know that. My gut tells me she might be the one."

"Remember, Chris," Stiles warned, "blood's thicker than water. She's going home someday, back to Chicago." He cocked his head to one side. "You do like her, don't you? Come on. A little, right?"

Gillette fought to hide a grin but couldn't. "She's a piece of work, I'll tell you that."

"What about Faith?"

Gillette let out a long breath. "Yeah, Faith." He reached for the phone, trying to forget about how many times he'd called her last night.

Stiles leaned forward and held out a section of the newspaper he'd folded into a rectangle the size of a piece of paper. "Put the phone away, Chris. Work on this instead."

"What is it?"

"A crossword puzzle. It'll take your mind off things."

Miles Whitman moved onto the flowery veranda of his spacious three-bedroom villa and gazed out over the

Mediterranean Sea in the fading light of another beautiful evening on the French Riviera.

Whitman had been nervous as hell on the flight from Kennedy to Milan last November. But once he'd gotten off the 747 and slipped into the airport crowd, he'd felt better. Even more relieved when he was out of the airport and in a cab headed downtown. He'd spent two weeks in Milan, two weeks in Rome, a month in Athens, and three months in Lisbon before settling in the south of France. He'd been here now for five months. Unless he did something incredibly stupid, he was safe. His cutout people, the ones who'd helped him hide the forty million dollars in return for allowing them to use North America Guaranty as their own little spy machine for the last nine years, would never roll over on him.

He took another sniff of the flowers, thinking about how Monique would be here soon. Thinking about how her heavenly twenty-four-year-old body would soon be draped all over him. Monique could do things his wife back in Connecticut would have a heart attack just thinking about. The little French kitten made for exquisite company—as long as she got to shop at the most expensive boutiques every day. C'est la vie, he thought. Everything had its price.

Whitman turned and walked back into the living room. A man he'd never seen before was waiting there, hands clasped behind his back.

Whitman took one look at him and spun around, ready to take his chances with the two-story leap from the veranda. But his path was blocked by two more large men who closed the double doors, cutting off any chance of escape. His head snapped left when another, smaller man ambled out of the bathroom, casually smoking a cigar. This man Whitman knew.

"Hello, Miles," the man said smoothly, moving directly

in front of Whitman. "I'm afraid this is going to have a bad ending for you. But it can be easy, so you don't feel pain. Or it can be hard. *Very hard.* Your choice. All you have to do is answer a few questions and I promise the end will be quick and clean." He eased down into a wicker chair. "Now, let's talk."

CHAPTER 9

"I don't like you. *At all.*"

Tell me how you really feel, Gillette thought. "We *just* met. You don't even know me."

"I know your *kind.*"

Becky Rouse was tall and thin, in her early forties, with shoulder-length dirty blond hair, hazel eyes, and a naturally determined expression. She was the mayor of Chatham, Maryland, a picturesque three-hundred-year-old fishing village set on the north bank of the wide Chester River a few miles upstream from where it met the Chesapeake Bay.

Becky had first been elected mayor five years ago—she was in the middle of her second four-year term. She'd moved to Chatham from Washington after a messy divorce from her lawyer husband, picking the town literally by tacking up a map of Maryland on her kitchen wall and throwing a dart. Originally from Georgia, she had no desire to go back. Her family had disowned her for marrying a Yankee.

Soon after moving to Chatham, she'd become friends with several female members of the town council who'd persuaded her to run against the incumbent, Jimmy Wilcox. Wilcox was a crotchety blue-crab captain who drank a case of Budweiser every day—winter or summer, rain or shine, healthy or sick. Thanks to the beer, he wasn't much fun to be around by the time the sun dipped low in the western sky, whether the crab pots were full that day or not.

As part of her campaign, Becky advertised that during his tenure, Jimmy had missed more than sixty percent of all town council meetings; accused him of buying a new pickup with treasury funds; and made it clear to everyone that tourist revenues were down twenty-five percent. She'd won the first election by fewer than three hundred votes, the second by a landslide.

Chatham's population was just under twenty thousand people, many of whom had never graduated from high school. Like most places, it was divided into the haves and the have-nots. The haves included families who'd owned huge tracts of land from way back; wealthy retirees who'd moved to the area from Wilmington, Baltimore, and Washington; yuppies and dinks who'd bought riverfront weekend homes; and proprietors who owned the waterfront shops. The have-nots were the fishermen, crabbers, and farmers whose families had been working the Chesapeake Bay and the land around it for years but had little to show for it.

The haves had tepidly supported Becky in the first election, not sure what to expect. But they'd become smitten with her when, soon after taking office, she attracted free state money for waterfront restoration, had the harbor dredged so large pleasure boats could tie up at the marinas and restaurants, moved the unsightly and smelly fish market to the other end of town, and advertised Chatham's new weekend festivals—her creations—in *The Washington Post* and the Baltimore *Sun*. Suddenly tourists were flocking to town. Just as suddenly, shop owners were making a killing and property values were skyrocketing.

"What *kind* do you think I am?" Gillette asked as they walked slowly along Main Street in the warm afternoon sunshine. He was wearing sunglasses, and his suit coat was slung over his shoulder.

Becky smiled sweetly at a mother and two children as they passed by, then glanced over her shoulder at the two QS agents following close behind. "You're about money. You've always had it, you always will, and the only thing that drives you is your desire to make more."

"Look, you should know that—"

"You want to put up that big discount store over on the west side of town," she continued, "and ruin what I've worked hard to build, all in the name of profits. That's what kind you are."

"How will putting up the store ruin what you've built?"

"It'll take business away from *my* waterfront."

"*What it will do,*" Gillette said, "is give the people in this area who don't have a lot of money a nice place to shop for decent products at affordable prices. They won't have to go all the way over to Delaware to buy home supplies and toys for their kids."

Becky sniffed. "The citizens of this town are fine."

"They're not fine. I spoke to a few of them and they're ticked off that you're blocking this thing." Before meeting Becky, Gillette had walked around the docks and spoken to some of the fishermen coming in from the morning catch. "They want this store."

She pointed a bony finger at him. "Don't try to make like you're some champion of the poor. You want this store so you can stay ahead of Wal-Mart. Chatham is very strategic for you geographically, I've looked at the map. You'll draw from everywhere. Your interest here is completely selfish. Once you get this store built, you'll never set foot in Chatham again. You'll go back to your homes in Manhattan, Easthampton, the south of France. But *I* have to live *here.*"

"Why do the people who matter to you even care?" he

asked. "The blue-collar folks don't shop on the waterfront. It's the rich and the tourists who come here."

"We'll become known as that town with the Discount America. I can already see the write-up in the *Post*," she said, holding her thumb and forefinger an inch apart and moving them across in front of her face. " 'Stay away from Chatham,' it'll say, 'it's the strip mall capital of the Eastern Shore.' "

"What you'll become known as is the town that's got a healthy treasury," Gillette argued. "The property taxes alone will pay for fire, police, and EMT, not to mention the economic benefit from the jobs the DA store and the smaller stores that pop up around it will create."

As they rounded a corner, Becky stopped and put her hands on her hips. "What are you willing to offer me?"

He'd been ready for this. "What do you want?" *Never* offer first. *Always* counter.

"That jackass Harry Stein said something about an elementary school. Which is fine for starters, but rest assured, I'll want a lot more than that, Mr. Gillette."

He'd asked her several times to call him Christian, but she'd refused so he'd stopped trying. "Like what?"

"A retirement home with at least two hundred beds, three new squad cars for the police force, a rescue boat for the fire department, and a couple of school buses."

"How about a pool and a hot tub for every home in town?" Gillette shot back. "Free steaks for a year. A hundred thousand in cash for everyone. We'll call this 'Little Kuwait.' "

She gave him a disdainful look. "Give me a couple of days. I'll come up with more."

"You know I'm not going to give you everything you just asked for, Becky. It wouldn't be worth it for me financially. No single store location is worth all that, not unless it's on the corner of Forty-second Street and Seventh Avenue."

"You've got *billions*, Mr. Gillette. I checked your Web site this morning. Everest Capital just raised another huge fund. I believe it was fifteen billion dollars. And you can't buy me a few necessities for my town?" She turned and headed into O'Malley's Bar & Grill. "Please, Mr. Gillette," she called over her shoulder. "Please."

Gillette followed her into the pub, reaching for his cell phone as he went through the door. Wright was calling. "What is it, David?" he asked, tossing his coat and sunglasses on the bar.

"I got the signed letter back from Maddox," Wright answered. "We're done."

"Good." At least something was going right today.

"And Tom O'Brien wanted you to know that the city of Las Vegas called. They want you to fly out next week for a few meetings they've set up with the appropriate people."

He was sure that *"appropriate people"* meant the individuals who could help him start the casino process. "Tell him to work it out with Debbie, will you?"

"Okay."

"This is a priority, so make sure it happens. Stay on Tom and Debbie about it."

"I'll take care of it, don't worry."

"Thanks." Gillette slipped the phone back in his pocket and checked his watch. It was two-thirty; he had to get out of here soon if he was going to be in Pittsburgh by seven for dinner with Jack Mitchell.

"Here's what we'd have to deal with, Bob," Becky said loudly to the bartender, pointing at Gillette as he sat next to her. "A man who brings his security detail with him everywhere he goes, like he's really that important, and thinks cell phones are more essential than people." She took a sip from the beer she'd ordered. "Rude, too. We were in the middle of a conversation when we walked in here."

Gillette glanced at Bob, who was cleaning a mug and shaking his head.

"So where did you send Stein?" she asked Gillette, picking up the large glass of water Bob had put down beside her beer.

She was smart, Gillette realized. She wasn't going to drink more than a sip of the beer. It was a weekday afternoon, and she'd ridden her previous opponent about all-day drinking in her first campaign, so she couldn't do it herself. But she wanted to put money in Bob's pocket, too. "On an errand," he answered. When they were introduced, he could tell she couldn't stand Stein, so he'd sent the CEO off to talk to more watermen.

Gillette pointed at what Becky had ordered. "Same, please, Bob. A beer and a water." He noticed an outside deck overlooking the river on the other side of the place. "Let's go outside," he suggested, picking up his sunglasses and the water glass. A couple of other people hanging around the bar seemed to be listening too carefully, and he didn't want this turning into an impromptu public forum. Becky had turned out to be cagey, and he didn't trust her motives. The move into O'Malley's had been too convenient. "Come on," he called when she didn't follow right away.

He moved through the screen door and sat at a wooden table with an umbrella, putting the water down amid the remnants of bright orange, smashed, steamed crab shells. The glare of the afternoon sun off the river's calm surface was brilliant, so he put his sunglasses back on, then took a deep breath, taking in the Old Bay seasoning from the crab shells, the salt water, and a trace of wood smoke from some far-off pile of burning leaves. He liked it here. Maybe he'd buy a place on the river. Someday.

A few moments later, Becky came through the door and sat on the other side of the table. "Why'd you want to come out here? It's awfully bright."

"I didn't feel like negotiating in front of half the town council." He'd recognized two of the men from pictures Craig West had included in the prep memo he'd reviewed on the short flight from D.C.

She smiled at him for the first time. "Well, aren't you a worthy opponent."

"That's the rumor. Look, here's what I'll do," he kept going, not giving her a chance to speak up, "I'll buy you half your elementary school and the three police cruisers. For that, I get my store."

She laughed loudly. "You must be joking."

He spotted a *USA Today* lying on another table, stood up, and walked to it, leafing through the sections until he found the one containing the crossword. "I never joke about Everest business, Ms. Rouse," he said, folding the newspaper and stashing it under his arm, then moving back to where she was and standing in front of her so the sun was behind him. That way she had to squint. "If you don't agree to my offer, I'll rally the people of this town against you and you'll have the biggest shit-storm this side of the Mississippi on your hands. At my direction, they'll call for a referendum, which they're allowed to do under the town charter. My lawyers have checked, and I guarantee you I'll win. I've got the numbers as long as I get people out to vote. And believe me, I'll rent buses if I have to." He took off his sunglasses. "I'll expect your call no later than Friday at five P.M. If I don't hear from you, we'll start the referendum process." He dropped a twenty on the table in front of her. "Beers are on me."

Tom McGuire walked along the wide, white-sand beach of Avalon, New Jersey, a quaint seaside resort town a hundred miles south of New York City. Avalon was built on a narrow strip of land that ran between the Atlantic Ocean and an extended bay in southern New Jersey. As far as anyone else knew, a man named William Cooper was renting a house on the bay side with a month-to-month lease. So far, McGuire hadn't run into any problems.

Avalon's busy season ran from Memorial Day to Labor Day. Now, in late September, the beach was almost deserted. Just a few elderly couples, who'd retired to the town, combing the beach for shells in the afternoon sunshine.

McGuire pulled the brim of his Baltimore Orioles baseball cap low over his sunglasses and looked down as he passed one of the older couples walking slowly the other way. He was taking no chances on being recognized. If he looked right at them, they might remember him later if they saw his picture on television. He'd already been featured once on *America's Most Wanted*.

When he passed them, he stopped and gazed out to sea, the cool water of a dying wave running over his toes just before it hissed, hesitated for a moment, then receded against his heels and washed back into the ocean. Everything had gone exactly according to plan, thanks to the hotel operator at the Parker Meridien who had listened in on Allison Wallace's telephone calls. The photographers had shown up at the Grill right on time and Gillette had ducked out the back, headlong into the trap. But it was as if the guy had a hundred lives. Gillette and Stiles had been outnumbered and outgunned, but Gillette had turned the tables by going on the attack—something McGuire hadn't anticipated.

McGuire's expression hardened into one of resolve as another wave hissed past his feet. He was going to take care of Gillette sooner or later, one way or another.

"Afternoon."

McGuire's eyes flashed left, toward the voice. The man standing a few feet away wore a baseball cap and sunglasses, too, but he was younger, in his mid-thirties. "Hello," he answered gruffly.

"Nice day, huh?"

"Yeah. Nice."

"Looking for shells?"

"Nah, just taking a walk."

"Live here?"

"Visiting," McGuire replied.

"Where you staying?"

McGuire glanced over at the man again. He was looking out to sea intently from behind his sunglasses, watching a ship on the horizon. "Up the beach."

"Really? Could have sworn I saw you going into a house over on the bay side yesterday. That's where I'm staying. On the bay side."

McGuire shook his head. "You got the wrong guy."

The man shrugged. "My mistake." He smiled. "Well, take care."

McGuire watched the man move off, wondering what the hell that had been about. Wondering if it was time for William Cooper to make another move.

It was the third time since Gillette had left Chatham that he'd tried Faith on both her cell phone and her private apartment line in New York. Still no answer, and no return call. She was getting the messages—she checked her phone religiously, every fifteen minutes when he was with her—she just wasn't answering. He knew what was going on. She was trying to teach him a lesson. But he wasn't guilty. As he sat back down at the table, Allison smiled and leaned toward him.

"Everything okay?" she asked, squeezing his arm.

Allison's touch caused a shiver to race up his back and reminded him that it had been a month since he and Faith had made love. He looked over at her. She was wearing her hair up and looked pretty in an off-the-shoulders dress she'd changed into after they'd gotten to the hotel. "Everything's fine. I'm going to Las Vegas next week to start that process we talked about." She'd taken a helicopter from Manhattan down to Chatham to meet him, and he'd brought her up to speed on the casino during the flight to Pittsburgh.

"I want to go with you on that trip," she said immediately.

"Well—"

"What do you have going on out in Las Vegas?" Jack Mitchell asked loudly. Mitchell was the CEO and controlling shareholder of Veramax. He was a big man who was nearly bald and wore large, unfashionable glasses.

Sometimes rich people did that, Gillette knew. Wore things that were out of style just to show everybody else that they didn't have to care about fashion.

"A couple of days ago, the NFL awarded us the new Las Vegas franchise," Gillette replied. He wasn't going to tell Mitchell about the casino because he didn't want other casinos in Vegas hearing about their plans yet. According to Allison, Mitchell was pretty connected, and you never knew who knew whom.

Mitchell banged the table with his palm. The silverware and plates rattled, and two of the water glasses almost fell over. "Damn, that's great. If we do a deal here, maybe I could get an invite to the first game."

"If we do a deal here, you'll have a standing invite to *all* the games," Gillette assured the other man. "Tell me about Veramax's products, will you, Jack?"

Mitchell cleared his throat and took a long swallow of Scotch. "Right now, our bread and butter is basic over-the-counter medicine. But we've got some hot new proprietary drugs just rarin' to go." A natural-born salesman, Mitchell used his hands a lot in conversation. "Dynamite stuff, but these FDA guys in Washington are dragging their heels."

"What's the problem?" Gillette asked. Allison hadn't explained the FDA problem yet or how she knew of his connection to Senator Clark. He reminded himself to drill her on that after dinner. "Why are they dragging their heels?"

"Ah, it's a long story," Mitchell said, waving a hand in front of his face.

"We haven't even gotten our salads yet, Jack. We've got plenty of time."

Mitchell set his jaw. "It's a damn personal thing with one of the senior people over there. A guy named Phil Rothchild. He's from Chicago, and we had a run-in a while back. It's stupid, but that's how things go sometimes. Silly and stupid."

"What happened?"

"It's embarrassing."

Gillette drew himself up in his chair. "Jack, if we're going to be partners, there can't be any secrets between us. If you expect me to go to Senator Clark on your behalf, I need to know what the deal is."

Mitchell grimaced. "Okay. I slept with Rothchild's daughter."

Gillette's eyes raced to Allison's.

"Jack's been divorced for five years," she explained, "and Rothchild's daughter was twenty-eight. Jack didn't do anything wrong."

"Rothchild was irritated because Amy, that's his daughter," Mitchell explained, "was seeing some young Wall Street punk at the time. Some guy from a well-to-do family in the Northeast. Like I'm not good enough or something," he said with a sneer, pointing his thumbs at himself. "Like Chicago isn't good enough. And it's such crap because Rothchild is from there. It's like he's turning his back on the Midwest, like he wants to join that Ivy League set or something, and I don't like that. Besides, I have way more money than that little prick Amy was seeing, even after my divorce."

"I still don't understand what caused the war."

"Rothchild thought I wasn't serious about Amy," Mitchell explained, "and, well, Amy was engaged to the Wall Street kid."

"Oh."

"Somehow"—Mitchell shrugged and rolled his eyes as if he had no idea how it could have happened—"the kid found out about our affair and dumped her."

"How did the kid find out?" Gillette asked.

Mitchell glanced down into his lap and grinned smugly. "I might have called him."

"Jesus." Gillette flashed Allison a look. "Are you still seeing Amy?"

Mitchell broke into a chuckle. "Nah, I decided that dating twenty-eight-year-olds wasn't a good idea."

From what Gillette could tell, Mitchell was probably at least fifty-five. "Yeah, I can understand why you'd—"

"They're too old," Mitchell interrupted. "My new girlfriend's twenty-three. Hot as hell, too."

Gillette put his elbows on the table and rubbed his face. People just couldn't keep themselves out of trouble—especially men with money.

"There's one more piece to the 'war,' as you called it," Mitchell continued.

"I can't wait to hear this," Gillette muttered.

"I kept Rothchild out of the Racquet Club in New York when he applied last year," Mitchell explained. "I've belonged there for almost thirty years, and I made a few calls to the membership committee. The guy never had a chance."

The Racquet Club was one of the most exclusive athletic clubs in New York. Gillette had been a member since becoming a managing partner at Everest five years ago. "Why did you do that?"

"Because of this whole thing with his daughter. I mean, he had no right to—"

"All right, all right," Gillette interrupted, holding up his hand. "I've heard enough. Look, here's what we're going to do. *First,*" he said emphatically, staring at Mitchell, "you're going to write Rothchild a letter, apologizing for keeping him out of the Racquet Club. *Don't call him,*" Gillette warned. "That would probably start World War Three. Just write him, and e-mail me a copy of what you've written before you send it. Then, you're going to get Rothchild in there."

"Aw, Jesus."

"*Jack.*"

"Okay," Mitchell agreed softly, "I'll do it."

"Then," Gillette continued, "I'm going to Senator Clark to get his help. I'll probably have to relocate one of Everest's companies to California, for crying out loud, but leave that to me. I promise you that within two weeks the FDA will have your products on the rocket-docket approval process, or whatever they call it there." He took a breath. "In return for my help, you're going to sell me forty-nine percent of Veramax for half a billion dollars in cash. It's a fair price given what you've gotten yourself into. Half the cash will go to you, the other half will go into the company to fund research and development of new products. I'll get new shares and they'll be nondilutive, meaning that if you issue more shares to other investors while I own mine, I'll still own forty-nine percent. The last part of my deal with you is that you'll sell me an option to buy another two percent of the company for a million dollars. I'll only be able to execute that option if you don't go public by the end of next year, at least at a valuation we both agree to in the stock purchase agreement. But if you don't go public by then, I'll execute my option and control the company. Got all that?"

Mitchell gazed at Gillette for a few moments stonefaced, then broke into a wide smile. "Get the lawyers started, my friend." He nodded at Allison. "That little girl over there told me you were sharp. She was right."

Gillette took several swallows of water. "So tell me about these hot new products. What do they deal with?"

"Alzheimer's, male impotence, a day-after pill that really works. Things like that."

"And the basic over-the-counter stuff that's your bread and butter right now. What's that?"

Mitchell glanced at Allison, then took a long guzzle of his Scotch. "Aspirin, nose drops, and cold medicines. Liquids and pills."

Though he wasn't sure why, something clicked in Gillette's brain.

"You sure?" Gillette asked. He was talking to Stiles on his cell phone as he waited for Allison. They'd finished dinner a few minutes ago and she was saying good-bye to Mitchell by the elevators before he went upstairs to his room. "No drugs?"

"You can never be *sure*." Stiles had flown back to New York that afternoon on the helicopter that had brought Allison down to Maryland. "But I spoke to a couple of people who would know, and there's no indication she's doing that. And," he continued, "she does have a history of allergy shots."

"Guess I was wrong." Gillette was sitting on a sofa in a secluded section of the hotel lobby. He spotted Allison walking toward him. "It's amazing how you get this stuff so fast."

"I'll check a few more sources tomorrow," Stiles offered, "but I think she's clean."

"Okay."

"You coming back tonight?" Stiles wanted to know.

"No. In the morning."

"Uh-huh. Well, stay out of trouble."

Gillette glanced at two QS agents who were standing against a far wall, trying to seem inconspicuous. "I told you, it's not like that."

"It never is," Stiles said, "until it is."

Gillette groaned. "Good night, Plato."

"Night."

"Who was that?" Allison asked, sitting beside Gillette on the sofa as he closed his cell phone. "That pop-star girlfriend of yours?"

"No, Stiles."

"You two trying to dig up secrets on me?"

Gillette raised one eyebrow. "Absolutely."

"Have fun. You won't find anything." She pushed her hair back over her ears and relaxed onto the sofa. "How did you think it went tonight with Jack?"

"Fine. He needs to start taking self-control pills or he's going to get himself in trouble."

Allison waved and made a face. "He's just a harmless old flirt from a different age." She laughed. "Lord, he made a pass at me a few minutes ago. He does every time I see him."

"In this age, old flirts cause multimillion-dollar lawsuits."

"Oh, don't worry so much." She put up a hand before he could respond. "I know, I know. It's what you do. Well, don't do it tonight. Give yourself a break. By the way," she said, her voice rising, "I may have another deal for us. A friend of Jack's here in Pittsburgh owns a large truck-leasing company, and he may want to sell it. It could fit really well with that leasing company in Atlanta you already control. I'll follow up tomorrow."

Allison Wallace was young, but she was already a rainmaker. No doubt. And he wanted those talents for his own. "Would you ever consider joining Everest full time?" Gillette asked. At times, he almost got a high by being blunt. By shocking people. "Let someone else in the family take your spot on the family trust's board?"

She smiled at him coyly. "Don't beat around the bush, Christian. Why don't you just ask me to marry you?"

Gillette felt his face flush, caught off guard right back. "No, I—"

"You never know," Allison said softly, "I might be convinced to join Everest. But I'd have a few conditions."

"Such as?"

She ran her hand up the lapel of his suit jacket, then brushed the backs of her fingers across his cheek. "I'll let you know."

He was in a prison cell. On death row. Trying to make the man sitting on the chair beside him, the man wearing the white collar, understand that he hadn't killed anyone. That he was innocent. He was pleading, the desperate words cascading from his parched mouth, but the priest wouldn't listen. Then the warden and his deputies—a short parade of tall, faceless men—were outside the cell, ready to take him to the execution chamber. As they were leading him away, he turned to make one last pitiful appeal, and as he did, the priest became his father.

"Jesus!" Gillette hissed, rising to a sitting position on the bed and rubbing his eyes. His head was pounding from the intensity of the images.

After a few moments and several deep breaths, he dropped his feet to the floor and sat on the edge of the bed, still half-in, half-out of the dream. Finally, he checked the clock—3:15—then turned on the light and picked up his Blackberry off the night table. He needed a few minutes to shake the dream before he tried to go back to sleep.

The first new e-mail was from Faith, sent only an hour ago. It read:

Chris, I love you. Sorry I was such a jerk at your office the other night. I was tired from the flight, and the last thing I needed was to run straight into the woman I thought about strangling (kidding . . . sort of) the whole way back on the plane. I got your phone messages—sorry I haven't returned them. I said I was a jerk, didn't I? Please call me first thing in the morning (as soon as you wake up). I have to go to London tomorrow afternoon for a few days—should be back Sunday or Monday. More promo stuff. Ugh!! I would have called you, but I didn't want to wake you up. I know how busy you are. I love you so much.

When Gillette had finished Faith's e-mail, he put the Blackberry down slowly on the night table and rubbed his eyes again. As he did, he caught a whiff of Allison's perfume, left over from when she'd squeezed his hand tight and kissed him on the cheek before heading to her room.

PART
TWO

CHAPTER 10

Dr. Scott Davis was the chief neurosurgeon at the Medical Center of Virginia in downtown Richmond and, according to the head of anesthesiology at St. Christopher's, also a leading authority on biochemical nanotechnology research.

Gillette had handed the project of finding a nanotechnology resource to an Everest vice president named Cathy Dylan. Cathy was every bit as aggressive as David Wright, just five years younger and, most important, much more malleable. Gillette would have handled the project himself, but he was worried that Boyd might be monitoring him—tapping phones, reading e-mails, having him followed—especially for the first few days after disclosing what they wanted. He couldn't have Wright track down an expert because Wright would ask too many questions. He needed a hunting dog, a loyal Lab who would act on orders without question. A younger person at the firm who wanted simply to please. Cathy fit the bill perfectly.

Like most Everest vice presidents, Cathy was nervous around him. But he sensed she was more street-smart than the others. Quicker on her feet with a believable truth stretcher if she needed to be.

Gillette had given Cathy a quick primer on nanotech, then the name of the anesthesiologist at St. Christopher's. The guy put her in touch with Davis right away. Which was a stroke of divine intervention as far as Gillette was concerned, because he didn't want six or seven degrees of separation on this. Casting a wider net would have given Boyd a better chance of finding out what was going on. After all, the nanotech research community couldn't be that big if most people believed commercial development of the technology was still thirty to forty years off.

Gillette had instructed Cathy not to use his or Everest's name during her search except with the anesthesiologist at St. Christopher's; to make all telephone calls related to finding an expert from a pay phone—never her SoHo apartment or Everest; not to do any nanotechnology research on her office or home computer; not to send any e-mails related to nanotech from her office or home computer; and to try to make certain the doctor she found was a practicing physician who worked long hours—someone who would be less likely to have time to be involved with DARPA. Gillette had called Cathy collect last night at seven forty-five from a pay phone in the hotel lobby, during a quick break from his dinner with Allison and Mitchell. Fourteen hours later, not only did she have a resource, she had an appointment. He was impressed.

Gillette sat in Davis's cramped and cluttered hospital office, waiting for the doctor to get out of surgery. Gillette had brought Stiles and just one other QS agent with him on the flight to Richmond and hadn't given the Everest pilot the destination until he and Stiles were on their way to LaGuardia and until the QS agent who was going with them was actually sitting beside the pilot. They'd stopped at a bodega in Harlem to call the pilot after the QS agent who was driving had made several nifty evasive maneuvers. And Gillette had warned the pilot on the call not to tell anyone but the tower where they were going.

He pulled out his Blackberry for the fourth time in the last twenty minutes and almost turned it on. But he caught himself just in time. He wasn't going to turn it or the cell phone on until he'd landed back at LaGuardia. He let out a long breath, glancing around the office as he put the Blackberry away. He hated sitting on his hands, hated wasted minutes. And he'd already been in here for half an hour.

"Where is he?" Wright demanded, frustrated that Debbie wasn't even bothering to look up from her computer.

"I don't know."

"What do you mean, you don't know? You *always* know where Chris is."

"This time I really don't. He told me he was going out this morning around nine, and that was it. He didn't say where he was going, and he didn't say when he'd be back."

"Look, I *have* to get in touch with him." Paul had called Wright an hour ago, looking for Gillette's schedule. "I have to talk to Chris about a deal point. We could lose it if I don't talk to him right away." A lie, but he had to say something.

"Then call his cell phone," Debbie snapped. "You've got his number."

"I tried, he's not picking up."

"E-mail him."

"I did that, too, of course," Wright said, "but he hasn't pinged me back. If he had, I wouldn't be here. Obviously."

Debbie finally looked up. "Well, I can't help you. If he calls me, I'll let him know you're looking for him."

Wright leaned over Debbie's desk. "You better not be lying to me," he warned. "The deal could hinge on this. I'm a managing partner now, and if you're holding back, I'll do everything I can to get you fired."

Debbie shot out of her seat. "*What is your damn problem, David?*"

Wright's cell phone went off, and he turned away, yanking it out of his pocket. It was Paul again. He shut his eyes, fighting the urge to scream.

Gillette was reaching for a magazine on the front of the doctor's desk when the door opened.

"Hello," said the man, a curious expression on his face. "I'm Scott Davis. I . . . I was expecting a Cathy Dylan. Are you—"

"I'm Christian Gillette." He rose and shook the doctor's hand. "Cathy works for me. She made the appointment for me. Sorry about the confusion, Dr. Davis."

"Oh, well, fine. And please call me Scott. I don't go for that formal stuff."

Davis was fifty-five, of average height and build, and had intense brown eyes, thick eyebrows, dimples, and a full beard. He was still dressed in his light blue surgery smock and pants, a mask draped around his neck, a surgical cap slightly crooked on his head.

"Thanks for seeing me on such short notice."

"Jamie Robinson's a good friend of mine," Davis said, referring to the anesthesiologist at St. Christopher's who had put Cathy in touch. "We did medical school together at Johns Hopkins." He eased into his wooden desk chair with a tired groan. "Sorry to keep you waiting, but the surgery was more complex than I had anticipated."

"What was it?" Gillette noticed several dark splotches on Davis's smock that looked like dried blood.

"A twelve-year-old boy with a brain tumor the size of an orange. It was a tricky procedure. The tumor was almost inaccessible."

Gillette winced. "That's awful."

Davis sighed, stroking his beard slowly with his thumb and forefinger, over and over, as he rocked in the creaky chair. "It is awful, but I believe we were successful. I believe the boy will recover."

Gillette liked Davis right away. He spoke in a low, soothing voice and had a calmness about him that was nearly hypnotic. "Congratulations," he said softly. "It's an incredible thing you do."

"God does it, Christian. I'm simply His conduit. But I appreciate your kind words." Davis was silent for a few moments as he continued stroking his beard. "Jamie tells me your firm has made quite a donation to his hospital. They'll be able to build a new wing for children with cancer now. That's wonderful. I believe in doing all we can for children. For everyone, of course, but particularly children."

"I'm a fortunate man, Dr. Davis." Davis had asked Gillette to call him by his first name, but somehow he couldn't. It didn't seem appropriate for a man who performed miracles every day. "I may not have the same faith in God as you, but I've been blessed in my life, and I believe in giving back."

Davis smiled serenely. "Good for you, good for you. Perhaps someday you'll find your faith."

"Perhaps."

Davis leaned forward and put his elbows on the desk. "Jamie also tells me you have an interest in nanotechnology."

"Yes."

"May I ask why?"

"I run an investment firm in New York, and I've been approached by some people about funding an opportunity in this area." He didn't like lying to Davis, but it was safer for the doctor if he didn't know the truth. Just as it was for Stiles. He'd taken a long look into Norman Boyd's eyes during their meeting yesterday and found a zealot, a man who was deeply committed to his objective and might use any means necessary to achieve it. If lying meant keeping innocent people out of jeopardy, so be it. "I need your expert advice."

"Let me be perfectly clear right from the start," Davis said candidly. "I've studied nanotechnology extensively, so I can sound dangerous. But I'm no expert. I know what atomic force microscopy is, I'm familiar with carbon nanotube transistors, and I can tell you that molecular tweezers will be very important one day. But I'm not researching day and night the way some people are, probably the way those people who are presenting you with that opportunity are." A far-off look came into his eyes. "You know, some people say I'm on the cutting edge of medicine today, but what I do will look like meatball surgery when true biochemical nanotechnology becomes reality."

"When will that be, Doctor?"

"Well . . . you hear rumors all the time."

"And?"

"Actually, there are people on the cusp of it right now."

Gillette's ears perked up.

"There's a company in San Francisco named Optimicronics," Davis went on, "basically four eye surgeons and a bioengineer. They've developed a subretinal chip that in clinical trials appears to restore sight quickly for many forms of blindness. The chip is tiny. Its diameter is about sixty times smaller than that of a *penny,* and it's about half as thick as a paintbrush bristle. Can you imagine? It's revolutionary, a major breakthrough if the trials prove out." Davis hesitated, studying Gillette's expression. "But judging from your reaction, that isn't what you're interested in."

"No, it's not."

"Then I assume your interest lies in the hard-core stuff. The ability to operate at the atomic level. In the range of ten-to-the-negative-nine meter and less."

Gillette broke into a grin, embarrassed at his ignorance. He wondered if this was how financial talk sounded sometimes to people outside the industry. "If you're talking eighty thousand times smaller than the diameter of a human hair, I think we're on the same page."

Davis nodded, chuckling. "Depending on whose hair you're talking about and when it was last washed."

"If you say so."

"It is fascinating stuff," Davis said. "I just hope I'm around to see it."

Gillette noticed Davis's fingers moving more quickly over his beard. It was clear the topic excited him. You could tell so much about people if you really watched them. It was like the good poker players always said: Play the players, not the cards. "How far off do you think nanotech is, Doctor?"

Davis leaned back, put his hands behind his head, and gazed at the ceiling. "Twenty to thirty years to the market, but in the lab right now."

Less than what Gillette had heard from others, but still at least a generation off. "Could nanotechnology really live up to the hype?"

"Yes, absolutely. Some people pooh-pooh it, but I'm a firm believer, and I don't have an ax to grind."

Gillette wrestled with the best way to ask his question, letting out an exasperated breath before he spoke up. "Can you, I mean, I just don't know if I get—"

"Do you want the layman's version of what's going on here? Is that what you're trying to ask me, Christian?"

"Yes," he admitted with a relieved smile.

"Happy to oblige. But remember, I only know enough to *sound* dangerous."

"I'm glad to start with that at this point."

"Okay, here it is in its simplest form. The human body is made up of billions and billions of complex molecules, and the elderly, the hurt, the frail, the sick—they all have one thing in common. The atoms, and therefore the molecules, are no longer functioning correctly because of a virus or a bacteria, or maybe because the genetic material degenerated, or because some linebacker blindsided them and now their knee is snapped. Nanotechnology will enable doctors to use incredibly small machines, active inside the body, to detect the problem, or maybe to direct the repair of the body's own DNA. Initially, these machines may only work on one type of disorder, but there will be many of them sent in to attack the problem. Eventually, they'll work atom by atom, molecule by molecule, cell by cell, organ by organ, until everything's right."

"Can you give me a specific example?"

"Sure, take a heart attack. The way it works now is that scar tissue replaces dead muscle after a heart attack. But nanotech will help the heart to grow new muscle tissue and overcome the scar.

"This technology isn't like a drug that goes bouncing around your body after you swallow a pill," Davis continued, "with you and your doctor hoping by chance it runs into the right receptor molecule. This is an advanced, sleek device that is programmed to zero in on specific physiological or biological problems."

"Or screw it up," Gillette said quietly.

"Well, now you've hit on one of the great debates with nanotech. The other being the immortality issue."

"Immortality?"

"People age because, simply through the passage of time, there is a greater and greater chance of DNA becoming damaged, due to all kinds of factors. As long as DNA remains intact, it can continue to produce directives for the assembly of new proteins to regenerate damaged cells. But when the DNA itself is harmed, it can't continue to produce error-free directives. Those errors add up over time, molecules become misarranged, organs break down, and, of course, people die. Nanotechnology machines will *repair* DNA. Even when your organs break down, we'll be able to fix them. You may never die. In fact, you may not even have wrinkles when the technology is perfected. It'll be preventive, too," he added. "For example, doctors will be able to detect that blood vessels in your brain are weakening and are about to explode. In other words, you're about to have a stroke. They'll send nanomachines into the brain immediately to guide the quick growth of reinforcing fibers, and you'll never know you were about to become a vegetable."

"Incredible," Gillette said, aware that the word was woefully inadequate for what Davis was describing.

"It really is. Now, the immortality issue has two main subproblems. The first is, who gets to be immortal? The answer, at least initially, is whoever has enough money."

"Which has terrible social implications."

"Right. If you knew there was everlasting life to be had, but you didn't have the money, what would you risk to get it? Anything, of course."

Gillette nodded. "Then the second piece to the puzzle must be, what do you do when *everyone* can afford it? When the technology becomes commonplace and for twenty bucks a year nanotechnology can touch up any little physical problem you have. Forty years ago, computers cost millions, now you can have one on your desk for a few hundred bucks. Eventually, it will be like that with nanotechnology."

"The way it is with every technology," Davis agreed. "Good for you."

"What about the Big Brother aspect?" Gillette asked.

"What do you mean?"

"Could nanotechnology enable you to inject chips into

the body that would allow you to remotely record what someone sees and hears, maybe even monitor what they think?"

Davis stroked his beard for several moments. "I'm convinced that anything will be possible with this technology, Christian. Anything."

"How would you do it so they wouldn't suspect?"

"You mean get the chip into their bodies?" Davis asked, making certain he was clear.

"Yes."

Davis shrugged. "All kinds of ways. You could put it in food, drinks, cold medicines, perfumes, nose sprays, air fresheners. There'd be many options. There're many ways into the body."

Gillette hesitated, almost distracted by the pulse pounding in his brain. "Could someone be close?" he asked, his voice almost inaudible.

"You always hear about secret projects, particularly inside the government," Davis replied, still rocking gently in his chair, "but I don't put much stock in those rumors."

"But could they be close?" Gillette asked again, his voice becoming stronger, his gaze focusing.

"They could."

"Then what's the barrier?"

"Primarily, the complexity of molecular structures. Do you remember those huge charts on the walls of your biology and chemistry classes?"

"Barely."

"Imagine a chart thousands of times bigger with millions of permutations. Before you can build, you must understand and then master the tools to control. It's an incredible proposition."

"But someone could be close. It is possible."

Davis stopped rocking and leaned forward. "What do you know, Christian Gillette?"

* * *

Boyd ended the phone call quickly when Ganze walked into his office. "What is it?"

"We lost Gillette in Harlem this morning around ten-thirty," Ganze explained. "We know at least one thing about the QS guys now, they sure as hell can drive. Our guy couldn't keep up."

Boyd cursed under his breath. "Where did he go?"

"Richmond, Virginia."

"Who did he see?"

"We don't know," Ganze replied.

"*Why not?*"

"We didn't find out Gillette went to Richmond until he got back to New York just a few minutes ago."

"But we have the pilots. They're supposed to let us know where he's going before he takes off so we can have people on the ground when he lands."

"The pilot couldn't call. Gillette didn't tell him where they were going until there was a QS agent sitting right next to him, and the QS agent didn't leave the pilot's side until they landed at LaGuardia. The pilot literally couldn't take a piss by himself."

"We've got to do better than that."

"I know, I'm working on it."

"What about the other thing?" Boyd asked.

"It's in motion."

"Good." Boyd thought for a second. "Did you speak to Marilyn?"

"Yes, she's ready."

They had to keep Gillette interested. Had to make him think he was so close to finding all these things he'd been trying to find for so long. "Tell Gillette it's all right to call her now." Boyd reached for the phone. "Anything more on Clayton Gillette?"

"I'm getting closer. I should have something tomorrow."

* * *

Tom McGuire reached into his pocket for the SUV keys. He wasn't going to stay in Avalon another day. The guy on the beach had rattled him; he'd had the look of a hunter about him, and over the last thirty years, McGuire had learned to trust his gut.

What bothered McGuire most was, if his gut was right, then who was the guy on the beach? If he was a fed, he would have arrested him. If it was somebody he'd put in prison a long time ago when he was with the Bureau who'd just gotten out, had somehow found him, and was settling a vendetta, he'd be dead. But the guy had just asked him about seashells.

McGuire pulled the SUV keys from his pocket, pushed the button to unlock the doors, then took a last look out over the bay in the late afternoon sunlight. He liked it here. It was too bad he had to go, but there was no choice.

Then he felt a burst of searing pain at the back of his neck, and everything went black.

It was five-thirty, and they were almost back to Everest after landing at LaGuardia thirty minutes earlier. Gillette was close to finishing the third crossword puzzle of the trip when his cell phone rang. He'd turned it back on when they'd landed.

"Hello."

"Christian, it's David."

"Hey."

"Christ, I've been trying to get in touch with you all day."

Wright had sent him seven e-mails. "I've been out of touch."

"No shit."

"What's the problem?" Gillette asked.

"I've got to talk to you about some of these reps and warranties Maddox wants in the Hush-Hush purchase agreement."

"Is it that urgent?"

"He really wants to—"

Gillette's phone beeped, indicating another call. "I've got to take this, David. We'll talk when I get to the office in a few minutes." He switched over. "Hello."

"Christian, it's Daniel Ganze."

"Yes," Gillette said, dropping the folded newspaper on the seat between Stiles and him.

"You can call Marilyn McRae now," Ganze said simply, relaying a number that Gillette jotted down. "She's really looking forward to talking to you. Also, I should have more on your father tomorrow, or maybe Monday."

"Thanks."

"We'll be speaking to you next week about the move north as well. Understood?"

"Yeah."

"Good, talk to you then."

Gillette stared straight ahead for a few moments after Ganze hung up, then looked down at the Los Angeles telephone number. It was shaking in his fingers.

"You okay, Chris?" Stiles asked.

"Fine," he answered, slipping the number into his wallet.

"Not even going to give me a clue about what's up? I mean, I didn't ask why we had to do all the CIA-wheelman driving this morning on the way to the airport, and I didn't ask who it was you went to see in Richmond. I figured all that was business. But this is personal, I can tell by the look on your face. What was that call about?"

"It was one of the guys I saw in Washington yesterday," Gillette answered, his voice raspy. "He called to give me my blood mother's telephone number. Like I told you he was going to."

"Oh." Stiles looked away.

Gillette could tell Stiles was disappointed that something tangible had come of the Washington trip. Stiles didn't trust these guys. "I'll tell you how the call goes after I talk to her."

"Thanks. I'd like that."

When Gillette reached his office, he pulled Marilyn McRae's telephone number from his wallet, put it on his desk, and stared. A lifetime he'd been waiting for this, he thought as he eased into his chair. A lifetime he'd thought it would never happen, and now here it was, thanks to Boyd and Ganze. Who were these guys?

"Christian."

Allison. She was leaning into the office. Debbie must have gone to the ladies' room and left the door unguarded. She usually didn't leave until seven, and it wasn't even six yet. "Hi."

"Can I come in?"

"Um, yeah." He slid a manila folder over Marilyn's number as Allison closed the door, then came in and sat in the chair in front of his desk. "What is it?"

"I wanted to let you know that Jack called me this afternoon, and he's very excited about working with you. To quote: He believes a Veramax-Everest partnership would be 'unstoppable.' "

"Jack's a salesman."

"Sure, but all you care about is that he's retaining counsel so he can start drafting documents for your investment. And he's almost finished writing that apology letter to Rothchild for keeping him out of the Racquet Club. He's doing what you told him to do. That's good, isn't it?"

Gillette couldn't stop thinking about how easily Mitchell had climbed on board the Everest train. How he hadn't negotiated at all. And how Veramax's bread-and-butter products—aspirin, nose drops, and cold medicine—were perfect nanotech delivery options. His mind was becoming cluttered with puzzle pieces he hoped wouldn't fit together. "Yeah, right."

"Don't get so excited."

"Do you think it's strange that he didn't negotiate with me at all?"

Allison shook her head. "Nope. I've known Jack a long time. He's a very gut-feel kind of guy. He liked you right away at dinner last night, I could tell. He must have liked your proposal, too."

"Mmm." Deals rarely went down like this.

"Jack talked to that friend of his again, too. The guy who owns the leasing company. He must have given you a great report because the guy wants to see you as soon as possible. I did some number crunching this afternoon while you were gone, and it's an even better fit with our company in Atlanta than I first thought."

Allison Wallace was a deal hound, and Gillette loved it. "Great. Talk to Debbie and set it up. It would be better if he could come here. But if not, I'll go back to Pittsburgh."

"Okay. By the way, where were you today?" she asked.

"Looking at a company."

Allison crossed her arms over her chest and leaned back into the chair. "Remember we talked about full disclosure the other night?"

"Sure."

"That explanation didn't sound like full disclosure. How about some more specifics? I *am* your partner."

Gillette picked up a pen and tapped it impatiently on the desk. "Look, I'm not going to tell you about every step I take during the day. I don't have time to keep you up to speed on every detail."

"Details, details," she repeated slowly. "You mean like

when you have your security guy check with people I know
to see if I'm a coke fiend?"

Gillette's eyes snapped to Allison's.

"The least you could have done was let me know what
was going on," she kept going. "You didn't like it when
People put you in that article without telling you. And that
was *good* pub."

"Yeah, I—"

"So I sniffed a little over my cheeseburger," she continued, her voice rising. "I told you, I have allergies."

"I know."

"But you didn't take my word for it."

"I'm sorry."

"What?" she said, putting a hand to her ear. "I don't
think I heard you."

"I'm sorry, *okay?*"

"That's it? That's all I get? An 'I'm sorry'?"

"What do you want?"

"I want to go out on the boat with you this weekend."

Gillette pursed his lips. "How did you hear about that?"

"I overheard Faraday on the phone talking about it." She
hesitated. "So, do I get to go?"

"First, I want to hear about those conditions you have."

"Conditions?"

"Yeah, what you'd need from me to join Everest full
time."

McGuire regained consciousness to a panoramic view of
the stars, the loud roar of engines, the smell of salt air mix-
ing with exhaust, and a throbbing pain at the back of his
neck. He tried to move his hands, but they were secured
tightly behind his back.

The engines droned on a bit longer, then he heard them
power down, then shut off completely.

McGuire heard voices as the fishing boat drifted silently through the water, waves lapping at its hull, then he saw shadowy figures standing above him.

"Who are you?" he asked. But they ignored him as they bound his ankles together tightly with wire. He didn't fight them; that would have been useless. His wrists were tied, and there were at least four of them. His best chance was to cooperate. "Talk to me, come on."

A moment later, two of the men hoisted him to his feet while another cut the rope binding his wrists.

"Now we're making some progress," he said to the one closest to him. "So, what's going on here?"

Suddenly two of the men grabbed his right arm and pinned it to a chopping block used for cutting bait. A third man snatched a meat cleaver off the fishing chair and slammed it down on McGuire's wrist.

McGuire screamed insanely, his body coursing with pain, his mind shuddering with anguish. He staggered backward as the two men who'd pinned his arm to the chopping block bent and picked up a huge anchor lying on the deck. Straining against the weight, they lugged it to the side of the boat. With a massive effort, they lifted it over the side and threw it in the ocean. It splashed loudly, disappearing into the black water, and a coil of rope began whipping after it over the side.

McGuire realized instantly that the other end of the rope was attached to his ankles, and he reached out with his left hand for the man standing next to him, but he was too late. The rope snapped tight around his ankles, sending him crashing to the deck, then yanking him over the side. He grabbed an aft cleat as he was going over, holding on with everything he had against the tremendous force pulling at his legs. One of the men moved to the cleat and with a grim look began peeling away the fingers of McGuire's left hand.

As he was about to go down, McGuire looked up into the face, expecting to see the man from the beach. But it wasn't him, it was someone else. Someone he recognized.

"You fucking—"

But that was all he got out before his hand wrenched free and he splashed into the water. He screamed as the anchor dragged him toward the depths, his voice muffled by the water. He thrashed, trying desperately to pull himself to the surface, but there was no chance; the weight was much too heavy. For a few moments, he could see the lights of the boat through the dark water, but then, as he passed fifty feet below the surface, everything faded.

Gillette sat on his patio, looking out over Central Park from high above. It was a beautiful early autumn evening. Crystal clear with a chill and the wisp of wood smoke wafting over Manhattan as people with fireplaces took advantage of the first wave of cool temperatures.

He reached for the cordless phone on the table and dialed Marilyn's number. He didn't need the piece of paper anymore. He'd looked at it so many times, he could have dialed the number backward.

"Hello."

"Marilyn?"

"Yes?" Her voice was already shaking.

"It's Christian Gillette."

"Oh, my God," she whispered.

And then he heard sobs as he'd never heard sobs before.

Paul pointed a finger into Wright's cheek on the darkened street in front of his apartment building. "That better not ever happen again, you understand?"

"Yes, sir."

"I told you, goddamn it. I have to know where Gillette is at all times."

"Yes, sir."

"All times!"

"Yes, sir." This was way out of control, Wright thought. Maybe he ought to go down to the local precinct and turn himself in. In the long run, he'd probably be safer.

CHAPTER 11

"Do you mind if I smoke?" Russell Hughes asked, reaching for a pack of Marlboros in his jacket pocket.

Gillette and Wright were sitting in Hughes's office, going through the Apex portfolio company by company with him, asking the tough questions. Gillette wanted to squeeze as much information out of Hughes as possible before he sank a billion dollars into another private equity firm. There was always the chance Hughes would slip up and give away something about Apex that would make Gillette back off the deal.

The truth was, Gillette hated cigarette and cigar smoke, though he liked the smell of a pipe—his father had smoked a pipe. But Hughes was under a huge amount of stress, so he allowed the man his vice. "It's all right."

Wright's cell phone went off suddenly, ejecting a loud, shrill whistle throughout the room.

"Jesus, David," Gillette snapped, "turn that damn thing off."

Wright already had it out of his pocket and was staring at the number. "I've gotta take this," he muttered, getting up and hurrying from the room.

Gillette watched him go, irritated. Wright still had a thing or two to learn.

"Can we talk, just the two of us?" Hughes asked when Wright was gone. Hughes's eyes were rimmed with fatigue.

"I'm sure David's a bright young man, but I'd rather report to you. We're closer in age, and I feel like I—"

"Russell," Gillette said gently, "save it. David's going to be running Apex. Full stop. Got it?"

Hughes nodded.

"I know this is difficult for you, but that's the way it's going to be."

"Okay," Hughes agreed quietly.

Gillette picked up the next company file off the stack—marked "XT Pharmaceuticals"—and began browsing through it. "This is one of your better investments," he said, not waiting for Wright to come back in. He had a lunch at one, it was already past eleven, and they still had twelve companies to go through. "It's a solid company, growing, with good cash flow."

"It's a *very* solid company," Hughes agreed. "So solid even the damn government's interested in it."

Gillette stopped scanning. "What do you mean?"

"There were some guys up from D.C. a while ago who wanted to use it as a cutout for a new technology they were trying to hide. Typical DOD clandestine ops kind of crap, but I called my contact at the CIA, and he said to stay away from them. I'm glad I did, too. They wanted me to sign some bullshit confidentiality agreement that could have put me in San Quentin doing hard time for the rest of my life if I'd sneezed the wrong way."

Gillette stared at Hughes for a few moments, then looked down, trying not to give away his shock. "What's 'a while ago'?"

"Few weeks."

"Did they tell you what kind of technology it was?"

"They made it seem like the biggest thing since electricity, but they didn't get into any specifics. It's probably all just hype, but like I said, I called my guy at the CIA and that was that. So I'm not sure if it was real or not."

"How do you have a CIA contact?"

Hughes fidgeted uncomfortably. "Look, I'm not supposed to tell anyone about this. It's classified."

"You want to keep your job?" Gillette asked. He didn't like to be this way, but he needed the information. Now.

Hughes nodded.

"Then tell me."

"Look, you can't say *anything* about this."

At that moment, Wright opened the door and stepped back into the office.

"David," Gillette said, "leave us alone for a few minutes."

"What?"

"I'll let you know when you can come back in."

"Chris, I—"

"*David!*"

Wright stalked out, shutting the door hard.

Gillette turned back around to face Hughes. "Tell me about your CIA contact, Russell."

Hughes took a measured breath. "Are you familiar with cutouts?"

"Yes."

"Well, that's why I have a CIA contact. One of our portfolio companies is a cutout."

"Which one?"

"The last one on the list." Hughes pointed at a piece of paper that had the names of every Apex portfolio company on it. "The information technology company."

"Omega IT?" Gillette asked.

"Yeah. Omega does IT consulting for financial institutions all over the world, including the Middle East. While the Omega people are installing and updating computer systems, they add a few extra options the customers don't know about. Options that let people in Washington watch money come and go."

"To track terrorist money," Gillette spoke up. "Probably al-Qaeda in particular."

"You got it."

"But why would Middle Eastern banks let a U.S. company do their IT work? That doesn't make any sense."

"They don't know it's a U.S. company. With the CIA's help, we've set up an elaborate corporate structure that winds its way through dummy relationships in Belgium and France and hides the ultimate ownership very effectively."

"I want to talk to your CIA contact," Gillette said tersely.

"If you're going to buy Apex, you'll *have* to talk to him. About Omega. In fact, he'll demand to talk to *you*. I'll set that meeting up right before we close the deal, when we're certain everything's a go."

What Gillette wanted to talk to Hughes's CIA contact about had nothing to do with Omega IT. "I don't want to wait that long. Set it up as soon as possible."

"What happened back there, Chris?" Wright demanded. They were heading back to Everest in the limousine. "Why did you make me stay out of the room for the rest of the meeting?"

"Russell and I got into some sensitive issues about a few of the Apex employees. Severance. Stuff like that."

"Shouldn't I be in on those discussions if I'm going to run Apex?" Wright asked, his voice rising.

"Calm down, David, there's no reason to get upset."

"I'm not getting upset, I'm just trying to understand. Am I still going to run Apex?"

Gillette said nothing as he scrolled through e-mails on his Blackberry. At this point, he needed to have direct contact with Hughes, and he didn't want Wright trying to find out why.

"Chris?"

Still nothing.

"Chris?"

"Russell is going to report to me for a while, until we've had a chance to understand exactly what we have at Apex."

"What the hell happened? I thought I was the man."

"I made a decision, David. I'll let you know when you're going to take over. It'll probably be a few weeks. For now, concentrate on Hush-Hush."

"Yeah," he muttered, "I'll concentrate all right."

"Chris."

Gillette looked up from his computer at Debbie. "Yes?"

"I know this sounds crazy, but there's a woman in the lobby who says she's your mother."

After talking for two hours last night, Gillette and Marilyn McRae had ended their conversation with a promise to get together next week. He'd told her he'd come to Los Angeles after finishing his business in Las Vegas and they'd have dinner. So it couldn't be her. Gillette stepped out from behind his desk and started to follow Debbie to the lobby. Then it hit him. Lana.

"Hey, Pop." Christian rose from the lumpy living room couch and moved toward his frail grandfather. Pop was shuffling in from the kitchen, pulling his blue oxygen tank behind him like a long-in-the-tooth hound dog on a leash. A lifetime in the coal mines of western Pennsylvania and thirty years of Camel no-filters had left him without much in the way of lungs.

"Let me help you," Christian offered, holding out his arm and guiding the old man to the couch. "How you feeling today?" They sat beside each other, Christian's palm resting atop his grandfather's gnarled fingers.

"I'm fine," the old man answered wearily, his voice like sandpaper on plywood. "I'm glad you came."

"Of course, Pop."

"I don't know how much time I have."

Mary Desmond bustled in from the kitchen carrying a tray of sandwiches and drinks. "Oh, you'll probably outlive me *and* Christian," she said, setting the tray on the coffee table in front of the couch and giving Christian a warm smile. "Pop thinks every day's his last," she blustered in a loud voice that belied her tiny frame. Mary was in her late fifties and lived next door. She often helped around the house with chores the old man couldn't handle anymore. "But it's probably good you came when you did," she admitted, her voice drifting lower as she sat in the chair next to the couch.

Christian was on his way back to the West Coast after graduating from Princeton, planning to put five thousand miles on his Ducati as he zigzagged from New Jersey to California, seeing the great expanse between the country's mountain chains. He knew the big cities on both coasts pretty well, thanks to traveling with his father, but he didn't know much about the small towns in between. So he was spending the summer on his bike until the highways and September finally forced him back to the real world. His first stop was this little house on Elmore Lane.

His father had told him it was important to do so quickly. Now he could see why.

"What are your plans?" Pop asked, taking a glass of iced tea off the tray and easing back on the couch with a low moan. "What will you do with yourself now?"

"I'm going to Stanford in the fall to get my MBA. Then I'll go to Wall Street, be an investment banker."

"Just like your daddy."

"Yeah, hopefully at Goldman Sachs."

"Why *'hopefully'*?"

"Goldman's the best investment bank in the world, so it's tough to get a job there. Everybody wants to work for them."

Pop took a labored breath. "I don't know much about Wall Street, but I know your father can get you a job anywhere you want." The old man shook his head proudly. "He's a good boy, your father. He loves you very much."

Christian felt a lump rising in his throat, the same way it had two weeks ago when his father had hugged him after graduation. Under a beautiful azure sky with the smells of freshly cut grass and blooming lilac filling his nostrils and that diploma clutched in his hand. "I know he does," he murmured.

"How's that mother of yours?" Pop spoke up, contempt surfacing in his voice.

Christian wondered if Pop knew, if that was the reason for the icy tone. Probably not. It wouldn't be like his father to share a piece of information like that with anyone—even Pop. "She's fine."

"Never did like her," the old man grumbled.

"*Now*, Pop," Mary piped up, "Lana's nice."

"She never calls or writes."

"She used to try," Mary argued, "but you wouldn't say more than two words to her."

"Didn't have anything to say."

Christian caught his grandfather's sidelong glance as the phone in the kitchen began to ring.

Mary was out of her chair quickly. "Don't forget, Christian," she said over her shoulder, "you promised to call bingo down at the lodge tonight." She laughed. "You'll drive all the old biddies crazy."

Christian smiled. He was looking forward to it. He and Pop were heading down there together. Team Gillette. Mary disappeared around the corner, and he heard her answer the phone. "Well, Pop, what are we going to do today?" he asked, settling back on the couch. "How about we wet a line in that pond down the lane? See if we can fool some bass?"

"Well, maybe in a—"

"Christian," Mary interrupted. She was standing in the kitchen doorway, a troubled expression creasing her small face. "Nikki is calling from California."

Christian moved quickly to the kitchen and took the old black receiver from Mary, who returned to the living room. "Hello."

"Chris, it's me."

Something was terribly wrong; he could tell by her tone. "What is it?"

"It's *Daddy*," she whispered. "It's Daddy."

A blast of blue flame seared Christian's chest. "What about him?" He turned toward the corner so Pop and Mary couldn't hear. But somehow he already knew.

"His plane went down a few minutes ago. On takeoff from Orange County." Nikki could barely get the words out. "He's gone."

Christian's forehead slowly came to rest against the wall. *Gone.* An awful word. He felt tears welling in his eyes, and he shut them tightly and ground his teeth together, trying to stem the tide. But the tears cascaded down his cheeks anyway, over his lip and into his mouth. They were warm and sweet, and the taste only invited more. "Oh, God," he whispered.

"I gotta go," Nikki said suddenly. "Come home, Chris. Come home."

He hung up the receiver and brought his hands to his face. The phone rang again, almost right away, and he picked it up, wondering what Nikki had forgotten to say. "Hello?"

"Christian."

It was Lana.

"I know you just talked to Nikki."

Lana's voice was so calm, Christian thought. But that was how she handled everything, good or bad. "Yes, I did."

"Then you know."

"Yes." He bit his lower lip. The last person in the world he wanted to show weakness to was Lana. "Are you okay?" he asked quietly.

"I'll be all right." Lana hesitated. "Christian, listen. You and I . . . we're not . . ." She took a breath. "Christian, things are going to be very hard for us around here, and I'm not sure . . . I don't think you should be here."

Christian pressed the phone to his ear, uncertain he'd heard her right. Certain no one could be that cold. "*What?* I don't think I—"

"Listen," she said, now with full force, "I need to be alone with my children."

He heard it plain and clear this time: *my* children. Troy and Nikki. Not you.

"I know what your father always wanted," she kept going, "but you and I don't belong to each other." She paused. "Good-bye, Christian."

Lana was sitting on one of the plush couches near the receptionist's desk. The last time he'd seen her was at his father's funeral sixteen years ago. They hadn't spoken there or since.

Lana had been a striking woman in her youth, statuesque with long brunette hair. But she had a tough look about her, too, manifested by an intense, almost cruel flavor to her eyes, the way her jaw jutted out, the ramrod-stiff posture.

The first thing Gillette noticed about her was how the years had worn down that toughness. Her eyes seemed sad, the corners of her mouth were puffy, and she slumped slightly. Deep creases coursed out from the corners of her eyes into the loose skin of her cheeks, and her hands seemed old, as if they belonged to a woman in her late seventies, not her late fifties.

"Hello, Christian," she said as he moved into the lobby.

Gillette was aware that Debbie and both receptionists were watching carefully. They knew he had no relationship with his family. That had been well documented in the articles in both *The Wall Street Journal* and *People*. "Let's go to my office," he suggested.

"This is so nice, Christian," Lana said, looking around the large space as they sat on one of the couches in a corner of his office. "I love the artwork and the antiques. I can see why you make people go through that search." She'd been searched at the lobby door by a QS agent, just like everyone else who came to Everest.

"Everyone has to do that before they come in."

"I see. Well, I've been keeping up with you in the press, and friends of mine tell me what they hear about you, too. You're so successful. I knew you would be. Your father would have been so proud."

"It's been a long time, Lana," he said quietly.

"Too long." A tear trickled down her cheek, and she reached into her purse for a tissue. "I'm sorry," she said, sniffling. "For everything. I was just so . . . hurt. No excuse, I know. What I did to you was awful, so I want to thank you for seeing me." She gestured toward the door. "That's why I showed up out there without calling ahead. I figured if I tried to make an appointment, you'd ignore me. I wouldn't have blamed you, either."

"How have you been?"

"Fine."

"What about Troy and Nikki?" Troy was a half-sibling as well, a good-for-nothing older brother. "They okay?"

"Okay. We're all surviving."

"Are you still living in the Bel Air house?"

"Trying to."

"What does that mean?"

Lana dabbed her eyes with the tissue, then let out a tiny sob. "It's just hard."

"Why?"

"It's expensive, and, well . . . Oh, Christian. Nikki isn't okay." Lana sobbed again. "She has cancer. Lung cancer."

Lung cancer. The words twisted Gillette's stomach. He and Nikki had been so close right up to the day of their father's death. He'd called to borrow a few dollars to get back to the West Coast after Lana cut him off, but for some reason she'd never answered or returned his messages. He hadn't let himself think about her in a long time. But it still hurt deeply to hear this. "I'm sorry."

"What makes it even worse is that she doesn't have any health insurance. She can't pay for the treatment she needs."

"What happened?"

"That idiot she married. Peter. He kept telling her he had it, but he didn't."

Gillette hadn't been invited to Nikki's wedding. He'd heard about it from friends. "Are you going to help her?"

Lana shrugged. "What can I do? I don't have much money left."

"Dad was worth a *hundred million dollars* when he died."

"Taxes took more than half, he gave a lot to charity, and then there was your mother. Several other women, too. I only ended up with about ten million. You'd be surprised how fast that goes."

"*Several other women?*" Gillette asked.

"You weren't the only child he had out of wedlock, just the only one I agreed to take in."

He could tell this was still hard for her. Any shred of

toughness she'd had about her when she'd come in was gone. "How many other children were there?"

The tears were flowing freely now. "One each with three other women."

Gillette's head suddenly ached. Secrets, always secrets. "Jesus."

Lana cleared her throat, trying to regain control. "Yes, your father had a problem." She shook her head quickly several times. "But I'm not here to rehash all that, I'm here to ask you to help your sister. She needs money, Christian."

"Have her call me."

"She won't, she's too proud."

"Then give me her number. I'll call her."

Lana hesitated, then reached into her pocketbook and removed a small black address book.

Gillette handed her a pen and one of his cards. "Write it on the back."

She scribbled the number, then handed the card and pen back to him. "I need money, too," she said firmly.

"Ten million is a lot, Lana. It isn't a hundred, but it's a lot. And you got the house, too. That's probably worth another ten. I don't believe you really need money. You can't."

"Well, I do."

She had always been a survivor. Whatever it took. She wasn't his real mother, but some of that had rubbed off on him. Maybe he owed her something. "I gotta give you credit, Lana. You cut me off completely the day Dad is killed, you don't speak to me for sixteen years, and you walk in here today with your hands out, looking for donations. One thing I'm sure we can agree on, you aren't proud."

"I don't have anywhere else to go," she said matter-of-factly, "and I did agree to take you in all those years ago. There is that."

"You're incredible."

"Will you help me?"

Gillette said nothing for a few moments. "I'll think about it. I'll be on the West Coast next week, we'll get together then. I'll call you."

She nodded slowly. "Okay," she whispered.

She seemed so much older, he realized. "Now I have a question for you. Who's my real mother?"

Lana looked him straight in the eyes. "I don't know."

She was always such a good liar, he remembered.

Faraday sat in Gillette's office, staring at the phone. It was almost five o'clock. "What's your bet?" he asked.

"She won't call," Gillette answered.

"I think she will. Chatham's too poor. She'll take what she can get."

"She's got too much pride."

"I thought you said she was smart."

"I did."

"So she'll do the right thing."

"Let's hope so."

Faraday dug a huge spoonful of rocky road ice cream out of a bowl in his lap. "How's Faith? She must be pissed about those pictures of you and Allison in the newspapers. She looked like she was going to kill someone when she stalked out of here the other night. I tried to say good-bye to her, but she blew past me without a word."

Gillette smiled, glad his girlfriend was once more a topic he was happy to discuss. "She's over it."

"Oh? So you finally spoke to her?"

"Yeah." Gillette jotted down a note to himself to call Russell Hughes to see if he'd arranged the CIA meeting.

"Is Faith coming out on the boat tomorrow?" Faraday asked.

"No. She's in London doing some promo stuff for the next album. It's coming out soon."

"Who else is coming?"

"You, Stiles, Wright, and me," Gillette answered.

"You still inviting David even after the way he acted at the Apex meeting?"

"He's just young, Nigel."

"Uh-huh." Faraday hesitated. "You want me to bring my significant other?"

"Sure. Who is it?"

"You've never met her. Are you going to be stag since Faith is in London?" Faraday asked, his mouth full of ice cream.

Gillette didn't answer.

Faraday stopped eating. "Oh no."

Gillette glanced up. "What?"

"You're bringing Allison."

"What are you talking about?"

"I can tell."

"You can't tell anything. And, if I asked her to come, it would be just as a colleague."

The intercom buzzed. It was Debbie. "Chris, Becky Rouse is on the line."

Faraday smiled triumphantly from behind the bowl.

"Thanks." Gillette picked up. "Hello."

"Mr. Gillette, this is Becky Rouse from Chatham."

"Yes."

"I'm calling to tell you what you can do with your offer."

Gillette felt his cheeks flush. Becky was one feisty character. "And what's that?"

"I'm a lady, so I can't say what I'm thinking. You'll just have to use your imagination. Good-bye, Mr. Gillette."

Gillette hung up the phone calmly after a loud click at the other end.

"So?" Faraday asked.

"We're going to war in Maryland."

Faraday groaned. "What a waste of time."

"For everyone," Gillette agreed.

David Wright stuck his head in the door. "Sorry to interrupt. Could I talk to you, Chris?" He glanced at Faraday. "Alone."

Faraday downed another spoonful of ice cream, then rose. "See you tomorrow, Christian. I'm going home. It's been a long week."

Wright stepped aside to let Faraday pass, then closed the door.

"What is it, David?"

Wright hesitated, looking sheepish. "I came in to apologize. I'm sorry for the way I acted in the limousine, it was stupid."

Good, Gillette thought. The right thing for him to do. "I appreciate that, David." He'd be sure to tell Faraday about this. "You still coming tomorrow?"

"You sure you still want me?"

"We can't go without you. It's a celebration cruise for your promotion."

CHAPTER 12

From the West Side pier, the *Everest* cruised down the Hudson, around the southern tip of Manhattan, then north up the East River. This course took it under the Brooklyn, Manhattan, Williamsburg, and Fifty-ninth Street bridges—massive suspension structures that were even more impressive from below than from street level. By noon, they'd made it to the Long Island Sound and were headed east beneath a hot Indian summer sun. At one o'clock, the temperature reached ninety-five degrees and the humidity was thick.

Stiles stood beside Gillette on the bridge, watching the captain navigate. "Tell me about this thing, Chris," he said over the hum of the two diesel engines.

"It's a hundred feet long," Gillette answered, glancing starboard toward Long Island. They were a mile offshore. "It's twenty-three feet at the beam, has two inboard engines with two thousand horses each, carries five thousand gallons of fuel, and has four staterooms. We've got a crew of three, including the captain, the cook, and a mate, and sailing on it is one of my favorite things in the world to do. It's a lot of money, Quentin, but it's worth it to me. I love it out here."

"You entertain a lot on it, too. That probably pays dividends."

"It does. Last Fourth of July, I took a hundred people

into New York Harbor for the fireworks, big investors we were lining up for Everest Eight. Let them bring their wives, husbands, kids. It was a great time, and most of the people who came committed to the new fund. Maybe they would have committed anyway, but I still hear about how much fun they had."

Allison appeared on the bridge in a red bikini. "Here you go," she said, handing Gillette a big cup of soda. "Having fun, Quentin?"

"Absolutely."

"You like the boat?" she asked.

"It's incredible. Chris was just telling me about it."

"Yeah, it's cute." She winked at Gillette before turning and walking back out.

"Cute?" Stiles asked. "What's that supposed to mean?"

"The Wallace boat sails out of South Beach," Gillette explained. "It's *two* hundred feet long. That's a real boat to her. This is cute."

"Oh." Stiles gestured toward the door she'd gone through. "She's beautiful."

"Yeah."

"Makes that piece of sewing thread she's wearing look awfully good." Stiles cleared his throat. "Tempting, you know?"

"Uh-huh."

Stiles hesitated. "Is something happening between you two?"

Gillette looked off toward Long Island again. They were getting farther and farther away from land. "No."

"I don't mean to pry."

Gillette ran a hand through his hair. "Yes, you do." He hesitated. "Look, I'm attracted to her, Quentin, I'll admit that. Who wouldn't be, for Christ's sake? But I won't let anything happen. It's business between the two of us. That's it."

They were silent for a few moments.

"We talked about how lonely it gets at the top sometimes," Stiles finally said.

"Yeah, *and*?"

"And you've got to be careful who you get close to, especially when a lot of people are depending on you. And watching closely. Especially when there's a lot of money at stake."

"I told you, I'll *never* let that happen."

"Might be tough to resist at some point." Stiles chuckled. "It's funny how different people look in bathing suits, isn't it?" he asked, his voice growing stronger as he switched subjects. "For example"—he laughed loudly—"on the other end of the how-do-you-look-in-a-bathing-suit spectrum is Nigel Faraday, who should thank the Lord for big baggy business suits. He's white as paste, with a belly Mr. Claus would be proud of."

Gillette laughed, too. "It's the gallon a day of ice cream."

"*A gallon*? Really?"

"Just about." Gillette watched a large sailboat off the port side. There was a decent wind, and the skipper had his spinnaker up, a blue-and-gold sail that puffed out majestically off the bow. "That's beautiful, isn't it?"

"I don't like blow-boats," Stiles said. "They're too slow, and they're lots of work."

"That's how our ancestors got around."

"Yours, maybe, not mine. Mine were smart. They paddled." He motioned for Gillette to move to the back of the bridge with him. "I've got some things I want to go over with you," he said when they were out of earshot of the captain.

"What's up?"

"The first thing's kind of a shocker. This morning one of my guys found some very powerful GPS trackers on both Everest planes. They were tiny, but he found them. They were put on recently, judging by the screws used to attach them. No rust or wear."

Gillette cursed under his breath. Norman Boyd. He should have anticipated this. "It was probably the guys in Washington."

Stiles shrugged. "I don't know. You won't tell me much about them, and I'm not going to ask again. Even though, as your head of security, especially now that we found those things, I think you should come clean with me." He waited for Gillette to say something. "Anyway," he kept going when there wasn't any response, "we removed the devices."

"No," Gillette spoke up quickly. "Put them back on. Right away."

"*Why?*"

"Just do it."

"Okay, okay, but—" Stiles stopped short. "Oh, I get it."

"Any idea when those things were put on?"

"No, impossible to tell."

"But it was recently," Gillette pushed. "That's what you said."

"It could have been a couple of weeks ago, it could have been this morning. I'm not sure."

Gillette's mind was racing, trying to think of other ways Boyd might be watching. "What else you got?"

"We ran a background check on that guy at the hospital ground-breaking ceremony, the one who handed you the shovel. He's definitely a member of the Carbone family."

Gillette took a sip of soda. "Well, we got our answer about the Mafia in Vegas, didn't we? Did you talk to any of those consulting firms out there? The ones that can help us with our issue?"

"Almost a dozen of them, and I've narrowed it down to two. Like you wanted. After we're finished here, I'll send you an e-mail from my Blackberry with the names and numbers of the people I talked to."

"Thanks." Gillette had instructed Debbie to get Stiles a Blackberry earlier in the week. "Like I told you, we're going out there next week. We'll meet with them then. Anything else?"

"Yeah, I've been doing some more checking on the Carbones. First of all, this guy Joe Celino, the boss of the family, makes John Gotti look like a puppy dog. Celino's ruthless as hell. His nickname's 'Twenty-two,' after his weapon of choice. His list of suspected victims is long, but he's never been prosecuted. Anyway, from what I've learned, Celino gets into things for the long term. So you won't just be doing business with him during the construction phase of the stadium and the casino. He'll want a piece of the action on the team, maybe concessions, and the casino, part of the take. He's not going away."

"I was afraid of that."

"Listen," Stiles said, leaning over so he was talking right into Gillette's ear, "I'm getting close to something that involves the Carbones. I'm working with some people in Philadelphia on this. People from the old days, before I started QS. It's something we might be able to use against Celino so he can't get into your businesses. We could release it anonymously once we've got it tied up, and it would probably block him from doing anything in Vegas."

"Fantastic. What is it?"

"I don't want to talk about it now," Stiles said, glancing at the captain.

"Come on, Quentin."

"No, we'll talk about it when we're back on dry land. I should have all the information by then." Gillette started to say something but Stiles held up his hand. "One more thing, Chris."

"What?"

"I checked with a few more people about Allison Wallace. Still no indication she's ever done drugs."

"Thanks. You can call off the dogs." Gillette didn't want Allison hearing from anyone else that they were still checking on her. "By the way," he called as Stiles headed toward the stairs leading belowdecks.

"Yeah?"

"Your girlfriend's nice. I like her son, too." Stiles's girlfriend had brought her six-year-old son, Danny, on the boat. "I'm glad he came."

Stiles grinned appreciatively. "Danny's having a blast, Chris. He's never been on a boat before. Thanks for letting him come along."

"Of course. Hey, if you see Wright, could you ask him to come see me up here?"

"Yup."

Gillette moved to where the captain stood and tapped him on the shoulder. "Billy, I need to use your cell phone."

It was lying on the shelf in front of the wheel. Billy reached up and snatched it. "Here you go."

"Thanks."

"Yours out of juice?"

"Yeah." It wasn't, but Gillette wasn't going through the whole thing for Billy. He dialed Cathy Dylan's number at her apartment in Manhattan.

"Hello."

"Cathy, it's Christian."

"Hi."

"I need a favor." The GPS devices on the planes were worrying him.

"Of course."

"I need you to call our friend in Richmond. I need you to thank him for meeting with me."

"Is that all?"

"Call me after you talk to him, and call me on this number. It's—"

"Already got it," she interrupted. "It's on my caller ID."

"Okay." Gillette wanted to make certain Scott Davis was all right, that Boyd hadn't done something crazy. He took a deep breath. He was putting people in danger, and it was wearing on him. "Thanks."

"Sure."

As Gillette hung up, Wright walked onto the bridge.

"You wanted to see me, Chris?"

"Yeah. Figured we'd do an update before people started having too much fun. What's up with Hush-Hush?"

"I'm already starting due diligence. I'm using Cathy Dylan to help me. That okay?"

Cathy Dylan was busy these days. "Fine."

"She should have a request-for-information list ready to go over to the Hush-Hush people by COB Monday. My buddy Hobbs is going to head up the team on their side. It should go pretty smoothly. Hobbs says Maddox couldn't be happier. He's already looking at real estate in the Caribbean."

"Good. Just so you know, I'm going to Las Vegas on Tuesday afternoon to see about some things related to the casino. After we meet with that insurance company you've got us set up with. I'll be out west for a few days. I'm going to the coast after I finish in Vegas. We'll talk every morning while I'm out there, just like we do now."

"Okay."

"There's one more deal I want to bring you in on. It's a company called Veramax. Are you familiar with it?"

"No."

"It's a privately held drug company based outside Chicago. Allison's introduced me to the owner out in Pittsburgh. That's why I was there. The company's growing fast and has some great new products coming out soon. Allison's family has known the family who owns Veramax for a long time. We're going to be able to get it pretty cheap because they've got some issues with the FDA I can help them with."

"Nice."

"But I want your take on it. Do some digging and tell me what you think about it when I get back from Vegas."

"I'll get right on it."

"Good. By the way, don't let Allison know I told you about this."

"Okay."

Gillette patted Wright's shoulder. "Well, that's it. Go back out and have some fun. It's nice seeing your bride again."

"Thanks." Wright turned to go, then paused. "Chris?"

"Yeah?"

"Is there something going on with you and Allison?"

My God, Gillette thought, don't these people have anything else to worry about? "Of course not."

"It's just that—"

Billy's cell phone rang before Wright could finish.

"Christian," Billy called, "it's for you."

"Excuse me, David," Gillette said, taking the phone. "Hello?"

"Christian, it's Cathy."

"Yes," he said, watching Wright head off.

"I spoke to Dr. Davis. Thanked him for meeting with you like you asked."

A wave of relief washed over Gillette. "Thanks."

Joseph "22" Celino sat on the patio of his modest Staten Island home, enjoying the hazy view of lower Manhattan in the distance. It was across New York Harbor, which was dotted by pleasure craft and the two orange ferries about to pass each other. He glanced to the left at the Statue of

Liberty, thinking about his Brooklyn childhood, about how the United States really was the land of opportunity—if you were willing to take risks. His father had tried to bring up nine children without taking any risks, in and out of work as a welder in the shipyards, but he'd gotten further and further behind every year, racking up huge debts, finally committing suicide when Celino was nine. As far as Celino was concerned, his father was a coward and had gotten what he deserved. No risk, no reward.

Celino had dropped out of high school to work as a bag boy in a grocery store for a buck seventy-five an hour, trying to help pay the family bills. But he'd quickly grown frustrated with the meager paycheck and agreed to make his first hit when a friend of a friend introduced him to a Mafia capo. The target was the owner of a Queens liquor store who refused to pay protection, and Celino had shot him with his twenty-two pistol as the guy was locking up one hot summer night. Celino found killing easy, sticking around a few minutes after the store owner crumpled to the ground to watch him vainly fight death, fascinated by the struggle. Celino was paid three hundred dollars later that night and never went back to the grocery store. By the time he was nineteen, Celino had murdered twenty-eight people.

Despite his small size—five six and a hundred forty pounds—he developed a reputation as one of the meanest, coldest men in New York. Never making a hit with a partner—not even another made man—so there were no witnesses. And always with his twenty-two. Now he was don of one of the most powerful Mafia families in the country—the Carbones. A name that struck fear in the heart of every other mobster and lawman in the country.

"How's Christian Gillette doing?" Celino asked, picking up a cheese-and-salami cracker from a platter in the middle of the table.

"He's going to Vegas next week." Al Scarpa was Celino's only direct report. Scarpa took care of all the details so Celino rarely had to leave the house. He was even smaller than Celino, and he carried a forty-four.

"Is he going to play?"

"I think so," Scarpa said, picking at something under one of his fingernails. "Quentin Stiles talked to our consulting friend out there yesterday. Gillette's going to meet with him next week. And one other," Scarpa added.

"He better pick the right one."

"He will."

"Has Stiles completely recovered?" Celino asked, chewing on the cracker.

"About ninety percent."

"Even at ninety percent he's dangerous. We've known that for a long time. The Philadelphia people warned us about him."

Scarpa nodded. "I agree, but don't worry about it, boss. I got everything taken care of."

Celino's eyes narrowed. There was no reason to ask any more questions when Scarpa said he had something taken care of. Scarpa had been his underboss for eight years, and Celino trusted the man completely. As much as a Mob boss could trust anyone. "Are we keeping up with things as agreed?"

"Yes."

"You have our top people on this, right? I can't have anything going wrong here, you understand? It's critical that we hold up our end of the bargain. Critical to many of our operations, to the advantage we have over our friends."

"I know, boss, believe me." Scarpa moved his chair to the right a few inches, to stay beneath the shade of the umbrella. "You know, I've always admired how you keep things so low-key, Joseph."

"What do you mean?"

"You're worth so much money, but your house . . . well . . . I don't want to insult you. I mean, it's a very nice house. But you could afford so much more. I know you do this so you don't bring attention to the family, but it must be frustrating sometimes when you see the Wall Street guys spreading money around on houses like it's manure."

Celino waved. "Doesn't bother me at all. They work hard, just like I do. Whatever a man wants to do with his money is his business, as long as it doesn't affect me." He gazed out over the harbor again. "Now, how is Allison Wallace fitting in at Everest?"

Scarpa smiled. "Very well, boss. Very well."

Gillette and Peggy Wright stood alone on the aft deck of the *Everest,* sipping drinks—Peggy her third martini, Gillette another Pepsi. They were thirty miles offshore, out of sight of land. Gillette liked seeing nothing but water. It made him feel as though he were truly unreachable, safe from the stress of business, if only temporarily.

"Thank you for promoting David." Peggy was a petite brunette with a pretty smile. "He was so happy."

"He deserved it."

"He works hard."

"Yes, he does," Gillette agreed. "And I depend on him."

Peggy looked around, making sure David wasn't anywhere in sight. "My husband thinks you walk on water, Christian. He's always saying, 'Well, Christian would look at it this way,' or, 'Christian would do it that way.' He's always thinking about Everest. Always thinking about how he can find deals or raise more money."

"That's why I promoted him. I know how dedicated he is." Gillette swirled the ice cubes in his cup. "Where are you from, Peggy?"

She'd been looking out to sea, watching a flock of seagulls diving at something dead on the surface. "Columbus, Ohio. Why?"

"We're involved in a deal on the Eastern Shore of Maryland, and David said he had relatives there. I was pretty sure his family was from Connecticut, so I thought maybe he meant the connection to Maryland was on your side."

Peggy shook her head slowly, a perplexed expression crossing her face. "I don't have any relatives in Maryland, and David's never mentioned anyone on his side who lives there." She swallowed hard when she saw the intense expression on Gillette's face. "Did I say something wrong?"

Gillette shook his head calmly. "You know what? It's my mistake. I was thinking of someone else. Sorry."

Billy hurried into the yacht's large dining room and leaned down close to Gillette so the others at the table couldn't hear him. "We have a problem," he said quietly. "Come with me."

Gillette excused himself and followed Billy into the next room. "What's wrong?"

"There's a line of thunderstorms coming straight at us that's really bad. It's a freak thing. They popped up out of nowhere with all this heat and humidity."

"Jesus." Gillette moved through a sliding door onto a side deck and glanced up into the black sky. There'd been stars out an hour ago; now they were gone. "How long until we get hit?"

"About forty minutes."

"We can't make it to a harbor?"

"No way, not enough time."

"How the hell can a storm this bad form so fast?" Gillette asked.

"It doesn't happen very often, but when it does, it can be deadly. You remember what happened in Baltimore a couple of years ago? Freak storm hit the harbor, *right down-*

town. Bunch of people drowned in a ferry." He checked the sky nervously. "Look, the Coast Guard's on the radio telling everybody who can't make port to batten down hatches and point their crafts due east, into the storm. They're saying we could get fifteen-foot seas, maybe higher, with sustained winds up to forty miles an hour and gusts up to a hundred. It ain't gonna last long, but it's gonna be hell while it's on us."

Gillette looked up and down the deck. He could feel the yacht beginning to pitch. "What do you want me to do?"

"Tell your guests things are gonna get real rough. Get them to put on life jackets right away."

"Where should we go? Does it matter?"

"Yeah, go to the enclosed aft quarters. I hate to say this, but I don't want you below if this thing turns over."

"Turns over?"

"I don't know how stable we'll be if we have fifteen-foot waves. I want people to be able to get clear of the boat quick if I give the order. They'll be better off in the water with a life jacket on if the thing isn't gonna last long. I know how that sounds, but I been doing this a long time, and I want to be ready."

"Do you really think it's going to be that—"

Billy held up his hands and shook his head. "I don't know, Christian, but the CG's making it sound *really* bad." He glanced over his shoulder. "I gotta get back to the bridge."

"All right, I'll get everyone ready," Gillette called, and headed back into the dining room.

People looked at him expectantly as he came back in, anticipating a problem because the boat had started to roll noticeably. "We've got a situation, folks," he said, standing behind his chair at the table. "Mother Nature's decided to throw a fireball at us. There's a nasty line of thunderstorms heading right for us, and we need to get ready. We need to put life jackets on." He pointed at the young boy asleep on a couch, a puppy curled up in his arms. "Especially Danny."

The *Everest* was being pounded by the storm. Wave crests reached twenty feet, gusts hit a hundred and ten miles an hour, and the rain and spray flew so fiercely that visibility was reduced to almost nothing. The yacht rose and fell violently as Billy fought to keep the bow pointed straight into the storm. The passengers, wrapped in bright orange life jackets, clung to anything they could as the boat plowed ahead and the engines roared belowdecks.

A massive surge of water rose off the starboard side of the bow, lifting the yacht high and then rolling it left. As the boat rolled, a wooden chair careened into the sliding glass door at the back of the room, smashing through it. At the same time, Wright, Peggy, Stiles, his girlfriend, Danny, and the puppy he was holding were tossed across the floor at the others, who were huddled against the opposite wall. As he tumbled, Danny lost his grip on the dog.

Wind and rain whipped into the room, and the terrified puppy yelped and tumbled through the smashed door onto the deck. Danny scrambled to his feet and raced after it, disappearing around the corner. His mother screamed and pointed, and Stiles was on his feet instantly, sprinting after the little boy, shielding his face against the driving rain, struggling to keep his balance.

"Quentin!" Gillette yelled, jumping to his feet just as another huge wave crashed into the boat. This time it was on the port side, and it tossed him and the others across the room. He landed heavily on the floor, then crashed into the far wall, and a searing shot of pain raced up his left arm through his shoulder. As he struggled to make it to his hands and knees, another shot of pain knifed through his left shoulder. Wincing, he glanced ahead as a wicked flash of lightning streaked the night sky. Stiles, Danny, and the dog were nowhere in sight.

"Oh God, oh God!" Stiles's girlfriend screamed. She'd seen the same thing.

Gillette crawled quickly across the wet carpet toward the smashed door, wind and driving rain in his face. He was trying to catch any sign of Stiles or Danny as the lightning continued to flash almost unceasingly. He pulled himself to his feet when he felt broken glass beneath his palms and edged toward the door, trying to keep his balance against the constant rocking, the din from outside like the sound of a freight train bearing down on him.

"What are you doing?" yelled Faraday. "You can't go out there."

Gillette burst onto the open aft deck, then dropped quickly to his hands and knees again. Staying on his feet would be impossible. He crawled around the side, the way Danny and Stiles had gone, as the yacht pitched left and knocked him toward the deck wall. He tried to protect his left arm, holding it tight to his side with his other arm as he crashed into the wall. Again he made it back onto his hands and knees. In the crackle of a lightning flash, he spotted Stiles up ahead and started to crawl forward.

The boat was rocked by another pounding swell. Gillette lunged for the bottom step of a stairway leading to an upper deck and clung to it desperately despite the pain in his arm and shoulder. When the wave had washed past, he looked up, still clinging to the stairs, his eyes stinging from the salt. Stiles was grasping the railing with one hand, Danny with the other. A burst of spray hit Gillette, and he ducked behind the stairs again. When he looked up, Stiles was heading toward him with Danny, half crawling, half sliding down the deck.

Just as Stiles reached Gillette, the boat pitched violently to starboard, then up. Gillette grabbed Danny as Stiles slid into the stairs, then past and down the deck thirty feet. As Danny wrapped both arms tightly around Gillette's neck, Gillette looked back, searching through the blinding spray for Stiles. For a moment, he saw the outline of Stiles's figure—he'd caught a rope and was struggling to his feet, grasping for the side of the boat.

Then, just as he was raising up, Gillette saw him go down again, falling forward and losing his grasp on the side. He crumpled to the deck as another wave crashed over the side, this the biggest one yet, and Gillette had to hold on to the stairs with one arm and Danny with the other, trying mightily to keep from being swept to the back of the yacht. For almost ten seconds, the water rushed past. When it finally eased, Gillette glanced back. Stiles was gone.

For ten minutes, Gillette held on to the bottom stair with one arm and Danny with the other, clenching his teeth against the pain slicing through his left shoulder as wave after wave continued to pound the *Everest*. The young boy shrieked every time the boat rolled, grabbing Gillette around the neck as tight as he could, screaming directly into his ear when another monster crashed over the side. Every time lightning flashed, Gillette glanced back over his shoulder, hoping he'd see Stiles through the storm. But nothing.

Finally, the storm began to subside. The wind and rain eased as quickly as they'd hit. As Gillette started to crawl back toward the aft deck, Faraday and Wright appeared around the corner, hunched over as they moved onto the deck.

"Christian!" Faraday yelled. He and Wright got to Gillette quickly and helped him back inside.

"Danny!" his mother cried, hurrying to Gillette and scooping Danny out of his arms. "Thank you so much," she sobbed, kissing Danny's face over and over. "Thank you, Christian."

"I'm sorry for all this," Gillette said softly. He turned to Faraday as Allison trotted up to him and put her arms around him. "Any sign of Quentin?"

Faraday shook his head. "No."

Gillette wheeled around and headed back out onto the deck, shaking off Allison and moving around the corner. He made his way farther aft, to the spot where Stiles had gone down, yelling Stiles's name over and over and peering into the waves, hoping to spot an orange life vest. Then he headed across the deck to the other side of the boat, then ahead all the way to the bow. But there was no sign of Stiles.

He scrambled up a stairway toward the bridge and burst through the door. "Billy!"

Billy glanced over his shoulder, then back ahead, both hands still glued to the wheel. "Everyone all right back there?"

"No."

Billy's eyes shot to Gillette's.

"Stiles is gone."

"*What?*"

Gillette quickly explained how he and Stiles had ended up on the deck. "I followed Stiles out and we got the kid, but then he washed past me. I saw him behind me on the starboard-side deck for a second, then he went down. It was weird, he just went down. Then a wave came over the side, and I lost sight of him."

"How 'bout the kid?"

"I got him. He's fine."

Billy's shoulders sagged. "Good. Look, Stiles is probably—"

"No," Gillette cut in, anticipating what Billy was going to say. "I've been all around the side decks. He's gone. We've got to turn around and look for him. We've got to call the Coast Guard right away."

"You check below?"

"No," Gillette admitted.

"I'll turn around, but I'm not calling the Coast Guard until we're sure he's not on board. They got their share of emergencies tonight, and I want to make sure we really got one before we call them out here."

But ten minutes later, Gillette was back on the bridge. "He's not on board."

Billy picked up the radio microphone and called the Coast Guard, relaying the information about Stiles and giving them coordinates from the GPS.

Gillette could hear the response over the loudspeaker. They had a cutter in the area, and they'd put a chopper in the air with a huge floodlight to cover the spot Billy had given them.

"You said he went down when a wave came over?" Billy asked when he hung up with the Coast Guard.

Gillette heard Billy's voice, but he was thinking about how Quentin had gone down. One second he was standing, the next he was going down. Limp, not even putting out his hands to cushion the impact. Not as if he'd fallen at all—as if he'd been shot.

CHAPTER 13

Derrick Walker sat in Gillette's office. One of the most senior QS agents, Walker was taking over Gillette's personal protection. It had been two days since the *Everest* had been caught in the storm on the sound, and Stiles was still missing.

Like Stiles, Walker was African American. His skin was darker than Stiles's, but while he wasn't as tall at six two, he weighed two hundred and fifty pounds, ten pounds more than Stiles weighed when he was healthy. Like Stiles, he had that same aura of control about him. As if things came to him, not the other way around. Gillette took a deep breath. It was almost impossible to believe that Walker was sitting in front of him—not Stiles.

"There won't be any drop in the quality of your protection," Walker began, "I assure you of that." He spoke in a low, tough monotone. "Everything will transition smoothly."

"I'm sure," Gillette said quietly.

"I'm up to speed on everything," Walker continued, "including those GPS devices that were put on your planes. And the fact that you *don't* want them removed."

"Good."

Walker hesitated. "I know Quentin was a friend of yours, a good friend."

"He was." Gillette winced as he shifted. His left arm was still hurting.

"I'm going to be candid. You and I won't have the same kind of relationship. I don't get close to my clients."

Gillette looked away, hiding a sad smile. Stiles had said the same thing when they'd first met. "I understand."

"Do you have any questions?" Walker asked.

Gillette thought for a moment. "Do you own any of QS Security?"

"Excuse me?"

He could see Walker thought it was a strange question. Walker had probably been expecting something more standard, like a rundown of his experience. But Gillette already assumed Walker's experience was excellent. Stiles would never hire anyone who didn't have that kind of background. Gillette was more interested in motivation at this point. "Did Quentin make you an owner? Did he give you any shares of QS?"

"No."

So there was nothing to keep Walker from going to another firm or, more important, being tempted by a huge bribe.

"Why do you ask?" Walker asked.

"Just curious."

"Chris." Debbie broke in on the intercom.

"Yes."

"We've got a problem in the lobby."

"What is it?"

"*Just get out here,*" she urged.

Gillette rose from his chair. "Come on, Derrick."

They hustled to the lobby, and as they neared reception, Gillette saw two QS agents standing in the wide double-doorway entrance, blocking someone's progress. He could hear yelling from outside the doors and recognized the voice instantly. Allison Wallace.

"What's going on?" Gillette asked, pushing his way through the agents.

"These guys won't let my new assistant through," she answered angrily, pointing at the agents.

The young man standing beside her was tall and thin, with wavy, jet black hair, brown eyes, and a dark, pocked complexion. As far as Gillette could tell, he was Arab. "I'm Christian Gillette," he said, extending his hand.

"Hamid Mohamed." The young man's expression—a slight sneer—didn't change.

"He doesn't have clearance," explained one of the agents.

"What's that mean?" Allison demanded.

"Every new employee has to have a background check before he or she can work here," Walker said, stepping beside Gillette.

"You didn't have one done on me," she argued, looking at Gillette.

"We didn't need to." Gillette spied Faraday, who'd come out to see what the ruckus was about. "You know that." He gestured at Faraday. "Get everybody in the conference room for the managers meeting, Nigel."

"Right." Faraday hesitated a moment longer, then turned and headed back down the corridor.

"How long does this background check take?" Allison asked.

"Up to two weeks," Walker replied.

"Christ, look, I—"

"Allison, these guys are just following orders," Gillette interrupted. "*My orders.* I'm sure Hamid will check out fine, but until he does we go by the rules. Like we do with everyone else." He turned to Mohamed. "Please don't take offense, Hamid, it's just procedure." He pointed at Allison. "She didn't know."

Mohamed glanced deliberately at Allison, then back at Gillette. "This is ridiculous. You're doing this because I'm Iranian. This is nothing but racial profiling."

"Frankly," Gillette answered, "I had no idea you were Iranian."

"You could tell I was Arab."

Gillette moved close to Mohamed. "Listen, pal, I don't like your attitude. But as long as your background check comes up clear, if Allison wants you, you could be a Klingon for all I care." He glared at her. "Let's go, it's three o'clock, we're going to be late for the meeting." As he passed Walker, he touched his arm. "Get this guy's info and get it processed fast," he instructed. "I want his background check done by COB tomorrow."

"Yes, sir."

"Christian." Allison was running to keep up as Gillette hurried toward the conference room. *"Christian!"*

"What?"

"This is ridiculous, there's no problem with Hamid. He's been working at Citibank for the last three years. He has great references. I've talked to them."

"Then I'm sure he'll check out fine, but he still goes through what everyone else does."

"This is silly. If I say he's okay, he's okay. I'm a managing partner here, and I've invested five billion dollars."

Gillette whipped around, glaring at her. "As you constantly remind me. But you still don't get special treatment, Allison."

"All right," she said quietly, her expression softening. "I'm sorry."

"Look," he said, his tone turning less confrontational, too, "I told Walker to get Hamid's background check done by COB tomorrow. As long as everything clears, he'll be in here first thing Wednesday morning."

She nodded. "Thanks." As he turned away, she called to him.

"Yeah?"

"You okay?"

He looked at her for a few moments. "Come on," he said quietly, "we're late."

Gillette strode into the conference room, Allison trailing him. Everyone else was already seated. "Last week," he began, standing behind his chair at the head of the table and putting both hands on the back of it as the room went from noisy to silent in a heartbeat, "I told all of you that the Wallace Family had committed five billion dollars to Everest Eight, and that a member of their family, Allison Wallace, would join us as a managing partner." He gestured to his right. "For any of you who haven't met her yet, this is Allison. Please welcome her."

She got the customary applause, the rapping of knuckles on the tabletop.

"Thank you." She'd already introduced herself to all the managing partners, but to only a couple of the managing directors.

"You'll sit by Debbie today," Gillette said to Allison, "but next week you'll sit to Tom's left." He pointed at Jim Richards, a managing director, who was sitting beside O'Brien. "Everyone will move down one. And on this side," he continued, shifting his attention to the other side of the table, "David Wright will now sit next to Maggie. David's been promoted to managing partner," he announced, pulling out his chair and easing into it. Seat changes at the meeting weren't allowed until Gillette had formally announced promotions to the group. In Wright's case, the announcement and the seat changes made clear that he'd jumped over several other managing directors who'd been at Everest longer.

"I'm surprised Wright wasn't the first one in here today and didn't plop himself down in that chair beside Maggie," Faraday whispered to Gillette as people rapped their knuckles on the tabletop again—not nearly as loudly as they had for Allison. "Actually, I'm surprised he didn't send out his own e-mail announcing his promotion."

Gillette would have smiled, but his mind was elsewhere. "All right, let's go through updates. I—"

"Mr. Gillette."

Gillette turned toward the door. It was Karen, one of the receptionists. "Yes?"

"I'm sorry to interrupt, but can I see you a moment? It's important."

"Take over," Gillette muttered to Faraday, getting up. "Update them on the fact that we finalized the purchase of the Vegas franchise. Then have Wright talk about Hush-Hush and have Allison talk about Veramax." He'd told Faraday about the dinner with Jack Mitchell. "Don't mention your connection to the French company on Hush-Hush, though. I don't want people knowing about that yet. Don't say anything about Apex, either."

Faraday nodded.

"Yes, Karen," Gillette said as he reached the door, Faraday's voice piping up in the background.

"Mr. Walker needs to see you in your office right away."

Gillette headed quickly down the corridor. "What is it, Derrick?" he asked as he came through the doorway.

Walker was just putting down the phone. "That was the Coast Guard. They've called off the search."

"You all right?"

It was four-thirty, and Gillette was sitting alone in a corner booth of the Irish bar on the first floor of the Everest building. It was a bar Faraday frequented but Gillette had never been to. He was leaning forward, elbows resting on the table, hands over his eyes. At the sound of the familiar voice, he dropped his hands slowly to his mouth and opened his eyes. Faraday was sliding onto the bench seat opposite him.

It was dark and almost empty in here, just a couple of early birds at the bar and two QS agents in the next booth, drinking water. "Been better," Gillette muttered.

A waiter appeared at the table. "Hello, Nigel."

"Hi, Mickey."

"Long time since I've seen you down here this early."

"Things change."

"What'll it be?"

"Guinness."

"Not a Scotch?"

"Guinness," Faraday repeated.

"Tall or small?"

"Small."

"You got it."

Faraday glanced at the full shot glass in front of Gillette on the scratched, wooden tabletop. "Scotch?"

"Yeah."

"Been a while, hasn't it?"

Gillette nodded.

"I know this thing with Stiles is really bothering you. I know how close you two were. I'm sorry. But should you—"

"I should do what gets me through."

"Okay."

They sat in silence until the waiter returned with Faraday's beer. Faraday picked up the mug, touched it to the shot glass in front of Gillette, and took a long guzzle. "What did you need to talk to me about?" he asked, wiping his mouth with the back of his hand. "That you needed Debbie to get me out of the meeting for."

"Stiles."

Faraday took another gulp of Guinness. "Well, I . . . I mean I'm honored that you want to confide in me, Christian. I know you miss him; he was a good man."

"He was shot, Nigel."

Faraday had been looking toward the bar. His head snapped left at this. *"What?"*

In his mind, Gillette replayed the image of Stiles falling to the deck so many times. Replayed the way Stiles hadn't held out his hands to break his fall, just went down like a board. Because he was already dead when he was falling. Already shot. It had come to him after Derrick Walker had told him the search had been called off. It was almost a perfect murder, Gillette thought. The gale-force winds had drowned out the report of the gun, and visibility was so terrible that he hadn't seen blood fly from the wound or spilled on the deck afterward because the torrential rains had washed it away immediately. Whoever killed him had shot him, then tossed him overboard, assuming his body would never be found. "He was shot on board, after he saved the kid. I'm sure of it."

Faraday's face contorted into a look of disbelief. "By who?"

"I don't know."

"Why would someone shoot him?"

"Revenge." Gillette's fingers closed around the shot glass. He slowly turned it a full revolution but didn't pick it up. "I'm pretty sure Tom McGuire was behind it."

"No shit."

Gillette relayed the story of the gang attack outside the Grill and how he believed McGuire was still out for him and Stiles. "You must have really seen him that day on Park Ave."

Faraday nodded glumly. "So you think maybe he got to one of the yacht's crew."

"Yeah. Probably paid them, like Stiles and I think he paid the Brooklyn gang."

"Jesus."

"Here's the point, Nigel. If all that's true, I'm in danger, even with the QS guys around." Gillette started to pick up the shot glass but didn't. "So I've got to let you in on a few things, in case all of a sudden I'm not around."

Faraday straightened up in his seat. "Okay."

"First, we need to talk about the NFL franchise."

"What about it?"

"I think the Mafia's trying to get involved."

"How?"

"Construction initially, of both the stadium and the casino. They'll extort us to keep people on the job and the equipment running. Then they'll try to get involved with the casino and the team. The NFL doesn't think so, but Stiles did some checking and I do. I'm meeting with some consultants when I go out there this week. People who'll run interference on that, but I think it's still going to be a problem. I'll keep you informed."

"Should we just get the fuck out of it?" Faraday asked. "Tell the NFL we don't want it?"

"No. It's going to be a huge win for us, even if the Mob is involved. We just have to figure out how to handle them."

"Okay."

Gillette could see Faraday's fear. He'd never come close to dealing with the Mafia. "The second thing I want to talk to you about is Apex," he said, slowly turning the shot glass another revolution. "As you know, I've been through the Apex portfolio with Russell Hughes, and I think we have a real opportunity."

"Right."

"What you need to understand is that one of their portfolio companies is a cutout for the CIA."

"What's a fucking cutout?"

Gillette quickly explained the concept.

"Which company is it?" Faraday asked.

"Omega IT. They do computer hardware and software system installation and integration. One of Omega's foreign subsidiaries has lots of clients that are Middle Eastern banks. According to Hughes, the Omega sub installs things in the computers that the banks don't know about so people in Washington can watch money flows."

"They're trying to catch fucking terrorists."

"Exactly. Anyway, I'm supposed to meet with Hughes's CIA contact, probably when I get back from the West Coast at the end of this week. If something happens to me, you do it. Call Hughes and tell him what you know."

"Nothing's going to happen to you, Christian."

"I hope not, but we can't be too careful at this point."

Faraday shook his head. "You deal with a lot of fucking shit, don't you."

This time Gillette almost picked up the shot glass, but again he resisted the temptation. He was testing himself, he knew. "I'd say you don't know the half of it, but now you do."

Faraday finished his beer. "Now there's something *I* want to talk to *you* about."

Gillette looked up. "What?"

"Allison."

"What about her?"

"I don't like her," Faraday said bluntly.

"You gotta be kidding me."

"Nope. I don't trust—"

"You guys want anything else?" Mickey asked, sauntering up to the table.

"I'll take another beer," Faraday said.

"What's your problem with Allison?" Gillette asked angrily when Mickey was gone.

Faraday shrugged. "Like I said, I don't trust her. It's hard to explain. Maybe it's the way she's tried to move in so fast."

"What do you mean?"

"Pushing Veramax so hard, for instance."

"It's a great deal."

"She had it teed up before she came here so you'd think she was good."

"So what?" Gillette snapped. "That's just good business. She wanted an early win. First impressions are important anywhere. She knows that, she's smart. *And,*" he continued, holding up one hand, "she's already got *another* deal going."

"Well, look who her fucking family is, for Christ's sake. It's easy for her, almost like she's cheating."

Sour grapes, Gillette thought. A normal human reaction, but he hadn't expected it from Faraday. "And we want to take advantage of that. It isn't like we're playing T-ball here and everyone gets a chance to bat. This is the big leagues."

"And I don't like the way she's tried to move on you," Faraday added. "It makes me want to puke."

"What do you mean?"

"Saturday on the boat she was all over you. And I wasn't the only one who noticed, let me tell you."

"Nothing's happened. Nothing will."

"People are talking," Faraday said. "They're worried that you and she are getting too close too fast, and that she's going to start having more and more influence on you. Maybe even helping to call the shots pretty soon. People don't like that."

"What 'people'?"

"The other managing partners."

Gillette was about to answer, but Mickey showed up carrying Faraday's beer. When he was gone, Gillette said, "She's not going to start calling the shots."

"She's twenty-five percent of the new fund. *Five billion dollars*. That's a big advantage over everyone else here. You might get addicted to the money, and the bikini," Faraday muttered.

"I deserve more credit than that, Nigel," Gillette shot back. "I've—"

"And I don't like this thing with the Iranian guy," Faraday interrupted. "Call me prejudiced, but I don't think it makes sense to bring him in here."

"Careful."

"It's a feeling, Christian. I don't like—"

"Hi, guys."

Gillette and Faraday looked up at Allison.

She slid onto the bench seat beside Gillette. "I'm surprised, Christian," she said, "leaving the managers meeting to come to a bar. Either you've got all the newspapers in this city snowed, or there's something big going on." She put her hand on his arm. "Or you miss your friend," she said quietly. "Sorry."

"I'm going back upstairs," Faraday said, giving Allison a forced smile. "I'll take care of that stuff we talked about, Christian."

"Call me *Chris*, Nigel."

Nigel already had one foot out of the booth. He stopped. "That was one of the bravest things I've ever seen anyone do, Chris. You and Stiles going out into that storm after that little boy. I wanted you to know that. I just wish both of you had come back." He nodded at Gillette, then gave Allison another quick smile. "See you upstairs."

When Faraday was gone, Allison picked up the shot glass in front of Gillette and sniffed. "Oh, God," she said, almost gagging.

"What can I get you, ma'am?" Mickey was back again.

"Chardonnay. Your best by the glass." She put her hand on Gillette's thigh when Mickey was gone. "I'm sorry, I know it's—"

"Tell me about Hamid," Gillette interrupted, moving his leg. He didn't want any more pity. "What's his background?"

Her eyes stayed on him a moment, then she shrugged. "He worked in Citibank's mergers and acquisitions department for the last three years. Before that he went to business school at the University of Michigan. I don't remember where he was before that. Why the interrogation?"

"How did you find him?"

"Friend of a friend."

"What friend?"

"A friend from Chicago. Look, I don't have to answer—"

"How did you know I was down here?"

"Debbie told me."

So she and Debbie really were talking. "What friend in Chicago?"

She rolled her eyes. "A guy I used to date, if you really must know. He works at Harris Fulmer. It's an investment bank."

Gillette felt a strange pang. "I know Harris." It felt like jealousy.

Mickey returned with Allison's glass of wine and set it down.

"How did this friend of yours know Hamid?" Gillette asked.

Allison was about to pick up her glass. "What's your problem? Is this really racial profiling? Was Hamid right?"

Gillette was thinking about the al-Qaeda conduit who, according to Norman Boyd, had approached one of the people on the DARPA nanotech project. And he was thinking about how uncomfortable Faraday was with Hamid. "No."

She took a sip of wine. "What's in Richmond?" she asked out of nowhere.

Gillette glanced up. "Huh?"

"Why did you go to Richmond the other day?"

"How do you know I went to Richmond?" he demanded.

"I told you," she answered calmly. "I'm Allison Wallace. Now, what were you doing there?"

"Research on a company. Like *I* told *you*."

She sighed and took a sip of wine. "I have an idea."

"What?"

"You should sell Everest's medical products company to me."

Gillette's eyes zipped to hers.

"What's it called?" she asked.

"You mean Beezer Johnson?" It was the company with the division in Minneapolis that Boyd wanted to hide his nanotech project in.

"That's it."

Gillette turned on the bench seat so he was facing her. "Why do you think we should sell Beezer Johnson?"

"It's a great company, and it's about time you had another win."

"What are you talking about? We've had several big wins lately. Like we talked about when you, Gordon, and I met."

"Actually, it's been a few months since you've sold anything. We need some good press."

"We're about to announce our intent to sell Laurel Energy. That'll create a fantastic buzz."

"But it'll be a while until you actually sell it. Probably six months before all the documents are completed. We want to keep the positive momentum going." She took a swallow of wine. "Here's the deal. My family has an investment in a medical products company, too. I can convince the board of that firm to make a very nice offer for Beezer Johnson. Very nice. And the whole thing can be wrapped up in sixty days."

Gillette grimaced, thinking hard about what Faraday had said—that he didn't trust her. How she knew he'd been to Richmond and how there were suddenly GPS trackers on his planes. How it suddenly seemed so coincidental that she'd want to buy Beezer Johnson just as Norman Boyd wanted to use it as a cutout.

She smiled back at him. "So, what do you think?"

"It would look like an inside job," he countered. Maybe Allison wasn't protégée material after all. Maybe she was an enemy. "The market wouldn't give us credit because your family controls the buying company."

"But technically we don't control it. We made that investment through a number of different entities. No one would ever be able to figure it out. I'll prove it to you." Her smile grew broader. "*Now* what do you think?"

"I don't know."

She cocked her head to one side and leaned close to him. "Well, I'll tell you what I think," she said, her voice dropping to a whisper. "I think you and I make a great team."

It was late, ten-thirty, and everyone else had left for the night. Gillette slipped into Cathy Dylan's cramped office and shut the door. "Hi."

She looked up from a spreadsheet she'd been working on. "Hi."

"Thanks for staying." He'd slipped her a note that afternoon.

"Sure. What do you need me to do?"

"I need you to call our doctor friend in Richmond again, and I need you to make me an appointment for Friday. Whatever time he can do it."

"Okay."

"I'll be in Las Vegas and on the West Coast most of this week, so e-mail me when you and Dr. Davis talk."

"Okay."

"But don't mention his name. I want you to call him Mr.

Jones in the e-mail, and I want you to use another day, some day in the following week. The only thing that will be accurate in the e-mail will be the time. Don't tell anyone we've spoken about this. Just like before. Got it?"

"Yes," she said hesitantly.

Gillette could see it was all she could do not to ask.

Maybe someday I'll tell her, he thought. But right now, the less she knew, the safer she was. There were enough people in danger. One was already gone.

She sat on the floor of Gillette's living room, between his legs, as he sat behind her on the sofa and rubbed her shoulders. It was late—they were watching Letterman sign off—but Gillette didn't want to go to bed yet. He was tired, but he knew he'd never get to sleep. Too much on his mind.

"That feels so good, Chris." Faith moaned and ran her hands up to his, then turned and rose to her knees so she was facing him. "I've missed you so much. I'm glad we've got tonight, at least."

Faith had gotten back from London a few hours ago, and Gillette was leaving for Las Vegas tomorrow. Then he was going on to the West Coast to meet Marilyn.

She gave him a deep kiss. "Let's go to bed," she whispered, taking his chin in her fingers and shaking it gently when he didn't answer. "Hey, boy, I just propositioned you."

He smiled. All she had on was one of his dress shirts. She looked so sexy.

She hugged him. "I'm so sorry about Quentin, honey. I know you loved him."

"Yeah."

"How did it happen?" she asked. "You told me he went overboard, but how?"

"He was trying to get to his girlfriend's little boy. The kid went after his dog when the thing ran out onto the deck in the storm."

"That's awful." Faith moved onto the couch beside him and ran her fingers through his hair. "Who else went with you on the cruise?"

Gillette took a deep breath. "Faraday and his new girl-friend, David and Peggy Wright."

"That's all?"

Gillette gazed at her. He didn't want to get into it now, but he couldn't lie to her, either. "Well, I—"

"You took Allison Wallace," she said before he could finish, her posture going rigid. "Didn't you?"

"Look, I—"

"*Did you?*"

"It wasn't like *I took* her, sweetheart. She's a partner at the firm. It was a firm outing."

Faith stood up. "It wasn't like you *took her* to dinner the other night here in New York, either, was it?" she asked. "She just came along, right? Why would you let her go with you on a cruise like that when you knew I was upset about those pictures?"

There was no winning this battle. The best thing to do was surrender immediately. "I wasn't thinking, Faith, I'm sorry."

"Did you ask your other partners? Tom, Maggie, or Blair?"

"No," he admitted.

"Did you sleep with her in Pittsburgh, Chris?"

"Of course not."

"How do I know?"

"Because I'm telling you."

Faith stared at him for a few moments, hands on her hips. Finally, she shook her head and groaned. "I love you so much, but I can't take this. We're away from each other more than we're together anyway, so I can't be thinking you're with someone else when I'm gone." With that she stalked out.

He started to get up, then fell back on the couch and put his hands over his eyes. Nothing was going right.

CHAPTER 14

Gillette sat up groggily in the comfortable leather chair and tossed the crossword puzzle lying on his lap to the floor. They'd taken the bigger of the two Everest jets—a Gulfstream IV—to Las Vegas. "How long till we land, Derrick?" he asked, stretching. He'd slept very little since Saturday.

"We're close," Walker answered, "only about fifteen minutes out."

"Any word?" At Gillette's suggestion, the police had begun interviewing the crew about Stiles's disappearance. The cops had talked to Billy yesterday but let him go, satisfied that he knew nothing.

"Yeah, they questioned the cook this afternoon. Gave him the same bare-bulb treatment they gave Billy. They're convinced he doesn't know anything either."

"Have they found the mate yet?"

"Nope."

Walker brought the piece of gum he was chewing forward and smacked it with his front teeth for a few seconds. Something he did when he was thinking hard, Gillette had noticed.

"He's our man," Walker said. "I can feel it. But Billy doesn't know anything about him. Never even got his home address, so it's going to be tough to find him. Maybe impossible."

It was Tuesday afternoon, and Gillette hadn't heard from Daniel Ganze about his father—Ganze had said it would be early this week at the latest when he'd have more information. He spotted Wright walking toward him from the back of the plane. "Have a seat." He pointed at the big leather chair on the other side of the plane. He'd decided to bring Wright along this morning, wanting to have a second while he interviewed the consultants who were going to deal with the Carbones.

Allison hadn't been happy about not coming along, but he didn't care. He needed a break from her. Needed to clear his head and think about what Faraday had said in the bar. Needed to think about her suggestion to buy Beezer right as Boyd had made contact. How Veramax's products would make excellent nanotech delivery systems. Nothing specific here, but a lot of coincidences.

"I meant to tell you," he said to Wright, "Nigel and I talked last night, and now that you're a managing partner, we're going to give you five percent of the ups on Everest Eight, with all the normal caveats, of course."

"Jesus, thanks."

"If we only double the fund over the next few years, we keep over four billion of the profits and you get more than two hundred large of that."

"That's awesome." Wright looked out the window at the barren desert below them. "I was excited about our meeting this morning." He and Gillette had met with the Bermuda-based insurance company before heading to La-Guardia. At the end of the meeting, the firm's lead partner had committed half a billion to Everest Eight, so the fund was now $20.5 billion. "And I'm working on another lead my father gave me. Could be another five hundred large."

Wright's drive never faltered. "We've got to close this fund at some point."

"Let's try to make it an even twenty-one billion," Wright urged.

"How long will it take you to smoke these people out, to see if they're real?"

"Give me a week."

"Who are they?"

"The Ohio Teachers Pension. My dad's good friends with the woman who runs it. From college or something, I'm not sure. Anyway, they're usually very conservative, but Dad says we've got a good shot at getting money from them, especially now that the Wallaces are in for five billion."

It was the whale factor, Gillette knew. Once other investors heard that a family like the Wallaces were in big, *everyone* wanted in. "All right, go for it."

"I will. So what's going on with the investigation?" Wright asked, nodding at Walker. On the way to the airport, Gillette had told Wright what he thought had really happened to Stiles.

"We think it's the mate."

"You still think Tom McGuire is behind it? That he's the one pulling the strings?"

"Yeah," Gillette said as one of the QS agents tapped him on the shoulder. The agent was holding the plane's phone.

"For you, sir."

"Thanks. . . . Hello?"

"Christian?"

"Yes."

"This is Percy Lundergard in Chatham, Maryland."

"Hi." Lundergard was a local attorney Gillette had hired to help Everest through the referendum process, to help fight Becky Rouse. Lundergard's family had been in Chatham for two hundred years, but unlike Percy, most of them were farmers and fishermen and fell into the have-not category.

Gillette had made sure of that before retaining Lundergard. "What's up?"

"I've been through all the town charter documents thoroughly, and you're right. We can call a referendum on this thing, and there's nothing Mayor Rouse can do about it." Lundergard spoke with a nasal twang. "But I have a suggestion."

"What?"

"Before you call for the vote, let's have a town meeting. Let's rile some people up. You've got the majority, Christian, but it's like any vote. You've got to get the population out there to win. Gotta get 'em interested. All the rich people will show, so you've got to get a lot of the poor folk out, too. My family can help. I've already spoken to them, but they think a town meeting at the high school would really do the trick."

"Fine. Let's do it."

"You'll need to be there."

"Oh, I'll be there. Don't you worry."

"You'll need to get up and make a speech, and you'll need to connect with them."

Gillette could hear it in Lundergard's voice: He didn't believe a big-shot Manhattanite had a chance in hell of connecting with a Chatham farmer or fisherman. Suddenly Gillette had a challenge on his hands. "I hear you, Percy. I'll see you there."

Gillette and Wright sat in Carmine Torino's spacious office overlooking the Vegas strip. Torino Consulting was furnished with big, gaudy pieces, and the colors were deafening—drapes bright red and the shag carpet a burnt yellow. Torino had thinning straight black hair and wore a flowered golf shirt—unbuttoned so you could see a gold medallion hanging in the dark chest hairs below his neck—and a sleeveless blue sweater. He wore a thick gold bracelet on his left wrist that jingled constantly and a Rolex on his right wrist with a face the size of a silver dollar.

"I love this view," he said, gesturing toward the wide window. The sun had just set, and the strip's neon lights were taking over. "It's the prettiest time of day. I can't imagine living anywhere else."

Gillette and Wright exchanged a subtle roll of the eyes.

"So, you guys got an NFL franchise."

Gillette nodded. He hated how slippery this whole thing felt, but it was a necessary evil. Tomorrow morning they'd meet with Federico Consulting, but Stiles had let him know that Torino was the best. If that was true, Gillette could only imagine what it would be like to sit down with Mick Federico.

"And you want to build a stadium and a casino, the stadium in eighteen months."

"Actually, I want *both* of them built in eighteen months. I want them both done at the same time. It'll be good from a marketing perspective."

"You're gonna use a local contractor, right?"

"No, I'm bringing in a group from Los Angeles that can handle both jobs."

Torino winced. "The local people won't be happy."

"That's why we're here," Wright said. "We understand the game."

Torino looked at Wright disdainfully. "It's no game, sonny, let me tell you."

"Can you take care of it?" Gillette asked.

Torino clasped his hands together, leaned back in his chair, and gazed up at the ceiling for a few moments. "I think so."

"How much?"

Torino smiled. "You're a bottom-line guy, huh? No bull-shit? Well, it'll be two million a year until the shit is built, then five million a year after that."

Gillette raised both eyebrows. "Exactly what do I get for my five million a year?"

"A guarantee that you'll have no worker walkouts, because even if you bring in an outside contractor, you'll have to hire local people to be the ants. Another guarantee that your equipment won't break down more than normal. And if it does, you'll be able to get spare parts quickly, not a year later." Torino could see he wasn't impressing anybody. "What the fuck do you want, some leather-bound presentation? I thought you were a bottom-line guy."

"I am."

"Why does the fee go up when the construction is *finished*?" Wright wanted to know.

Torino chuckled. "And I thought you guys were supposed to be these stiletto-sharp types. Sophisticated and—"

"It goes up," Gillette interrupted, "to give us assurances that the construction will actually get done on time. That we won't be held up for a ball-buster payment with a month to go before the first preseason game, and we end up having to play the whole year at UNLV. And if we miss a year, there'll be problems with the plumbing, electrical outages, bomb scares. Right, Carmine?"

Torino smiled smugly. "Exactly." His bracelet jingled as he pointed at Wright. "See, sonny, that's why he's the boss."

"Here's what I'll do," Gillette offered. "I'll pay you a million a year during construction and three million per thereafter."

Torino shook his head. "This isn't negotiable, Mr. Gillette. It is what it is. You want it, you call me by eight forty-five tomorrow morning. If I don't hear from you by then, the offer's off the table."

Something clicked, and Gillette realized Torino knew their meeting with Federico started at nine.

Torino clapped his hands together enthusiastically, as

though he knew the deal were done. "I'm going to a couple of strip clubs and see some of my favorite girls. You guys wanna come?"

"No," Gillette answered quickly, standing. "But we'll be in touch. Thanks for your time."

Five minutes later, Gillette and Wright were standing in front of the building with two QS agents, waiting for the car to pull up. "So, David," Gillette asked, "how do you feel?"

"Like I want to take a shower."

Wright was lying on the bed of his Caesar's Palace hotel room when the doorbell rang.

"Room service."

Wright sprang out of bed. He was famished. "Beautiful," he muttered. He was wearing just boxers but didn't bother putting on his pants. "You guys are fast," he said, opening the door. "I thought it would be at least another—" He stopped in midsentence. There were two men in dark suits at the door—and no food.

"We need to talk to you," said one of the men, ushering Wright back into the room before he could close the door. The other man followed and locked the door.

Wright's eyes flickered between the two of them. "What about?"

"Put some clothes on," the man ordered.

"Where are we going?" Wright asked anxiously, reaching for his pants.

"Don't worry about it."

Thirty minutes later, the two men led Wright into the living room of a suite on the top floor of the Hard Rock Hotel.

"Have a seat." One of the men pointed at a couch. "Mr. Celino will be with you in a moment."

Wright swallowed hard. He knew the name. Gillette had

explained the reason for the Vegas trip—the fact that the Carbone family was probably who Carmine Torino was fronting for, that Joe Celino was don of the Carbone family, that Celino was one of the most ruthless crime bosses in Mafia history.

When Celino ambled in and sat in a chair opposite the couch, Wright rose, head tilted forward, doing his best to put on an appearance of subordination.

"Sit down."

Wright did.

"I'm Joe Celino, and I obviously know who you are." He motioned for the two men who'd brought Wright to move off. "You've met with one of my men in New York several times, the first time in Saks Fifth Avenue last week."

"Yes." Wright's voice was instantly hoarse. "Paul."

"I trust he's been polite to you."

"Yes."

"Congratulations on the NFL franchise; that's exciting news for Everest Capital. As long as you play your cards right, you should enjoy quite a return on that investment. Both from a multiple of invested capital and an IRR perspective."

Wright nodded numbly. Celino wasn't at all what he'd expected. He wasn't macho and boorish. He was nattily dressed: wool blazer, button-down shirt, neatly pressed slacks, Gucci loafers. His English was perfect, he was well groomed, and he was painfully polite.

"You look . . . surprised. What's the matter?"

"Nothing . . . sir."

Celino patted the arm of the chair. "Yes, that was quite a coup Christian Gillette pulled off, winning the NFL franchise." He smiled. "And he wasn't even the high bidder. Imagine that."

"What? How do you know?"

"So we have a few things to talk about," Celino said, ignoring Wright's question.

"But I really—"

"And I hardly ever leave my house on Staten Island. In fact, I think it's been five months since I did. So I hope you understand, this meeting is very, very important."

"I understand."

"Good. Well, as my associate told you at Saks, we, uh . . . well, we know what you did. At the sex shop." Celino raised one finger. "And we have proof. But believe me, Mr. Wright, what a man does in his spare time is no concern of mine. Even if it's perverted. *Unless*, of course, I can take advantage of it. In this case, I can."

Wright was looking down into his lap. He felt a tear form in his left eye.

"You're going to do anything me or my men tell you to do. You're going to do it pronto, and you're going to do it *con gusto*. Are we clear?"

"Yes," Wright said, his voice so quiet that he almost didn't hear it himself.

"How clear?"

"As clear as you want."

Celino nodded his approval. "Good." He pointed at a manila folder lying on a side table next to Wright's chair. "Pick that up and open it."

Wright reached for the folder. Inside was a single eight-and-a-half-by-eleven glossy head shot of a face. The man's eyes had been cut out and his teeth removed. Wright felt a wave of bile rising from his stomach.

"He was still alive at that point, David. Both eyes and all twenty-nine teeth gone, *but he was still breathing*. That's how good my guys are. Am I getting through to you?"

Wright gagged, then nodded.

"You can put it down. Now, I need a few things from

you. First, you need to keep telling us where Gillette is at all times, no exceptions. You miss one appointment of his and . . . well . . ." Celino pointed at the folder. "You don't want to end up like him, do you?"

"No."

"Second, I don't want Christian Gillette even *going* to that meeting with Mick Federico tomorrow morning. I want Carmine Torino to get the business. Gillette goes to the meeting with Federico and—"

"But—"

Celino raised his hand, and for the first time a look of rage filled his face.

"Torino will get the business," Wright said meekly.

The rage disappeared as fast as it had come, replaced by contentment. "Now we're getting somewhere, David." Celino pulled out a cigarette and lighted it. "I hope you don't mind."

"No."

"If you do, please say so."

"I love cigarettes." He hated them.

"You want one?" Celino asked, holding out the pack and smiling.

"No, thank you."

Celino put the cigarettes back in his jacket pocket. "You know, when you ask someone to take extraordinary measures for you, I believe you should tell them a little bit about what's going on." He opened his hands and gestured toward Wright. "It makes them feel like they're part of it. Like when you guys give your senior managers stock in the companies they're operating for you. It gives them a stake, right? Makes them more passionate about making things run well."

Wright nodded. That was exactly what they did for their senior managers.

"You see, I believe in the *stick*." Celino pointed at the manila folder on the table beside Wright. "But I believe in the *carrot,* too. Call me an amateur psychiatrist, but, well, I've done okay for myself, you know?"

Wright could barely breathe. "Very okay."

"So here's the first thing I'm going to let you in on. *We* took care of Stiles. We retained the services of the mate on your partner's yacht. Of course, he's gone now, too." Celino chuckled. "It was a short engagement, and the cops won't find anything. If they do, I'll blame you."

"Why did you kill Stiles?" Wright asked, shuddering at the thought of Celino blaming him for anything.

"He was doing some poking around I didn't like. He was a very resourceful man. I'd had enough." Celino took a long puff off the cigarette. "The second thing I'm going to tell you will blow your mind."

Wright leaned forward. His stomach was feeling better.

"We're working on something big. We and the Wallace Family, that is."

Wright's mouth fell open.

Celino smiled widely. "Let me just tell you, when all this is over and Allison Wallace is running Everest Capital, there'll be a place for you. If you're a good boy." Wright started to say something, but Celino cut him off. "That's all I can tell you about that right now, but it's your big carrot. Treat Miss Wallace with great respect and do what you're told. At the end of the day, you'll be a happy man. Whatever ups Gillette has promised you will look like peanuts compared to what you could earn after he's gone."

Wright's heart was pounding. He was still in shock at what he'd heard, but he was thinking about the possibilities, too.

"There's one more thing," Celino said.

"Yes?"

"We know Gillette is starting to depend on you, but we don't think he trusts you yet. Not as much as we want him to, anyway."

"He trusts me."

Celino gave Wright a dismissive wave. "Like I said, not as much as we want him to. So we're going to set up an incident tomorrow."

"An incident?"

"Yes. You'll get details tomorrow morning after the Federico meeting is canceled. Before you and Gillette go downtown to meet with the city council representatives about the casino." Celino rose from the chair. "Do you have any questions?"

Wright thought for a moment. "There is one thing. Last week I was on the phone with Gillette, trying to find out exactly where he was going so I could report back to your . . . uh . . . associate, Paul."

"Yeah, so?"

"He was going to the Eastern Shore of Maryland, and I was trying to find out exactly what town it was. He asked me why I was so interested and I told him it was because I had family down there."

"And, of course, you don't."

"No," Wright admitted. "I wouldn't be too worried about it except he brought it up with my wife this weekend when we were out on the yacht. You see, he invited a few of us out on it to celebrate—"

"I know," Celino said coolly, "remember?"

"Right."

"You want me to solve this problem for you?"

"Yes, sir. I'm afraid it might blow everything."

Celino considered the request, then nodded. "All right, I'll do it. Now," he said loudly, pointing toward the door, "please leave."

Wright took one last glance at the manila folder on the table and headed quickly for the door.

When he was in the elevator with the doors closed, he leaned back against the walls, let out a deep breath, and shook his head. So Allison Wallace was going to be running Everest Capital.

CHAPTER 15

It took every ounce of self-control Gillette had not to smash the cell phone on the marble floor when it rang. He'd take so much pleasure watching it disintegrate into a thousand pieces. Then no one would be able to reach him on it anymore. *"What is it?"*

"We need you in that northern city we discussed when we met last week. We need you there tomorrow morning, ready to go by nine."

It was two o'clock. Gillette and Wright were sitting in the hotel lobby, waiting for the limo to take them to the Las Vegas airport. Earlier, they'd finished a grueling three-hour session with several members of the city council concerning the casino. After some horse trading, it appeared everything was a go, thanks in no small part to his having retained Carmine Torino at eight-thirty that morning, Gillette figured. He glanced over at Wright, who was in the chair beside him. David was going back to New York on a commercial flight, and he was headed to the West Coast to see Marilyn—and Lana. David had pushed so hard this morning at breakfast not to even bother with Federico.

"I can't," Gillette replied, refocusing on the call, "I've got plans."

"Cancel them," Ganze ordered. "We need to go *now*. You have to arrange for us to move into the space up there right away. Figure that out tonight or *early* tomorrow morning so we're ready to go at nine. We only need about three thousand square feet, but it's got to be remote, it's got to have its own access. We've had our people up there scoping out the facility, and there's a building near the river we think would be perfect. We can take care of security, no need for you to worry about that. All you need to do is get a heart valve research lab out of there. It's just a few people. That's the only thing in there at this point."

So Ganze had been watching the Minneapolis facility for a while. "I'm going to meet these people, right?" Gillette asked. "The three we talked about? The biochemist in charge of the project and her two top assistants?"

There was nothing but dead air.

"Ganze?"

"I have to talk to my boss about that."

"You promised me."

"I know," Ganze agreed quietly.

"I'm not doing this unless I meet them," Gillette vowed, "and unless I hear more about my father. You told me I would by now." Once again he glanced over at Wright, who was fiddling with his own cell phone. Gillette pressed the phone tightly to his ear. "You got that?"

"I'll give you more on that tomorrow after our meeting," Ganze promised. "I do have additional information."

"Tell me now."

"Not on a cell phone. Look, I know you're frustrated," Ganze said, his voice growing compassionate. "Just meet with us tomorrow. You'll be glad you did." He waited a moment. "Hello?"

"*All right.*"

"Good. Find a hotel on the south side of the city. In Bloomington or Edina. You'll hear from me later on."

"Yeah, okay." Gillette clicked off.

"What's going on?" Wright wanted to know, stowing his cell phone away immediately.

Gillette checked the lobby for the QS agents. He didn't see them at first—just loudly dressed tourists moving in all directions. He sat up, his breath instantly short. Then he saw the agents over by a pillar. His shoulders sagged.

"Chris?"

"Damn it, David, keep your shorts on."

"Jeez, bite my head off."

Gillette relaxed into the chair. "Sorry." He sighed. Sometimes it seemed as though his life weren't his own anymore. More and more he thought about giving it all away. "Change of plans," he explained. He'd have to call Marilyn from the plane to tell her he wasn't coming. A tough trade, he thought ruefully: meeting his real mother the first time for learning more about his father. "I'm not going to the West Coast now."

"Where are you going?"

"Something's come up."

"I thought you were seeing . . . your family."

"I was."

"Well, whatever came up must be pretty important if it's getting in the way of that."

"Drop it, David," Gillette said bluntly.

"I just thought we were going to be in contact all the time."

"We are. With cell phones and Blackberries."

"Yeah, but it would be helpful to know where you are in case—"

"Where's the damn limousine?" Gillette barked, surprising even himself.

"It'll be here soon," Wright assured him. "I talked to the QS guy in charge. Ten minutes tops. What's wrong?"

"Nothing."

"You just seem—"

"I told you, drop it."

"Okay, okay." Wright stayed quiet for a few moments.

"You want to talk about our meeting with the city council people? You know, compare notes?"

Might as well do something with the downtime, Gillette figured. "Okay," he agreed, noticing a blonde who was sitting across the lobby from him. She was older—in her mid-forties—but very attractive. She smiled at him as their eyes met, and he smiled back politely.

"So, what did you think?" Wright asked.

"I thought it went pretty well," Gillette answered, trying to hide a yawn. He hadn't slept well again last night. Each night, he replayed the scene on the yacht deck in his mind, trying to figure out if he was missing something. Something that might help the police figure out what had happened to Stiles. "I think the casino's ours if we want it. The one guy in the maroon leisure suit at the other end of the table was a pain in the ass, but they'll probably send Carmine Torino to see him and that'll be that."

"It was amazing how they already knew you'd hired Torino when we got there," Wright commented.

"It's a rigged town. Always has been, always will be, no matter what anybody says." Gillette looked over at the blonde again. She was touching her chest, seemed to be breathing hard. "I want to ask you something."

"Yeah?"

"Why did you tell me you had relatives on the Eastern Shore of Maryland?"

Wright's mouth fell slowly open. "Because . . . I do."

"I talked to Peggy on the boat Saturday, and she said you've never mentioned having family there to her."

Wright shrugged. "I guess I never mentioned it to her. I mean, they're distant cousins, you know? I don't think I've seen them in ten years."

"Which side?" Gillette asked, leaning forward in his chair.

"Huh?"

"Which side of the family? Your mother's or father's?" Gillette stared at the blonde. She seemed to be trying to get up out of her seat, but she was having trouble. *"Jesus,"* he said, standing up and pointing, "I think that woman's having a heart attack."

The blonde clutched her chest as she finally made it to her feet. She staggered a few steps forward, then crumpled to the ground. Gillette, the two QS agents, and Wright rushed toward her.

As they did, a man who'd been sitting in a chair nearby stood up and drew a pistol from his jacket, aiming at Gillette.

"Chris!" Wright shouted, knocking Gillette to the ground as the first shot rang out. He sprinted at the shooter as the QS agents dropped to their knees and drew their weapons.

"Don't shoot!" Gillette yelled at the agents as Wright closed in on the assailant.

One more shot rang out, then Wright was on the guy, knocking him down and grabbing his wrist, slamming it against the marble floor. The gun skittered away. The QS agents were on the man a heartbeat later, rolling him onto his stomach and cuffing his hands behind his back.

Gillette let his head fall back gently against the floor. Tom McGuire just wasn't going to quit.

The private jet lifted off from Boston's Logan Airport at six P.M. eastern time. An hour and forty-five minutes later, it was flying at twenty-four thousand feet just east of Lake Michigan.

In the cabin were two men and one woman who'd been tucked away in a far, forgotten corner of Harvard Medical School for the last two years. They were the three biochemists who'd been leading the development of DARPA's nanotechnology project, which was on the edge of a major breakthrough.

A second, larger plane was fifteen minutes behind them, carrying their records, computer files, and all the equipment they'd used over the last two years—and would need to finish the project. They'd been told that there had been a breach of security in Boston and that they were being secretly transferred to another agency, GARD, that would be in charge of the project to its conclusion. They'd also been told that they wouldn't be allowed to see—even make contact with—their families for at least several weeks, maybe longer, until they'd gotten settled into their new location, which hadn't been disclosed to them. For a while, they tried to guess where they were going as they sped west, but after thirty minutes, they had settled patiently into their seats, reading magazines, newspapers, and files.

When the plane was twenty miles out over Lake Michigan, a remote-control device tripped two emergency fuel ejection valves, and fuel began pouring from the tanks. A red light went off in the cockpit thirty seconds later, indicating to the pilots that the plane was quickly losing fuel, but they were helpless to do anything. The valve wouldn't close, and they were flying on fumes. They turned the aircraft around and descended, trying desperately to get down, but at ten thousand feet the engines shut down and everything went eerily silent.

The plane stayed up for a few seconds, then rapidly lost speed, and the nose turned down. The pilots worked furiously to maintain altitude, but at five thousand feet they lost control and the plane went into a vertical dive.

When the jet hit the surface of Lake Michigan, it disintegrated—as did everything inside.

The man who had pulled the gun in the hotel lobby sat at a small table in an interrogation room, smoking a cigarette. On the other side of the table was an armless wooden chair where he figured the cop would park his fat ass when he finally got around to making it in here. The man had been waiting an hour, and he was getting irritated. It wasn't supposed to take this long. He was supposed to have been in and out.

Finally the door opened.

"I'm Detective Jim Pearson."

"Congratulations."

Pearson tossed a folder on the table, turned the chair around so the back of it was to the table, and straddled it. "What in the hell were you doing?" he asked, crossing his forearms over the top of the chair back.

"What do you mean?"

"You try to shoot Christian Gillette in the main lobby of Caesar's Palace while he's being covered by two private security guys, not to mention all the hotel security people buzzing around. You only pop off two shots, neither one of which comes anywhere near him. You know you didn't have a chance of getting away. I'll ask you again, what were you doing?"

"Trying to kill him."

"Bullshit. If you were, then that was one stupid plan."

"Okay, I'm stupid."

"At least you could have shot that guy who tackled you. I mean, he was right in front of you."

The man took a deep breath. He was one of the best shots in the Carbone family, so it was difficult to take this. "Okay, I'm stupid *and* I'm a lousy shot."

Pearson grunted, not satisfied. "What's your name?"

"Johnny Depp."

"Fuck you."

The man shrugged. "Hey, maybe I'm stupid and a lousy shot, but give me some credit for being creative."

"Who's behind this?"

"What do you mean?"

"I don't think you've got anything against Gillette, I can't find any connection. So who does?"

The man looked down. Hopefully the detective would make something of his silence.

Pearson leaned in. "You're looking at a lot of time, pal. You're gonna be charged with attempted murder. I'd cooperate if I were you."

The man winced, then shook his head. "I can't."

"Come on, Johnny. Come clean. Maybe I can help."

"How?"

"Maybe the evidence gets lost, I don't know. I'll think of something. I want the person behind the scenes."

The man dropped his cigarette on the floor and stepped on it. "His name's Tom McGuire. He told me he used to run a company Gillette owned, and Gillette screwed him somehow. I don't know, though. I didn't get all the details. Frankly, I didn't care once he paid me."

Pearson pulled out a pen and paper. "What was that name again?"

"Tom McGuire."

"Where did McGuire approach you?"

"I don't understand."

"Did he talk to you here in Vegas first, or what?"

"No, no, it was back in Jersey. We have a mutual friend there."

"What's your friend's name?"

The man rolled his eyes. "Fucking Christ, you got to be kidding me."

"Okay, okay." Pearson backed off. "You said McGuire ran a company for Gillette?"

"Yeah."

"What's the name of the company?"

The man shrugged. "Ask Gillette."

"I will." Pearson put the pad and pen away. "How much did McGuire pay you?"

The man thought about it for a second. It had to be enough, but not too much. "A hundred grand."

They'd been in the air for two hours, and Gillette had finished the crossword puzzles in *The New York Times* and *USA Today* and was just about done with *The Washington Post*. When he'd gotten the last answer of the *Post*'s puzzle, he dropped the paper on the floor and looked over at Wright. Since Wright had gone after the guy in the hotel lobby, Gillette had decided to bring him along. He wouldn't be allowed into the meeting with Boyd, Ganze, and the biochemists, but he deserved to come to Minneapolis. Christ, he'd put himself in terrible danger, directly in the line of fire. He was as dedicated as Stiles had been. Suddenly he felt bad for asking Wright about his family in Maryland. For being suspicious. Wright had done nothing but continue to prove himself a worthy protégé.

"Hey, David."

"Yeah?"

"You okay?"

"What do you mean?"

"You look a little pale."

Wright smiled wanly. "I guess I'm just not much for staring down the barrel of an angry gun."

Gillette could relate to that. "Why don't you catch a nap?"

"That'd be nice, but I need to get this Hush-Hush deal done," Wright answered, pointing at the due diligence material spread out on his lap.

One of the QS agents trotted up from the back of the plane. "Phone, Mr. Gillette."

"Thanks," he said, taking the receiver. "Hello."

"Christian, it's me."

"*Me*" meant Allison. So they were at that stage already. She was, anyway.

"Having a good time without me?" she asked.

"Yep."

"How did it go with the Vegas city council?" Her voice turned serious. "Do we have our casino?"

"I think so. We hired one of the consultants I told you about. That was key."

"How much is it?"

"A lot." No need to get into it right now. "But it's worth it."

"Are you on your way to the West Coast?"

"No."

"Well, where are you going?"

"Something came up."

"What?"

"Something."

"What's the big secret?" she snapped. "Jesus, first Richmond, now this. I should have you tracked."

Gillette's eyes narrowed. No doubt she could if she wanted to. Maybe she already was and this conversation was just cover. "I'm going to Minneapolis." Really no reason to be so evasive. Wright was with him. She'd get it out of him.

"What happened?"

"A friend of mine called this morning. We got an opportunity. Another deal, but I have to get to Minneapolis right away." He was safe on this one. Wright had no idea why they were going to Minneapolis.

"More rush-rush."

"Always."

"Is David with you?"

"Yeah."

"Minneapolis, huh?" Allison spoke up, her voice intensifying. "That's weird. Doesn't Beezer Johnson have a division up there?"

"Uh-huh," Gillette answered hesitantly.

"Have you thought any more about my proposal?" she asked. "My family buying Beezer?"

"I haven't had a chance to really—"

"I talked to my uncle and grandfather about it," she cut in, "and they think it's a great idea. They had a couple of our analysts in Chicago take a look at it, you know, tear apart the numbers, and they think Beezer would be a nice fit with our business."

Gillette let out an exasperated breath. "How did your analysts get the numbers?"

"I had Cathy Dylan e-mail them. I didn't think you'd mind." She paused. "Do you?"

"Before you do that again, talk to me first. Those files are confidential."

"Okay." She paused again. "Let's talk price."

"It's not for sale, Allison." He didn't want to hear her price. Once he did, if it was good, he'd have a fiduciary responsibility to consider it.

But she barreled ahead anyway. "Six billion."

"Six billion?" Everest had bought Beezer Johnson a couple of years ago for just two. "At that price we'd make almost as much on Beezer as we will on Laurel Energy. But Beezer only has income of about a hundred million. That's a ridiculous multiple to pay."

"Thanks for calling my family ridiculous."

"You know what I mean." Why did they want Beezer so badly? Gillette kept asking himself. "I said the *deal* was ridiculous."

"Look, we can combine Beezer with the company we already own and generate some fantastic synergies, so our actual buy-in multiple is a lot less."

"I want to see that analysis." He could poke holes in any analysis, no matter how good it looked on a spreadsheet. He'd be able to keep her at bay for a while.

"Um, sure. I'll have our analyst e-mail it to you."

"As soon as possible."

"Yeah, sure. By the way, have you talked to Senator Clark about setting up the meeting with the FDA guy?" Allison asked, switching subjects. "Jack Mitchell e-mailed me today about that. He's still hot to trot, but he wants to see the FDA thing start moving."

"Don't worry about it."

"Okay. Well, I hope everything goes all right in Minneapolis. Whatever secret thing it is."

"Thanks."

"How's Faith?" she asked out of the blue.

"Fine."

There were a few seconds of dead air.

"I miss you, Christian," she finally said.

Gillette glanced at Wright. "Thanks," he said, then clicked off.

"Was that Allison?" Wright asked after Gillette had hung up.

"Yeah."

"You know, I really like her. She's something special."

"Not still worried that I'm going to be distracted by her?"

"Nah."

Gillette eyed Wright. "Why'd you change your mind?"

"I had a chance to talk to her for a while Saturday on the yacht. She's nice. Smart, too. And you're too much of a pro to let that happen. I know that."

Finally, he thought, someone was giving him the benefit of the doubt.

"By the way," Wright spoke up, "I remembered where my family is on the Eastern Shore of Maryland."

"Oh?"

"Yeah, it's a town called Easton. The woman is my mom's second cousin. You should go visit her when you're in Chatham next. It's like an hour away from there. Mom says the woman's a great cook. Fried chicken's her specialty."

Gillette nodded. "Maybe I will," he said, but his first instinct was to call Wright's mother to check the story out. When would he ever learn to trust anyone? "Thanks."

"Sure."

The phone in Gillette's lap rang. Hopefully, it wasn't Allison. When he saw the number, he knew it wasn't.

"Hello."

"May I speak to Christian Gillette?"

"This is Christian."

"Mr. Gillette, this is Jim Pearson. I'm a detective with the Las Vegas Police Department."

Gillette sat up in the leather chair. "Uh-huh."

"I got your number from one of the officers who responded to the shooting out at the hotel this afternoon. I need to ask you a few questions."

"All right."

"Does the name Tom McGuire mean anything to you?"

Gillette froze. "Yeah, why?"

"The guy we arrested claims McGuire paid him to kill you. Claims McGuire ran one of your companies and that you and McGuire got into it over something. Does all this make any sense to you?"

"Yes, it does."

"Good," Pearson said, sounding surprised. "Maybe we've got something to go on after all."

"McGuire ran a security company for me," Gillette explained. "He and his brother, Vince, started it. I think McGuire tried to kill me in New York City last week, too."

"You *think*?"

"It was like what happened today. Someone else attacked me, but we think McGuire was behind it. And I . . . well, I believe he was behind the murder of my friend

Quentin Stiles this past weekend, too. Anything you can get out of the guy you're holding could be very important."

"All right, good. I'm gonna question him again tomorrow morning, after he's cooled his heels in jail overnight and had a chance to think about how much trouble he's in. If I have any more questions, I want to call you, okay?"

"Sure. Let me know how the interrogation goes tomorrow morning, will you?"

"Okay."

"Who was that?" Wright asked.

"The detective who interrogated the guy you caught at the hotel."

"Really? What did he say?"

Gillette looked hard at David, mulling over his response. He needed a new confidant. Someone he could trust with anything. "Tom McGuire paid the guy to kill me."

He'd been in this jail before, a few overnight stays for drunk and disorderly, so he knew the drill. And this wasn't it. Not even the usual route to the cells. As they turned a corner of the lonely hallway, the cop stopped, took out a key, and undid the handcuffs. Then he pushed open a door marked EMERGENCY. "Get lost."

The man didn't hesitate, just moved out into the night and quickly hailed a taxi.

"Airport and step on it," he urged, fat with pride thinking about what a great acting job he'd done for Pearson. He checked his watch. A few hours more than he'd expected, but Celino would be happy. And that was all that mattered.

Wright moved into the bathroom at the back of the jet, then closed and locked the door behind him. He leaned over the sink and gazed into the mirror, then turned on the cold water and splashed his face. He stared at himself again, not exactly sure who was staring back.

Gillette had bought everything—just like Celino said he would: that the guy in the hotel lobby had really been trying to kill him, that Wright had saved his life, that Tom McGuire was behind everything. Wright shook his head. Celino using McGuire's name was perfect cover, a stroke of genius. McGuire was in hiding, so there was no way to confirm or deny that he was behind it.

Wright splashed more cold water on his face. Celino knew how to dangle a carrot, but it was the stick that was causing nightmares.

He turned to go but caught himself in the reflection once more. He hesitated and leaned close to the mirror, studying himself. Finally, he grimaced and headed out. He couldn't look any longer.

CHAPTER 16

Late September and, at seven o'clock in the morning, it was just thirty-four degrees. The predicted high for the day was only forty-nine. It amazed Gillette that people actually chose to live in a place like Minneapolis. New York got cold, but not like this. He clenched his teeth, trying not to shiver. They'd come straight from Vegas, so he didn't have an overcoat. God, he hated the cold.

From the steps of a building that rose up along the banks of the Mississippi River, Gillette watched a dark blue Cadillac sedan move slowly down the single-lane road toward him. This was the original building of Beezer Johnson's Minnesota division—a quaint, three-story, redbrick structure built in the 1920s and added on to several times since. In the sixties, after several spring floods in a row, management had relocated most of the division to a newly constructed facility on high ground overlooking the area. Now there were four gleaming two-hundred-thousand-square-foot plants up there, and the only people left in the original building were the heart valve research staff. Management had kept the old building around mainly for posterity.

The Cadillac pulled to a stop in front of the steps, and a man emerged bundled up in a long overcoat. A QS agent descended the steps quickly, frisked him, then gestured for him to go up the steps.

"Hello, Mr. Gillette," said the man, holding out his hand as he reached the top step. "I'm Andrew Morgenstern."

Morgenstern was president of the Minnesota division. Gillette had never met him before, had spoken to him for the first time only last night on the plane. Typically, Gillette dealt with Beezer's CEO and CFO, whose offices were at the corporate headquarters in northern New Jersey.

"Welcome to Minnesota," Morgenstern said.

Nervously, Gillette thought.

"It's a beautiful morning, isn't it?"

"If you're a polar bear."

Morgenstern smiled, but not as though he were amused.

"Let's go inside," Gillette suggested, rubbing his hands together, his breath rising in front of him. Morgenstern's nervousness was typical for line managers when they met him, and he wanted to ease the other man's anxiety. "I appreciate your getting up early."

"You betcha." Morgenstern pulled out a set of keys and unlocked the front door. "Jeez, you ought to be wearing a coat, you know."

"I would if I had one," Gillette replied as Walker waved the QS agents in ahead of them. It didn't seem much warmer inside. "I thought you had people working in here."

"Sure, yah, we do."

"Don't you heat it for them?"

Morgenstern laughed loudly, then frowned when Gillette remained stone-faced. "Oh, you're serious."

"Yes."

"It's sixty-six degrees in here, Mr. Gillette. With sweaters on, people are fine. There's no need to cook 'em and pump up Northern State Power's revenues at the same time. We're big on cost savings around here. Turn out the lights when you're done, you know? I got signs everywhere."

"Uh-huh." Gillette glanced at the QS agents, who were moving down the tiled hallway ahead of him, checking rooms. Walker was staying right by his side. "How many people work in this building, Andrew?" he asked as they walked slowly down the corridor.

"Around twenty, I think."

"Can you move them into one of the other facilities up the hill?" Gillette asked bluntly.

"I guess. Do you mind if I ask why?"

"I'm afraid I do." He was used to politely telling people to pound salt.

Morgenstern's eyebrows floated up. "Jeez, okay."

"Look, I know how this sounds, but I need you to abandon this building until I tell you it's okay to come back. It could be a couple of weeks, it could be a year. I don't know, but that's the way it has to be."

Morgenstern shrugged. "You're the boss."

Gillette glanced at Walker, who had taken a call on his cell phone and peeled away. "I need everybody out of here by eight this morning, no later. If they leave anything behind, they'll have to call and make a special request to get it."

"*Eight o'clock?* Golly, some of the folks don't even *get* here until nine. They gotta get their kids off to school. You can understand that, can't you?"

"They won't be allowed in here after eight, Andrew. No exceptions."

"Okay, okay."

"Does this building have its own entrance to the main road?" He could see Morgenstern's curiosity was killing him, but to the man's credit, he didn't ask anything.

"Yes."

"Good."

The front door opened loudly behind them, and Gillette whipped around.

"It's all right," Walker called over his shoulder, trotting

toward the door. "It's one of my guys. I just talked to him on the phone."

Gillette turned back to Morgenstern. "Andrew, you can't tell anyone what's going on here."

"I don't *know* what's going on."

"You can't tell *anyone* you've seen me or these men. You can't even tell the CEO or CFO. I'll fire you if you do."

Morgenstern's eyebrows rose. "Hey, it's your company."

"And Andrew . . ."

"Yes?"

"I need that key." Gillette pointed at the set of keys Morgenstern was holding. "And any others that go to doors in this building."

Morgenstern handed the entire set to Gillette. "Here."

"Thanks." Gillette shook Morgenstern's hand. "I appreciate your help." He spotted Walker coming back down the corridor. "Congratulations on the great job you're doing. The CEO tells me your group is way ahead of plan for the year."

"Division."

"Excuse me?"

"My *division* is way ahead of plan."

"Right." Morgenstern was a stickler, but Gillette appreciated that. "Your division. Have a profitable day, Andrew."

When Boyd and Ganze arrived, Gillette was waiting in the lobby, going through e-mails on his Blackberry, while Walker and several other QS agents milled around—they'd finished checking the building. Gillette stowed the device in his pocket and stood up when he saw them.

"We need to go somewhere we can talk privately," Boyd said right away.

"The building's empty except for the people in this

room," Gillette answered. "I don't think privacy will be a problem."

Walker started to follow them as they headed off down the corridor.

"He can't come with us, Christian," Boyd growled, "you know that."

"It's all right, Derrick," Gillette said, waving him off.

"That's not the same guy you brought to Washington last week, is it?" Boyd asked as they walked away, heels clicking on the tiles.

"No."

"Where's that guy?"

"Dead."

Boyd was headed into a vacant office when Gillette answered. He stopped in the doorway and turned around. *"What?"*

"Dead," Gillette repeated.

Boyd moved into the office. "Jesus, what happened to him?" he asked over his shoulder.

"It was a freak thing." No need to get into it.

"God, that's awful," Ganze said, shaking his head and following Gillette inside. "Sorry."

"Thanks."

"The nanotech people we've brought from DARPA are waiting outside in a van," Boyd spoke up impatiently. "I don't want to leave them there like that for long. What's the deal?"

"I met with the president of this division an hour ago," Gillette replied, "and told him he had to abandon this building until I said otherwise. And that he had to keep it quiet. That he couldn't tell anyone he'd met with me, including the top officers of the entire company."

"Good."

"What's his name?" Ganze asked, pulling out a pen and pad.

"Andrew Morgenstern," Gillette said. "He's good. Anyway, the building is yours at this point. You can do what you want with it. Now, I want to meet these people."

Boyd sat behind the desk, then motioned at Ganze. "Go get them, but I don't want anyone else seeing them, Daniel. Doors closed down the hall."

"Yes, sir."

When he was gone, Gillette sat down. "So, did you stage these people's deaths yet?"

"What?" Boyd was off in another world.

"You told me you were going to stage a plane crash," Gillette reminded him. "So other people on the nanotech project wouldn't suspect anything when the people in the van weren't around anymore."

Boyd nodded somberly. "Oh, yeah, we did that."

"Where was the crash?"

"Out in western Pennsylvania somewhere, in the mountains."

"How are you going to convince anyone that there were people on board?"

"There *were* people on board," Boyd answered.

Gillette looked at him hard. "Are you kidding me?"

"Don't get bent out of shape. We used cadavers, and the pilot bailed out before the thing went down." Boyd chuckled. "God, you actually thought I killed people?"

Gillette stifled his sudden outrage. He was disliking the man more and more all the time. "How would I know? You wanted to be able to stick me in prison for thirty years."

"Mmm."

"What about dental records and DNA? They won't match."

"It was a hell of a crash. Huge fireball. The plane was only in the air for a few minutes before it went down, so it was full of fuel. The bodies were too badly burned for anybody to make a positive identification."

"I think they can still—"

"It won't be a problem," Boyd snapped, aggravated. "Talk to Ganze if you're really that interested."

"Won't the other people on the project think it's strange that the three of them were on the plane together?"

"Not at all. They were supposed to be on their way to a nanotech conference in Los Angeles, with a stopover in Cleveland to check out another project. They were going to catch a commercial flight from Cleveland. Small teams of them did that kind of thing all the time."

Gillette stood up as Ganze walked back in with the three biochemists. A petite Asian woman and two scholarly-looking men wearing tweed blazers.

"Dr. Evelyn Chang is our project leader," Ganze said to Gillette, introducing him to the woman, "and these are Dr. Silverstein and Dr. Rice."

Gillette shook hands with each of them.

"There," Boyd said, standing up, "you've met them. Now we've got to get them moved in."

Gillette gazed at each of them intently for a few more moments. "Welcome to the facility. I hope it works for you."

Dr. Chang shook Gillette's hand again. "Thank you very much, Mr. Gillette. We appreciate your dedication to national security, to keeping this country ahead."

"You're welcome," Gillette said quietly, thinking about how he'd gotten into this purely for selfish reasons. But now, with these three individuals standing in front of him, it seemed different. Maybe he *was* doing the right thing.

"All right," Boyd pushed, "let's go."

"What about my questions?" Gillette asked when they were out of earshot of the biochemists.

Boyd stopped. "Didn't Daniel give you Marilyn McRae's number?"

"Yes."

"Well, call her."

"I did, but I want to know about my father, too."

Boyd motioned to Ganze. "Go with him."

Gillette and Ganze moved to another office a few doors down.

"Here's the deal," Ganze said when they were inside and the door was closed. "We were right. Your father was killed by a group inside the government that was planning to assassinate President Bush. At that point, the group believed Bush would easily win another term. Of course he didn't, but they didn't have a crystal ball. He was incredibly popular when they were plotting."

"How do you know that these people killed my father?"

"So far," Ganze replied, "we have two sources. First, we have a guy who was a mechanic at the Orange County Airport at the time. He was working the day your father's plane crashed. The guy claims he knows who rigged the plane to go down. We're going out there to talk to him, in the next few days."

"I want to talk to him, too. I want to be there."

"I don't know if I can do that. I'll have to get back to you on that."

"You always have to get back to me."

Ganze looked down. "Sorry, Christian, it's all very complicated. I hope you can appreciate that."

"Who's the other source?" Gillette demanded.

"A man who was in the Secret Service back then," Ganze replied. "Same kind of situation as the mechanic. This guy has information for us about a couple of agents who were going to be involved in the assassination. We should get to him in the next few weeks."

"Why wait so long?"

"These things take time. People don't just give up this stuff that fast. We negotiate."

"The agents who were involved must have been thrown in jail. Check it out."

Ganze shook his head. "No, that's the thing. There wasn't anything to convict them of. No proof of a conspiracy, just the appearance of one. People in the service were let go, re-assigned. Some were probably guilty, some weren't. It just isn't as clear cut as you and I want it to be. It may never be, especially since it's been sixteen years."

Frustration coursed through Gillette. As he'd suspected all these years, his father had been murdered, but maybe this outcome was worse. Now he *knew* there'd been foul play, but there might not be anyone to hold accountable. No one to take his anger out on.

"Look, I know you want answers fast," Ganze continued, "but you have to be patient. And for a while, maybe for good, you may have to be satisfied with the fact that your father probably saved the president's life. We think he contacted a higher-up at the White House just before the plane crash, maybe even that morning. We think he stopped the assassination. Your father's a hero."

CHAPTER 17

"Chris!"

Gillette stopped short and turned around. He'd been heading toward the Everest lobby, but Faraday was jogging down the corridor toward him, puffing hard.

"Where are you going?"

"Downstairs to get something to eat," Gillette answered. It was just before two. They'd gotten back from Minnesota an hour ago. "What's up?"

"Without the QS guys?" Faraday asked loudly.

Gillette looked around furtively to see if anyone had heard him. "I was going to take the guy at the door."

Faraday's face scrunched up. "And let him leave the lobby?"

"It'll be fine for a few minutes." Gillette searched Faraday's expression for a sign of what was bothering him. "What is it?"

"Derrick Walker's got the FBI on the phone in Conference Room One. He wants you in there right away."

The FBI. Maybe they'd found out something about Stiles. "Okay."

When Gillette and Faraday entered the room, Walker was leaning against the conference room table near the speaker box, arms folded over his broad chest.

"Close the door, Nigel," Walker ordered. "George," he

called loudly when Faraday had shut it, "I've got Christian Gillette in here now."

"Christian?"

"Yes."

"I'm Special Agent George Butler." Butler spoke with a heavy southern drawl. "I'm with the FBI downtown here at Twenty-six Federal Plaza in Manhattan. I've got some information you'll be very interested in."

"I hope it has to do with Quentin Stiles." Walker had told Gillette he'd been in touch with Butler about Stiles and that Butler was working with the local authorities. "That would make my day."

"Unfortunately not," Butler replied, "but it should make you sleep better."

"Go ahead."

"We believe Tom McGuire is dead."

Walker remained stone-faced, but Faraday pumped his fist.

"How do you know?" Gillette asked.

Butler hesitated. "We don't know *for sure*, but I'd say it's ninety-five percent at this point."

Gillette eased into the chair from which he ran the managers meetings. He felt as if a boulder had just tumbled off his shoulders.

"We have informants inside most of the big Mafia families," Butler explained. "*Soldatti*, usually, but sometimes more senior members. Yesterday afternoon we heard from one of those guys. He told us McGuire had been hit. Apparently, they put him in a boat, took him offshore from Jersey about forty miles, then threw him overboard. Our guy's always been very accurate about this kind of stuff."

"Why would the Mafia kill Tom McGuire?" Gillette asked.

"Revenge. We think it goes back to when McGuire was

in the FBI years ago. He busted up a big drug operation in Boston."

"You guys bust the Mob on that kind of stuff all the time," Walker spoke up. "Why would they care so much about it that time?"

"Right," Gillette agreed, "and why would they kill him after so much time?"

"Good questions," Butler said. "During the Boston raid, McGuire killed the brother of a man who's now don of one of the big families. Rumor was, it wasn't during a shoot-out or in self-defense. Rumor was, McGuire took him in a bathroom and tortured him to get information. Cut off fingers, that kind of stuff. When the guy wouldn't talk, McGuire dunked him in a tub. The last time a little too long."

"That's why they drowned McGuire," Walker said. "So he got it the same way as the don's brother."

"Eye for an eye," Butler agreed. "And it gets better. Yesterday, McGuire's wife gets home from the grocery store and there's a shoe box on her front stoop. She opens it up and there's a human hand inside, a right hand. There's also a wedding ring inside the box. After the EMTs revive her, McGuire's wife identifies the wedding ring from the inscription."

"Still don't understand why they'd wait so long to kill him," Walker said.

"The guy who's the don of the family now wasn't in power when McGuire killed his brother," Butler answered. "Plus, McGuire was careful. He usually had his men around."

"That's true," Gillette agreed, remembering.

"But George, your guys couldn't find him," said Walker. "How could the Mob?"

"Derrick, didn't you tell me he hired a Brooklyn gang? A gang named the Fire?" Butler asked. "You know, the guys who attacked Christian and Stiles outside that restaurant in TriBeCa last week?"

"Yeah."

"Maybe one of the gang talked. Maybe they knew where he was."

"Maybe," Walker said skeptically.

Gillette settled into the chair. It sounded as if Tom McGuire was really dead. Maybe he could finally relax, get back to a more normal life. "Who did McGuire torture up in Boston?" he asked.

"A guy name Tony Celino. His brother is Joe Celino, aka Twenty-two, boss of the Carbone family."

Then again, Gillette thought, maybe not.

Gillette hustled down Park Avenue to Grand Central Station. He headed through the station's north entrance, jogging past restaurants and shops to the escalators moving down to the main floor of the station. He turned right and covered the open area to the stairway leading up to the west entrance in a matter of seconds. He was up to the top of the stairway quickly, then past Michael Jordan's restaurant and out the door, his eyes flashing around, scouring the area for his contact. Suddenly there was a tap on his shoulder, and he whipped around. It was the QS agent he'd been looking for.

"Here you are, Mr. Gillette." The man handed Gillette a small package, then reached into his pocket and pulled out a set of car keys.

"Thanks." Gillette grabbed the package and the keys. "Where is it?"

The man pointed at a black Escalade parked at the curb a short distance away. It had tinted windows, as Gillette had requested.

"You didn't tell anybody about meeting me, did you?"

"No."

"Or about taking these for me?" Gillette held up the package.

"Nope."

Gillette could see the guy was anxious. "Don't worry."

"I don't want to lose my job, Mr. Gillette. I can't begin to tell you how pissed off Derrick will be if he finds out I did this."

"I'm the client. I pay you."

"Yeah, but I work for Derrick."

"Derrick won't find out. If he does, I'll make sure he knows I didn't give you any choice."

The QS agent eyed Gillette for a few seconds. "That's fine . . . if you're around to tell him."

"I'll be around," Gillette assured him. "Now, get to La-Guardia. Call me when you're there."

"Come in," Faraday called from his desk at the sound of the sharp knock.

Allison stepped into his office but didn't say anything right away.

"What do you want?" he asked. He was trying to answer a ton of e-mails, and he didn't have time for idle chitchat.

"Do you know where Christian is?" she asked, staying by the door.

Faraday shook his head. "Nope. Just that he isn't here."

"If you talk to him, will you transfer him over to me?"

"Just tell me what you want to ask him."

"That won't work," she said quickly. "Just transfer him over to me. Don't forget."

Faraday's eyes narrowed as she backed out of the office and closed the door. He didn't trust Allison Wallace one bit.

Dr. Davis had agreed—through Cathy Dylan—to meet with him that afternoon. Gillette's cell phone rang as he passed Exit 9 on the New Jersey Turnpike, headed south toward Richmond.

"Hello."

"It's Richard."

The QS agent who'd met Gillette at Grand Central Station an hour ago. "You there?" Gillette asked.

"Yes."

"How about the other guy?"

"Yes."

"Is the door to the cabin closed?"

"Yes."

"All right, give me the pilot. Tell him I'm in the back."

There was a rustling noise and some muffled words, then the pilot came on. "Hello?"

"It's Christian."

"Yes, sir."

"We're headed to Chicago. Let's get going."

"Okay."

Gillette smiled to himself as he ended the call, satisfied. He could hear the pilot's irritation at having to wait until the last minute to get destination instructions, but it had to be this way.

Next, Gillette dialed the cell phone number of another QS agent who was sitting in the cockpit beside the pilot of the second Everest jet. Gillette instructed the second pilot to fly to Atlanta.

Boyd's door shook with a loud knock.

"What is it, Daniel?" Boyd demanded after Ganze opened the door.

"I just got a call from our mechanic friend at LaGuardia. Both Everest planes are on the move."

"*Both?*"

"Yes."

"Did Gillette gag the pilots again?" Boyd asked angrily.

"Has he got his QS boys holding their dicks for them when they piss?"

"I guess. I haven't heard from either of them."

"Well, are we tracking the planes?"

"Of course."

"Good." Boyd put his elbows on the desk and rested his chin on the back of his hand. "Strange, isn't it? That Gillette would have both planes in the air at the same time?"

"Maybe."

"He's gotta be on one of them," Boyd observed. "The question is, what's the other plane doing? Is it on a real mission or just decoying?" He glanced up. "Any chance they could have found the tracking devices?"

"Sure," Ganze replied. "If they know what they're doing."

"Gillette's a smart fucker. He might have left them on there just to screw with whoever he assumed put them there."

"Or to try to find out who did."

Boyd nodded. "I hope we have people on the ground wherever he lands."

"I appreciate your meeting with me again on such short notice, Dr. Davis."

"It's my pleasure, Christian."

"How's that boy you operated on last week?"

Davis broke into a wide smile. "Very well. Thank you for asking. Still in the ICU, but the prognosis is quite good. He's responding well."

"That's great. You really are a miracle man."

"Please don't embarrass me like that." But Davis's smile grew wider. "So, are you back for the 'intermediate' lecture on nanotechnology?" he asked. "I can give you that one, but you'll have to find someone else for the 'expert' lecture."

Gillette thought carefully about what he was going to say. He was about to bring Davis inside the circle, and judging by that look he'd seen in Boyd's eyes at their meeting in Washington and again yesterday in Minneapolis, this could be dangerous. "No. The 'beginner' lecture was plenty. I need something else."

"What?"

Gillette hesitated.

Davis leaned forward over his desk, stroking his beard. He frowned. "Last time, I asked what you knew and you stonewalled me, Christian. You gave me a half-assed answer I knew was crap. Be straight with me this time, son."

Gillette looked up, surprised at Davis's words, even more so at his tone. The doctor seemed like such a gentle man, but clearly he had an edge to him. "I told you I was here last week because I had an investment opportunity. That wasn't true."

"Well, I—"

"Can you keep what I'm about to tell you completely confidential? I mean, *tell no one.*"

Davis gazed at Gillette for a few moments.

"It's vital that you stay quiet . . . for a lot of people's sakes. But, Doctor, I think this is something you'll want to hear."

Davis nodded slowly, his anger fading. "I'll keep my mouth shut."

The other man's eyes were flashing. Gillette wondered if it was out of fear or curiosity.

"I was approached by the government," Gillette began, "by people representing something called GARD, the Government Advanced Research Department. Don't bother going on the Internet to try to find it. I did. There's nothing."

"What did they want?" Davis asked, his voice hushed.

"Have you ever heard of DARPA, the Defense Advanced Research Projects Agency?"

"Sure. Those are the Defense Department's sci-fi geeks." Davis smiled. "And I use that term fondly. I consider myself one."

"Uh-huh. Well, they've been working on biomedical nanotech research for a few years, and they claim they're close to breaking through in a big way."

Davis's mouth dropped slowly open. "My God. Are you sure?"

"No," Gillette admitted. "I'm not sure at all. I only know what I've been told by the man who runs GARD. Or says he does," he added. He didn't really know if Boyd ran GARD or if there even was such an organization. Everything had come from Boyd or Ganze, so it was all questionable.

Davis's expression intensified. "Why did the people from GARD approach you?"

"Supposedly, they work with DARPA. They help them out when there's a problem. When something needs to go supersecret because there's a security issue with something the DARPA people are working on."

"Is that what's going on, a security problem?"

"Yes. They're worried that—"

"They're worried," Davis interrupted, "that one of the terrorist organizations is trying to get the technology."

"That's right. How did you know?"

"I didn't, but it makes sense." Davis shuddered. "If they did, biological warfare would suddenly look like something out of the Middle Ages. Once terrorists had bionanotech that worked, all they'd need is a delivery system. Then they could wipe out millions of us very quickly."

"Help me with that," Gillette said. "What do you mean? How could they wipe out millions of us?"

"Last week I told you how nanotechnology could save people. How those tiny little terminators could be programmed to kill cancer or head off a stroke by rebuilding blood vessels in the brain. Remember?"

"Of course."

"Well, those little terminators could also be programmed to kill healthy cells very easily. They can be programmed to do anything. But to make them killers of healthy cells on a massive scale, you have to have a way of getting them into lots of people's bodies without their realizing. You can't just release them into the atmosphere and hope they'll be inhaled. It doesn't work that way."

"Then what do you do?"

"If it was me, I'd buy a pharmaceutical company, then hide the nanodevils in things like nose sprays and cold medicines. Or I'd buy a food or a drink company. I'd buy something that produces things people ingest in huge quantities. Soft drinks, coffee, cookies. Anything like that."

Gillette looked past Davis and out the office window overlooking the James River, his mind flickering back to the dinner with Allison and Jack Mitchell. Veramax's primary products would make perfect nanodevil delivery systems.

"What does GARD want from you?" Davis asked.

"They want to use one of the companies we own to hide the project while they finish it up."

"*One* of the companies you own?"

Gillette gave Davis a quick overview of Everest. "Unlike GARD, you'll find Everest on the Internet," he finished.

"I'll take a look after you leave," Davis said. "Have they moved the project into the cutout yet?"

Gillette had started to explain cutouts to Davis, but the doctor was already familiar with them. "Yes, into a company we own that has a division in Minneapolis. There's a building on the division's property that was only being used by a few people. I kicked them out and let the bio-chemists use it. I met with them yesterday morning."

Davis tapped his forefinger on his lips. "Why are you telling me all this?" he asked. "How do I fit in?"

"I need you to find out who these people are."

"Which people?"

"The biochemists on the project," Gillette replied.

"I thought you said you met them."

"I did, and I can give you the names they gave me. What I need to do is make sure they are who they say they are."

"Being careful, are you?"

"I *have* to be, Doctor."

"You're smart. So, what's in it for Christian?" Davis asked quietly. "Why would you let these people use your company?"

Gillette had been anticipating this question. "Loyalty to the country. If these people are real and they're close to cracking the code, then I feel like I need to help if they think there's a security problem. The top executives at those financial firms who are big investors of mine would expect me to help. I'm sure some of them are already in-volved in the intelligence world, based on what I've learned in the last week or so, anyway." False as they were, he was glad the words were rolling off his tongue so easily.

Davis nodded. "You're in a tough position."

"Yeah," Gillette agreed, letting out a frustrated breath. "So will you help me, Doctor?"

Davis leaned back in his chair. "Now I know what's in it for you. So tell me: What's in it for me?"

Wright sat in a taxi in downtown Richmond, outside the Medical Center of Virginia. Same taxi he'd hailed outside Grand Central Station almost eight hours ago after watch-ing Gillette hop into the black Escalade and tear off. Wright had been forced to offer the cabbie more and more money as the day wore on and the miles added up. By the time they reached Richmond, the negotiated fare had reached a thousand dollars and his Rolex, and the guy demanded payment.

So Wright had gone to a cash machine, withdrawn the thousand dollars, and given it to the cabbie. Now the guy was happy, smacking his lips as he devoured a messy cheesesteak sub in the front as they waited for Gillette to reappear.

Wright looked down at his cell phone and Blackberry, lying on the backseat beside him. He smiled. He'd simply conducted business today from the cab, not missing a beat. The Hush-Hush deal was on track—he'd spoken to the Everest associates who were crunching the numbers several times—and he'd arranged for a meeting with the Ohio Teachers Pension. Christian would be quite satisfied—and he'd never know he'd been followed.

Gillette flipped through new e-mails as he headed north on I-95 toward Washington, D.C. He scrolled to the last one, shaking his head at the rush hour traffic crawling the other way. The background check on Allison's new assistant had come up clean, the message from Derrick Walker indicated. As Allison had said, Hamid had spent the last few years at Citibank, and his references were solid.

Gillette dropped the Blackberry on the passenger seat and picked up the package the QS agent had given him, sliding the stack of photographs out of the envelope. Picture after picture of Boyd and Ganze outside the Minneapolis Beezer Johnson facility yesterday.

He gazed to the left again, at the traffic, thinking about Stiles. The memorial was on Sunday, and Stiles's grandmother had asked him to make a speech. He'd met her several times at the hospital over the last ten months, and they'd gotten to be friends. Stiles's grandmother had raised

Quentin—his mother had died when he was young—and had been responsible for him going into the army. Stiles always claimed that she had saved him from a dead-end life.

His cell phone rang. It was Walker. "Hello."

"Where are you?" Walker demanded angrily.

"I don't want to say on the cell phone."

"Look, I need to—"

"When I pull off I'll call you from a pay phone, all right?"

"Yeah, all right."

"Besides," Gillette spoke up, "McGuire's dead, remember? I'm fine."

"Which is one of the reasons I called."

"Oh?"

"Yeah, the DNA test checked out. It was definitely McGuire's hand his wife found."

"Well, he was right-handed. If somehow he's still alive, he won't be able to shoot very well."

"Very funny. Look, pull over right now so I can get a detail to you."

"I'll call you when I pull off for gas." Gillette heard Walker curse at the other end.

"Did you get my e-mail on that guy Allison Wallace wants to bring in?" Walker asked.

"Yeah, I got it."

"Sorry it took so much longer, but we wanted to be very careful. Faraday's nervous about him."

"Nigel told you that?"

"Several times."

"Jesus." That wasn't good. They didn't need the ACLU coming down on them if Hamid got wind of Faraday's suspicions. "You think the kid is okay?"

Walker was silent for a few moments.

"Derrick?"

"I don't like his attitude. More important, there's four months we can't account for."

"Four months? What do you mean?"

"The kid was at Citibank for a little over three years before Allison hired him. Before Citibank he worked at something called the Pan Arab Bank, in their New York branch here in Manhattan."

"I thought Allison said he went to the University of Michigan."

"He did, before Pan Arab. Anyway, he left Pan Arab in April, but he didn't start at Citibank until the following August."

"Did you ask him about those four months?"

"Yeah, this morning."

"And?"

"After he got through giving me attitude, he said he had traveled around the U.S. on his own during that time, sightseeing."

"On his own?"

"Yeah."

"Did you ask him where he went, what he saw?"

"He wouldn't talk about it. He hit me with the profiling thing again. And Christian?"

"What?"

"His parents still live in Iran. They work for the government."

Gillette gritted his teeth. Maybe Faraday was right to be suspicious. His other line rang. "Let me take this call. I'll be in touch later."

"Be careful."

"I will." He switched lines. "Hello."

"Christian, it's Percy Lundergard from Chatham."

"Hey, Percy."

"I set up this town meeting we talked about. So we can get your store built."

"When is it?"

"Sunday night at the high school auditorium."

"That doesn't leave much time to get the word out," Gillette said. "Will we get enough people there?"

"My family's been working this thing pretty good. There'll be plenty of people there."

"On a Sunday night?"

Lundergard chuckled. "Never lived in a small town, have you?"

"No."

"It'll be the social event of the month."

Joe Celino was back in New York, back at his home in Staten Island, sitting on his veranda with Al Scarpa. They were taking in the sights of Manhattan drenched in late afternoon sunshine.

"I think you musta made a pretty good impression on David Wright," Scarpa said. "This morning he hired a taxi at Grand Central to go all the way to Richmond, Virginia, to follow Gillette. At least that's what Paul told me."

"Who did Gillette see in Richmond?"

"A doctor. A brain surgeon."

Celino looked over at Scarpa.

"Yeah, I know."

"Did we get that guy who capped Stiles for us yet?" Celino asked. "That guy who was crewing on Gillette's boat?"

Scarpa shook his head. "No."

"*No?*"

"Joseph, it's the strangest thing. Nobody's seen him." Scarpa shrugged. "He musta figured out he was gonna get it in the end and run."

"We only gave him half the money, right?"

"Maybe that was enough."

Celino grimaced. He didn't like the sound of this. "Find

the bastard," he snarled. "I don't care what it takes. *Find him.*"

"What are you doing?" Wright pounded on the Plexiglas separating the front seat from the backseat of the cab. They were slowing down, and the black Escalade was disappearing into the traffic ahead. "You can't lose this guy."

"There's nothing I can do," the cabbie yelled back. "The engine's crapping out. I knew I shouldn't have fucking come all the way down here."

"Shit." Wright grabbed his cell phone and dialed the number, but Gillette had already disappeared.

The meeting place was a parking garage near the Potomac River waterfront below Georgetown, on the west side of Washington. Basement level, next to the elevator banks—nine P.M. sharp. Gillette had been standing in the shadows beside the Escalade for half an hour. He checked his watch in the low light: It was nine-fifteen.

A white sedan made the U-turn from the level above at the far end of the garage and approached slowly, headlights on. Gillette stepped back all the way to the wall and watched the driver swing into a spot, then climb out of the car.

The man looked around as he stood up, then closed the car door and walked toward the elevators.

From a distance, he reminded Gillette of Gordon Meade, the man who had come with Allison to Everest that first morning. He was tall and thin, slightly stooped, most likely in his fifties. Gillette spotted the bottled water the man said he'd be carrying as he stopped a few feet from the elevator banks. Gillette moved out, toward the man.

They made eye contact as soon as Gillette appeared in front of the Escalade, and they stared at each other until

Gillette stopped a few feet away. "Ted Casey?" Gillette asked.

Casey nodded.

"How do you want to do this?"

"What do you mean?"

"We can stand out here in the open, or we can go in that SUV over there." Gillette pointed at the Escalade.

"Yeah," Casey agreed, eying the tinted windows, "let's do that."

When they were inside the SUV, Casey spoke first. "I looked at your Web site. You guys are big. Bigger than Apex."

"Thanks to the new fund, that's right."

"How big is that fund?"

"Twenty billion plus," Gillette answered.

Casey whistled. "Russell Hughes tells me you're going to take over Apex with some of that money."

"Yeah."

"Will you be in charge of Apex after you buy it?" Casey asked nervously.

"Initially. After a few weeks I'm going to turn it over to one of my partners, guy named David Wright. But Wright doesn't need to know about what Omega IT does in the Middle East. Ultimately he will, but not yet." Casey seemed happy to hear that.

"Good. We need to keep that circle as small as possible."

"Don't worry. What's going on at Omega is safe with me." Gillette hesitated. "Are you actually in the Directorate of Operations?"

"Yup, I'm a spook."

"How long have you been with the CIA?"

"Since I graduated from Yale thirty-five years ago. I'm a career man."

That was good. There was a better chance Casey would

be able to answer his questions. "Are you responsible for a number of cutouts, or just Omega IT?"

Casey chewed on his answer. "Not just Omega."

"What else?"

"Can't tell you." Casey put the plastic water bottle in a cup holder.

He seemed to be growing more anxious by the moment, Gillette noticed.

"What did you want to ask me, Christian?" Casey asked impatiently.

"Do you know of a man named Norman Boyd?"

Casey looked over at Gillette. "Maybe. Why?"

"What do you know about him?"

Casey said nothing.

"Look," Gillette spoke up, "I'm going to keep Omega a secret, but I need you to cooperate. I'm loyal, but it has to go both ways. If you know anything about Norman Boyd, I want to hear it."

"How do you know Boyd?" Casey asked.

"He wants me to help him the way Russell Hughes helps you, the way you want me to help you. In fact, I think Boyd approached Russell before he approached me, and you told Russell to stay away from him. Right?"

"Yes."

"Why did you tell him that?"

"Boyd's part of Defense Department intel," Casey began. "He's been around a long time over there. Got the ear of a lot of very important people at the Pentagon, people who want to see the DOD come out ahead of the CIA in the intelligence landgrab that's going on right now." Casey exhaled heavily. "Maybe you've heard, there's a massive power struggle going on. Iraq, 9/11, and Osama have turned everything upside down. Everything's in chaos. No one knows who's going to end up with what. Careers will be made *and* destroyed by this."

"I've heard a little about it. But not much," Gillette admitted.

"Well, Boyd's a sacred cow over there at DOD. Always in charge of very *secret*, very *important* projects. He's aggressive about grabbing everything he can for the Pentagon. We respect that at the CIA, it's natural. But he's a renegade. He thinks he's outside the law, outside what's tolerable, maybe because he's older. But we can't accept it."

"What do you mean?" Gillette could tell that Casey was getting exasperated. "What's he done?"

Casey grimaced. "His people went too far with one of our important friends, a guy who helped us for many years."

"What do you mean, they went too far?"

"They killed him." Casey held up a hand. "Don't get me wrong, this guy was no angel. But he didn't deserve to die, and it really smacks our reputation."

Boyd's people were killers after all.

"They were interrogating him," Casey continued, "and they went too far."

"Was this guy someone you were close to?"

"No, I wasn't his handler. And you didn't hear all this from me," Casey added sternly. "I'd never admit I told you anything. I'd never admit we had this meeting. Anyway, that's why I told Hughes to stay away from Boyd. As far as I'm concerned, he's crazy."

Casey seemed believable enough, but he was CIA. Was anything he said believable? "Any question about Boyd's loyalty to the U.S.?" Gillette asked.

"None," Casey replied firmly. "Boyd bleeds red, white, and blue. But there is one thing I heard about him," he said, his voice dropping.

"What's that?"

"He's got a chip on his shoulder about how much money he could have made outside the government. He feels like he sacrificed a lot by staying in all these years, and he wants something for it. Something big." Casey snorted. " 'Course, so do all of us." Casey picked up the water bottle from the cup holder. "There was a rumor that he was trying to move something out of one of his projects and into a private shell so he could sell it later on and make big bucks. But I haven't heard anything more about that for a while."

CHAPTER 18

"Chris." Debbie's voice crackled over the intercom.

Gillette was sitting behind his desk, rubbing his bloodshot eyes. He'd only gotten two hours' sleep the previous night. There'd been construction on the Jersey Turnpike—causing a twelve-mile backup—after his meeting with Ted Casey in Washington. A meeting that had gone longer than he'd expected. He hadn't gotten to his apartment until three o'clock this morning—just four hours ago.

"What is it?" he answered, his voice scratchy.

"Nigel wants to see you."

"Let him in."

"Since when do I need to be announced?" Faraday blustered, bursting into the office.

"Calm down."

"Where were you yesterday?"

"Out."

"Come on, Chris, I've got to know where you are—"

"What do you want?"

Faraday stood in the middle of the room, hands on his hips, fuming. "I need to tell you something."

"Okay."

"It's about Allison."

Gillette's eyes narrowed.

"She called a few more of our investors yesterday," Faraday explained, "trying to buddy up to them. They said she made it sound like she was running Everest Capital. Or would be soon."

"I'll talk to her." Gillette wanted to believe it was just an error of enthusiasm. "She's young and aggressive, like David. That's all."

"I don't trust her."

"I know."

"She was going crazy yesterday trying to find you."

Gillette already knew that. She'd left five messages on his cell phone.

"By the way, I found out something very interesting about our NFL franchise and the bidding process," Faraday said.

Gillette had been thinking about his trip west. Meeting Marilyn and seeing Lana. "What?"

"We weren't the highest bidder." Faraday hesitated. "By a long shot."

Somehow that didn't surprise him. Of course, not much did anymore. "By how much?" Gillette asked.

"Fifty million."

Gillette's mind flashed back to his lunch with Kurt Landry. He'd gotten a strange vibe about the whole deal that day. "Somebody was willing to pay five hundred million and they didn't get the deal?"

"Yup."

"How did you find out?"

"A little bird told me."

"Nigel, I have to know."

"I can't tell you, I really can't, but he's credible. He's an investment banker, a senior member of the team who put a bid together for a very wealthy family. Not *Wallace* wealthy, but wealthy."

"Did you tell him what we bid?"

"No." Faraday moved closer to Gillette's desk. "I think that's pretty strange, Chris."

"I hear you." Suddenly, there were a lot of strange things going on.

"Chris." It was Debbie on the intercom again. "Now Allison wants to see you."

Gillette met Faraday's eyes.

"I guess I better get out of here," Faraday muttered, turning to go.

"Let her in," Gillette said.

Faraday and Allison passed at the doorway, giving each other their standard quick nod.

"You never phoned last night," she said.

Gillette glanced up. "Was I supposed to?"

"I wanted an update on your day."

"I didn't get home till late. *Very* late."

Allison plopped down in the chair on the other side of his desk. "Well, I'm right upstairs now," she said, smiling widely. "That ought to make Faith happy."

Faith still hadn't called him back again. Problem was, maybe she was right this time. Maybe he shouldn't have invited Allison on the cruise while Faith was in London. Nothing had happened, but he could see how it would aggravate her. "You moved in yesterday?"

"Yeah."

"How did it go?"

"Smooth as silk. The movers took care of everything. We're as good as roommates now."

Gillette didn't want to get into this now, but he owed it to Faraday. "Have you been calling our investors?" he asked, trying to figure out if her expression was registering shock that he'd found out so fast or fear that he was going to be angry. Either way, she'd clearly been taken by surprise.

She didn't answer right away. "Yeah," she finally admitted. "So what?"

"Why'd you do it?"

"To tell them I'd joined the firm as a managing partner," she said nonchalantly, regaining her composure. "I didn't think you'd mind."

"Do me a favor and talk to Nigel before you do that again. That's his turf, and he's very sensitive about anyone stomping around on it."

"Fine," she agreed, rolling her eyes. "So, where were you last night?"

"You're not going to like my answer," he muttered. "Nobody does."

"Why not?"

"I can't tell you."

"I'm so sick of this," she snapped. "Were you with Faith?"

"No. Not that it's any of your business if I was."

"Then where were you?" Allison put both hands up. "I know, I know. Something came up. Look, I'm getting really tired of this," she said loudly. "I mean, I invest a ton of money in this place, find a great deal in Veramax, and offer to buy Beezer Johnson at a very nice price. I'm going the extra mile here, but I'm not getting anything in return."

Gillette stood up. "I appreciate—"

"Were you in Richmond again?"

He didn't answer.

She put her head back and groaned. "Is this how it is with you? Mystery after mystery?"

"Maybe."

"Was I an idiot to invest so much money in Everest?"

He wanted to come back at her with a flip remark, but discretion won out. "You're going to be very happy with your investment."

"Have you at least set up a meeting with that FDA guy?" Allison asked. "Jack Mitchell called me *again* yesterday."

Gillette nodded, satisfied with her surprised expression.

"I'm meeting with Rothchild in Washington two weeks from tomorrow. Has Mitchell written his apology letter?"

"I don't know, I—"

"Find out, and while you're at it, make sure he's doing everything he can to get Rothchild into the Racquet Club. Like he said he would. I'm going to call a friend of mine who's on the membership committee to see if he can help. If Jack hasn't done anything on that, tell him to get off his ass fast."

"I'll call him right now," she said, rising from the chair.

"Good. And Allison?"

"What?" she asked, turning back around.

"I haven't seen that analysis on Beezer Johnson yet. The one that shows how great the combination of it and your family's company would be."

"I'll get right on that, too."

Once Allison was gone, David Wright wanted time.

Wright moved into Gillette's office carrying two copies of a Hush-Hush presentation, a summary of the due diligence he'd done so far. "Over there," Gillette said, covering the phone with one hand and pointing toward the couches and the coffee table. "Give me a second."

By the time Wright had spread out the materials, Gillette was off the call. They sat together and reviewed the material for several minutes.

"Did Cathy do any sensitivity analysis on the exit multiple?" Gillette asked after scanning the financial projections.

"Doing it as we speak."

"I want to see what the return is if we can't flip Hush-Hush quickly to the French. If we have to hold it for a while."

Wright rose from the couch and headed for Gillette's desk.

"Where are you going?"

"To get your calculator so we can crunch that return," Wright answered. "Top drawer, right?"

"Yeah," Gillette said, noticing that Wright's wallet was lying on the table in the middle of the Hush-Hush due diligence material. He spotted a familiar-looking piece of paper sticking out of it. "Do me a favor after you get the calculator, will you?" he called. "Go see if Debbie has my daily planner. I think I gave it to her yesterday. I want to go over next week's schedule with you."

"Sure."

When Wright was out of the office, Gillette quickly pulled the slip of paper from the wallet. It was a toll receipt from the New Jersey Turnpike. He checked the date. Yesterday.

When Gillette was finished with Wright, he headed for Cathy Dylan's office. "Cathy." He knocked on her door as he leaned into the office. He'd gotten her message from Debbie. "What's up?"

She motioned for him to come in and close the door. "I spoke to Dr. Davis, and he needs to talk to you as soon as possible. He says it's urgent."

Gillette stared at her intently. "Not a word of this to anyone."

"I know."

He turned to go, then stopped. "Do something else for me, will you?" For the first time, he thought he saw fear in her eyes. "Check the Internet and see if there were any small plane crashes in western Pennsylvania in the last couple of weeks."

"Dr. Davis."

"Christian? Glad you called so quickly."

Gillette was at a pay phone in the lobby of the Intercontinental Hotel. "Cathy said it was urgent."

"I tried tracking down those names you gave me from

your meeting in Minneapolis. No luck. No one knows them, which is strange. You're right, the nanotech research community isn't that big. I thought someone would have recognized at least one of them. Usually, somebody went to school with somebody."

Gillette had anticipated this. Boyd didn't seem like the type to throw around crucial information haphazardly. "Well, thanks. I appreciate your help."

"Don't go so fast. That's not the only reason I called."

Gillette perked up. "Oh?"

"Maybe this is nothing, Christian, but you never know."

"Go on," Gillette urged.

"One of the people I called to check the names out with is a guy named Nathaniel Pete. Nate's in Boston. Runs with that whole Cambridge crowd. He's a biochemist graduate school professor at Harvard, and very into nanotech. He could be running one of these government nanotech programs, but he's a little flaky. Great credentials, but he wouldn't pass the gut-check test. Right out of the sixties. Long hair, tie-dyed shirts. Not somebody you'd trust one of your most important projects to. But trust me, he's brilliant."

"What did he say?"

"Said the wife of a friend of his called him yesterday, very upset. She said her husband has been working on a highly confidential project for the government over the last two years, and suddenly he can't see her or call her. He's going away and he's not sure how long it'll be. She said they had a two-minute conversation a few days ago, and that was it. She hasn't seen or heard from him since."

"What's his name, Doctor?"

"Matt Lee."

"Gillette's gone!" Wright shouted into the phone. "And I have no idea where he went."

"Calm down, Davey."

"There's only so much I can do before he gets suspicious. I can't follow him around every second."

"Easy, easy. We know that."

Wright swallowed hard. "I mean, Christ, I went all the way to Richmond yesterday in a damn cab for you guys."

"And we all appreciate that, the man you met with in Las Vegas particularly. He wanted me to tell you of his thanks. You've done a good job."

Wright started breathing a little easier. His mind had gone wild with possibilities. They'd shoot him on the street, kidnap his wife. Awful things he had no way to stop.

"Davey?"

"Yes, sir?"

"From now on, you don't need to worry about following him. All you need to be is his friend. Someone he confides in all the time."

Wright took a long breath. That I can do, he thought.

Gillette sped north on I-95, toward Boston, toward Matt Lee's home. Dr. Davis was to have called Lee's wife, Mary, to prepare her for Gillette's knock on the door.

Gillette's cell phone rang. "Hello."

"Christian, it's Cathy."

"Hi."

"There was only one plane crash in western Pennsylvania in the last two weeks. The plane went down about twenty miles north of Pittsburgh last Wednesday."

"Fatalities?"

"One," she said, reading off an article on the Internet. "The other four people on board were okay, broken bones but nothing serious. It looks like the guy who died was thrown from the plane, and that's what killed him."

"Who was he?"

"A senior executive of Three River Bank. They were all TRB people on the plane."

Three River Bank was headquartered in Pittsburgh. No way that crash had anything to do with Boyd. "That's it?"

"Yup."

"Thanks, I'll talk to you later."

Gillette checked the rearview mirror as he ended the call. He'd made certain Wright was in a meeting behind closed doors before he'd left—which didn't mean somebody else wasn't back there. So he'd taken a couple of quick turns on his way out of Manhattan, and it didn't look as if anyone were following him.

He slid a disc into the CD player and tried to relax, but it was no use. He started thinking about everything that was happening. About how he was going to have to wait until Monday morning to confront Wright about the New Jersey Turnpike toll receipt. He was flying to the West Coast this afternoon, then there was Stiles's memorial service tomorrow, and he had to head to that Chatham town meeting right after the service. Besides, Wright was leaving the city with his wife for the rest of the weekend after the service. So Monday would be his first chance to talk to Wright face-to-face. He couldn't wait to hear that explanation. The stamp on the receipt registered the same time he would have been going through the same toll.

It was afternoon and the sky was a blazing blue when Gillette pulled the SUV to a stop in front of a quaint house in Concord, Massachusetts, a residential neighborhood outside Boston. He was on his cell phone, calling for the larger Everest jet, and he was using the same drill. There was a QS agent sitting beside the pilot as he relayed the destination. Gillette didn't care if somebody figured out he'd gone to Boston after the fact, when the plane landed at Logan. They'd never be able to figure out he had visited Mary Lee by that time. And he didn't care if anyone knew he was going to the West Coast—that trip was about family, not business. Nothing he needed to be careful about.

When Gillette was done talking to the pilot, he stowed the cell phone in his pocket and headed up the cement walkway toward the Lees' modest-looking, two-story home. He knocked on the door, but there was no answer right away. He checked his watch—one P.M. Exactly the time Davis had told him to be at Mary's front door. He knocked again, hoping he hadn't just wasted most of a day.

Finally, the door opened partway and a timid-looking Asian woman appeared. Most of her remained obscured behind the door.

"Mrs. Lee?"

She nodded almost imperceptibly.

"I'm Christian Gillette. Dr. Davis was supposed to call you. At the suggestion of Nathaniel Pete."

Again, the barely noticeable nod.

"Did Dr. Davis explain to you who I was?"

"Yes." Her voice was as timid as her demeanor, only slightly more than a whisper.

"Do you have Internet connection, Mrs. Lee?" Gillette asked.

"Yes."

"Then you can go online and check me out. My picture is on our Web site. I'll stay here while you do it. Our URL is—"

"I already checked the Web site," she cut in, "and I called some friends who know Wall Street. They said you were real."

"Good."

She opened the door wide. "Please come in. You can call me Mary."

"Thank you." He moved into the foyer and shut the door. "Please call me Christian," he said, gesturing around. "You have a very nice home."

"Thank you," she said, then suddenly teared up. "I'm so worried about my husband." She began to sob, putting a hand to her mouth to hide her quivering chin.

"I understand," Gillette said softly, surprising himself by putting his arms around her. For several minutes he held her, feeling the sobs racking her body.

Finally she stepped away from him. "I'm so embarrassed," she said, dabbing her eyes with a tissue.

"Please don't be," Gillette urged. "I know this is so difficult for you." He hesitated, not certain if he should say this. "I'm going to be very candid with you, Mary, I'm worried about your husband, too. But I'm going to do my best to find him."

"Thank you. It's just not like him to go off like this and not call. I've talked to him every day for the last fourteen years. Now this."

"Do you have a picture of him?"

"Yes."

She hurried to a table in the living room, picked up a frame, and returned, holding it out for Gillette as she neared him. It was a photograph of Matt and her standing together, holding hands. The man in the picture wasn't one of the two men he'd met in Minneapolis.

"Does it help?"

Gillette kept staring at the photograph, unable to meet Mary's eyes. "I'm not sure."

"Men came here yesterday," Mary spoke up.

He finally looked up from the picture.

"They went through all of Matt's things while I had to sit in the kitchen with one of them. They went through his den, his closets, his clothes, everything. They took some things."

Gillette reached into his coat pocket and pulled out the pictures the QS agent had taken for him in Minneapolis.

"Were either of these men here yesterday?" he asked, showing the pictures to her.

She gasped, then pointed at Ganze immediately. "Him."

Matt Lee had been part of the nanotech project. The fact that Ganze had come to the Lees' house linked them. And it was clear to Gillette that Matt wasn't coming back. The real question now: What was Norman Boyd really up to?

"What's wrong?" she asked.

Gillette grimaced. "I'm afraid there are some very bad people in charge of the project your husband was working on. I'm sorry." He could see that she understood what he was trying to say. That she'd heard him use the past tense.

"Follow me," she said suddenly.

Gillette followed Mary up the stairs to the couple's bedroom but stayed in the doorway as she moved to her dresser and opened a jewelry box. She pulled out the top drawer of the box and put it on the dresser, then removed a small package from inside. "Here," she said, moving to where he stood, holding out the package. "I don't want this."

"What is it?" Gillette asked, taking it from her shaking hands.

"A flash drive. Matt kept calling it the silver bullet."

"Flash drive?"

"A portable disk drive."

"What did he mean by 'silver bullet'?"

She shook her head and started sobbing quietly again. "I should have known something was wrong."

"Why?"

"He brought this home the night before he called to tell me he was going away. He suspected something."

"What's on it?" Gillette asked. "Did he tell you?"

"Everything the team had done up until the day he called to tell me he had to go away. He said they didn't have far to go on the project. That anyone who knew what they were doing and had this could finish it."

Gillette swallowed hard as he slipped the flash drive into his shirt pocket. "Mary," he said firmly, "you can't tell anyone I was here."

As Gillette walked down the path toward the Escalade, he thought about Boyd and remembered something from the other day in Minneapolis. When Boyd had seen Derrick Walker in the Beezer facility, he'd asked about the security guy Gillette had brought to Washington last week—meaning Stiles. It had seemed like nothing more than an innocent question at the time. Problem was, Boyd had never seen Stiles in Washington. Boyd had stayed in his office the entire time, and Stiles had never gone in—Ganze hadn't let him. Only Ganze had seen Stiles. So how the hell could Boyd know Walker was a different guy?

Dr. Scott Davis sat strapped to the chair, a hood over his head. The ropes binding his wrists and ankles to the chair were extremely tight, cutting into his skin, and he moaned as the tension became excruciating.

"I want to know what you told Christian Gillette," said the man standing behind him. He was holding a knife to Davis's throat. "I want to know everything you and he talked about."

CHAPTER 19

Nikki lay on her back in the hospital bed, her eyes mere slits. Gillette watched her for a few moments from the doorway. Every breath seemed like a struggle, and she was painfully frail. He'd talked to one of the nurses and learned that Nikki's lung cancer was advancing rapidly. That she probably didn't have more than a few months. He shook his head. If they'd just caught it earlier . . . But it was too late now. He pressed his hand against the flash drive in his shirt pocket, wondering if it might hold the key to her cure.

He hadn't seen her in sixteen years. They'd been so close growing up—even though she was Lana's child—but she'd let him down when he needed her most.

"Nikki."

She turned her head slowly toward him, a wan smile forming on her lips, her eyes glassy but joyful. "Chris," she murmured.

He took her hand. It was cold. She tried to squeeze his hand back when he took hers, but it was a feeble attempt. He leaned down and kissed her on the cheek. It was cold, too.

"How did you find out?" she asked.

"Lana showed up in New York last week out of the blue. She told me you were sick."

Nikki groaned, then coughed several times. "My husband screwed it all up. He said we had coverage, but he was lying. He's gone now. I don't know where. . . ."

"Christ, Nikki, how could you be with someone like that?"

"I didn't have you around to guide me."

"You didn't *want* me around. How many times did I call?"

"I'm not blaming you, I'm blaming myself. I've always let Lana control me."

Gillette brushed away a tear rolling down her cheek.

She tried to squeeze his hand again. "I wish I could go back and change everything, I really do. I'd give anything."

"Why didn't you call me when you got sick?" he asked.

She shrugged weakly. "How could I? I wasn't there when *you* needed *me*."

"So what? This is your life we're talking about. No second chances."

"Yeah," she said softly, "I know."

He cursed under his breath. An awful thing to say. "All right," he said in a determined voice, looking around at the other three patients. "The first thing we're going to do is get you a private room."

Two hours later, Nikki was in a private room with a beautiful view of dusk settling over downtown Los Angeles. The aroma of fresh-cut flowers filled the room, and a stack of her favorite magazines and books sat on the nightstand.

"Thanks, Christian," she said, her voice stronger. "This is nice. I feel better."

She looked better, too, he was glad to see. "Well, you should get some rest."

"How long will you be in Los Angeles?"

"I'm going back to New York in the morning." He was having dinner with Marilyn tonight, then seeing Lana after that. Stiles's memorial service started at ten Saturday morning, and he wasn't going to chance missing it.

"Will you come and see me again before you leave," she pleaded, "even if it's just for a few minutes?"

"Of course." He leaned down and kissed her on the forehead, then turned to go. But he stopped at the doorway. "I need to ask you a question," he said, moving slowly back to where she lay. "Was I the only one Dad had outside his marriage to Lana?"

Nikki took a shallow breath. "No. There were others. Daddy had a problem."

"How many others?" He had to see if he got the same answer from Nikki that he had gotten from Lana.

"Three, all from different women."

Confirmed. "God."

"Daddy started making a lot of money, and I guess he couldn't control himself. I guess he felt like it was his right. Plus, he and Mom . . . well, they had issues."

"That's no excuse."

"She was a bitch to him, Christian. She was never satisfied with anything."

"Do you know who the women were?" Gillette asked.

Nikki shook her head. "I think they were all from the Los Angeles area, but I don't know their names." She hesitated. "Mom does."

Lana had lied. So predictable. "Do you think she ever cheated on him?"

"I thought so, once."

"Why?"

"A man came to the house a couple of times in the months before Dad's plane crash, but then he stopped." Nikki smiled. "I took pictures of him sitting out on the patio with her from one of the upstairs windows one time. I was going to confront her, you know? But then Dad died . . . and that was that." She frowned. "Not that I probably ever would have been brave enough to actually do that." She looked up at him. "Do you think you'll ever get married, Christian?"

He thought about the question for a few moments, then gave her the best smile he could manage. "I don't know. But if I ever do, you better be there. You hear me?"

Her eyes filled with tears instantly, and she nodded.

Gillette had enjoyed dinner with Marilyn even more than he'd anticipated. She was pretty and dripping with diamonds. She'd gotten ten million dollars after Clayton died—as had the other three women he'd fathered children with. Gillette had been uncomfortable when he'd seen all the jewelry, but she'd assured him she'd invested most of the money wisely and didn't have any financial worries. She hadn't asked him for money, as he'd anticipated she would. Why wouldn't he expect that? Others had.

"It was wonderful to see you," Marilyn gushed as they finished coffee. "And to find out how successful you are."

"Thanks." Gillette had studied her all through dinner, looking for the physical similarities. He couldn't decide if he'd found any.

"We have to stay close," she urged. "Please call me when you have time. I know you're so busy. I don't want to bother you."

"I'll call," he assured her, folding his napkin and putting it on the table. "Did you love my father?" he asked.

"So much, Christian. He was such a charismatic man." She smiled. "Like you."

Gillette smiled back. "I always remember those cigars he smoked. The Cubans. I loved the way they smelled, you know?"

Marilyn pondered his comment. Finally she sighed. "I miss that, too."

* * *

"You lied to me in New York." Gillette and Lana were sitting on the patio of her Bel Air mansion.

"I don't know what you're talking about."

It was late, but in the glow of the outside lights Gillette could see that the mansion and its grounds had been neglected. There were dead trees and bushes in the large backyard, the paint on the shutters was peeling badly, and many of the stones on the patio were cracked and chipped. "You told me you didn't know the names of the women Dad had children with outside your marriage. Nikki says you do, and I believe her."

Lana stuck her chin out fiercely. "She's wrong."

"I need to know, Lana."

"Well, I can't help you."

"Then I can't help you."

Lana folded her hands tightly in her lap. "How would you help me?" she asked.

"The only way you care about. Money."

"I'm not as evil as you think I am."

"I'm not here to debate that," Gillette replied. "I have my opinion, you have yours. Let's leave it at that."

Lana bit her lower lip for a moment. "How much would you be willing to help me?"

"I'll lend you ten million dollars as long as you pledge this house to me as collateral."

"Do you have your father's curse? Does it always have to be about business?"

"That's what it is with you, Lana. Business. Always was, always will be."

"You aren't mine," she snapped.

"Wasn't *my* choice."

They were silent for a few minutes.

"Are you going to give me the names?" Gillette finally asked.

"I don't know yet." Lana picked up her wineglass and took a large gulp. "I could get in so much trouble if I do."

"Why?"

"There might still be people around who would make me pay."

Gillette's eyes narrowed. "Who?"

"Important people."

"*Who?*"

"People who hated your father."

"Why did they hate him?"

"He had information that could have destroyed them."

"What kind of information?"

"I don't know, they wouldn't tell me. Neither would he."

Gillette's brain began to pound. "Were they the ones who killed him?"

"The crash was an accident."

"*Lana!*"

"I gave them the names of the women, that's all I did."

"What did you get in return?" Gillette demanded. "I know you too well, Lana," he said when she didn't answer right away. "You don't give away anything for free."

"They said they were going to use the names of the women against your father. Publicize Clayton's infidelity in an awful way, so I'd be able to divorce him and get everything. Which sounded pretty damn good to me at that point, Christian," she said, her voice trembling. "He'd just started seeing someone else, a girl who was nineteen, for Christ's sake." She put her hands to her face. "You can't imagine what it's like to know that every time your husband walks out the door, you won't see him again until he's made love to another woman. I'd had enough. I couldn't take it anymore."

For a moment, Gillette tried to understand what she'd endured, tried to feel sympathy for her. But it wouldn't come. He simply couldn't get past what she'd done to him. "Just give me the names."

"Do we have good news yet?" Boyd asked irritably.

Ganze shook his head. "No. I just came in to tell you that Gillette's been visiting his stepmother at the Bel Air house for the last thirty minutes."

Boyd's eyes rose from his desk. "Oh, my God."

Gillette sat behind the desk in his father's old study, taking in the sights and smells. It had been a long time, but he was sure he could still smell the sweet aroma of the pipe.

He'd tried to work with the computer there to copy what was on the flash drive Mary Lee had given him, but the hard drive was too old and the memory insufficient to handle the transfer. He reached for the phone and dialed Nikki's direct line at the hospital.

"Hello."

Her voice was groggy, and he felt bad for calling so late. But he had to talk to her. "Nikki, it's Christian."

"Oh, hi."

"I'm sorry to wake you up."

"It's all right, what's the matter?"

"When I was there with you earlier, you told me you took pictures of a man who visited Lana at the house before Dad's plane crash. He was out on the patio with her."

"Yes. Actually I took a whole bunch of them, maybe ten."

"Do you still have them?"

She was quiet for a few moments. "I didn't take them with me when I moved out of the house. Which was like ten or eleven years ago. If they're still around, they're in a box in the bottom left-hand drawer of my desk. But Mom probably threw them out."

*   *   *

Davis lay on the cot, his wrists and ankles chained tightly to the frame. His captors had tortured him three separate times, hadn't given him any food or water, and had pulled one of his teeth with a pair of needle-nose pliers. But they hadn't broken him yet. Not because he had any allegiance to Christian Gillette; no, they hadn't broken him because the very fact that he'd been kidnapped and tortured proved to him that someone was close to a major breakthrough on nanotechnology—someone who shouldn't have it.

And for Gillette to stay in front of that person, he needed the biggest head start Davis could give him.

Gillette opened the drawer of Nikki's old desk and reached down for the small box. His fingers shook as he opened it. The pictures were there, as Nikki had promised, ten of them. Clear shots of Lana and the man Nikki had mentioned sitting on the patio outside the house.

Gillette exhaled heavily. Unbelievable.

There was no need for Lana to give him his mother's real name now. He just wanted to know that Marilyn McRae wasn't his real mother. Her slipup at dinner about the cigars—his father never smoked cigars—was almost enough. But the pictures gave him the answers he'd been looking for—and a lot more than that.

Davis had always had an irrational fear of water, which he assumed stemmed from a childhood incident where he'd almost drowned. He never swam and never took a bath, always showered because he hated the feeling of having any part of his body submerged in water. Now they had him kneeling in front of a tub of water, his hands tied tightly behind his back. Somehow they had figured out his Room 101—the thing he feared most in life.

As they forced his head into the water, he screamed as

he'd never screamed in his life, trying desperately to get his head back up. Just as he thought he would pass out, they jerked him out of the tub.

They didn't even have to ask. He began to babble on his own, telling them every detail of the conversations he'd had with Christian Gillette.

"Norman!" Ganze yelled, bursting into Boyd's office. "They got Davis to break. A little water and he crumbled like a stale cookie."

"Excellent. Did he tell them anything important?"

"He told them that he had sent Gillette to Matt Lee's wife."

"*Jesus Christ!*" Boyd roared, shooting out of his chair. "Weren't you just there?"

"Yes. Apparently, Gillette was there too."

"You searched the place, right?"

"Yes."

"But you didn't find anything?"

"No."

"Could she have told him anything important?"

"I don't know. These people aren't supposed to talk to anyone about the project, even to their spouses. But you know they do."

"Did you question her?" Boyd asked.

"No."

"Well, get back on the phone with Celino's people right now. Get them up to Boston immediately. Take any means necessary to find out what she told Gillette. Hell, have them do the same thing to Lee's wife that they just did to Davis."

"You mean—"

"Yes, damn it, I mean torture, then disposal. By now she must know something's happened to her husband anyway.

We don't want her running around trying to get the newspapers interested in her story. Get her off the fucking face of the earth."

David Wright gazed out over the East River and Queens from the terrace of his Upper East Side apartment. It was four in the morning, but he couldn't sleep. He leaned forward in his chair and put his face in his hands. He couldn't go on like this, being a coward. It was killing him. Ratting on Gillette like some little pussy because he was so afraid Joe Celino would send the pictures to the cops or take him out. Or worst of all, do something to Peggy. That's what really kept him up, the thought of that. He shook his head. He wasn't a coward. Never had been. He'd always faced things head-on.

"David?"

Wright whipped around in the chair, toward Peggy. "Hey, Peg."

"It's four in the morning," she said, coming to him and putting a hand on his shoulder. Her face was creased with concern. "What's wrong?"

"Nothing," he lied, "I was just thinking about this deal I'm working on."

She sat on his lap and put her arms around him, sighed, then smiled at him sweetly. "I guess now's as good a time as any to tell you," she said, patting her belly.

"Tell me what?"

But before she could answer, he realized suddenly that he had a whole new reason to get things straight.

CHAPTER 20

Less than a year before, Gillette had delivered Bill Donovan's eulogy to a packed church in midtown Manhattan. This time it was Harlem, but the church was just as crowded.

"He was my best friend," Gillette said quietly. "I'll never have another friend like Quentin Stiles."

When he was finished, Gillette moved down the steps from the dais and knelt before Stiles's grandmother. Her face was soaked with tears, and he took her hand gently. "You going to be okay?"

"I'm a tough old bird," she whispered. "I'll be all right."

After he'd kissed her on the forehead, Gillette headed down the center aisle toward the back of the church, glancing at Wright as he passed. Wright's eyes were down, glued to the floor. So were Peggy's.

Outside the church, Gillette leaned back against a tree and closed his eyes, wondering if the time had come to get out. He was thirty-seven, and he'd never be able to spend all the money he'd made. Why keep working? Why deal with it anymore?

"You ready?"

Gillette opened his eyes. Derrick Walker stood in front of him.

"We got to get you down to Chatham, Christian. The meeting doesn't start until six o'clock, but I spoke to Percy

345

Lundergard and he wants you there by four. Says he's got a lot of things he needs to cover with you before you go on."

"Yeah, okay." Over Walker's shoulder, Gillette saw Wright and Peggy walking toward their car. "Give me a second," he said, brushing past Walker. "David," he called.

Wright kept moving.

"David!"

The second time Gillette called, Wright stopped on the sidewalk and turned.

"I need to talk to you," Gillette said loudly as he neared them.

Wright gestured for Peggy to go ahead without him. "What is it?" he asked when she was gone.

The younger man seemed to be hanging his head, Gillette noticed. He seemed tired, almost beaten. "What's wrong?"

Wright shrugged. "Nothing."

"You sure?"

Wright shook his head. "I . . . I haven't been . . . I'm just . . ." He groaned. "I've just been working hard on this Hush-Hush thing. I want to get it done fast, that's all. I don't want someone else coming in and stealing it."

"That's all? You don't have anything else you want to tell me?"

"No. Why?"

"I went to Richmond."

Wright swallowed hard. "Yeah, so?"

"I drove. After I got out of the city, I went down the Jersey Turnpike."

"Makes sense. That would be the fastest way to get to Richmond if you were driving. But why are you telling me?"

Gillette hesitated, letting the pressure build. "Were you on the Jersey Turnpike this week?"

Wright shifted on his feet, then shoved his hands in his pockets. "Why would you think I was?"

"I saw a—"

"Look, I gotta go, Chris," Wright said suddenly, turning and trotting toward Peggy, who was standing by their car.

Gillette swung the dark green Oldsmobile into a spot of the Chatham High School student parking lot and climbed out. Percy Lundergard had suggested that Gillette not come in a limousine, that he dress casually, and that his security detail be as invisible as possible. So he'd driven himself to the meeting in Lundergard's own sedan, worn a golf shirt and slacks, and been accompanied by only one QS agent, who was also casually dressed. As he made his way across the parking lot with the rest of the crowd, he thought how nice it was to blend in for once.

There was already a line forming at the front door, and as Gillette reached the back of it, he noticed a figure standing alone on the grass by the side of the building. When he took a second look, the figure seemed familiar. He stared hard for a moment. David Wright.

They locked eyes for a few moments and acknowledged each other with a subtle nod, then Wright motioned for Gillette to break away.

Gillette gave the QS agent standing beside him a tap on the shoulder. "See that guy over there?" he said, pointing at Wright.

"Yes."

"I'm going to talk to him. You're coming with me."

"Okay."

"What are you doing here, David?" Gillette asked as he neared him, aware that the people in line were watching. He and Wright clearly weren't locals. In a town as small as Chatham, everyone knew everyone. "I thought you and Peggy were going out of the city for the weekend, out to Long Island or something."

"We were," Wright mumbled, glancing at the QS agent. "Hey, can we have a little space?"

Gillette waved the agent off. "What's going on, David?"

Wright took a deep breath. "This is tough."

"Tough?"

"Look, let's not beat around the bush. You know I was on the turnpike the other day. I don't know how you know, but you know."

"Were you following me?" Gillette asked.

"Yeah."

"Why?"

"You're not going to believe this."

"Try me."

Wright put a hand to his face and rubbed his eyes. "I've been keeping tabs on you for the Carbone family."

Gillette's throat went dry as Wright's image blurred in front of him. The man he'd tabbed as his protégé, a man he'd trusted completely, was a traitor. It was almost unfathomable. "Is this about Las Vegas?" he asked, his voice hushed.

"I, I think so," Wright said hesitantly.

"Why would they care so much where I was?" Gillette asked, knowing it couldn't be just about the NFL franchise and the casino. He looked around warily, suddenly wondering if this was a setup. Wondering if Wright had really driven all the way down here to come clean.

"I don't know."

"We're paying that guy Carmine Torino his fee, which I'm sure the Carbones are getting most of." Might as well try to dig as much information out of Wright as possible, Gillete thought. "I assume that's what they wanted. I can't understand why they'd need to know where I was all the time. There's got to be something more."

"Like I said," Wright answered shakily, "I don't know. I asked that question a lot, but I never got an answer."

"Why did you do it, David?"

"I've got a problem," Wright mumbled. "Something they're using against me. You know I didn't want to."

"What is it, what do they have on you?"

"I can't tell you."

"David, you—"

"I *really* can't tell you, Chris. You've been a great friend to me, and I couldn't look myself in the mirror anymore, if I told you. I thought I could screw anyone to get ahead, to save myself, but I guess I can't after all. I suppose that's one thing I can take away from this whole mess." He kicked at a tuft of grass. "But I can't tell you what they have on me, I just can't. You'll probably hear about it on the news at some point, but I don't want to tell you now."

"It's that bad?"

"It doesn't have anything to do with Everest, though," Wright said quickly. "I want you to know that."

"Is it something I might be able to help you with?"

"No."

Gillette glanced over his shoulder at the line. It was getting long. "Look, I gotta go." He put his hand on Wright's shoulder. "Thanks for coming down here. We'll need to talk again on Monday. In depth."

"If I'm still around," Wright muttered.

"What?"

"Nothing. Look, there's more."

Gillette turned back. *"More?"*

"When we were in Vegas, I met with Joe Celino."

"What?"

" 'Met' isn't really the right word," Wright corrected himself. "I was basically hauled in front of him. He told me I was a dead man if I didn't do exactly what he wanted. He showed me a picture of this poor fucker they tortured to death to scare the shit out of me. Which it did. So I'm probably pretty much screwed at this point. I'm sure they'll find out I came to you, so when I don't show up Monday, you'll know why. But here's the point: Celino told me some things you oughta know."

"Like what?"

"First, he claimed he was working with Allison Wallace somehow."

Gillette suddenly felt as though someone had hit him in the gut with a sledgehammer. "Jesus Christ." Veramax, Dr. Davis, and Beezer Johnson raced through his mind.

"I don't know how, and I don't know on what," Wright continued. "But he told me she'd be running Everest at some point soon, so I ought to suck up to her. That if I cooperated with him, there'd be a place for me when she was in charge."

Probably why she was calling investors and inferring that she'd be running the show soon, Gillette thought. Setting the stage. So Faraday was right. Maybe Nigel was the guy to run Everest after all. His instincts seemed to be dead-on. "What else did Celino tell you?" Gillette asked angrily.

"He told me his people had gotten that mate on the yacht to kill Quentin Stiles."

"*Are you serious?*" Gillette asked incredulously.

"Yes."

Gillette's mind was spinning. The Carbones had gotten Stiles. It kept echoing in his head. But somehow Norman Boyd had known in Minneapolis, without ever laying eyes on Stiles in Washington, that Derrick Walker was a different head of security. *Somehow Boyd had known that something had happened to Stiles.* The connection suddenly made sense. The Carbones were rarely ever in the news, but they were the most successful and feared crime family in the country. And Norman Boyd would need assassins, people who were good at killing. As Ted Casey had said in the Georgetown parking garage the other night. Maybe it wasn't a coincidence that the Carbones made so much money and that Boyd had a reputation for being able to intimidate anyone he wanted to. Maybe there was a hideous partnership. One in which Celino's people tortured and killed for Boyd. And, in return, got cover from the government on their criminal activities, maybe even had things pushed their way every once in a while. That would also explain why the Carbones would kill Tom McGuire. Boyd couldn't have somebody out there trying to kill Gillette—not when Boyd was relying on him.

Then it hit Gillette. Boyd wouldn't need him if he had Allison in his pocket.

"Why would they want Stiles dead?" Gillette asked, barely able to hear his voice over the pounding of his heart.

"Celino said Stiles was getting too close on something. He didn't tell me what, though."

Maybe that was what Stiles had been talking about on the boat last weekend. Maybe he was getting close to linking Celino with a government agency. A connection that Celino and Boyd's agency would certainly do almost anything to avoid having exposed. Something like that, were it revealed and proven true, would end any advantage the Carbones had over the rest of the country's Mob families. In fact, it would probably end the Carbones as a family. There would be endless congressional investigations and scrutiny that would make it almost impossible for the Carbones to continue to operate. And there'd be no telling what it would do to the United States intelligence agencies.

"Did you follow me all the way to Richmond the other day?" Gillette demanded.

Wright nodded. "In a damn cab."

"Do you know who I met with?"

"A neurosurgeon named Scott Davis."

Gillette banged his fist against the building. "Did you tell the Carbones that?"

"Yeah." Wright's voice was barely audible.

Gillette yanked his cell phone from his pocket to call Cathy Dylan. He had to get in touch with Davis immediately, to warn him. "Did you tell them about Tom McGuire, too? About McGuire coming after me?"

"Yeah."

"Christian," Percy Lundergard called, trotting across the grass toward Gillette, "you've got to get inside. It's almost time."

Gillette held up a hand, waiting for Cathy to answer, but she didn't pick up. "Damn it." He pointed at Wright as he cut the connection. "Get out of here, David. Call your wife immediately and tell her to get somewhere safe right away."

"Christian, come on," Lundergard urged, looking at Wright strangely.

"Percy, I've got an emergency. I'm not going to be able to—"

"*No way,*" Lundergard snapped. "I've moved heaven and earth to put two thousand people in that auditorium tonight," he said, pointing at the building, "and to get the NBC affiliate to televise this thing. You're not backing out on me, Christian, not for *any* reason."

"Celino's people got it out of Mary Lee," Ganze reported.

Boyd was standing behind his desk, squeezing the back of the chair so hard that his knuckles were white. "*What, damn it?* What did they get?"

"That she gave Gillette a flash drive with everything on it. All the work the team had generated up to the point they took off from Boston the other day. Matt gave it to her right before he got on the plane you sent into Lake Michigan. Apparently, he smuggled it out of the research lab the night before."

"Well, doesn't that make my fucking day," Boyd hissed. "Christian Gillette knows more about nanotechnology than we do at this point."

"What do you mean?" Ganze asked.

Boyd nodded at the secure telephone on his desk. "I just spoke to our lead person in Minneapolis. She says there's something missing from the research material, a vital piece of the code they can't find and can't re-create without Matt Lee. He must have figured out he wasn't getting off that plane." Boyd pounded the desk. "Get Celino's people after Gillette, *immediately*. I want that flash drive, and I want it yesterday. I don't care what they have to do to get it."

It was Gillette's turn to speak in front of the packed auditorium. Becky Rouse had made her case, telling the crowd that allowing a Discount America store into town would destroy the successful tourist trade she had developed over the past several years. Citing facts and figures that demonstrated how so many more outsiders were spending money on the waterfront. That tourists would no longer think of Chatham as quaint if it was at the center of a superstore war. That the mammoth retail outlet would suck dollars away from the waterfront, too, and attract a group of people from other towns Chatham didn't want. She was given a strong round of applause as she sat down.

Gillette took the microphone and smiled calmly at several people in the huge crowd before speaking, trying to focus. So many things were racing through his mind. "Good evening, I'm Christian Gillette," he began, wondering if someone in the audience was here to kill him. "I'm the chairman of Discount America, and I want to thank you for giving me the opportunity to speak. I realize that it's Saturday evening, so I won't keep you long. I want you to be able to get home to your families and your televisions and your parties, I really do. I just want to take a few minutes of your time and present you with a few basic facts as you decide whether or not you want our store in your town. We hope you do. We think it'll be a great partnership.

"First, the store will be built out on Route 212, at least five miles west of the waterfront. Almost a hundred percent of the tourist traffic comes from the east, they'll never see this store. Second, the store will be huge. You'll be able to buy almost anything you want, from fresh vegetables to computers. You won't have to go to Delaware to buy basic stuff anymore. Third, thanks to our ability to buy in bulk, our prices are tremendously low." Gillette motioned to the crowd. "Can someone please tell me what a four-bar pack of Ivory soap costs at Fletcher's market on the Chatham waterfront?"

A young woman raised her hand.

"Yes?"

"Five dollars and a quarter," the woman said, her voice cracking with nerves.

"Five dollars and twenty-five cents," Gillette said loudly. He shook his head. "You know what it'll cost at the new DA store? Two fifty at most."

A rumble ran through the crowd.

"Believe me," he said, acknowledging the positive response, "you want us here. It'll be a great store and a fantastic shopping experience. It'll create jobs and tax revenue. It'll be—"

"How much money will you make from the store?" Becky interrupted.

Gillete turned. Becky was out of her chair, arms folded firmly over her chest. Obviously, she'd felt the tide turning in his favor and was going to do anything she could to stop the momentum.

"Come on, Mr. Gillette, tell us all what you're going to make off this store."

"I don't have the exact figures yet, but it's—"

"At least a hundred million!" she shouted.

A murmur rolled through the auditorium.

Gillette smiled calmly and put up his arms. "It's nowhere near a hundred million." He glanced at Percy Lundergard, who had his hands over his eyes.

Becky pointed at a man in the second row. "You all know who Fred Jacobs is. The best accountant in the county. Fred looked into this for me. What do you think Mr. Gillette will make on the store, Fred?"

Jacobs stood up. He was a scholarly-looking man with wire-rimmed glasses and a crop of white hair. "I think Becky's pretty close. About a hundred million a year."

"Believe me," Gillette said loudly, "that's way off."

"Then how much is it?" an elderly woman in the middle of the crowd shouted in a high-pitched voice.

"I'm not sure right now."

The crowd groaned.

Gillette saw Lundergard running his finger across his neck.

"Mr. Gillette won't even help us with a few things we need around here," Becky spoke up. "His investors just gave him *fifteen billion dollars* and—"

"Actually, it's *twenty*," Jacobs corrected from his seat. "I checked the Everest Capital Web site right before I came over. Some rich family from Chicago just gave Mr. Gillette another five billion."

"*Twenty billion dollars!*" Becky shouted, whipping the crowd into a frenzy. "Can you imagine having that much money at your fingertips? I can't. I asked Mr. Gillette to help us build a new elementary school, and you know what he said? He said he'd build half of it. *Half* a school. Can you imagine that? Now, Mr. Gillette, which half were you thinking about? The top half or the bottom half?"

A loud chorus of cackles and boos arose from the crowd.

"*What I said was—*"

"I know about you, Mr. Gillette," Becky said, pointing at him and silencing the crowd as they hung on her every word. "I know there are people who question what you've done with some of the money they've given you."

"That's not true."

"I understand there's going to be an investigation," she said loudly, turning to the crowd. "This is not the kind of man we want in our town, people. Believe me. A man who'd build *half* a school and who's about to be investigated for fraud!"

Gillette and Becky Rouse stood on a darkened, tree-lined side street a few blocks from the high school. It had been thirty minutes since the scene on the auditorium stage.

"What do you want?" she asked, grinning smugly. "What do you want to talk about?"

"Pretty proud of yourself, aren't you."

"Yup."

"You know I'm not being investigated."

She pointed back toward the high school. "Yeah, but they don't."

Gillette glanced over his shoulder. He'd parked Lundergard's car back up the street and told the QS agent to stay there. "I want a truce; I want to call off the war," he said. "I want my store, and I want you to support it." It had started to drizzle, and he spotted a couple beneath an umbrella walking down the other side of the street. "I'll give you everything you want. The elementary school, the retirement home, the squad cars. I just want this back-and-forth to be done. There's no reason for it."

"You better not go back on this," she said, her voice rising.

Gillette glanced through the darkness at the couple across the street, their silhouettes outlined by a streetlamp. "Easy," he urged, trying to calm her down, noticing that the couple had stopped and was looking toward them. "I'm not going back on it. There's no reason to think I would."

"There's *every* reason to think you would. I know your kind, Christian. You think the world revolves around you!"

"Becky, come on, that's not fair. I'm the one that ought to be upset here. With what you said to the crowd about me being investigated."

She shrugged and turned away.

"Hey, look," he said, moving to her side, "I'm just trying to—"

There was a flash and the blast of a gunshot. A bullet tore through Becky's back and out her chest, grazing Gillette's arm and hurling her against him. He tried to catch her, but she fell from his arms, dead even before she hit the street.

Another gunshot exploded, closer this time.

Gillette wheeled around and sprinted the other way. Whoever was shooting was trying to hit *him*, not Becky. Out of the corner of his eye, he saw the couple standing on the other side of the street dive for cover behind a car, then he cut right, hurdled a waist-high hedge, and darted between two homes. At the back of the house, he scaled a six-foot chain-link fence and dropped into the thick brush on the other side.

He pulled himself to his feet and waded through the raspberry bushes, thorns tugging at his clothes. Finally the bushes gave way to woods, and he raced ahead, wincing as his feet crashed through dried leaves, careful to avoid the trees in the darkness. When he reached the edge of the trees and the next street over, he hesitated, pressed behind a large oak, gazing back into the gloom of the woods, listening carefully for any sound. But there was nothing more than the consistent patter of drops as the rain began to fall more steadily.

Gillette waited ten minutes, then saw a police car cruising slowly down the wet street, lights flashing in the growing fog. A huge stroke of luck. He moved out from behind the oak tree, waving his arms as he stepped into the glare of the headlights.

The police car stopped, and the driver's-side door opened instantly.

"Down on the ground," the cop yelled. "Now!"

Gillette put his hand up over his face and squinted against the high beams. He could barely make out the officer kneeling behind the door, aiming a pistol at him over the mirror. "Officer, my name's Christian Gillette. I was just shot at. I'm not the one you're looking for."

"Get down, now! Arms and legs spread."

Gillette made a snap decision and bolted back for the woods. He heard the *pop, pop, pop* of the policeman's revolver, but he was quickly back into the cover of the trees, impossible to see in the darkness. As he hid behind another tree, he peered around the side of it.

The policeman was on the radio, calling for backup. Gillette wanted to give himself up, but the flash drive was in his pocket. The officer would have confiscated everything on him, and he wasn't going to let the flash drive go. Not for anything in the world. It could easily fall into the wrong hands.

Then he heard sirens, several of them, quickly growing louder. He turned and ran as the rain became a downpour.

CHAPTER 21

Faraday relaxed into his favorite easy chair, propped his feet up on the ottoman, clicked the television on with the remote, then reached for a heaping bowl of cookie-dough ice cream sitting on the table beside the chair. He'd thought about going out tonight—he had several invitations—but he was dead tired. It had been a long week, and all he wanted to do was relax in his apartment. If the past was any indicator, he'd be asleep in an hour, wake up around midnight, and drag himself to bed.

He watched the last few minutes of *Seinfeld*, finishing the ice cream as the credits rolled, then settled in for the news.

When Christian Gillette's face appeared on the screen over the anchor's shoulder, Faraday shot out of the chair, dropping the bowl to the floor. The woman relayed that the Everest Capital chairman was a fugitive. That he was wanted for the murder of Becky Rouse, the mayor of a small town in Maryland called Chatham. That there were two witnesses to the shooting. That he had evaded an attempted arrest and was considered extremely dangerous.

Gillette found Percy Lundergard's cell number on his phone and called. He was somewhere on the east side of Chatham, at the edge of a trailer park and a cornfield. His plan was to get off the Eastern Shore of Maryland as soon as possible—by going either north to Wilmington, Delaware, or west over the Chesapeake Bay Bridge toward Washington, D.C. He pressed his arms close to his body and stomped his feet. It was still raining, and the temperature was dropping fast.

"Hello."

"Percy?"

"Christian?"

"Yeah."

"Where are you?"

"What in the hell is going on?" he asked, ignoring the question. "Why did a Chatham cop try to arrest me an hour ago?"

"The police think you killed Becky Rouse."

"*What? That's insane.*"

"That's exactly what I told them."

"Whoever shot her was trying to kill *me,*" Gillette said.

"The cops say they have two witnesses."

The couple walking on the other side of the street under the umbrella, Gillette assumed. They'd heard Becky shout his name.

"And," Lundergard continued, "they're saying they've got the murder weapon with your prints on it."

Planted, obviously. "What about the guy who was with me?" Gillette asked. "My bodyguard."

"No one can find him."

The guy was dead, was helping whoever shot Becky, or was the one who shot her. Gillette patted his shirt pocket, making certain the flash drive was still there. He had a pretty damn good idea of who was responsible for her death. Maybe he didn't know who'd actually pulled the trigger, but he knew who was pulling the strings.

"Why don't you come here? To my house?" Lundergard offered. "We'll figure out what to do next when you get here."

Gillette thought for a second. "Okay, see you in a little while."

Faraday reached for his apartment phone, hoping it was Gillette. It wasn't. It was Allison.

"Have you heard what's going on?" she asked excitedly as soon as he picked up.

"You mean about Christian?"

"Of course that's what I mean."

"I'm watching the news right now."

"Nigel, what do you think happened?"

"Somebody's made a terrible mistake."

Lundergard put down the phone and glanced up at Jim Cochran, the Chatham chief of police, who was standing in his living room. On either side of Cochran were two men claiming to be federal agents. Lundergard hadn't seen the big gold badges for long—the agents had flipped them open and shut quickly—but Cochran seemed satisfied.

"So?" Cochran demanded gruffly.

"Gillette says he'll be here in a little while. You better get all the police cars out of here."

Gillette's next call was to Derrick Walker. He'd thought long and hard about whether or not to make this call. If the agent who'd been with him in the car had turned on him, then Walker could easily have turned, too. Walker wasn't like Stiles; he didn't own QS Security—he could be bribed. But in the end, Gillette had no choice. He needed someone's help.

Walker picked up on the first ring.

"Hello," he answered fiercely. "Are you all right?"

Obviously, Walker had seen the number on the cell screen. "Where are you?" Gillette asked.

"The Chatham police station."

"Can you talk?"

"Yeah," Walker said quietly.

"I didn't shoot this woman." It was stupid to have to say it. If it had been Stiles, he wouldn't have even bothered.

"Of course you didn't."

"What happened to your guy?" Gillette asked. "The one who was with me tonight?"

"I'm pretty sure he's dead. He's not answering his phone or his pager."

"Maybe he's working with whoever shot Becky Rouse. Maybe *he* shot Becky."

"Not a chance. I've known Lionel for seven years. I'd trust my life with him. That's why I had him with you. Now what the fuck is going on?" Walker asked angrily. "Do you know?"

Gillette hesitated. "I'm pretty sure I do, but I don't want to say anything on this line." He watched as a man came out of one of the trailer homes close to where he was standing and stuffed a garbage bag in the trash can, then hurried back inside. "I need to meet up with you."

"Where?"

"At that place I told you I had that meeting yesterday."

Walker hung up with Gillette, then made another call immediately. It lasted just twenty seconds. After he slipped the cell phone back into his pocket, he stood up from the desk he'd been sitting on and turned around. Jim Cochran was directly in front of him, flanked by several deputies.

"You're under arrest, Mr. Walker. Turn around and put your hands behind your back."

"*For what?*" Walker demanded.

"Aiding and abetting."

"Aiding and abetting who?"

"Christian Gillette."

*　　*　　*

Gillette sprinted across the open field toward the rest stop and the idling tractor-trailer. He had no intention of going to Percy Lundergard's house or anywhere else the authorities might be waiting. He'd watched the truck driver jump down and trot toward the bathrooms through the driving rain. He shivered as he pulled himself up between the cab and the trailer. This was going to be a cold ride.

CHAPTER 22

Gillette had been waiting two hours for Derrick Walker on the ground floor of the same Georgetown parking garage where he'd met Ted Casey, the CIA cutout specialist, a few days ago. They must have gotten Walker, too, he realized. Walker had had a day and a half to get here, but he was a no-show.

Gillette had spent the last two nights outside in the elements. Saturday night, beneath a railroad bridge in southwest Washington fighting a torrential rain; last night, beneath the stars on a steam grate near the Washington Monument along with three indigents, bundled up in blankets. It had turned unusually cold for early October after the rain had passed through. He hadn't used his credit cards, cash card, or cell phone until this morning, not wanting to give anyone any clue to where he was. Now he didn't care.

It was five after ten, and he needed to get to Tysons Corner out in northern Virginia—a twenty-minute cab ride from here. He let out a frustrated breath. He really could have used Walker.

Tysons Corner was fifteen miles west of downtown Washington, D.C., and only a few miles from where Gillette, Boyd, and Ganze had first met. One anchor of the Dulles Corridor—the area's high-tech center stretching to

Dulles Airport fifteen miles farther west—Tysons was also the location of two large, popular shopping malls—Tysons I and II—that were less than half a mile apart.

Tysons II, built on a hill overlooking the area, was a sprawling three-level structure full of upscale shops and restaurants, all attached to a Ritz-Carlton Hotel and two office buildings rising up on either side of the Ritz. Gillette had stayed at the hotel several times in the last few years for technology conferences, so he knew the mall well. Also called the Galleria, the mall would be crowded now at lunchtime, which was perfect for what he was planning.

It was twelve-twenty. Gillette had called Boyd and Ganze forty minutes ago, giving them until twelve-thirty to get here. They'd agreed to come immediately. Gillette now knew how important the flash drive was.

He grimaced. Mary was so timid, but she'd shown so much courage in giving him the drive. He had no doubt they'd gotten to her. Davis, too. Getting to Mary and Davis was the only way they could have connected the dots and known about the flash drive so fast. He just hoped they'd been merciful and ended it quickly for both of them. And he hoped that if something went wrong in the next few minutes, they'd do the same for him.

Gillette walked slowly, a Washington Nationals baseball cap pulled low over his eyes, looking around constantly as he approached PF Chang's, a popular, high-end Chinese restaurant located at the mall's northwest entrance. He wasn't worried about Boyd's people—including the Carbone family—trying to kill him. Boyd needed the flash drive almost as badly as he needed his next breath, so they weren't going to do anything stupid. Not yet, anyway. But the police or some bystander might. If he was still being accused of Becky Rouse's murder, the cops would be on the lookout for him, even over here on the western side of the bay. And if his face had been on the news, there was always the chance some do-gooder might try to take him just to get his name in the paper.

Gillette moved through the mall to the escalator and took it up to the third level, then followed the concourse to a Hallmark store in front of the south escalators. Boyd was standing in front of the store, alone, as Gillette had instructed.

"Well, well, look what the cat dragged in," Boyd said as Gillette stopped ten feet away. "You look like crap."

"But I'm alive."

"Only because I want you that way. Now give me the drive," Boyd demanded.

"Not yet."

"I told you, pal, I have a lot of friends in the right places. I can take Everest down in a heartbeat. Find something wrong with it and you in no time." He sneered. "Hell, there's already a kiddie porn aggregator on your hard drive at Everest, Christian, pulling enough nasty videos onto your machine to put you away for a few years. We installed it yesterday, remotely. But no one will ever know it was done that way. All the feds will know is that Christian Gillette is into kiddie porn. How's that gonna look in *The New York Times,* pal?"

"I have the flash drive. The rest will take care of itself. The truth will out."

"I'm glad you think so. I'm glad you're that naïve."

"You live in your world, Norman, I'll live in mine."

"And of course," Boyd continued, "you've got that little issue of murdering the Rouse woman down in Chatham."

"You know I didn't kill her."

"But the cops think you did. That's all that matters. *Now, give me the damn drive.*"

Gillette moved a few steps closer. "What? You think I'm going to just hand it over so your Carbone friends can pop out of a couple of these stores and mow me down?" He saw shock register on Boyd's face. "That would be pretty stupid, wouldn't it? Those guys don't mind making a hit in a public place. They don't mind killing anyone anywhere, right?"

Boyd shook in silent rage.

Gillette could tell he'd hit a nerve. His suspicions were dead-on. "Look, all I want is closure, Norman. That's all I've ever wanted from you."

"What do you mean?"

"I want answers. Answers you and Ganze promised to give me about my mother and father."

"I don't know anything about that. You'll have to talk to Daniel, but you didn't want him with me."

"But he's here at the mall, right?"

Boyd nodded. "Like I said, I don't know anything about those questions of yours."

"I think you do. I think you made Ganze and everyone else believe you didn't, but I think you know everything. I think you threw Marilyn McRae to Ganze and me. I'm sure she would have sworn to Ganze and me until the day she died that she really was my mother, but I know she's not. What did you give her, Norman? Money? A career? Promised her the world if she'd do a few favors for you and your government cronies? You've probably manipulated her for years." Gillette hesitated. "Like you manipulated the sale of the Vegas franchise to Everest so your Carbone buddies could get their money through Carmine Torino, and ultimately get their claws into the casino. We were the only ones who put in a bid that included a casino, weren't we, Norman?"

Boyd smiled slightly.

"It was perfect. You're always looking for ways to pay the Carbones back for their dirty work. The tortures and the assassinations. Right? You called a few of the owners you have in your hip pocket and influenced them to give

Everest the nod in the auction, even though there was another bid that was fifty million dollars higher. You rigged that thing, didn't you?"

Boyd shrugged. "You'll never prove it."

"How can you possibly influence NFL owners?"

"A favor here, a favor there. Make a woman who's about to file a palimony suit disappear, help a father when his kid gets into drug trouble. There's all kinds of ways, Christian. Everybody has their problems. As long as you know about them, you can make things go your way."

"How long have you been working with the Carbones?" Gillette asked.

"All right, that's enough. Give me the fucking drive."

Gillette stared at Boyd hard. "Is that what my father really uncovered, Norman? That you were working with the Mafia? Is that why you killed him? There wasn't any plot to kill the president. You were the plot."

Boyd's eyes flashed to Gillette's. "What?" An odd expression came over his face.

"Is that why you killed my father?" Gillette repeated, louder this time.

"Are you out of your mind? What kind of question is that?"

"I have pictures of you and Lana sitting on the patio at the house in Bel Air just months before my father was killed. That's when Lana gave you the names of the women my father had children with. You tried to extort my father, telling him you were going to leak the details of his affairs to the newspapers so he'd have to resign his Senate seat. But it didn't work, did it? He was going to expose you no matter what. Expose your relationship to the Carbones, all the things you'd stolen from the government, then sold. Like you're trying to steal the nanotechnology now. You've murdered innocent people in the name of national security, but it has nothing to do with national security. It's all about you. All about making you and your pals rich."

Boyd's face went blank.

Gillette moved closer, until their faces were just inches apart. "Tell me if I'm right, Norman. I have to know." He nodded slowly, submissively. "I know you can take me down. I know you can nail me for Becky Rouse's murder. I'm sure you've done a lot worse to people who've done a lot less."

"You're damn right I have."

"So tell me if I'm right. Then you get your drive."

Boyd's mouth slowly broke into a slight grin, then he chuckled. "You're a smart man, Christian. Brave, too. You could have worked for me." He took a deep breath. "Now, give me my goddamn drive."

Gillette spotted two men emerging from the Hallmark store. He slammed Boyd's chin with a right cross, then turned and raced toward the escalator, leaping four steps at a time, bowling over two men in front of him. As he reached the second floor, two more men came at him from Bebe, a women's clothing store. One of them hit him high and the other low, and the three of them tumbled to the ground, knocking over a young woman who shrieked as she rolled away. Gillette felt them forcing his hands behind his back roughly.

Then suddenly a stream of agents poured out of several stores, wrestled the two men off Gillette, lifted them to their feet, and slammed them up against the wall face first.

As soon as he was free, Gillette jumped to his feet and sprinted down the concourse to the entrance to the Ritz. He raced inside it and through the main lobby to the elevators that would take him to the hotel's arrival lobby.

Boyd touched his chin and moaned. Gillette's punch had knocked him out, and he was just getting his senses back.

He made it to his hands and knees groggily, then stood up slowly. As his vision cleared, he noticed a man standing in front of him.

"Hello, Mr. Boyd. I'm Ted Casey. I'm with the Central Intelligence Agency." Casey signaled to several men behind him. "Take him away."

Gillette moved through the main entrance of the Ritz-Carlton and trotted across the courtyard toward the ground floor of the office building to the right of the hotel. Once inside the revolving glass door, he turned left toward the Palm restaurant.

"Tim."

The host looked up from behind the stand. "Yes?"

"I'm Christian. I was here about an hour ago. I rented a wine box."

"Oh, of course."

"I need to get in there."

"Sure, follow me."

Tim led Christian to the wine boxes—ten across and ten high, available for personal wines people wanted to have on hand for a special meal. "Which one is yours?"

"Twelve."

Tim handed Gillette a key.

Gillette unlocked the small door and reached inside for the flash drive. It was there, exactly where he'd left it. "Thanks."

Gillette moved out of the restaurant and turned left, past the elevators toward the parking garage. Casey was to have left him a car on the third level. He moved out the back door, then headed up the steps.

"Stop right there."

Gillette's eyes snapped up from the steps. Daniel Ganze stood in front of him on the first landing, gun drawn.

"Give me the drive, Christian."

Gillette stopped short, shocked, glancing from the gun to Ganze's eyes. Finally, he shook his head. "It's over, Ganze. Boyd's in custody by now."

"I don't give a rat's ass about Boyd."

Gillette shook his head. Ganze didn't understand. "You don't have to go down, too. It's Boyd they want."

"And it's the drive I want. We have to make sure it's protected."

"There was no spy, Ganze," Gillette assured him, "no terrorist outfit. That was all part of Boyd's cover."

Ganze smiled. "Perfect, wasn't it?"

Gillette's eyes narrowed. "Huh?"

"I can assure you that there absolutely is a terrorist connection," Ganze snapped. "And it's about to pay off." He stepped forward and grabbed the flash drive from Gillette's shirt pocket, then stepped back, raised the gun, and aimed it at Gillette.

The explosion was deafening in the stairwell. Gillette dropped to his knees, bracing for excruciating pain. But there was nothing. Nothing but the sound of Ganze falling to the ground and his gun clattering down several steps.

Gillette opened his eyes and looked up the stairway. Quentin Stiles was looking back.

CHAPTER 23

Gillette and Stiles sat on a courtyard bench in front of the Ritz-Carlton. It had been three hours since Stiles had shot Daniel Ganze dead. Ted Casey's men had removed the body, and the flash drive was back in Gillette's pocket.

"Okay, thanks," Gillette said, ending the call.

"Who was that?" Stiles asked.

"Casey," Gillette replied curtly.

"Oh, yeah? What did he say?"

Gillette bit his lip. He was overjoyed that his best friend was alive, but torn up by what he'd been put through. Made to think Stiles was dead. "His people just finished interrogating one of the Carbone guys they shot at the mall."

"They find out anything good?"

Gillette stretched. In a few minutes, he was getting a room at the Ritz and sleeping for two days. "David Wright killed a woman in a West Village sex shop a couple of weeks ago."

"Oh, Jesus."

"The Carbones knew about it. That's how Celino got Wright to do what he wanted. They had pictures and a tape of Wright doing it."

"What's going to happen to him? They gonna prosecute?"

"Casey's already turned everything over to the New

York Police Department. He doesn't know anything more than that. But I'm sure David will end up behind bars."

"What about Miles Whitman?" Stiles asked.

"The Carbones killed Whitman in France at Boyd's direction. Tortured him until he told them how to find Tom McGuire. Whitman was feeding McGuire money once a month from the forty million the CIA helped him stash away before he ran last year."

"Why was the CIA helping Whitman?"

"He let them use North America Guaranty as a cutout for years. Basically helped them spy on a lot of individuals in this country, especially high net worth people."

Stiles spat. "Nice world we live in, huh?"

"Yeah."

"But why would the CIA tell Boyd where Whitman was?"

"Agencies cooperate. But the CIA brass obviously didn't know Boyd was working with the Carbones."

"What about Allison Wallace?" Stiles wanted to know. "Was she working with the Carbones like Wright told you?"

"No," Gillette answered. "That was Celino disinformation. He was just trying to manipulate Wright with that one. She's straight. Turns out her assistant, Hamid, is okay, too." He held up his hand. "Oh, wait a minute, you don't know about Hamid. You've been dead for a week."

Stiles chuckled. "Derrick Walker told me about that. How Allison was out in the lobby and my guys wouldn't let Hamid in." He laughed louder.

"It isn't funny, Quentin."

"Come on, Chris, ease up."

"Fuck you," Gillette snapped. He'd been wanting to say that for three hours.

"Hey, I just saved your life again," Stiles shot back. "You could at least be a *little* grateful."

"You put a lot of people through a lot of pain."

"I had to. It was the only way."

Gillette gritted his teeth. "Why? Why'd you do it?"

Stiles looked out over the courtyard. "My guys swept the yacht the morning of the cruise and we found a rifle in the bunk room. We figured out pretty quick it was the mate's. We took him downstairs before you got there, did a little influencing. He came clean about how he'd agreed to kill me for the Mob, so we decided to use it. Put the guy into 'protective custody' so the Mob figured he'd run because he thought they'd knock him off. I told you, I was working on something in Philly with my contacts, and I figured I might be able to find out more quickly if the guys I was investigating thought they'd killed me. What I was on to was basically what I had already told you. That the Carbones were working with the government. I just didn't know which agency. Like I said, Walker kept me up to speed about what was going on. He called me from Chatham right before they put him in jail. That's how I caught up with you."

Gillette shook his head and stood up. He'd heard enough, and he could barely keep his eyes open. "I'm going to bed."

"You better take a shower first," Stiles said, standing up, too. "You need one."

Gillette started to walk off without answering.

"Yo, Chris!" Stiles called.

Gillette turned around. "What is it?"

Stiles moved slowly to where Gillette stood, hesitated a moment, then embraced him. "I'm sorry, man. I'm sorry I did that to you. I was just trying to help."

Gillette took a deep breath, then hugged Stiles back. Life was too short to be angry at your best friend for long. "I know."

After a few moments, they stepped back.

Gillette swallowed hard. "Quentin, I um . . . I, well . . ." He could feel his heart pounding. He wanted to say it, but he didn't know how. "You know I—"

"Yeah, I know," Stiles interrupted, grinning.

"Thanks," Gillette said quietly, letting out a long breath. "Hey, where you going?" Stiles was heading off across the grass.

"Chatham. I gotta get Walker out of jail."

CHAPTER 24

Faith and Gillette sat outside the Everest building on Park Avenue in the back of a limousine, saying good-bye. She was leaving on a two-week tour to promote her new album, which had just hit stores and was racing to the top of the charts. He was going back to Everest for the first time since facing off against Norman Boyd in northern Virginia.

He'd been wearing a wire that day, so everything Boyd had said was on tape. Ted Casey had more than enough to go to the Justice Department with. Casey had called to tell Gillette that Boyd was probably going to prison for the rest of his life—even with all his high-level connections. That Ganze was in the ICU of a hospital close to the mall, almost certain to follow Boyd to prison if he recovered. And that Gillette now had friends at the CIA, for life.

"I had such a wonderful time," Faith said quietly, stroking Gillette's arm as she nestled against him on the comfortable seat. They'd spent the last week together at a cozy resort in Antigua.

"Me too." He smiled down at her.

"I'll miss you. It'll be so hard not seeing you for the next couple of weeks."

"I know."

She gathered herself up on the seat so her face was close to his. "Christian?"

"Yes."

"I'm sorry for how I acted. Not calling you back those times. I was just jealous." A frustrated expression crossed her face. "I'm so embarrassed. I wanted to tell you in Antigua, but, well ... . There won't be any more episodes like that. I promise."

He shook his head. "I shouldn't have let Allison come out on the boat like that. That was—"

Faith touched her fingers to his lips. "Stop. She's your business partner. I understand that now, I really do. I'm just glad you're safe. That this thing with the people in Washington is over."

Gillette grinned wryly. "*You're* glad?"

"And it's so wonderful that Quentin's okay."

"Yeah." It was much more than wonderful, but he appreciated her saying that.

"I'm glad you have had closure on your father, too."

He nodded. After sixteen years, he finally knew what had happened to his father. He thought knowing would make it easier. Make the hollow feeling go away. But it hadn't. "Thanks."

She stroked his arm a little longer. "I have to go."

"Right."

"Chris?"

"Yes?"

Faith hesitated. "I'm ready."

"For what?"

She sat up and slipped her hands around his neck. "To be yours. I want us to be committed to each other. Completely."

"Well, it's good to have you back, old man," Faraday said, beaming from the chair on the other side of Gillette's desk. Gillette had been giving him a blow-by-blow of the mall scene with Boyd and the Carbone's people. "That's all I know."

Gillette glanced around the office. "It's good to *be* back." After a few days in Antigua, he'd started to miss the pace. It was great to be back in it again. "Give me a quick update, will you?" Faith hadn't allowed him to have contact with anyone from Everest while they were in the Caribbean.

"Sure. Well, I assigned Hush-Hush to Blair Johnson. I hope you're okay with that."

"Absolutely."

"Blair's doing a great job. Maddox and Hobbs love him. They haven't missed Wright at all. *And*," Faraday said, looking up from his notepad, "the French are bugging me every day for more info. We're going to make a killing on this one. Fast. Just like you thought."

Gillette liked the sound of that.

"Not much has happened as far as Vegas goes," Faraday continued. "You'll keep that one, I assume."

"Yup."

"As far as Apex is concerned, the Strazzi estate is still very committed to selling."

"Good. I was worried they might have second thoughts."

"And Morgan Stanley is working hard on the Laurel Energy sell-side book. They're pretty cocky about getting us a big payday."

"Have you spoken to Wright's father?"

"Yeah. He didn't bring up David at all."

Gillette nodded somberly.

"Christian." Debbie's voice blared through the intercom.

"Yes?"

"Allison wants to see you."

Faraday rolled his eyes and rose from the chair. "We still on for lunch today?"

"Yup."

"I'm not going to be preempted by Miss Wallace, am I?"

Gillette shook his head. "Never, Nigel. You're my right-hand man."

"Yeah, yeah, heard that one before."

"Well, well," Allison spoke up as she replaced Faraday in the doorway. "The conquering hero returns."

Gillette tried to hide a grin.

"Pretty proud of yourself, huh?"

"Just glad to be here."

Allison sat in the chair and sniffed. "Thought I was working with the Mob, did you?" she asked, her tone turning edgy.

"After sleeping outside for two nights, I wasn't really sure what to think," he replied, catching her quick glance at his left hand. "I was just trying to stay alive. And no, I didn't go do anything stupid in Antigua."

"What do you mean by that?"

"I didn't get married."

"What are you talking about?"

"You were looking at my ring finger," he said. "I saw you."

Allison grinned. "Oh, you did, did you?"

"Uh-huh."

"Well, why would getting married be stupid?"

Gillette shrugged. "Ah, I meant impulsive."

"Why *weren't* you impulsive?" Allison wanted to know. "Don't you love her?"

Gillette hesitated. "Why shouldn't I?"

"You *should*. A lot of guys all over the country do right now. I got a load of her on the new album cover yesterday." Allison held out her hand and shook it slowly. "Whew. She's hot."

"She does look good."

"Of course, they can do a lot of things with those digital photos now. You know, to hide the flaws."

Gillette grinned. "Well, Allison Wallace, I never would have thought you'd—"

"I want to give you a quick update," she interrupted. "Veramax is moving forward fast. Rothchild is into the Racquet Club, and *what do you know*. The company's products are on the fast track at the FDA."

"Yeah, what do you know."

"We've got a meeting with this guy who owns the leasing company in Pittsburgh on Wednesday," she continued. "Here. Ten A.M."

"Okay."

"And I've got two other deals going. No need to go over the details with you yet. Probably another few days until we do that."

He watched her tick quickly down the list. She was such a natural-born rainmaker. "Just let me know."

Allison stood up. "That's it. Maybe we can have lunch at some point."

"Hey," Gillette called as she neared the door.

"What?"

"What about those conditions?" he asked, standing and coming out from behind the desk.

She stopped and turned around. "Conditions?"

"The things you said you'd need before you'd commit to joining Everest full time."

"Oh, right. Why are you so interested?" she asked, moving to where he stood.

"I think you're good at this," he said honestly. "People naturally listen to you." He took a deep breath. "You could be chairman of this place someday. Especially now that David's not around."

Allison's eyes went wide. "Wow."

"I'm not kidding. I've thought about it a lot. I can't

promise anything, but you have a lot going for you." He held up his hand. "And think about this. You'd be doing this on your own. No family help. More respect."

"Yeah."

"So?" he pushed.

"I really only have one condition," Allison said after a few moments, her voice still subdued.

"What?"

"You don't get married for six months."

He leaned back, caught off guard. "Why?"

"I don't have to tell you *why*, I just have to tell you *what*."

Gillette shook his head. "We're business partners. That's all it can ever—"

"Will you meet my condition or not?" she cut in.

Gillette thought about it for a second. "Okay." He had no intention of getting married soon anyway. Commitment was one thing, marriage another. "But that's it, right? I agree to that one condition and you'll sign a contract to join here."

Allison turned away and headed for the door again.

"Allison."

She stopped at the door. "As long as you put in the contract that you agree not to get married for six months. As long as that clause is in there." She winked, then disappeared through the doorway.

Gillette stood in the middle of his office, staring after her. Allison wanted the clause in there so she could show Faith up. So she could demonstrate to Faith her ability to manipulate him.

He shook his head as he headed back to his desk. There it was again, that tendency to always suspect there was a hidden agenda. Maybe Allison simply wanted him focused on the business. Or maybe it was her way of politely saying no, certain he'd never actually put anything about his personal life in a contract.

He eased into the chair and started reviewing a prep file Debbie had dropped on his desk earlier. He focused on it for a few seconds, but then looked at the doorway again and smiled, thinking of Allison, thinking of Faith.

There are always issues, he thought, but most men would kill for problems like mine.

WRITER'S NOTE ON NANOTECHNOLOGY

I first heard of nanotechnology from a great friend of mine, Matt Malone, who is a top middle-market private equity professional. He reads more than anyone I know, and he'd recently seen an article in a popular national magazine on nanotech related to potential military applications—i.e., creating super-warriors who would be able to do physical things that even the strongest men and women of today couldn't dream of doing.

After Matt alerted me about it, I did some research and found the subject absolutely fascinating. I then called another friend, Teo Forcht Dagi, who is a neurosurgeon turned venture capitalist. Teo provided excellent technical assistance and introduced me to other specialists in the field; and soon I was off and running with the book.

It's incredible to think about it from a biological perspective (which is really all we can do right now), but if nanotechnology will ever be perfected to become available and allow us to live decades, maybe even centuries, longer, it will pose some terribly traumatic social questions. The weightiest of them will be: Who gets to take advantage of it? Only the wealthy? Because, like any technology, it will be extraordinarily expensive at first. Or will the government try to make it available to everyone? That, of course, would be incredibly costly. And what will happen when nanotechnology gets cheap and nearly everyone can afford it? Will funeral homes and cemeteries go out of business and beachfront property get *really* pricey?

If you're inclined to delve further and do some of your own research on the subject, here are some excellent websites to start with:

www.nanotech-now.com
www.nano.gov
www.nsti.org
www.nasatech.com

Enjoy!

—Stephen Frey
June 2005

Read on for a
preview of Stephen Frey's
next thrilling novel,

THE POWER BROKER

Available at bookstores everywhere
Published by Ballantine Books

CHAPTER 1

Christian Gillette sat on the balcony of his suite at Caesar's Palace in Las Vegas, watching first light scale the craggy peaks in the distance. In a few hours, tourists would be mobbing the casino on the ground floor. He hoped soon it would be *his* casino they'd be mobbing.

Christian ran Everest Capital, a Manhattan-based investment firm that owned thirty companies in a wide range of industries—smokestack to high-tech. The companies were all large, at least a billion in sales, and Christian chaired eighteen of them. He also chaired Central States Telecom and Satellite, a communications company in Chicago that Everest had taken public six months ago—after owning for three years. Everest had made four hundred million on the CST initial public offering—Christian had gotten twenty of that. Forty years old, he'd already made fifty times more than most people did in a lifetime, but it hadn't gone to his head. Money was just money, and success could be fleeting.

He dialed Nigel Faraday's cell number. Nigel was one of Everest's five managing partners. There were sixty-four people at the firm, but, other than his assistant, Debbie, the five partners were Christian's only direct reports. Beneath the partners was a burgeoning pyramid of managing directors, vice presidents, and associates, but he rarely dealt with them. Five years ago, he'd known everyone at Everest by name. He missed those days.

Nigel answered on the third ring. "Well, well, you gambling, Chris?" Nigel had lived in the United States for almost twenty years, but his British accent remained heavy. "Sitting in front of some one-armed bandit with your bucket of quarters?" He laughed. "Ah, *the slot machine.* Another wonderful contribution to mankind from you Americans. Right up there with rap music and the Big Mac."

Playing the slots actually sounded like fun to Christian, if only for its pure simplicity, but there wasn't time. It seemed like there never was anymore for things like that. "Hey, I don't mind rap once in a while, and I don't know why you, of all people, would bash the Big Mac. You've eaten your share."

"Hey, chap, what I eat is my business."

"Relax, *chap*, I'm just kidding." Christian heard traffic in the background at the other end of the line— horns blaring, engines revving, tires skidding. "Where are you?"

"Walking down Park. Bit of a late start to the office this morning, I'm afraid."

Nigel was huffing as he strode toward Everest's Park Avenue headquarters. The Brit was thirty pounds overweight thanks to a steady diet of rocky road ice cream and those Big Macs. "Up late last night?" Christian asked. Nigel was fresh into a new relationship with a pretty brunette he'd met a few weeks ago. They were in the infatuation stage, calling each other five times a day and staying out late every night. "I don't want that woman distracting you, no matter how wonderful she is."

"Look, I—"

"No, no, I'm glad you're finally enjoying yourself," Christian broke in. Nigel had put in a lot of long days the last few years, taking care of administrative details so Christian could focus on the big picture. Nigel had been Mr. Inside so Christian could be Mr. Outside, and the formula worked. Both *Forbes* and *Fortune* had tabbed Everest Capital as one of the top investment firms. "Now, any updates?"

Dead air.

"Nigel?"

"Just one."

Christian picked up something in Nigel's tone, and a tiny alarm went off in his head. "What?"

"After you left for Vegas last night, I got an e-mail from Bob Galloway."

Bob Galloway was the chief financial officer of CST. Despite being chairman of CST, Christian didn't know Galloway well, just saw him for a few hours at quarterly board meetings. Nigel, on the other hand, knew Galloway very well. Though Nigel wasn't technically a CST officer like Christian, he was Everest's day-to-day person on the investment. The one at Everest who constantly kept up with how CST was doing. The one who knew CST's financial staff and had been in charge of dealing directly with the lawyers and investment bankers during the IPO.

"Some woman from the Securities and Exchange Commission called Galloway yesterday," Nigel explained.

Hearing from the SEC was like hearing from the IRS or the Grim Reaper: Safe bet it wasn't good news. "What did she want?" Christian asked.

"She called to demand a meeting. Didn't tell Galloway any more than that."

"Okay, call Galloway as soon as we're finished. Tell him to get back in touch with the SEC right away and find out what's going on. Let me know as soon as you hear anything. And, Nigel?"

"Yeah?"

"Make sure Galloway doesn't mention this to anyone else at CST."

"Sure, sure."

Christian heard a trace of fear in Nigel's tone. "It'll be fine, pal. Don't worry."

"Oh, I'm worried all right," Nigel admitted.

"Being worried doesn't help."

"Sorry I'm human. I'm glad you can stay so cool about it, Chris, but those people scare the hell out of me. They can destroy anybody anytime. Remember that guy who got twenty years for telling his girlfriend he had a stock tip over the phone, when what he really said was he had a sock that was ripped?"

"What guy? I don't remember that."

"And with my accent," Nigel continued, "I could see it happening to me."

"It's not like that."

"Oh yeah? Ask the guys at Enron and MCI."

"They got what they deserved."

"You'll be whistling a different tune when they bust into Everest and lead you and me out in shackles in front of the whole firm."

Sometimes Nigel panicked too quickly. He didn't have many faults, but hitting the eject button prematurely was one of them. "That call Galloway got was probably nothing, probably just some kind of follow-up on the IPO."

"I hope so. Hey, what about the casino license?" Nigel asked, his voice growing stronger as he switched subjects. "Everything all right there? Opening day isn't far off."

Two years ago Everest Capital had won the National Football League's new Las Vegas franchise and named it the Dice. They'd spent over seven hundred million for the team and a new stadium they were building east of the city. As part of the deal with the NFL, Christian had gotten permission to build a casino, also naming it the Dice. The casino was supposed to open the day of the team's home opener, which was just a few months away. On top of the seven hundred million for the team and the stadium, Everest had forked out a billion on construction of the casino—which was almost finished. Now, at the last minute, the Nevada Gaming Commission was holding off on approving the operating license. What seemed like a dream come true a month ago was turning into a nightmare. Christian hadn't told anyone else at the firm how bad the situation was.

"We'll get the license," he assured Nigel. Trying to figure out what was going on with the license was Christian's main reason for coming to Las Vegas. At two o'clock he was meeting with the chairman of the Gaming Commission. "Don't sweat it." Sometimes it seemed like he spent half his life convincing people there wasn't any smoke and the other half putting out fires.

"You think the mob's involved?" Nigel asked. "Think they're holding the commission up for some last-minute dough?"

"I don't know. That's why I'm here, to find out."

"Didn't we hire somebody in Vegas to take care of those things, to deal with the mob? Like most people out there do when they're building something big. What's his name?"

"Carmine Torino." Christian had been trying to reach Torino for a week, but suddenly no one could find him. Until now the guy had never taken more than fifteen minutes to return his call. Torino had vanished into thin air.

"Yeah, right, Carmine Torino."

"I've gotta go, Nigel. Ray Lancaster's going to be here in a few minutes."

Ray Lancaster was the Dice's head coach and general manager. Christian had hired him away from the Tampa Bay Buccaneers last February. Nigel had gone to Florida to do the negotiating on the contract, so this was going to be Christian's first face-to-face meeting with Lancaster.

"Ray's tough," Nigel warned.

"He better be. I want the Dice in the play-offs this season so we get all that extra publicity for the casino. Call me back when—"

"What about Laurel Energy?" Nigel interrupted. "Anything on that? Are we close to selling it?"

Christian let out a ten-ton sigh. "Let's talk about it later." Laurel Energy was a Canadian oil and gas company—and another Everest problem child. Christian—and everyone else at Everest—had been anticipating a huge profit on the sale of Laurel, but it had been on the market for a while and there weren't any takers. Just a few nibbles from bottom feeders, and no one could figure out what was wrong because it was reserve-rich. "I've got to go," he said firmly. "Call me back when Galloway knows why the SEC's snooping around CST so I can—"

"Where's Allison?"

Another of Nigel's annoying habits. Sometimes it was impossible to get him off the phone. "What?"

"Where's Allison? I've been trying to get her for days. She's been out of the office and hasn't returned my calls."

Allison Wallace was another of Everest's five managing partners. "She's on the West Coast working on that deal, you know, that company she's been trying to buy for a month. Aero Systems. I talked to her last night. It's going pretty well. She thinks the sellers are about to agree to terms."

Nigel snorted. "I guess the bitch doesn't think I'm important enough to call back."

"*Hey, Nigel, none of that. She's just—*" There was a loud rap on the suite door. "Talk to you later, Nigel." Christian slipped the phone in his pocket as the person in the hallway knocked again, louder this time. "Who is it?"

"Ray Lancaster."

"Hi, Ray," Christian said, extending his hand when he'd opened the door.

Lancaster had played defensive back for the Lions in the early eighties, but age and the stress of coaching had clearly caught up with him. His curly black hair was thinning and streaked with gray, his cheeks were pudgy, and there was a bulging spare tire beneath his shirt. Like Nigel, Ray probably ate a lot of his frustration.

"Christian Gillette. Thanks for coming so early."

"No problem, been looking at tapes since five this morning. First game's closing in. Cleveland Browns. We're gonna kick some ass. At least on defense."

"Good. I want to make the play-offs this season."

Lancaster stopped short. "Well, I don't know if we're—"

"Let's go out on the balcony," Christian suggested, motioning toward the back of the suite. "I like it." Christian pointed at the Dice logo on Lancaster's aqua golf shirt as they sat down. Two tumbling die—one showing a single dot, the other six—with a sharp orange flame trailing behind them.

"Yeah, it's way cool."

"How's your family doing?" Lancaster and his second wife had two boys—one thirteen, one eleven. Whenever Christian relocated an executive he always worried about the family adapting to the new city. If the family wasn't happy, neither was the executive. "Las Vegas is a big change from Tampa."

"They're fine. Thanks for asking."

Lancaster seemed anxious, like something was on his mind. "Everything all right, Ray?"

"I should have called you after we inked my contract, but, well, better late than never." Lancaster looked directly into Christian's eyes. "Thanks for giving me this chance. I owe you."

Lancaster hadn't been the Buccaneers general manager in Tampa, just head coach, so this was a big promotion. "Win me a Super Bowl and we'll call it even."

Lancaster laughed nervously. *"Yeah, right."* He tugged at the front of his shirt like it had suddenly gotten tight. "I didn't think I'd ever get a shot to be a GM in this league," he continued, skirting Christian's Super Bowl demand. "Hardly any black men get to be head coach in the NFL, let alone GM."

"You've won a lot of football games. You got the Bucs to the NFC championship last year without a lot of talent. You deserve this."

"And I really didn't think I'd get a shot from a *white* man," Lancaster went on. "I thought I might eventually get it from a black owner, but not a guy like you."

Christian could tell it had been tough for Lancaster to admit that. "I don't judge a person by his skin, Ray, I really don't. I look at track record and work ethic, and I listen to what people close to him say." Christian understood the value of letting a camel get his nose into the tent every once in a while, the value of giving someone a brief window into his life, even if it was just momentary. "I grew up in a big house in LA, Ray. We had a couple of Hispanic maids, and my stepmother treated them like dirt. Not because they were maids, because they were Hispanic. I hated that."

Lancaster thought on that, then nodded.

"*Now,*" Christian said emphatically, "how many games are we going to win this season?"

Lancaster gazed out over Las Vegas, his eyes finally focusing on the tower of the Stratosphere Hotel in the distance. It was easily the tallest structure in Las Vegas, over eleven hundred feet, with several terrifying rides at the top. "It's gonna be a wild year. We'll have a lot of close games."

"Why?"

"We got a good defense but no quarterback worth a damn. We're not going to score many points. It'll come down to the last possession in a lot of games."

"You going to start Ricky Poe at quarterback?"

"He's the only game in town. We picked him up in the expansion draft from the Cowboys, but he's—"

"Not taking anybody to the promised land," Christian broke in. "Yeah, I know. So make a trade. We've got a couple of all-pro linebackers you can use as bait. If I have to choose, I'll take a top quarterback over a top linebacker any day."

Lancaster nodded, impressed. "Did you play something at Princeton?"

"Rugby."

"Man, that's tough. Basically football with no pads."

Christian turned his head so Lancaster had a profile. "Broke my nose twice. The second time it was almost in my left ear when I came to."

Lancaster made a grim face.

"Thank God for plastic surgeons."

"Uh-huh, well, look, I've been trying to make a trade for weeks and won't nobody talk to me."

"What do you mean?" For the second time in a few minutes that tiny alarm went off in Christian's head.

"I've been calling other coaches around the league, guys I'm close to. Guys who need linebackers and have a good backup quarterback. Guys who would be real likely to trade, but they ain't calling me back. Christian, these are guys I was on staff with at other teams, guys I go way back with. I even played with a couple of them. But it's like somebody got to them, like somebody told them not to talk to me."

"That's ridiculous."

"I know how it sounds, but I don't know how else to explain it."

Christian's cell phone rang. "Excuse me, Ray."

"Sure."

"What's up, Nigel?" he asked, turning away from Lancaster.

"Galloway talked to the gal at the SEC."

"And?"

"She wouldn't say much, but it sounds like they're going to start an investigation of CST. Accounting irregularities, she claimed. It sounded serious."

"*What?* That's impossible. We run things squeaky clean at all our portfolio companies."

"Hey, don't shoot the messenger," Nigel complained. "I'm just telling you what Galloway told me."

Christian closed his eyes. There were a lot of strange things going on lately. Too many.